BEAUTIFUL JOY

Beautiful Joy

VINCENT JAMES

PROLOGUE: TUESDAY

"Love," Joy said aloud to herself.

She said it without initially realizing that she had said it out loud. She only intended to say the word to herself internally within her thoughts (as she often did).

She was immediately embarrassed.

As she uttered the word (one that still felt so mysterious, awkward and sad to her all at once), she managed a slight smile that just as quickly turned back sideways to the frown she usually conveyed.

She was sitting in the front passenger seat of her mom's car.

It was raining all over the car, all over the cars and trucks on the street around them, and all over the kids walking to school along the sidewalks outside.

It was the pouring, relentless sort of rain.

It was early December and even though the rain wasn't coming down as ice rain at this point; it was coming down cold.

"What?" Her mom asked, sounding perturbed. "What about love?"

The car smelled like a combination of the wet sidewalks outside and the leather seats inside with just a hint of her mom's coffee.

Joy had been too late getting ready for school and missed the bus at her stop, so her mom was already moody about having to drive her to school before she went to work.

Even when irritable and moody, Joy's mom had an undeniable beauty that even strangers pointed out to her on a regular basis. Joy's mom was one of those "rare beautiful" type of people who had a timeless quality to them that would have rendered them "beautiful" regardless of the time period and culture they lived in. It was the kind of beautiful that could transcend trends, bridge cultures, and echo through lifetimes. Joy heard people describe her mom's face as "cute," her mom's body as "sexy," her mom's choices in style and clothing as "pretty" and her mom's overall appearance as "youthful" and "ageless." Her mom was one of those people who never had a wrinkled part of her clothing, a smudge in her makeup, or a stray strand of hair sticking to her face. Joy's mom was one of those people, and she carried herself in a way that reverberated a quiet energy that she had full confidence in knowing this about herself.

Joy's long dark hair always seemed to be wild, frizzy and everywhere as it ran over and past her shoulders. She rarely tied it back or placed it in any style. She allowed her hair to be free and frizzy. Today, the 'frizzy situation' was somehow even more the case due to the weather and her lack of any sort of preparation. This was much to the annoyance of her mom who had made a comment about it before they entered the car.

"You asked me what keeps me going in life even though all the other girls don't like me. I think about love."

Joy maintained her trademark resting-frown as she said this. Her mom didn't reply right away as she glared out at the road over the steering wheel. They were stopped at a stoplight, and her mom was holding her to-go cup coffee close to her lips to allow the steamy warmth of the coffee to climb up her lips and cradle the lower part of her nose. She was close to taking a sip when she decided against this and put the coffee back into one of the car's drink holders. Joy had noticed that her mom didn't let herself savor any of the food or beverages she consumed, even the ones she loved. It was like even enjoyable moments or activities in her life were a chore, and her mind was anxiously already on to the next event or set of events she was planning to engage in.

"Joy, I'm going to tell you a secret that most women don't learn until later in life and that most men never really learn, so are you ready for it this morning?"

"Probably not..."

Her mom sighed an exaggerated sigh before launching into her planned speech anyway: "Most of the men you'll meet don't know what it means to appreciate a woman. Trust me, most of these idiots only go by sexual attraction, especially in high school. Most men never learn anything about how to truly see a woman they are drawn to for who they really are. They literally can't know or see a woman's qualities past the way their own minds and bodies are responding to the woman they are attracted to. Their sexual attraction blinds them from your character and your abilities to the point that they'll only say the right things to you just to have sex with you or to keep to staring at you.

"Pretty much the one thing they have to offer is, well— words. It's the words they think they need to say to get you in bed. Their words have no meaning or connection to who you really are. Men don't have the ability to understand the depth of a woman or even begin to understand how sophisticated, diverse and complex we really are. They just get frustrated and confused. I know it's sad, but it's true. Nearly all the men you will meet will never get past that level either, and that's why most men can't have authentic relationships or even real friendships with any woman they are attracted to. I thought your dad was different at one point, but he isn't. I learned right before you were born that he was never interested in anything about me except my body and maybe my popularity when we were in school. But that was it. Nothing else.

"I know you already think you know what love is now, Joy. But I'll be honest with you— you don't. Girls your age don't know right now. Many of them end up like me where they don't learn until after they've spent years in a soulless marriage or relationship. Many of them settle with that kind of relationship because they don't know any better, think they can't do any better, or think they don't deserve real love. Many of them don't want to believe that real love exists. Even some of those women who learn any of the things I am sharing with you right now don't teach their children what they've learned because they are either bitter and resentful that they had to learn the hard way, or they still don't want to admit to themselves that 'real love' is really out there even if they've seen it or experienced it before.

"I've never experienced it, Joy, but I know it's out there. I've seen other people experience it and I am doing you a huge favor by sharing this all with you now. If you don't experience real love in a relationship then, at best, you might get a guy who never learns real love but knows just enough about relationships to still give you his full attention and kind of fake it— like your dad still does with me. But that is hard work to them and never quite fulfilling for us, even if it sometimes feels like it could be enough. 'Real love' is different. 'Real love' is unconditional trust, unconditional respect, and unconditional faith. It's rare. They say it's even more rare nowadays, but Joy...I think it's always been rare. Do you know what I mean by 'real love?'"

Joy remained silent, but not because she didn't want to give a response. She wasn't sure how to respond. Her mom had never told this to her before, and she didn't want to say the wrong thing. However, she could sense that this silence still annoyed her mom anyway.

Her mom groaned at the lack of response. She looked at Joy for a split second in anger as if to say something, but initially remained quiet. She then groaned again. What she said next was much more familiar to Joy: "Some people are the type of people that you can tell just by looking at them that they will end up alone. You know within seconds of seeing them," her mom explained with an air of exhaustion and resignation that people often have when repeating themselves on a subject they feel like they shouldn't have to discuss, "and if you don't want to end up like one of them, you'll have to stop dreaming. Be more realistic about who you are in this world and what you can get. You'll have to take what you can get if you are going to get anything at all. And you, Joy, you are going to be limited in what you can get. So, you better accept that now. The sooner you accept it, then you'll at least make a few friends who are like you, and then maybe have a boyfriend if you're lucky. It won't be nearly as easy for you as it was for me, and I've admitted to you that it didn't turn out to be all roses for me either. You are going to be much, much, much more limited with your options. But you can get around some of these things if you start listening to me."

Her mom had told her this second part of today's lecture repeatedly almost daily.

Within the content of some of these lectures, her mom pointed out the people who she perceived as having ended up alone or on their way to ending up alone whenever they were out in public. On this occasion, the largest girl in her class happened to be standing eight feet away from the other kids at a nearby bus stop as they pulled up to another stoplight. Everybody else had umbrellas or were standing under somebody else's umbrella, except this girl.

That girl was soaked.

Completely drenched.

She was so soaked that her clothing had the appearance of being freshly painted over her body. Joy couldn't comprehend how the girl was able to stand out there without wearing a jacket and imagined she must have been freezing.

"You are only slightly better off than her," her mom reminded her, "and trust me, it's going to get worse as you get older if you keep going down this road you're on."

Joy replied by quietly maintaining her resting-frown.

Her mom then pointed out a homeless man looking defeated, alone, and soaked like an unaffected, weathered statue as he stood motionless on the sidewalk in the torrential rain outside of a holiday-decorated convenience store: "You're on your way to ending up like that," she added as they drove by him.

He didn't look back at Joy, but Joy still felt like he observed her looking him, just like she felt like the largest girl in the class had noted her gaze too.

It felt like there was a vague connection of loneliness between all of them (despite leading very different lives) that didn't need to be overtly acknowledged.

When she was eleven years-old, she remembered she was with her mom at the grocery store in the frozen aisle and her mom couldn't take her eyes off a very lonely-looking woman with black-rimmed glasses dressed in clothes a size or two too tight on her. Her mom was staring at her so intently that Joy felt uncomfortable as though she was the one being stared at. But the lonely-looking woman didn't seem to notice her mom staring at her from halfway down the aisle. Instead, the lonely-looking woman was staring intently at a bag a frozen broccoli she was holding and had indecisively motioned toward the freezer door at least two or three times to put it back. But instead of putting it back, she simultaneously kept reading the nutrition label on the bag of broccoli. On another near-attempt to put it back, she anxiously dropped it on the ground. As it fell, she bent over so quickly to try to catch it that she split the back of her pants across her bottom— right in front of them. She stayed bent over after the splitting occurred, still staring down at the bag of broccoli without even reaching for it anymore. She continued to look at it awkwardly– as though she was still reading the label. Joy's mom burst out laughing in such a sudden rage, that it scared Joy and she felt like it was echoing through the entire store as though they were in some deep majestic cavern that carried an endless echo. Joy wondered if she was more embarrassed than the lonely-looking woman since the woman was still reading the label (or at least pretending to) and was seemingly unaffected by her mom's laughter.

"See, if you don't start getting yourself together," Joy's mom had laughed at the time, "that will be you someday. You have no other choice, you have to live this life to the best of your limited beauty."

Back in the car, her mom paused and started a little hum to herself. Joy had noted her mom normally did that hum before she would start saying things that were weird and arbitrary.

"I wouldn't be this beautiful and or be as popular as I was when I was in high school if I hadn't been a princess in my previous life," her mom explained. "You see, there is no greater opportunity to be raised on how to have class, etiquette, education, and self-care than to be born as a princess. I've done everything I can to teach you all of those important characteristics from birth, but you've ignored me. I'm telling you, Joy, they are so important, especially for a girl like you who wasn't born with natural beauty. You can still live like a princess, even with your limitations. I have all the tools and know all the ways; you have to start listening to me."

Yes... Joy thought to herself. *She does the humming thing to herself before things usually get weird.* She briefly smiled a little bit at this thought and didn't respond to her mom.

By the time her mom turned to look at her for a response, the silent resting-frown had returned to her face.

*** *** ***

"What are you looking at?!"

The couple that Joy had been watching as they were making out in the hallway at school had stopped and they were now staring directly at her waiting for a response that wasn't coming.

The girl had asked the question with an expression of disgust while the guy she had been kissing simply grinned. The guy looked like a little kid who had only opened one present on Christmas Day up to that point and still had at least a dozen presents left. The girl was beautiful, but she carried herself in a way that took away from her natural beauty, like she was probably insecure. She was immaculately dressed in expensive looking clothes, was wearing makeup that looked like it had been carefully applied for approximately two hours before school started and was wearing the type of gorgeous shoes that Joy would be afraid to wear outside of the house out of fear getting them dirty.

The girl looked at Joy with disdain. They had never spoken to each other before but had known of each other since at least the first grade. She may have even been in one of Joy's elementary school classes one year, but Joy couldn't remember which one and had forgotten her name. *It was something like Rachel or Colleen,* she thought. She frequently had trouble remembering the names of most of her classmates, but they all seemed to know her name.

"You don't even know who I am, do you?" The girl asked with a snarky tone that suggested it was more of a rhetorical question.

Joy took a step back, as though she was taken aback by the thought that this girl had been reading her mind. She still couldn't remember what year they shared an elementary school teacher. The girl emitted a toxic aura filled with compressed tension that was oozing with insecurity and anger. The guy looked at the girl longingly with adoration. He seemed completely oblivious to all the negative energy Joy was sensing from her. The girl ignored him while staring directly at Joy. Joy looked back at her with her characteristic resting-frown. Joy could sense that the girl knew that Joy sensed she was insecure, and that this girl was intent on putting Joy down even further than how far down she already felt about herself.

"Come on, Natalie," the guy said, still glaring at the girl, "Joy is a loser, she's not worth it."

Joy had been watching them make out while standing in front of her locker at the end of the school day. Her locker was still open to her side as she stared back at Natalie. Natalie and her boyfriend had been making out in front of her boyfriend's locker which was about seven lockers away from Joy's locker in the same row.

Nearly everybody else had long gone and all the buses had probably left by that point.

She was going to have to walk home again.

The hallway smelled like a strange combination of books, dirty shoes, and bleach (from the floors being continuously mopped), but was also topped off with a vague smelly odor from the restrooms nearby.

"You're right," Natalie agreed with her boyfriend, finally acknowledging him again after several more seconds of continued focus on Joy after he had said that. "Joy is and has always been the biggest loser in our class since kindergarten. She doesn't even exist."

They looked at each other and resumed making out in front of Joy as though she wasn't there.

Joy continued standing there, looking at them quietly. But this time, she had completely lost focus of them after Natalie had uttered the words "she doesn't even exist." After she had heard Natalie say that, it felt as though she really had physically disappeared along with those words.

Even though she was still standing there and looking in their direction, her mind wouldn't stop moving through those "reminders" her mom had given earlier: *Maybe I really am one of those people. You can tell which people they are on the street or at the store.*

They are always alone, look lonely, look strange, and look out of place. I already feel like one of those people. I want to walk up to these people and ask them how they get by. I know from my aunt, my chemistry teacher, our mail carrier, one of my Dad's second cousins, and our next door neighbor (who are all identified by mom as being one of them) that they often either have many dogs, or many cats, or lots of plants, or indulge in fantasy worlds with strange interests and hobbies most people don't care about...but how is that enough? How can they go so long without feeling the touch of another person? How can they not sit and cry every day when they are ignored every day like the world doesn't want them to exist? How do they get by? I am becoming an adult and I need to know.

She had started visibly shaking with these thoughts and dropped one of her books on accident to the floor but didn't pick it up. After it hit the floor, she stopped shaking as she looked down at the book without picking it up. The hardcover calculus book had fallen open to pages near the end of the book revealing a chapter she looked at and concluded she would struggle with once her class got around to it. She felt awkwardly frozen in that stance in front of her locker as she became aware again that Natalie was making out with her boyfriend nearby. She felt frozen in the way she had seen the nameless lonely woman frozen with the dropped bag of broccoli as her mom's laughter echoed around her in the frozen aisle at the grocery store. But she heard no reaction from them as the hallway was filled with the continued sounds of them kissing and adjusting their embrace.

She took a deep breath and turned to her locker; she saw how big of a mess she had allowed it to become over the course of the semester. She winced as though she had never noticed the mess before up until this point.

She looked away in disgust and sighed.

Back in her field of view, the couple were still kissing each other and now also occasionally whispering to one another between kisses.

And just like that, she was back to where she had started before they had spoken to her: she returned to watching them again. She was mesmerized as she watched a process she was completely unfamiliar with; she wondered what a kiss felt like.

Her locker door was still open.

Her calculus book was still opened on the floor beside her feet.

But now she was so focused on them that she was no longer aware of the fact that she was even in the hallway at school.

For a moment she felt the fog of emptiness and loneliness surround her as anxious, prophesying thoughts reminded her that she may never get to experience what the couple was experiencing a few lockers away from her.

She wanted it so badly.

That girl Natalie has no idea how good she has it. She doesn't deserve him. Will there ever be a guy who wants me as badly as that guy wants Natalie? She couldn't remember Natalie's boyfriend's name either.*But, wow! They look so happy and in love. Will I ever get to love someone who loves me back?*

Yes, she wanted what they had.

Even if just for a moment.

One moment in her life could be enough because then she'd have a recurring memory she could relive as often as she wanted to.

She closed her eyes as tight as she could as if that would help to block the negative thoughts.

After she had closed her eyes, she started to pucker her lips.

The process of puckering her lips was gradual, as though they needed to be in perfect form to be effective. She had practiced this with her lips at home a thousand times.

All they felt was empty hallway air.

Part I: Wednesday

1.1

J oy had gone to bed that night thinking about that couple by her locker and hardly slept at all.

By the next morning, they were still in the back of her mind as she was laying wide-awake in bed, looking around her bedroom. She no longer kept a clock in her room and had stored the coconut-themed alarm clock she used to have on her nightstand up on a shelf in her closet. This change had happened about a year ago when she realized she was watching the clock at night (hoping that time would slow down so she didn't have to go back to school again so quickly) instead of sleeping. Therefore, she wasn't sure what time it was but could sense it was early morning by how tired she felt despite having the intuitive obligation to get up.

She wanted to go back to sleep and sleep all day.

She closed her eyes and that was when the cascade of the morning thoughts she usually had while still awake in bed before school hit her all at once: *I wish I had a pretty face. I wish I had a different body. I wish I would eat better. I wish I didn't get so sweaty and tired when I tried to exercise. I wish I was a different ethnicity. I wish I had a different last name. I wish my facial features were different. I wish I had better clothes. I wish my parents made more money so they would be happier. I wish I was more athletic like I was when I was younger. I wish my mom liked me. I wish I had a brother or sister. I wish I had a better body. I wish I liked my face. I wish I was taller. I wish I had friends. I wish I knew what clothes to wear. I wish I would sleep better. I wish I liked the things the other girls like so I know what they are talking about when they talk about movies, TV shows and music. I wish they would tell me what movies, shows and music to like ahead of time so I can keep up with them. I wish they would be my friends. I wish the other girls didn't bully me. I wish all the guys didn't pretend that I don't exist. I wish I knew how to talk to people. I wish I had a boyfriend like the other girls do. I wish they would be my friends so they can show me how to have a boyfriend too. I wish Gray liked me. I wish Gray liked me...*

Gray was a guy at school she had liked since the sixth grade. Okay, she had actually liked him now for longer than that (maybe more like kindergarten) but she had really liked him since the sixth grade. Either way, as far as she knew, he didn't know she existed. They had never interacted, not even when they shared the same sixth grade teacher. She loved everything about him. She loved the way he wore hats all the time outside of class, she loved the way he breathed a little too much whenever he laughed, and she loved his smile. She loved the idea that her mom wouldn't like a kid like him (maybe her dad would). He wasn't like everyone else. He was different. He was beautiful.

But in addition to the fact that Gray never acknowledged her, there was one other issue that impacted her chance of being with Gray: he was dating Casey. They had been dating since the eighth grade.

Her heart sank as she thought about Gray. She felt her stomach getting upset, so she rolled over in her bed on her belly. She laid the side of her head on the pillow and as she opened her eyes again, she noticed something felt different.

She couldn't quite tell what was different.

Her eyes scanned the dim room.

Her bedroom was usually dim or dark.

She liked to keep it that way.

As she thought about how dim it was, she glanced at and took greater notice of the razor-thin rays of sunlight creeping up one of the walls through her window. Usually, enough light crept in through the curtains in the early morning before school so that she could see the white in her eyes in the mirror that hung over her dresser. She could also see the oval of a face, the curves of her chest and hips, and see the strands of her hair falling over her shoulders. But that was all she could see.

That was all she needed to see, because in those circumstances with that specific lighting, she looked beautiful.

In fact, when that was all that she could see of herself, it was the only time she ever felt like she looked beautiful. She felt like she only looked beautiful in that mirror when the early morning light was partially coming in through her window like it was in that moment. It didn't happen every day. She hated getting up early, but on mornings like this, her morning beauty made it worth it.

Whenever she felt motivated enough to get out of the bed earlier and walk up to that mirror, it was the one time of the day she'd allow herself to look directly into it. On every other occasion, she avoided looking at herself in the mirror if she could help it. She could never quite replicate the appearance she had with the assistance of the thin rays of sunrise peering through her curtains during the other times of the day, so she had given up trying.

Each time she had a morning like this, she thought: *If only it was possible that Gray could see me when I look like this.*Of course, in that imaginary scenario, Gray would also be single or immediately willing to become single to be with her.

Sometimes when she was in class or on the bus and her stomach cramped with anxiety about the fact the school day was far from over, she tried to redirect her mind to think about how she only needed a thin ray of light to be beautiful. She'd even tell herself how all those pretty girls from school that went out on dates almost every night needed constant light and all the attention on them to feel special.

They always needed a spotlight on them.

But she only needed a little light.

She needed a little and to think, all those beautiful girls needed as much of the world as possible to see them just to feel special.

But at the same time, it seemed like it was impossible not to think about all the things they had that she didn't. She would see a guy holding a pretty girl's hand, see a guy talking in a pretty girl's ear to make her smile, and see a guy holding his hand around a pretty girl's waist as they walked down the sidewalk.

She didn't need a guy to smile. But every time her hand felt cold, her lips felt dry, or her body felt unhugged, she wanted one. It seemed so easy for the other girls. She watched how many of the other girls only had to stand around and look pretty to meet guys. She even noticed how the teachers who saw them grinned and then carried expressions that looked like a cross between judgment and fascination at the way those girls looked and acted. Some of those teachers seemed like they envied that their own high school experiences didn't include that level of attention from others or that ease of meeting someone to date. So as practice, she gave herself those opportunities to stand around and look pretty too, but she hadn't made it past doing so alone and in the dimmed sunrise.

She had hoped if she did it enough, she would gain the confidence to do it when she wasn't in her room.

She bristled at the follow-up-thought she usually had that it was probably never going to happen anyway. But before she could over-indulge herself in her doubt like she usually did, that weird feeling she had earlier returned to her again.

It was then that she realized that the "different" feeling she had was a feeling that the whole world had somehow become a darker place that morning, as dark as her room was.

She felt this way even though she still hadn't left her room or even her bed.

She was having an even harder time getting out of bed than she usually did.

Something was off.

The thin ray of light coming through her window seemed different at one glance, but then when she blinked, it looked perfectly normal.

She laid there thinking about it until she realized that thinking about it too much jumbled up her head and was preventing her from having any clear thoughts about what it might be.

It was only as she emerged reluctantly and tiredly from her bed that she finally confirmed the thin ray of light wasn't shining through her window the way it usually did. *Maybe there was a really big cloud suddenly blocking the sun, or it had become a super-cloudy day but with darker clouds than usual.*

She scuffed and stub-toed through the day-darkness and mess on the floor. The closer she got to the window, the darker the room seemed to be. She followed the sounds of rush-hour traffic coming from outside to her window.

By the time she reached the window, it had become so dim that when she closed her eyes, she was able to imagine the window more clearly in her mind: she saw the purple curtain she was pinching blindly in her hand, and she saw the cars through the window, backed up at the intersection down the street like they usually were. But when she pushed the curtain aside and opened her eyes to look out the window, she didn't see anything at all. Even the last remaining glint of light that had been peeking through the window had disappeared.

Everything was black.

No streetlights, no headlights, and no sunlight.

But there was still the traffic noise.

Maybe this is the biggest, darkest storm ever coming in right now.

She curled her toes into carpet as a function of her anxiety.

She then turned and scuffled back across the carpeting to the other end of the room, gently kicking the miniskirts, tank tops, chap sticks, socks, and skin lotion bottles that formed the mess she had left scattered on the floor. Her right hand searched and swayed in the space immediately in front of her until a light switch crept in awkwardly between her middle and ring fingers.

In this new dark world, she wasn't sure the light would come back if she flipped the switch.

There was only one way to find out.

She hesitated.

For several seconds she stood still and wondered why she was hesitating. She imagined the darkness thicken and wrap around her skin like a straitjacket, pulling her back, resisting her movement.

She flipped the switch.

Nothing.

She blinked and blinked again, but it was still dark.

Oh, maybe the power is out again.

Or maybe I'm not really blinking, maybe I can't open my eyes at all so all I see is the back of my eyelids.

Or maybe I lost my eyesight completely.

Or maybe I died in my sleep of a broken heart, and this was an afterlife purgatory I was in.

Whatever it was, she knew she needed to do something to try to navigate these changes with some kind of assistance.

She walked back carefully to her bed and felt around cautiously in the area she knew her nightstand was in. She eventually found her smartphone on top of it. It had been turned off. She turned it on, and she did so, the phone screen flashed on with its corresponding light.

She shouted with joy.

She shouted with joy but then ducked down in embarrassment at the thought that her parents might hear her.

She allowed herself a half-smile; her twilight was back.

Once the home screen of her phone loaded, she clicked on the phone flashlight feature. It had the right level of brightness to give her the desired glow she wanted in the otherwise dark bedroom. She looked in the mirror and smiled a bigger smile that she could barely see from the distance she was away from the mirror. Despite all the different ways she had tried to find beauty in herself while looking in the mirror, she had never tried this before with her phone flashlight and thought about how it could be called her "beautiful glow."

Any fear she once had of the new weird darkness disappeared from memory. There followed a strange moment as she stood there holding the phone flashlight in which she realized that this random Wednesday might be the happiest day of her life.

Now, she controlled her twilight.

She picked up a white miniskirt off the floor with her other empty hand as she also continued to hold her phone-light. Her mom had bought her the miniskirt months ago. She would never wear it in public because she didn't like how she looked in it in daylight. The top of the dresser itself went up to her belly button, so she had to stand on her bed to see her whole body in the large mirror that was on top of her dresser. She awkwardly climbed the bed with the phone still in one hand and the skirt in the other. The bedsprings wobbled a little underneath her feet. After she was sure of her balance, she held the skirt up against her waist, like her mom did at the store. She had refused to try it on that day. That was on her birthday. She had tried on the skirt many times since then, but it had never left her room. With awkward gentle bounces she started pulling the skirt up and over her pajama bottoms with both hands. The phone flashlight was still gleaming as she held it in one of her hands alongside a part of her skirt.

Once the skirt was on, she smiled and started leaping softly on her bed in front of the mirror before performing her favorite jump: a full leap and a twist mid-air in which her entire body and the skirt were spinning a full 360 degrees around (or at least the closest she could do to a 360, maybe it was more like "a 240," but it felt like a 360 so she called it that).

Yes, today will be different.

1.2

There was a fascinating glow, displaying multiple colors at any given time, that at first glance appeared to be drawing closer toward her. As the glow brightened, its shine began to reflect off the sheen of her space helmet. She reached for it. The yellow glow turned to blue, then to red, then to green, then to pink, then to orange, twinkling and rotating every few seconds to a different shade of color.

What a pretty rainbow light.

She wanted to get closer to it, close enough to allow it to further illuminate the otherwise endless darkness around her. But the closer she got to it, the more distant as a fading kaleidoscopic swirl it became, and then she felt herself become further removed, deeper into space.

The rainbow had been so distractingly beautiful that it wasn't until it disappeared that she became fully aware of the fact that she was no longer jumping on her bed but was now floating in outer space.

She looked over her shoulder and saw a dolphin floating beside her wearing a modified spacesuit for a dolphin's body. She was wearing a full spacesuit as well and that they were both simply floating in place in space with no spaceship or planet in sight. There were several thousand or billion (she couldn't tell) distant twinkling stars around them that provided a collective source of dim light.

She gave an awkward nod of acknowledgement in The Dolphin's direction.

"Eeee," The Dolphin replied, adding a smile.

They continued to float there together in silence for a few minutes.

"That was a pretty rainbow," Joy reflected.

"It was a nice moment," The Dolphin observed in a human sounding, female voice. "Nice colorful swirling thing, or whatever it was, it was kind of strange. Strange and beautiful. Beautifully strange."

"The nice moments disappear like that, as quickly as they arrive. Before you can take a second breath, they are gone," Joy determined. "I don't know how you can store them. There are so many days without nice moments when I wish I could pull out the nice moments like that out of storage, retrieve them, and relive them, but not like a memory. I mean, I wish I could fully re-experience them in the present moment."

Joy smiled at this concept of a "storage warehouse of re-experiences." The warehouse would have a different room for each beautiful memory to re-experience whenever she needed it.

"That wasn't really a rainbow," The Dolphin said.

"It was a rainbow..." Joy asserted, then hesitated as she pronounced the end of the word 'rainbow' before adding: "I think."

"Eeee," The Dolphin replied, adding a grin.

Joy initially gave the Dolphin a dubious look that gradually turned into an expression of warmth and familiarity.

"Well, Dolphin, this isn't really the sea, is it?"

"I'm a Space Dolphin now," The Dolphin clarified.

Joy looked at The Dolphin long and hard. The Dolphin took note and laughed.

"You remember me now," The Dolphin whispered softly, "it's been a very long time since you've seen me."

Joy didn't reply as though she was still stunned and unsure of how to start making sense of these strange feelings of déjà vu with The Dolphin. Instead, she observed the universe around them and saw how many of the stars seemed to be glowing brighter. She wondered where the sun was, wondered why The Dolphin was there, and wondered why she was there. Despite all these unanswered questions, she still couldn't help but smile once she had given herself the extra time to observe everything around her.

"What are we doing in outer space anyway? Joy asked, still smiling.

"I was wondering the same thing," The Dolphin replied. "Why did you bring us here? Was it to see that rainbow—"

The Dolphin tried to catch herself as she said "rainbow," but it was too late.

"Got you!" Joy giggled.

The billions of stars around them began twinkling with a greater shining intensity in a sort of rhythm of cascading levels of brightness that caught the attention of both Joy and The Dolphin. The stars twinkled in such a rhythm that they created twinkling waves of light at first, but then twinkled in scattered bundles like mini blinking spotlights. Then, a little later, the twinkling stars were individualized twinkles at a slower pace, with some rows twinkling in a pattern right to left and other rows left to right. They were like flashing white Christmas lights.

Then, all the stars grew in size and moved closer to them as if to improve their view.

Joy watched this light show in awe, and her smile broadened at the changes in patterns. She couldn't remember the last time she had smiled in this way.

Then one of the stars turned purple.

"Oooh," she beamed.

As she responded another star turned blue, and another green, another red, and so on until all the stars changed in color. Once this transformation was complete among all the stars, they twinkled like multi-colored Christmas lights.

"Your rainbow." The Dolphin nodded with approval.

"My rainbow," Joy mused.

Joy looked at The Dolphin after a moment of deep thought.

"But how do you make the colors appear like this?" Joy asked.

The Dolphin laughed at this and Joy laughed a little bit along with her too.

"I'm a dolphin," The Dolphin laughed.

"A Space Dolphin," Joy corrected her.

"All of us dolphins can't quite see different colors the way you can," The Dolphin explained. "We only have one type of cone in our eyes. You are creating the colors you see. I'm just responding to what you see."

Joy paused as she was about to reply, returning to contemplation.

"I'm not creating what I see," Joy concluded, "but I suppose with something like a rainbow, everyone might see it differently, and it probably won't look like what I see."

"Either way, you like rainbows apparently," The Dolphin added.

"I do like rainbows," Joy confirmed, "but it doesn't bother you that you can't see the rainbow too?"

"I may not see the rainbow like you can," The Dolphin conceded, "but I can observe how happy you are to see the rainbow and imagine how beautiful one must be based on happy it makes you."

"What do you mean? You can't see it."

"For better or worse, we can only see what we are able to see, but we also get to choose what we see and what we don't see in life."

"You can't even see the stars, can you?"

"Nope."

"Then how you can you enjoy them?"

"Because you are."

"And we aren't even in the sea…"

"In my mind, we are."

Joy laughed.

She turned back to watch the colorful star lights and then tried to look out even further beyond them. She tried to look out as far as she could into outer space just like she would try to see as far out to sea as she could whenever she was on a beach.

As she did so, she started wondering what the term "outer space" really meant: *Was it for people only like me? Did it simply describe the space that people like me belong in? Is the only place we can reside in relative to the rest of the world?*

She closed her eyes as the thoughts became overwhelming.

When she opened them again, she was back in her room, standing on her bed, and holding her flashlight with her skirt still pulled over her pajama pants.

She started jumping slowly as if there was less gravity in her room and the bed was the surface of the moon.

On the fifth jump, she closed her eyes.

When she opened her eyes again, she was back in outer space but this time without The Dolphin.

She looked down and this time, she saw the moon underneath her. She had jumped so high from the surface of the moon that it was now several thousand feet below her.

She smiled again.

Even though The Dolphin was gone this time, the sun had also made an appearance like a distant spotlight. It was a sort of night-light with a thin glow that slightly gleaned off the side of her helmet. The colorful stars continued to twinkle all around her, in varying levels of brightness, with no two stars appearing to be lit the same.

She blinked and the stars had transformed into thousands of colorful beautiful fairies flying around her in the blank space.

They were smiling too.

She then realized she had continued soaring in an upward motion through space from her initial jump, but the billions of colorful glowing fairies were still surrounding her.

She looked down and could no longer see the moon underneath her. She realized the sun was no longer reflecting off of her helmet. The only light came from the fairies, who flew gently around like mini-floating lanterns in what was otherwise pure darkness surrounding them.

The fairies still twinkled like the stars did.

"This is wonderful," Joy said aloud, the heat of her breath slightly clouding the visor of her helmet.

But as she said that a shot of pain raced up and down her back and then through her legs. She closed her eyes and clenched her knees with both arms as her body folded within her space suit into a floating fetal position.

She opened her eyes, and she was back in her room, where it was still dim. She looked around and realized she was now sitting on the floor, next to her bed. It occurred to her that she had tried to jump so high on her bed that she had bounced on her butt off the edge of the mattress and tumbled to the floor. As she thought about this, she also noted her mouth tasted sour with morning breath.

She reluctantly realized she still had to brush her teeth, shower, and do her hair to get ready for school.

She slowly got up and sighed. Her phone was still shining its flashlight on top of her bed.

After a momentary lack of knowledge of what day of the week it was with the potential it could be Friday, she sighed again when she remembered what day it was.

She said to herself aloud: "It's only Wednesday."

She walked over to her bedroom light switch and out of habit without thinking about it, made the involuntary move to try to turn it back on again.

This time, to her surprise, the light worked.

She had nearly jumped when the light flipped on.

She looked around her messy room which was now thoroughly exposed by the newly acquired light. She felt no motivation to clean it, despite the mess being even worse than it usually was.

She picked up her phone and turned off its flashlight.

"It's only Wednesday," she said aloud again. This time in a softer voice.

1.3

After her visit to outer space, she found that all the lights in the house worked again, and the sun outside was back to normal. She wondered if the outer space encounter with The Dolphin was a random, fluke flashback to her childhood. She missed her younger childhood when she used to spend a lot of time with The Dolphin and reflected on it for a moment with a wistful grin.

Or maybe she didn't get enough sleep again.

She had thought way too much about the couple in the hallway and how she didn't have something like that when she was laying in her bed trying to sleep.

In a lumbering fashion, she scuffled her way out of her room into the bathroom and nearly tripped over the side of the tub as she entered the shower.

When the cold water fell from the showerhead, she backpedaled quickly toward the back end of the bathtub before gradually moving forward into the shower stream to test it in its progress from very cold to temperate water. She was wearing her bathing suit, a ritual she had been doing for every shower since she first started taking showers. She moved forward with her arms crossed over her chest. Each of her hands grasped the opposite bare shoulder in her cautious approach until the water pressure flattened her frizzy hair strands of billowy bed-head. As the water continued falling through her hair, she raised her arms over her head as though she was trying to stop the flow of water that was still too cold to her.

"I can't even get into the shower right," she said aloud to herself as the temperate water flowed past her hands and all over her body. "I hate the way I look anyway, what's the point of taking this shower anyway?! I still won't look right no matter how much time I spend in here. I can't change the way my body or my face looks in here."

Out of frustration she tried to pick up a bar of soap, but it slipped out of her hands and fell down into the tub by her toes. She kicked the soap out of frustration, and it slid around the front and side of the tub before disappearing somewhere behind her. She glanced at the fancy-looking body wash her mom had bought her a while back (but had never used) before proceeding to look for the soap.

"Whoa...whoa, hold on a second!" A baritone voice objected from behind the orchid patterned shower curtain as she recovered the soap.

Joy nearly jumped and fell at the same time at the sound of the familiar voice. But as the voice was familiar, she quickly recovered and even felt a vague sense of relief.

She paused, started to smile for a split-second but defaulted again to her resting-frown. The gradually warming water continued to rain on her.

"I can't approach anyone..." She started to explain as her shaky hands struggled to create a desired lather with the soap she had now recovered.

"You do need to change your face," the voice indicated, "but not the kind of change you're thinking of."

She peeked out around the shower curtain for a moment and immediately recognized The Bear. Now that she had seen The Dolphin, she felt more prepared to see The Bear as well.

The Bear was an american black bear of such considerable size that he took up nearly half of the confined space that made up the rest of the bathroom. He was hunched over the sink, looking in mirror as he often used to. As she looked at him, she recalled from her early childhood that he liked to look at the mirror and make faces at himself to be silly: showing teeth, blinking eyelids, nodding his head, etc.

"Bear," Joy said, "you're back,"

The Bear smiled in the mirror.

Joy hesitated, and couldn't help but wonder: *Is this my "new normal?"*

Her "new normal" this morning was kind of like the "old normal" she experienced as a younger kid. But now she was older, and life still felt much weirder and more awkward, even around her old familiar animal friends. She disappeared behind the shower curtain to resume her shower.

As she stood there staring blankly at the tiled wall in the shower while the water continued to fall on her, she decided to try to settle back into that feeling of comfort she had as a younger kid.

She took a deep breath.

Her shoulders relaxed as she allowed a new comfort to set in. It was the comfort of knowing that The Dolphin and now The Bear had returned.

"You are supposed to be guarding me, Bear, while I am in the tub like you used to, right?" Joy laughed. "But instead, you're goofing around in front of the mirror again."

The Bear laughed along with her from the other side of the shower curtain. It was a hearty laugh that tried to hide the fact that he was a little embarrassed.

"You gave me the worst jobs back in the day," The Bear laughed. "I already protected you whenever you were in here for a few years or so and now you have me back here doing it again! By the way, you still lock the door as well."

"All you have to do is watch the door," Joy requested from behind the shower curtain over the sounds of water pouring and splashing.

The Bear regained his composure and turned back to the door. He checked the doorknob with his paw out of habit to doubly make sure it was still locked.

"You have been looking out for me since I was like three years old, Bear," Joy recalled over the running shower. "I mean, we have a history. Doesn't that mean anything to you?"

"Earlier than that." The Bear corrected her. He hesitated for a few seconds before deciding to proceed. "I don't think any of us ever told you this, but we were all present in the hospital room when you were born."

The Bear closed his eyes in front of the door and remembered the sight of Joy's father holding Joy's mother's hands as she was having contractions and yelling at him for not doing enough to help her cope with the pain. She had been yelling at him as if the doctors and nursing staff weren't there. He recalled Joy's father looking sheepish and fumbling around the side of hospital bed trying to give himself the sense that he had greater control of the situation. He also remembered leaning in and observing to The Dolphin that this probably going to be their only kid, given the struggles the couple had in their relationship while adjusting to the pregnancy. He smiled to himself and almost laughed— he had totally called it since Joy's mom refused to even think about having another kid after Joy was born.

"Of course, we all had easy access to witnessing your birth since no one, but you, could actually see us or sense when we were around," The Bear added. "You were too young to remember."

Joy grinned on the other side of the shower curtain as if she had already known they had been there for her birth. She wasn't surprised.

"Regardless of how long we've known each other, I'm just a bear that apparently only protects you anymore when you close your eyes while you are shampooing in the shower. I don't even remember what I am protecting you from. Some kind of monster that might pop out of the toilet? Or was it to prevent your mom from coming in to make sure you washed your hair? I feel like it was more about your mom potentially coming in since you have me watching the door. But I know you were dealing with the monster thing too. I can't even remember what you named it."

"It was 'The Toilet Monster', and I'm still afraid of him now that you're reminding me of him," Joy admitted.

"Ha, knowing you back then, I would have thought you were a little more creative with your imagination than just naming him that,"The Bear chuckled.

"You are so cranky, Bear. You weren't always like this."

"I was naive," The Bear reasoned. He had returned to the sink and was looking with some fascination at the various hair and skin products that Joy owned. They were huddled all over the top of the counter around the sink. He didn't remember her having products like this before. He scratched the hair on his chin with his paw in contemplation over whether or not he wanted to try any of them on himself.

"Now that I think about it more, I remember now how I really thought there was a toilet monster. You had me fooled for at least five years and I never saw the guy. You should be fine by now. Several years of you using the shower on your own should help you realize this wasn't a real thing," The Bear deduced.

"Listen, The Toilet Monster could still very well be in there," Joy asserted, poking her head out of the shower curtain again and glaring at The Bear with squinting eyes. "I know, I saw him there."

"Twelve years ago!" The Bear roared. "You were four years old!"

Joy had progressed to the point of her shower that her hair was now covered in conditioner. Her long strands of hair were dripping water onto the side of the bathtub and the tile floor immediately beside the tub as she continued to look at The Bear with her head protruding around the shower curtain.

"What do you want me to do, Bear?"

The Bear looked at her and proceeded to awkwardly sit down on the toilet that he was clearly too large for. His whole complexion changed to a much more somber appearance. He appeared as though he had something to say but chose not to say anything. He looked back at her meekly.

"You have no idea how much it means to me to have you back. You are my friend, Bear...I didn't have friends anymore before you and Dolphin returned."

The Bear looked into her eyes and thought about how he had barely recognized her. He had never seen her looking so lost. That was the word to describe her that he had been looking for: "lost." He thought about how she had so much positive energy, so much desire for exploration and adventure, and how she had been such a deep well of happiness as a little kid. All of that was gone— completely. He hadn't seen her in five or six years, but he still couldn't believe how much had changed. It seemed like all that was left from before was The Toilet Monster and she seemed more afraid of The Toilet Monster right now after being reminded of him than she was back then when the monster's "existence" made more sense.

As he thought about all of this, he hid any desire of having anything to say despite wanting to say something.

Joy's head disappeared back behind the shower curtain, and he listened to the sounds of water splattering against the bathtub as she washed the conditioner out of her hair. He loyally sat on the toilet seat and watched the door, encumbering any potential intervention from The Toilet Monster and/or Joy's mom.

1.4

When Joy emerged from behind the shower curtain after finishing her shower, The Bear was gone. This had been the routine back when she was younger, so it wasn't a surprise. She had only ever needed his protection while she was in the shower.

Joy looked through her makeup case and sifted through her various other beauty accessories, determining whether she was going to apply anything to herself that day. She wondered if she was doing it right when she did apply these products. Her mom had demonstrated how to use them to her repeatedly and she felt like she followed the process exactly the way she was taught, but her mom still told her she was doing it wrong whenever she tried on her own. When recently asked, her mom had declined to show her again anymore. She had thought about asking one of the girls at school who seemed like they did a good job on themselves but all the accomplished makeup artists that she had identified didn't like her. She also didn't want to go through the embarrassment of trying to talk to any of them anyway and probably get ignored or insulted. Joy used to be more afraid of being insulted, but lately, she had been ignored more often and that felt even worse. The pain of not knowing what she was doing and not being able to keep up with the trends of teenage life hurt less than being ignored. Either way, she still had mornings when she teased herself with the idea of trying the makeup.

As she dabbled around in her makeup case, she noticed a strange, unexpected movement out of the corner of her eye in the mirror. She did a quick double take while reluctantly looking at her reflection in the mirror, but everything seemed normal. She was breaking one of her own rules by looking into the mirror with the bathroom light on, so she was careful not to look at herself in the mirror too long.

She sighed.

By now, with the direction this day already seemed to be going in, she reminded herself that it was advisable to expect anything. She resumed fumbling around in her makeup case, but this time continued looking suspiciously out of the corner of her eye at the mirror.

After about twenty seconds, it happened again— a strange movement. She looked up and now, out of elevated fear and curiosity, glared at her reflection in the mirror.

At first, her reflection looked as exactly as she would've expected, and she cringed at looking at herself for so long in the mirror under the bright lights of the bathroom. It made her stomach turn. She was about to instinctively look away in disgust at herself when she noticed her reflection in the mirror seemed to move slightly without her moving.

It was weird.

It was also weird that it wasn't scary.

She took a deep breath. *I really need to start going to bed earlier to try to get more sleep at night.*

But before she could rationalize any further, it moved again. This time her reflection clearly lifted its left hand up and started waving to her even though her actual left hand was still clearly squeezing the edge of the bathroom countertop.

Now it was scary.

"What am I looking at?" Joy asked the moving reflection. "This is supposed to be a mirror."

She looked up at the bathroom ceiling to look away from it, not wanting to believe what she was seeing.

"I don't want to look at you." Joy declared.

But she could still feel her reflection staring at her, so she looked back at her reflection.

"I'm not afraid of you," she lied.

The mirror reflection smirked as its reply. It turned away from Joy so that its back was facing her. It remained in this position and Joy noted that its arms were moving like as it was working on something that it didn't want Joy to see.

"What are you doing?!" Joy demanded.

A burst of bright white light flashed through the entire bathroom. Joy closed her eyes at the flash and stumbled backward from the sink, nearly falling into the bathtub several steps behind her. She caught herself on the orchid shower curtain and fell into a seated position on the side of the tub with the assistance of the pull of the curtain. A few of the shower curtain rings snapped off of the curtain itself as it carried Joy's weight.

Once she regained her composure, Joy gradually opened her eyes and once she had obtained a full focus back on the mirror, she couldn't believe what she saw: her reflection showed her as a cute princess, so cute she looked cartoon-like. Her reflection was in flawless makeup, with beautiful, highlighted hair, glitter on both its hair and skin, and had sparkling earrings. It was wearing a beautiful exotic dress that looked like it was made specifically for her body.

"Wow!" Joy exclaimed. "I can't believe that's me!"

Her reflection winked at her.

Joy walked back up to the sink and leaned over it to get a better look at this version of her most beautiful self in the mirror.

She was completely entranced and mesmerized.

But soon after she had leaned forward, her reflection abruptly reached through the mirror and aggressively latched on to her. Joy was so stunned that it was easy for her reflection to get a good grip on her with both hands. The reflection's left hand had a substantial clump of Joy's hair, while the right hand was wrapped behind her neck. The right hand of her reflection was extremely cold on the back of her neck, as though it was nearly frozen.

Now with a firm strong grasp of Joy, her reflection in the mirror tried to pull her into the mirror with it, dragging her across the front of the bathroom counter with one of Joy's knees falling into and then pushing up against the wet sink. Joy used both hands to grab the edges of the counter. The tips of her fingers turned red on each hand until her left hand could no longer hold on. Despite the shock of what was happening, Joy marveled at how strong her reflection was.

Joy shifted all her strength to her right hand while grabbing blindly at anything on the counter with her left hand that could help her hold on. At first, she grabbed her toothpaste and once she realized it was a loose object, she threw it away so that it bounced against the wall like it would against the backboard of a basketball hoop before falling and splashing directly into the toilet.

"Joy?!" she heard her mom at the door. "What was that? Are you almost done in there?"

"Almost, Mom!" Joy cried.

"Okay," her mom replied and over the commotion of her current struggle, she could still hear her mom's footsteps walking away from the door on the wood-paneled flooring of their upstairs hallway.

Despite the loud commotion, her mom had chosen to ignore it.

She desperately grabbed onto a bottle of hairspray next and almost threw it away as she groaned at grabbing another loose object that initially seemed to be useless to her. She had anchored her left foot up against the edge of the countertop to compensate for the lost grip of her left hand. The arch of this foot pulsated in pain as she struggled to awkwardly keep it docked in position.

Her reflection suddenly made another surge to pull her in harder, and Joy muffled a scream by vigorously tightening her lips.

That was when a great idea occurred to her: she hurled the hairspray bottle at the face of her reflection, and to her surprise, the bottle hurtled through the mirror cleanly and was a direct hit right in the middle her reflection's forehead. Her reflection momentarily loosened its icy grip on her hair and neck, moaning in ghostly pain. She then felt around the sticky bathroom countertop for another object and once that object was secured (her hairbrush) she tossed it at her reflection. The hairbrush struck her reflection's nose.

Joy slipped slightly backward as her reflection released her hair upon that second blow, but it still had a grip on her neck. With her left hand, Joy gripped the arm of her reflection that was still holding her neck. Joy pushed herself completely up on the countertop, causing various beauty items that were on it to fall into the sink or onto the floor. Releasing her grip on the side of the countertop, she then grabbed the arm with her right hand as well. She confidently gazed into the eyes of her wincing reflection.

She gripped harder with both hands onto her reflection's arm and started a twisting motion that managed to gradually soften her reflection's hold on her neck. She took a deep breath before pushing her full weight into this twisting effort, until finally, her reflection released her. Joy, in turn, released her reflection and her reflection turned its back toward her defiantly as Joy slid sideways across the countertop and sink, causing more items on the countertop to fall or roll onto the floor.

Once she caught herself from rolling off the bathroom countertop, Joy carefully slid away from the mirror until her feet returned to the floor. She stood up back in front of the mirror, still trying to catch her breath. She was sweating and felt like she needed another shower.

Her reflection turned back towards her with both hands now covering its face.

Joy watched as her reflection gradually and theatrically removed its hands from its face.

Her reflection revealed that it was no longer the princess-version of Joy, but the face of Casey, the girl from school who not only dated Gray, but teased her far more than any of the other girls at school. The rest of the reflection's body morphed into Casey's body and was dressed in the kind of expensive clothes that Casey wore. It was notably a different outfit that Joy had never seen her in. This made sense, as Joy could not recollect ever seeing Casey wear the same thing twice since they had started high school.

Casey's reflection smirked upon Joy's recognition of it as it remained within the mirror where Joy's reflection was supposed to be.

Casey (and her reflection in Joy's mirror) had natural highlights in her long hair that all the other girls, including Joy, envied, but Casey was not the natural beauty that Joy's mom and Casey's friends like Natalie were said to be. Joy's mom had cited Casey as an example for Joy to aspire to of how someone who wasn't born with natural beauty had made themselves more beautiful by maximizing her strengths, hiding her weaknesses, and keeping up with all the current beauty trends. But Joy noticed that no matter how much Casey invested into looking good through her wealthy parents, and no matter how much effort she put into herself, that she still had a bitterness and resentment about her perceived lack of natural beauty.

Joy could now hear both her mom and dad knocking on the door, occasionally calling her name between questions asking whether she was "okay," and other questions related to what she was doing in there. It sounded like they were taking turns asking each type of question and sometimes they were unintelligible because they were both talking at once.

"You know that feeling you get when a guy really likes you by the way he looks at you when he first sees you?" The ghostly voice of Casey's reflection asked her. The voice sounded like Casey as if she was doing a serious impression of a ghost.

Joy remained quiet and still as though she had encountered a tiger in a rainforest.

"Of course you wouldn't. But let me tell you about it, Joy. I'm talking about a stranger that you'll only see once in your lifetime whether it's passing him by on the street or waiting in the same line as him at a concert. Most of the time you aren't attracted to the guy. But they are so into you in that brief period of time that your lives cross paths that you feel like a young queen being crowned for the first time in front of a large audience with every person there looking at you and believing that you are the most beautiful woman in the room. That's the feeling you can get from that one stranger. Now imagine you have an event like that happen to you at least once or twice a day. It's the best feeling in the world. You will never know what that's like, not even for one day. That's why I feel sorry for you."

Casey's reflection reached through the mirror and grabbed Joy by the arm with its right hand. By this point, Joy was so exhausted and sore that she looked down at its icy grip on her arm and sighed.

"Haven't you noticed by now? You aren't ever going to be good at anything. I mean what do people like you end up doing in your lives? You're really a waste of space..." The ghostly reflection of Casey looked Joy up and down and smirked. "...a lot of space," it finished.

Joy looked at the bathroom door but hesitated to yell back to her parents.

"If anything, think of me as your best friend. I'm trying to help you. I'm just making sure you understand it now, so you don't go living your life ignorantly thinking you're something you're not. You'll always be a loser, Joy."

Casey's reflection paused after that last sentence to let it stay longer with Joy before continuing: "I am giving you the opportunity here and now to admit it. Admit that you are a loser, and I will leave you alone from now on. The other girls will leave you alone too. You'll be free to be the loser you are without us bothering you. So why don't you—"

Before Casey could finish, Joy leaned forward and grabbed Casey's arm with both hands and bit it as hard as she could. It was like biting as ice cube.

Casey's reflection shrieked.

The entire mirror started flashing violently with bright white lights as though the sun in its true white color had suddenly formed right behind Casey's reflection. This blazing spectacle of light was so immense and kinetic that Joy closed her eyes and covered her face as she crouched down upon the bathroom floor. As she had closed her eyes, she saw Casey's reflection disappear among the flashing lights.

The bathroom door flew open and barely missed Joy as she remained crouched down on the floor. Joy opened her eyes and uncovered her face in time to see her dad as he nearly fell forward right over her. She backed up against the side of the bathtub as her dad took a giant step right beside her to maintain his balance. He had broken the door open by jumping shoulder-first into the door. Her mom was right behind him, still calling her name.

Her parents tightly gathered around her in the small bathroom, as she remained on the floor, trying to catch her breath.

"Joy..." Her dad started to say in a self-interrupted mumble.

Joy unraveled slowly out of her crouching position and stood back up. Her parents backed off to give her space as she stood up. Once she was standing, she looked sheepishly back at her parents.

Her parents then observed how various items that had been on the counter were scattered around the floor or had fallen into the sink. They also saw how the shower curtain was partially torn away from the shower rod.

The tube of toothpaste was still in the toilet.

"...what in the world happened in here?" Her dad continued in his most diplomatic tone. But despite his best effort to remain calm, his voice also gradually revealed more and more disappointment with each word spoken and an undercurrent of restrained anger was detectable by the time he uttered the word "here".

"Joy, have you finally lost your mind?!" Her mom shouted vigorously with a wide-eyed and menacing glare. "I knew it. I don't even know you anymore. This is crazy!"

Joy looked both embarrassed and puzzled. She closed her eyes for a moment in response to them, hoping maybe they would be gone when she was ready to open them again. She waited for what seemed like several minutes before opening them.

They were still standing there.

"Hi mom...hi dad," she said awkwardly, trying not to acknowledge the mess around her. She opted to try to change the subject. "How's your week going? Can you believe it's already Wednesday?!"

Her mom and dad looked at each other, counting on the other to respond. They clearly weren't expecting that kind of response from Joy and now looked more perplexed than angry or concerned. Eventually, they looked back at Joy with a mutual loss for words.

Joy looked back at them for a moment and decided it was a good time to try again.

She closed her eyes.

1.5

J oy vaguely realized she was chewing on her fingernails but continued to do so anyway until she finally stopped herself several minutes later. She then inspected her right hand in disgust. She discovered that she had been biting every nail on this particular hand to such a degree that she decided not to look at her other hand. She dug both her hands into her pockets so no one could see the now perceived glaring fingernail bite marks she didn't know she had until now. She stopped in front of her locker in the hallway at school, looking down at her shoes with her hands shoved in pockets.

She knew she had to eventually open her locker, take out her book for her first class, and start her day at school. But all she could think about was Casey's reflection in the mirror that morning and that couple making out in this same hallway the day before.

"Are you losing weight?" A voice she didn't initially recognize asked just as she sensed someone was approaching her.

Joy looked over and recognized Autumn, another girl nobody else liked, standing a few feet away from her. This was probably the first time Autumn had approached Joy and acknowledged her in about a year. Joy had known Autumn since kindergarten but through all those years they had known each other, they usually passed each other in the hallway in silence like two solitary ships passing in the night.

Joy didn't know how to respond to this question, so she remained quiet and blankly looked at Autumn with her hands still in her pockets.

Autumn didn't really have any friends either, but she was often seen in the hallway, classrooms, cafeteria, and even the restroom talking to people. She was usually talking to other girls who had either bemused or disgusted expressions on their faces as she was talking to them. Regardless of what each expression revealed, there was always general movement away from Autumn. There was a tendency in others to back or lean away from her while she was talking to them, since she came in close. There was also a pattern of avoiding her in general in terms of where she sat in the classroom or at the lunch table, where she stood in the hallway, and when it was time to work in groups or with partners in any given class. Joy didn't do any of that, but Autumn rarely approached Joy and when she did, she notably didn't get as close to her as she did with other people. Despite this lack of close contact, Joy had still been able to observe that Autumn strangely smelled like graham crackers even though Joy had never observed her consuming one.

Autumn had waited for a response from Joy and was looking at her curiously up and down, then up and down again.

Joy despised these fully body scans. She couldn't believe how people had the audacity to do them right in front of the people they were doing them to.

"What are you thinking about?" Joy finally inquired to break up the continuous body scan. She took a step forward toward Autumn, who responded by taking a step back.

"I'm thinking you could try the same pill I have been using to help me. As you can see, it's worked really well for me." Autumn then lifted her hands away from her body and moved her hips as she turned herself around in various unconfident poses trying to look like a model at a fashion show who had reached the end of the catwalk.

Joy looked Autumn up and down and side to side as Autumn posed for her until she caught herself doing the very thing she despised and stopped herself. She could detect no difference at all in Autumn's appearance from a year before. Autumn looked the same as she always did to her except that she was wearing even more makeup than she used to. The drawback that Joy observed of Autumn wearing the extra makeup, however, was that there were more places where the make-up appeared smeared and smudged on her face. The smudged areas of makeup matched her style of wearing wrinkled, disheveled clothes that looked like they had been picked up from a pile of clothes on her bedroom floor rather than stored in a closet.

Autumn had been dying her long wavy hair a bright red color since the sixth grade. She never dyed it completely red though, so her dark natural hair color was still showing in her roots. She wore a ton of beaded bracelets on both of her wrists and always had a black elastic hair tie also around her wrist that she never used in her hair. She often wore sweaters and scarves as often as she could, even in transitional parts of the seasons when the weather was still too warm or getting warm enough for short sleeve shirts. She wasn't overweight, but she wasn't super thin like she had said she wanted to be, so she preferred to cover herself up in layers of clothes whenever possible. Autumn's overall tired appearance made Joy suspect that she had been up all night either streaming or viewing video games.

"Wow, you look great," Joy said, trying her best to believe in what she was saying to give Autumn a good moment in what she imagined would otherwise be a miserable day at school for her.

"Thanks, Joy. You are too nice. Maybe that's part of the reason why nobody likes you."

"Well...." Joy started as she looked down, pulled her hands out her pockets, and fumbled around with a lock of several strands of her long hair between the fingers of both hands, "...you can tell them that I like them."

"Even Casey?"

Joy hesitated. "Sometimes Casey, except when she's mean."

"Isn't she always mean, especially to you?"

"She probably has people somewhere who at some point, weren't nice to her either. That's usually how it works, right? Someone isn't nice to her, so she isn't nice to me, and so on. It's like a domino effect of not being nice."

"Maybe some people are mean," Autumn observed, rolling her eyes. "Like you are too nice. To everyone, actually. You are too nice."

"I'm trying to stand up for myself more," Joy asserted.

"Trying?" Autumn asked rhetorically, "I don't understand you, Joy. You could be one of the most beautiful girls in school if you wanted to be. You only need to make a few changes. Yeah, a few. You have such a beautiful face, I mean your eyes are amazing. I would love to have your lashes; you have the best lashes in school. Even Casey knows it. I think that's part of the reason why she hates you so much. But anyway, I'm telling you this stuff I've been taking to lose weight has been magic. You deserve a little magic, Joy."

"I have plenty of magic," Joy contended.

Autumn gave her a baffled stare for several seconds before looking her up and down one more time.

"You say that, but you don't truly know what you have." Autumn muttered as she made tense eye contact with her. "You can still turn your life around, but if you don't act on it soon, you will become hopeless. Once you become hopeless, there is no going back."

Autumn abruptly turned and walked away as Joy stuttered around for a response.

"I have hope," Joy finally said in a delayed reply that instead went to a group of seven students that were now walking past her in the area where Autumn had been standing. She recognized them as members of the varsity football team. They were all wearing jackets with the school's colors and team logo on them. They walked past her as if she wasn't there.

Joy turned back to her locker and opened it. Upon opening her locker door, a folded-up piece of paper came tumbling out of it. It bounced off of Joy's knee and hit the floor.

Someone left me a note!?

As she looked at the note for a moment as it remained on the floor, her entire body felt a flood of excitement. *Maybe it was a note from Gray.*

She enthusiastically bent down and started opening it so quickly as she stood back up that she nearly tore it. She took a deep breath before she read it:

"Be ready to fight today in the locker room after gym class starts" -C.

Joy's shoulders slumped.

Her head dropped.

Both of her arms fell beside her body.

She released the note and allowed it to tumble down her leg back to the floor.

Her mind flashed back to the image of Casey and her friends lingering around the locker room while the rest of the girls had left to go to gym class. Joy knew they did that often. She knew that because she was slow to get motivated and dressed in her gym clothes to go to gym class. She would hear them a couple of aisles away beyond the row where her gym locker was talking about their boyfriends, complaining about their parents or teachers, talking about clothes, or talking about other girls who weren't there with them. She would even hear them talking about her and how they wanted to beat her up someday to put her in her place. Now, they were going to finally do it.

Joy knew it was unquestionably Casey who wrote it. Casey signed everything with a "C." and put hearts in place of a dot over every "i" she wrote. There was a large heart over the "i" in the word "in" on the note and Casey had colored in the heart. The note was written in purple ink and Casey preferred writing in either purple or pink ink. Teachers let her get away with this because she was one of the most popular girls in school and consistently got straight A's on her report cards. Casey was one of those girls who didn't need to study because she had a naturally high IQ. As she anxiously thought about Casey, Joy was amazed at how much she knew about her. It was far more than she would ever want to know.

Joy's first inclination was to show this to either her parents or to a staff member at the school. But then she reminded herself this was out of the question. Joy's parents would probably encourage her to fight as an opportunity to improve her standing among the other kids at school since all of their previous efforts to help Joy hadn't worked. She could picture her dad teaching her how to fight (he had already tried to do that on more than one occasion). Her mom had also encouraged her to learn how to fight. She had told her: "You don't really have anything else going for you, Joy. Let your father teach you. If you can defend yourself at least they'll leave you alone." Showing it to staff at school would also be an issue. It would result in Casey getting into trouble and therefore it would further strain Joy's already poor social standing with the rest of the junior class at her high school (and probably a considerable number of students within the senior and sophomore classes as well). She would make more enemies than she already had. It also occurred to her that she might lose more respect from some of the teachers if she did that. Some of the teachers gave her the sense that they looked at her as an instigator who provoked the perpetual bullying that she received from the other girls.

She decided she was either going to have to fight or skip school before gym class and go home. She hesitated and found herself ambivalent. She was fortunate in that she had time to decide. She didn't have gym class until 9:30am. She looked at the time on her phone. She winced with surprise that she had left her phone on before noting that it was Wednesday, December 8th at 7:36am. *I have plenty of time to decide.*

She turned off the phone.

She preferred to keep it off as much as possible.

It then occurred to her that she was six minutes late to her first class. Somehow, she had spent the previous ten minutes looking at the note and then thinking about it without hearing the bell ring in the hallway. Somehow, she hadn't noticed that the hallway had completely emptied, and she was the only one standing there in the total silence.

She started running down the hallway toward her next class and she was about halfway down the hallway when she remembered she didn't have her history book. She ran back to her locker that was still left open and grabbed her history book out of it. Upon closing her locker, she started running back down the hallway again. At approximately the same spot she had stopped at before, she stopped again.

She sighed.

She ran back to her locker and picked up the note off the floor. She carefully folded it back up and put it into her pocket. She didn't run to class on this third try. Instead, she walked in a slow, meandering fashion. She felt a sensation around her hip as though the note was burning inside of her pocket.

It felt like she had already been beaten up in a fight.

1.6

Joy stood on a beautiful, elevated mahogany deck that appeared to be at least three hundred feet above the ground. It was high enough to rise over the thousands of pine trees surrounding it. The sky was filled with dozens of clouds that were perfectly and strategically placed in a morning sky. She recognized it was still early morning by the emerging daylight, the smell of renewal in the air, and the dew blossoming on the wooden boards of the deck. She heard the distant chirping of birds in the background. When she listened closely, she realized she was hearing over a hundred different species of birds with different dialects and tones of singing and chirping that coalesced well together to sound like a metropolitan orchestra playing a gentle, but complicated symphony.

She breathed in the pine smell.

The deck was enormous in area and looked like it might have been around two thousand square feet. It had beautiful white string lights curled around the wooden railings. Portions of the edges of the deck were lined with various forms of potted trees that were decorated with white string lights as well and adorned with red ribbons and bows. All the white strings lights were twinkling throughout the deck.

Joy noted a foggy morning mist among the pine trees around the deck, and it was a little cold, but she was sufficiently dressed in a sweater and scarf. This was the kind of morning cold that you could sense would warm up by mid-day to be the perfect temperature. The deck floor was covered with a red carpeted walking path that meandered around long, rectangular, fine oak tables set with beautiful red tablecloths and silver settings. There were also water glasses, wine glasses, and champagne glasses with unopened and expensive-looking wine and champagne bottles. They all surrounded beautiful orchid themed floating candles that lined the middle of the tables as centerpieces. The candles were lit and glowing.

Joy couldn't believe the experience she was having from simply being in this mysterious place. This was the type of place that only the beautiful people and the rich people ever had access to. It was the kind of world she thought she would never know and now here she was. There was no one else around, but that didn't matter.

She was finally here, in a place like this.

This was exactly the type of place where she would want to have her wedding reception, birthday party, anniversary party, baby shower or even funeral (because she would want the people who care about her to experience this too). It was so beautiful. *How could I ever have a party in a place like this? I would have to make friends and obviously make money too. That would be hard. It feels so comfortable in this place, like I've been here before.* It was exactly the type of place she would dream about when she was a little kid. She took in another deep breath of the morning pine air before she began exploring.

She walked past at least a dozen tables crowded with decorative formal place settings and candles. The tables were surrounded evenly by gorgeous oak tiffany chairs that had red ribbons tied behind them.

Eventually, she arrived at the largest table at one end of the deck where Casey was sitting in an elaborate, lace embellished, white silk wedding dress. Casey was seated across the table from where Joy was standing and carefully picking at an acai bowl. She looked up at Joy and smirked.

"I've been expecting you, Joy." She greeted her in the warm tone that Joy usually heard her use with people she liked. "Please, have a seat."

Joy looked down and hesitated.

There was a hot coffee with cream in an elegant silver cup in front of her. Casey noted her looking at it.

"Yours," Casey offered.

Joy sat down across the table from Casey, trying to hide the fact that she was forcing herself to do it. The coffee helped. Joy loved coffee and it was a treat to her because her mom restricted her to one coffee per week on Saturdays.

Joy looked around again after she sat down and decided that the setting there looked enough like it was a Saturday to her.

She took a sip.

Right away, she realized it was the most incredible coffee she had ever tasted with a strong, earthy, yet exotic taste that was perfectly complimented by the right amount of high-grade cream.

"Wow!" Joy exclaimed involuntarily and looked wide-eyed back at Casey.

Casey smirked again. "I've seen you at school staring at the coffee cups that the other girls have so I thought you might like that."

"I love it," Joy gushed. She hesitated, but then continued: "I love coffee but my parents don't like me drinking too much of it because I have a lot of anxiety and they also say I'm still kind of young for it."

She then took another enthusiastic sip of her coffee like she was a little kid enjoying a new drink for the first time.

Casey didn't respond and was now looking out to the misty pine treetops and the dark blue sky off to the side of Joy. It was unclear to Joy if she had paid any attention to anything she had said. Casey looked bored by her already.

"Where are we?"

"The morning of my future wedding," Casey revealed. She looked annoyed that Joy wasn't aware of this.

"Oh." Joy tried to take a more casual sip of her coffee but took in another generous gulp instead. She hoped that maybe there was more coffee available on the deck. She hadn't seen any servers around during her walk earlier.

"I can't describe to you what it feels like because I know you've never felt anything close to it before," Casey explained with a sarcastic tone, now looking at her directly with a piercing glare. "There are really two different ways a guy will look at you. There's the look I get all the time where he obviously wants you so bad, he can't stand still. You can see him doing a little dance in front of you that he doesn't want you to notice. You feel the tension and it's so thick but at the same time you know he can cut right through it and embrace you at any second. You know why? Because they are animals, and their instincts tell them I'm beautiful and they want their children to look like me. There is an intuitive primal dance of tension-filled courtship between lovers that requires both calculated restraint and incredible grandiose gestures of commitment. It's like a beautiful chess match that's unique only to the two people involved at a shared pace that will never be replicated with anyone else. Nearly all women get to at least experience that. But you'll never even know that first time a guy looks at a girl and wants to be with her, and you know I'm right."

An immaculately dressed young male-server dressed in a three-piece black tuxedo with a white apron conveniently arrived before Joy felt any pressure to respond.

"More coffee, Joy?" The server asked.

Joy's eyes widened and her brows were raised at the fact that the server knew her name and she had never seen him in her life. He was very handsome, and she could barely find the words to reply. He appeared to be in his late 20's or early 30's and looked like a model out of a men's fashion magazine ad. The thought of her mom disapproving of her drinking more than one cup of coffee briefly entered her mind as she tried to part her lips to speak to him. Knowing her mom, she would make an exception for her to drink a second cup of coffee in this scenario since she was spending time with a popular girl. In fact, she would probably encourage Joy to get a second cup since she was here with Casey.

"Yes, please," she mumbled. The server picked up her empty coffee cup and walked away.

"But there's a better feeling than that. There's a second more perfect way a guy looks at a girl," Casey continued once the server had left. "I probably get it at least once a week and I know you'll also never have this happen to you either so let me tell you about it..."

Casey smiled and rose slightly to adjust a part of her dress underneath her within her seat. She then ran her fingers down and through the long hair falling over her left shoulder, slightly twisting the ends of the strands playfully. Joy wondered if she was going to continue as Casey maintained a deep inward smile. She was looking in Joy's direction but it was like she had lost awareness that Joy was there. Joy gradually realized that Casey was having a moment in which she was so enamored with herself that she had become lost in herself. She looked like she had rediscovered the true depth of knowing how beautiful the rest of the world thought she was even though she was already aware of how other people regarded her and talked about that constantly. What made Casey different from most of the other beautiful girls that Joy encountered was that she was so intelligent that she was able analyze and evaluate the impact and implications of her beauty in any circumstance on levels others couldn't comprehend or would usually consider. Joy had also wondered if Casey was more vocal and reflective about her beauty because Casey's beauty wasn't as natural as the others, and she wasn't regarded as one of the most beautiful girls in school until around the eighth grade.

Eventually, Casey was able return her attention to Joy, who by now had defaulted to her usual resting-frown.

"Okay," Casey said once she had regained her composure, "it's when a guy looks at you tenderly and longingly because he wants to spend the rest of his life with you. You get the sense he would be so happy to hold you all night and doesn't care whether he has sex with you because he so overwhelmed by you in the present moment that he doesn't have enough room in his mind to have his own agenda. He's transformed into a gentleman, and his heart tells him I'm 'beautiful' and he wants to raise children with me and only me. It goes beyond that first way I was describing where he just wants to subconsciously procreate with you. In this case, he definitely wants to have children with you and be the best possible father he can be to them because he shares those children with you and wants to be the best possible husband to you and co-parent with you. He will consistently do everything he can to make you feel safe and make sure you feel loved."

Casey quietly glanced at Joy after she had finished talking and then let out a long sigh.

"But you'll never know this," she continued, "and you understand this about yourself better than anyone. You will never be the main woman in any guy's life. You will never be number one. If you're lucky, you'll get some guy separated from his wife looking for a one-night stand or maybe a drunk frat guy in college for one night because he probably lost a bet with his buddies. If you're real lucky, you'll get a guy who is already married that will string you along as his ugly, but passionate and loyal mistress. That might give you your best chance at something close to a long-term relationship. That's all you'll get, Joy."

Joy was staring down in dismay at the table where there was still an absence of the coffee that she thought she was getting refilled.

"The server isn't coming back, is he?"

"No," Casey bluntly responded with a tone that suggested she derived pleasure in answering that way, "and you already know you won't be invited to this wedding when it happens either but..." As Casey trailed off, Joy looked up so their eyes met.

Casey nodded sideways in the direction to the left of Joy and when Joy turned to look in that direction, she saw that the server had returned without her realizing it. The server slid a clipboard on the table in front of Joy that looked like it included about 40 pages of printed forms attached to it. The server placed a fancy-looking pen beside the clipboard. There was no coffee included.

"This isn't coffee," Joy protested as the server disappeared again.

"...but you could be included in everything I do," Casey continued, ignoring Joy's comment. "You could be invited to every event I have. Be a part of my world. The staff here had started setting up a couple hours before you arrived, so you are only getting a very small sample size of what my wedding would be like. You could be invited to any future event you want to be at, including this wedding. I leave it up to you."

"Wait, who would you be marrying?" Joy asked. Her stomach was suddenly in knots when the thought that Casey might marry Gray crossed her mind.

Casey giggled and pointed to the pen.

"What is this?" Joy picked up the pen and looked down at the front page.

"It's a contract I am hoping you will sign," Casey answered. Joy started perusing the forms. She noted there were various places for her to initial and sign on each of the pages. She looked at them long enough to observe that her full name and Casey's full name were printed several times throughout the seemingly endless paragraphs of the contract. *Casey expects me to read all of this here and now? Without another coffee?*

"I am going to have to get my parents or a lawyer to look this over first before I sign anything," Joy indicated as she flipped back and forth through the forms. She looked distraught and overwhelmed by content of them.

Casey rolled her eyes.

"Joy, it's simple. If you sign the contract, you will be invited to my future wedding, you'll be included in everything I do as one of my friends, and people will know who you are and actually want to talk to you. You won't get bullied by me and my friends and we will make sure everyone else in school leaves you alone. By signing this contract, we will be starting new: you'll be legally forgiving me and my friends for everything we've done to hurt you over the years, and you'll be loyally committing to us. I don't know if you've noticed, but I am the most popular girl in school and my friends have really benefited from my popularity. I can't make any promises, but you know what? I'll even say this. If you sign that, I'll try to get you a date with Gray. We all know you have loved that guy for years now. I can probably make that happen. Can you imagine going on a date with Gray? Even with your imagination, you probably can't do that right now. You can start opening yourself up to so many possibilities and opportunities. It's that simple. I'll make it easy for you, sign page 31 now and I'll let you get to the rest of the forms later."

"What would I be signing on page 31?" Joy asked. Her eyes had started beaming at the thought of Casey being willing to break up with Gray so she could date him. Her gut instinct that Casey didn't really love Gray the way she did was true after all. She tried not to look too excited.

"All you are doing with page 31 is admitting that you are a loser and verifying that you will still be one even after your life gets better once you've become my friend," Casey explained.

Joy stopped breathing. She tried to push air out through her nose and when she failed to breathe through her nose, she tried with her mouth. She had opened her mouth to breathe, but it was completely dry and parched. She stood up from her chair and tried to force a deep inhale in through her nose. She tilted her head upward and vaguely noticed how the white clouds were now spinning in the sky.

She closed her eyes.

1.7

When she opened her eyes again, Joy was in her history class sitting at her desk. She was holding her phone so that it was propped up on her desk and she was staring at it as if she was watching a video or reading a message on it.

She was looking at a blank screen.

She let out a deep exhale through her mouth.

There was nothing on Joy's phone but a black screen, and yet she appeared to her history teacher, Mr. Kingsapple, to have been using it from the moment she had arrived eleven minutes late to class. He initially left Joy alone because he was confused more than anything and thought to himself: *Does this girl really have friends she would be texting in class?*

The class had been asked to form small groups of three or four students to complete three discussion questions together as an in-class assignment. The rest of the history class had shuffled around the classroom to sit with their groups. They had carried around their chairs, pushed desks together, and began conversations often unrelated to the discussion questions with little, if anything, to do with history. If history was discussed, then that "history" was compartmentalized to events that had taken place over the semester at this specific school, usually involving students who were either not in this particular class, or out of hearing range of conversations that involved them as subjects.

But Joy hadn't moved at all. She had remained locked in at her desk, unmoved, unaffected, and uninvolved with what the rest of the class was doing or not doing. She hadn't lifted her head up when the class had started moving around to create groups for the assignment. She was just sitting there looking at her phone, surround by a cluster of empty desks (some with missing chairs) in the back corner of the room.

At first, Mr. Kingsapple was inclined to give Joy the benefit of the doubt. Whenever he asked the class to get together either with a partner or a small group, Joy was never able to find a partner or group. Even so, she consistently completed whatever the assignment was independently and often with superior results compared to the rest of the class. He wondered to himself: *Should I let it go again?* He wanted to let her off again. *The girl looks like she has enough going on in her life.*

The problem was that this was one of those times when she didn't give him the impression that she was aware that there was an assignment. She had made no effort to open her book, take out a notebook or a pen, or open her backpack since she had arrived in class. All she did was stare at her phone. He was unclear if she had scrolled around on her phone or typed a message into it. She only appeared to be looking at it. *Was she watching a video in silence? Was she reading something but scrolling whenever he wasn't looking at her? She was such a strange student.*

In 25 years of teaching, he had seen a lot of weird kids (more than any non-teacher could ever imagine), but no one this odd. He had seen her distracted like this plenty of times, but never like this situation where she seemed completely detached from being present in class for nearly a half hour. She had always been aware of and eventually responded to in-class assignments.

Finally, he had enough, and he stood up from his desk, hoping she'd look up and meet his gaze so he could sit back down. She didn't move so he began to approach her with reluctant hesitation.

His index finger was held up to his chin and his head was tilted with curiosity.

"Alright Joy, time to hand over the phone."

She was startled and dropped the phone on her desk. She quickly recovered and quietly flipped the phone over as though there was something important and private on it. She held both of her hands over it.

She looked up at Mr. Kingsapple, then down at the covered phone, then at Mr. Kingsapple again before glancing around the room for the first time at all the groups of students. A few of the other students had started to turn their heads in her direction. She observed that the turned heads were still talking (probably about her).

She looked up at Mr. Kingsapple a third time, then at the phone again, and finally handed it to him awkwardly while still staring down at the desk area where the phone had been.

She had noticed how tired Mr. Kingsapple looked. He had looked like he hadn't shaved in three or four days and seemed like he had more gray hair than he did when the semester first started. From where he was standing near her desk, he smelled like cigarettes, cheap cologne, and coffee. He was wearing an ugly tan-suit that looked like it was twenty years old (Mr. Kingsapple looked like he was probably in his mid-40s, so Joy wondered if he wore the same suits from when he first started teaching). He also looked like he was always sweating (regardless of the time of year it was). He had short, thinning hair on his head that didn't seem to match his incredibly thick mustache.

"What was on this, Joy?" he asked, glaring quizzically at the blank screen and trying unsuccessfully to turn the phone on out of his own ignorance of operating smartphones that weren't the same brand as his.

Joy looked at the door to the classroom. She imagined herself getting up and simply walking out of class. She watched an imaginary apparition version of herself get up from her desk as her physical-self remained seated. The imaginary apparition version of herself then walked toward the doorway. About halfway there, her apparition-self stopped.

Where would I go?

It then occurred to her that as many times as she had looked longingly toward the door to the hallway from her desk, she had never thought about where she would go. *Would I really want to go home?*

"I'm really embarrassed to tell you Mr. Kingsapple," Joy mumbled, looking up at Mr. Kingsapple again but avoiding eye-contact. She watched him as he tried in vain to turn on her phone while his head remained tilted in a quirky pose. *He is one of the strangest teachers I have ever had. He seemed kind of lonely. Maybe he will understand me. Maybe he gets it.*

Mr. Kingsapple wondered if Joy had turned the phone off when she saw him approaching her through the corner of her eye. But he had observed no movement from her and no perceived recognition from her that he was approaching her until he had spoken to her.

He was stunned.

He didn't want to believe it.

"Joy, has your phone been turned off the whole time?!"

"Don't you ever go through life wishing you were someone else?" Joy abruptly asked as though she hadn't heard his question.

Mr. Kingsapple raised his brow, straightened his head, and cleared his throat. He placed her phone gently back on her desk and looked like he wanted to walk away.

"You really shouldn't think like that, Joy."

"Well, have you?"

Mr. Kingsapple glared at her, hoping that the silence would speak loud enough for her to let her curiosity pass. He hoped he could ask her about the assignment without answering her question while still coming across as empathetic to her.

He looked around the room to make sure the students were still working, or at least not paying attention to this conservation. Thankfully, they weren't or at least doing a good job of pretending they weren't as soon as they realized he was turning in their direction.

"I think you feel that way too," Joy surmised. "It's like there is someone inside of me who isn't lonely, who looks better, and who has more to offer this world. But when I look in the mirror and when you and all the other people in the world see me, all they see is this. That's why if I can't be someone else, I at least want to be the person inside of me to everyone else. But whenever I try to show that person to people, they hate me even more."

Mr. Kingsapple looked like he had transformed into a statue. He also looked like wanted to start the interaction over again.

Meanwhile, thin tears had streamed down both of Joy's cheeks from each eye.

Mr. Kingsapple knew he couldn't pause for much longer. He felt he had to set some kind of boundary with her but do so as diplomatically as possible.

"Joy, I'm trying to understand how it's relevant if I have or not and why that should have any bearing on how you feel about your own self-image."

"You are different, like me," Joy reasoned.

Out of frustration, she took a short, interrupted breath that created an unintended huffing and puffing sound that made Mr. Kingsapple take a step back before she continued: "You're supposed to understand. I always feel like I have to be someone I'm not. I wish I could be that person I think they want me to be, but now I know I'm never going to be that person. I am also realizing it's too hard to be the person inside of me that I want you and the others to see. Can you at least tell me you understand what I am talking about?!"

1.8

After Joy had asked Mr. Kingsapple that question, she looked down to hide more tears that had formed in the corners of her eyes. But as she did so, she noticed she was no longer sitting at her desk, but on a large rock. She also noticed that the tiled floor had turned into a dimly lit surface of rock of the same type as the rock she was sitting on. The rock floor was covered with a few inches of clear water that surrounded her shoes. She saw that the water covered the entire area of rugged rock flooring for as far as she could see. She could see the ends of the room were shrouded in darkness, suggesting that she was in a much larger room than what she was able to immediately perceive. She then looked up at a dim rock ceiling that was vaguely visible against the closest wall to her. The rock ceiling gave way to darkness as it arched higher toward the center of the room. She was able to see the characteristics of the cave immediately around her with the help of a glowing lantern sitting on the large rock beside her. This lantern formed her only source of light.

Several feet away in front of her she observed an immense glittery looking object. She felt drawn to it. She picked up the lantern and approached it. She perceived the cathedral-like acoustics of the cave that echoed with each step she made through the water. She felt an odd sense of security for being in such a large, dark, and strange place.

As she drew closer to the immense glittery object, it gradually revealed itself to be a mirror.

A gigantic, magnificent mirror.

It was by far the largest one she'd ever seen. The mirror had no frame. It was shiny, even in the dimly lit darkness, and was tall enough to resemble a skyscraper in length. It must have been forty stories tall. It felt like she was standing in front of large building that had been randomly erected in the middle of an immense cave. But when she walked the one hundred or so feet required for her to look around the side of it, she observed that it was flat like most mirrors. At first, she was disappointed when she saw it was just another mirror. But then when she briefly scanned the rest of the cave and looked again at her lantern, it occurred to her that the lighting was perfect.

It was dark enough to be the same way her bedroom was when she woke up in the morning with the little bit of morning light shining though her curtains.

This was exactly the level of darkness she needed and what made it better was that she was in solitude (she looked around one last time again to make sure). She held up the lantern like it was a trophy that she had earned. The light from the lantern really resembled that morning glow.

She excitedly ran (nearly slipping in the water) to a position near the center of the width of the mirror. Once she arrived, she put the lantern down by her feet in the water and slowly lifted her eyes to look at herself in the mirror.

She was surprised to see her reflection was dressed in a silk purple gown. A diamond speckled crown was on top of her head and her hair was made up in a style she'd never seen it in before with lavishly highlighted curls. She looked down and saw that her shoes were now diamond studded high heels. She imagined herself wearing this outfit at that beautiful wedding reception location on the mahogany deck among the misty pine tree-tops that she had been at earlier.

She looked up again and confidently twirled around in front of the mirror like she had a thousand times at home whenever she pretended to look something like this. She slipped again and nearly fell over after twirling, but that didn't faze her.

She was mesmerized.

She wanted a better view.

She tried to hold the lantern right up to the mirror to get a closer look. But as she leaned forward toward the mirror, her hair, her crown, her dress, and her heels all gradually faded into her frizzy untamed natural hair, her drab school clothes, and her wrinkled sneakers.

The water covering the floor of the cave was now rapidly rising. The water level elevated up over her shoes and continued rising toward her knees.

Joy backed away when she saw all of this.

She shook her head in disbelief and turned to walk away.

She then changed her mind and turned to face her reflection again.

She looked directly at the mirror, lifted her wet right sneaker out of the water and pressed the bottom of it against the mirror with all her strength. To her surprise, the entire mirror easily tipped backward. But before it could come crashing down, it vanished midway through the fall into the darkness.

Meanwhile, the water was now flowing over her ankles as it continued to rise.

She breathed a long sigh as she walked away from the where the mirror was and calmly sat down on the large rock that she had been sitting on earlier. The rock was elevated like a chair, so it was still safely above water-level.

She placed the lantern beside her on the rock.

She knew she should try to find a way out of the flooding cave, but she was too defeated from her experience with the mirror to explore any further.

"Joy?!" She heard a voice echo through the cave. She lifted up the lantern and held it eagerly in the direction from where she had heard her name called. At first, she didn't recognize this voice, but it sounded strong, confident, and reassuring.

A dignified african lion bearing a large regal mane was standing nearby. He had a stoic aura about him despite being almost chest deep in water.

"Joy," The Lion gently repeated, "we should head back through the passageway to the castle, we will be safe there."

1.9

"**J**oy?!" Mr. Kingsapple asked with a tone of genuine, almost-panicked, concern. "Are you still with me?"

Joy wiped her eyes and looked up to see that Mr. Kingsapple was now hovering over her, waving his hand in front of her face.

Mr. Kingsapple still looked too overwhelmed to be relieved. He stopped waving his hand in front of her face when she looked up at him and they briefly made eye contact. He generally did a good job of not showing too much emotion in the classroom to his students despite otherwise being an overly sensitive, empathic man who loved his profession deeply. But with Joy, it was harder to maintain a semblance of neutrality. The more he interacted with her, the harder it seemed to be to try to protect her without some outward demonstration of sympathy for her high school survival. He felt embarrassed for her. He could sense the rest of the class behind them now looking at them and all their voices had fallen silent. He wanted to turn around and tell them to continue working, but he knew that wouldn't work. He felt guilty for drawing the unwanted attention to her. He could see that she could sense all of their faces looking at her but she was pretending not to notice.

His instincts told him to simply get her out of there.

"Joy, do you mind taking a walk with me out into the hallway? Bring your backpack with you."

Joy picked up her overstuffed backpack that looked like it weighed thirty pounds. Mr. Kingsapple wondered: *What on earth does she keep in there? Does she have to make life harder on herself with everything she does?!*

As they walked out of the classroom he turned to the class, urging them to get back to work with the hope they would simply return to what they were doing before (whether they were really working or not).

As the door closed behind him in the empty hallway, Mr. Kingsapple started to sigh but caught himself midway and ended up with a sort of muted sigh.

"Joy," he whispered (as though they were still in classroom), "I'm sending you to Ms. Jewel's office, again. I know you don't like going to see her, but I think it's better for you to be with her today rather than staying in there. I expect you to head directly there, don't get sidetracked on the way there. This time I am messaging her advance as soon as I go back in the classroom so she will be expecting you."

Joy let out a muted sigh of her own before replying: "But Ms. Jewel doesn't like me, she doesn't like how I—"

"Don't say that Joy. You know it's not true," Mr. Kingsapple interjected before she could go any further. "Everyone who works at this school likes you. We all like you, but sometimes we don't know what to do with you."

But the way the inflection in his tone changed when Mr. Kingsapple said "everyone who works at this school likes you" gave Joy the strong impression he was politely lying to her.

Joy looked down at the floor without immediately responding. He became concerned he might have lost her in the conversation again, but she looked back up at him without making eye contact.

"But I am missing today's assignment," she mumbled.

Mr. Kingsapple considered this and initially thought about asking her to do it as her homework for the night but realized she probably hadn't written down the discussion questions. As he looked at her, he observed how lost she looked standing there in the hallway with a clear continued desire to not want to go to where he was sending her.

"I tell you what Joy, you get a free pass on this one."

He had never said that to a student in his career. He couldn't believe the words coming out of his mouth. He almost smiled after he said it. Maybe that was his way of saying "I understand" in response to her questions earlier.

Joy placed her backpack down on the floor, opened it, and knelt beside it as she tussled and fumbled around the books, folders and crumpled papers in it. Eventually she recovered a folder that took some extra energy to remove. When she looked back up at Mr. Kingsapple she saw that his head was tilted again with his index finger scratching his chin. She pulled out a typed, three-page response to the in-class discussion questions the other students were working on in the classroom. She handed it to Mr. Kingsapple with his free hand.

"I appreciate it, Mr. Kingsapple," Joy acknowledged, "especially since I know you probably never usually do something like that. But I finished the assignment on Monday night. I enjoyed reading and writing about the medieval period. It helped me take my mind off the more stressful things I have been dealing with."

Mr. Kingsapple looked at her blankly. "Well, how—"

"You wrote the discussion questions down on the board on Monday and told us to keep them in mind as we completed the reading assignment for today's class," Joy clarified before he could go any further (she had Mr. Kingsapple's history class on Mondays, Wednesdays, and Fridays). "You always do that. You give us the questions to think about before you have us do an in-class assignment in the next class, right?"

Mr. Kingsapple held his blank expression.

"Right," he finally managed to say.

"Try to do something you love after work this afternoon, even if it just involves eating your favorite food or listening to your favorite song, Mr. Kingsapple," Joy advised. "You seem like you could use a break yourself today. I'll see you on Friday."

Mr. Kingsapple blinked a few times and nodded as she walked down the hallway in the direction of Ms. Jewel's office.

"Right," he repeated. This time he was only talking to himself as Joy had already turned the corner into the next hallway.

1.10

"**S**taring at a blank screen on your phone for 30 minutes without moving while the rest of the class is working on a group assignment," Ms. Jewel read from her computer screen as Joy sat quietly in one of the two chairs on the other side of her desk. The back of both guest chairs in Ms. Jewel's office were up against a row of ceiling-to-floor windows that separated her office from the hallway. Joy sat in the one closest to the office door.

"Joy, are you daydreaming again, but this time with props?"

"No," Joy muttered. She was sitting uncomfortably in her chair because she had declined to take off her overstuffed backpack when she sat down. The backpack was compressed between her back and the backrest of the chair. The size of the backpack left only so much room for Joy, so she was just partially on the chair herself. She kept her balance by placing additional weight on her feet and straining her knees.

Joy didn't look at Ms. Jewel at all. Instead, her gaze was fixated on a lit candle that Ms. Jewel had on the corner of her desk. She was mesmerized by how quickly it danced in a radiant, hypnotic, swirling motion. She figured this calming candle could be her anchor as she was about to navigate an inevitable barrage of questions from Ms. Jewel.

She braced herself.

"And why is your hair like that?" Ms. Jewel asked.

"I had to walk outside across campus and it's very windy."

"Why didn't you use the skybridge?"

"It has a lot of windows that are kind of like mirrors, and I don't like seeing myself in those mirrors."

"I worry about you, Joy…" Ms. Jewel indicated without any hint of worry in her facial expression, "…you need to embrace both yourself and nature. It seems to me that you are resisting both. You won't even look at your own reflection in the mirror and your hair tells me that you see the wind outside as a nuisance. The wind is absolutely not a nuisance at all."

Joy looked at her oddly.

It was still surprising that this woman, who was a self-identified nature-loving free spirit, seemed more interested in what her hair had to say to her than what she had to say. Joy wouldn't have minded so much but she also was using language like "not," "absolutely" and "at all" within the same sentence while sounding as judgmental about her hair as everyone else.

"There is all of this energy in me," Joy shared, "and it's leading me in a direction, but I don't know what that direction is."

"Like you mean, anxiety?"

Joy paused before she was about to reply.

The candle flame was swirling like a tornado.

"Maybe," she responded, having decided to avoid an argument.

"You are shaking right now."

"Your office is really cold every time I'm in here," Joy replied, squinting her eyes at Ms. Jewel. "But anyway, all the energy inside of me— I'm still trying to think of how I can describe it. It's like there is a real person inside of me waiting to get out and be around the rest of the world, but the other girls won't let her come out, because they don't want me to be around them or anyone else."

"Why not?"

"You know why—" Joy began.

"Tell me why," Ms. Jewel interrupted, "this may surprise you, but I can't read your mind right now."

You are supposed to help me decide what classes to take and help me figure out what I want to do with my life. You are supposed to help me figure out what I might major in if I go to college. You are supposed to listen to my concerns and help guide me. You aren't supposed to bring things out of me that I don't want to talk about. Joy had almost vocalized these thoughts as a response but held them in her thoughts because she thought it might sting Ms. Jewel. After all, Ms. Jewel was already more on edge with her than usual.

Ms. Jewel was a guidance counselor by profession. But she liked to also think of herself as a therapist and presented herself that way much more so than she ever presented herself as a guidance counselor. Joy wondered why so many adults worked in certain jobs even though they more strongly identified with a different profession. *Why not land a job in therapy if you are more interested in that vocation?* It was like they chose to bend the job they were currently in toward resembling the job they really wanted rather than taking on a job (or at least pursuing an education) in the field they preferred.

"What if figuring out what you want to do with this person inside of you involved having to confront things you don't want to think about?"

"Then I won't do it," Joy answered. She looked at the door but didn't leave. As annoyed as she must have appeared to Ms. Jewel, she realized in that moment that she strangely kind of liked her in a way. But she still didn't like that Ms. Jewel was doing a job that wasn't her true calling. The candle, meanwhile, had transitioned to a slower burn.

"There are going to be people who don't like you. We all must accept that about ourselves. They may not like you because you are you. They may not like who you are or what you represent to them. They may not like you because they are in a bad mood that day. They may not like you because it's situation where you would otherwise get along with that person, but you happen to meet that person at the wrong place and at the wrong time when maybe you aren't ready for that person or that person isn't ready for you..."

"...or all the above!" Joy blurted out before Ms. Jewel could finish. "For me it seems like it's all the above. Everyone is always in a bad mood around me. They aren't ready for me and I'm not ready for them. That is, I mean, if I can get past them not liking who I am."

Tears were budding in the corners of the Joy's eyes. "All of the other girls seem like they have something I don't have," she continued, "I can't describe it. But I see it when they smile. I never know how to smile like that. I don't know what makes them so happy to be able to let out that smile. Sometimes I feel like they were born with it, like it's some kind of gene or some kind of trait that you can't learn or pick up because it has to be something that you were born with. It's like it has to be something innate and the rest of the world around you recognizes your luck and continues to shower you with luck. Then there are people like me, who bought the wrong charger for their phone and who can't figure out how to do a new task the first time or even the fifth time. People like me can hardly get out of bed in the morning. I don't know how people keep going. I don't know how they get out of bed in the morning. I don't know how they deal with people saying mean things to them. I don't know how they have the ability to understand what someone else wants from them. I don't know how they can pretend to know or understand what someone else is thinking. I don't know how they can fit in or keep trying to fit in. I am not going to fit in anywhere. I don't even fit in with the other people who don't fit in. How can the other people who don't fit in judge somebody else who doesn't fit in? I don't know, but they do."

There was a momentary pause that followed between them as Ms. Jewel joined Joy in glazing at the candle flame while deep in thought.

"And yet you have all this energy inside of you that you don't know what do with, right? Maybe that energy is 'the something' you feel like you don't have and maybe it's a greater energy than what most people have. You have it, but you don't know what to do with it. And perhaps they see with envy what you can potentially do with it, but you don't yet because if you did, a lot of these questions you are asking yourself would be answered." Ms. Jewel sat back in her chair as though satisfied with her own response.

Joy non-verbally reacted like a deer curiously stopping at the first sight of a hiker in the forest for a brief analysis with the plan to run away if the hiker moved any closer.

Ms. Jewel's phone buzzed with a notification.

Ms. Jewel looked at her phone as though Joy wasn't in the room. As she quietly swiped the screen with her thumb, she reached up with her free hand and ran it through her short auburn hair a few times before scratching her head. She then stood up from her seat, revealing how her long, over-sized knit sweater draped over her thin body below her waist and over her hands. She was shorter than Joy, so her sweater almost looked like a dress. She poked her hands out from underneath her sleeves to pick up her planner and mug of hot tea from her desk.

"Joy, I have to go a meeting now. I called your mom before you got here, she should be arriving in about fifteen minutes or so to pick you up."

"You what?!"

For a moment Joy looked like she had stopped breathing and might implode. When she did finally exhale, she blurted out something she never thought she would say: "But I still have to go to gym class!"

"You what?!" Ms. Jewel looked like she definitely didn't expect that. Joy placed her hand up to her mouth. She didn't expect it either.

As they briefly made eye contact, it occurred to Joy that she would rather go get physically beat up at gym class by Casey and her friends than be subjected to the mental and emotional beating she was anticipating from her mom on the car ride home.

"Nevermind," Joy conceded. She stood up as well and looked out the window into the hallway behind her.

"Actually, Joy, you can wait in here for your mom. I instructed the front office staff to come and get you here when she arrives," Ms. Jewel explained as she walked out the door.

"Oh," Joy said to the empty office as she watched Ms. Jewel walking down the hallway through the window. She stood there awkwardly for a moment as someone might do after an interaction ends without the closure of an exchange of goodbyes. She took the opportunity while still standing to remove her overstuffed backpack and place it on the other chair beside her chair. She had so much homework, and she wondered again how the other students didn't seem to have to carry all of their books. Everyone else seemed so relaxed, hands-free and unburdened by this weight of heavy books tugging down on her tense shoulders. *How did they get their work done without carrying their books with them? How did they still pass their classes without turning in their homework?* She bristled at the thought of how much more extra work she would have from missing the classes she was going to miss for the rest of the day. She felt like the school was trying to get rid of her rather than truly try to help her.

She took a deep breath as she stood between the chair she had been sitting in and Ms. Jewel's desk. She turned and glanced back at the candle. *Did Ms. Jewel leave her candle on for me, or did she forget to blow it out?*

The flickering flame expanded once it was locked within her gaze until it became a full-blown torch. Joy took a step back and upon doing so, realized the chair was no longer behind her and Ms. Jewel's desk was no longer in front of her.

1.11

Joy was no longer in Ms. Jewel's office but standing in a cool, dim, stone-walled passageway lined with torches. She was standing right in front of the torch nearest to her. As she turned her gaze away with the torch's hypnotic flame, she was amazed at the fact that there were hundreds of torches like this one lining both sides of the hallway. She observed how the ceiling and flooring were made up of large stone bricks like the walls were. Her shoes, socks and pant-legs up to her knees were still soaked from earlier. She then saw that The Lion was walking away from her and had progressed further down the hallway. He must have assumed she hadn't stopped at the torch and was still walking behind him.

"Tell me again, where are we, Lion?"

"You don't recognize this place?" The Lion turned to her and looked surprised to see her so much further behind him. "We are in the secret passageway from the underground caves that leads up to your castle."

"My castle?!" Joy did a double-take around the passageway. "Secret passageway?!"

"The castle that you were a queen in," The Lion recalled with a partial smile that didn't seem natural to his stoic demeanor.

"Oh?"

The Lion approached her, and as he got closer to her, she noticed that his lower chest, legs and tail tuft were also still wet.

"We're almost there," The Lion reassured her as he stopped beside her.

They continued down the passageway together. Joy looked with fascination at the torches, breathed in the damp musty air, and hoped her shoes and socks would dry faster.

"Who makes sure all these torches remain lit?"

"Your guards take turns lighting the torches according to their shifts," The Lion answered.

"My guards?!" Joy smiled.

The Lion continued walking silently. He maintained the partial smile he had earlier.

"Why was the cave flooding back there?" Joy asked.

"I don't know," The Lion admitted, "I have never seen it like that before."

She stopped again. She could hear faint sounds that sounded like explosions in the background. She tried to listen more closely.

"Maybe someone moved in here since I haven't been here. I think I hear a TV."

The Lion stopped and turned to her. He looked puzzled that she had stopped and had fallen behind again. He also looked like he wasn't sure how to reply to her comment.

Joy caught up with The Lion and they continued walking for a while without any interaction between them. Joy was looking fervently and curiously around the passageway as if she was trying to take in every possible detail.

"Just to prepare you before we get there: the castle has fallen into disrepair because you haven't been here for several years. Many of the knights, guardsman, servants, maidens, nobles, and even the apothecary have left. There is barely enough staff taking shifts here from the village to keep it minimally maintained," The Lion disclosed after their long silence.

Joy stopped again.

The Lion stopped a few steps ahead of her and looked back at her. He had defaulted back to his stoic demeanor.

"I know you said the castle won't be the same, but do you think we still have any towels around here, Lion? We are both still pretty soaked from being in the cave."

"Towels?!"

By The Lion's reaction, Joy quickly deduced he hadn't considered a towel for himself.

"Why are you taking me to the castle exactly?"

"You brought us here," The Lion replied.

"I did?"

The Lion didn't provide any further information, and they continued through the passageway. Joy tried to recall having a conversation with The Lion about bringing her there. She was also trying to remember a recent time when she would have thought about the castle to have the desire to return there. She was quite perplexed, and The Lion didn't seem interested in clarifying things for her. He had an air about him in the way he looked at her that suggested she was supposed to already know everything.

When they reached the end of the passageway, they entered a small vestibule with a set of two large dark oak double doors to their right, and an identical set of doors to their left. Every door had matching detailed wood carvings of orchid flowers at the center of it. A smaller version of the orchid flower emblem was carved at the center of each upper and lower panel of the doors. Upon closer examination, this art was augmented by even smaller orchids etched in columns and rows along the outer edges of the panels and along the outer edges of the doors.

"Wow, the artwork on these doors is incredible," Joy gushed. "I love orchids so much."

The Lion was at the entrance at the right side of the vestibule while Joy had been primarily observing the pair of doors on the left side.

"This set of doors opens to a corridor that leads to the great hall of your castle," The Lion explained as he nodded in the direction of the doors he was standing at.

"And this one..." Joy pointed to the doors she was facing.

"...leads to one of the towers of the castle."

"Can we—"

"Sure."

They proceeded to go through the left doors which, upon opening, revealed a stone spiral staircase filled with pockets of speckled sunlight from small windows of various sizes installed in the tower. The brightness of the sunlight peering in through these windows suggested it was sunrise.

Joy smiled broadly at this sight and ran up the staircase with The Lion mumbling "careful" while staying close behind her.

At the top of the tower, they entered a canopied room that indicated the tower was covered by a conical roof. The room was larger than one might've expected after climbing the relatively narrow spiral staircase to get there. It contained small windows like the rest of the tower, but there were not enough windows to fill the room with sunlight. As a result, there were also three lit torches strategically placed around the room. Two of the torches were on either side of a large, elaborately decorated book display table. The table had an acrylic display case on top of a rectangular stone base dotted in swirling designs of blue gemstones. The decorated stone base was surrounded by dozens of floating navy-blue tea candles in clear cylinder glass vases filled with water. The candles were lit. The book itself within the display case was massive, closed, and appeared to be hardcover. The book had a dark navy-blue cover that contained no writing on it. It looked like it had thousands and thousands of pages. Joy wondered if it was 10,000 pages long.

"Everything is blue," Joy whispered as she walked slowly up to the display table.

"Each tower has a corresponding color, and we are in the 'blue tower,' but everything is that darker shade of blue you prefer."

"Makes sense." Joy was gazing at the book in wonder.

The Lion sat beside her as they both faced the display.

"Joy, this book contains everything that everyone else has ever said about you behind your back. Everything is in dialogue format like you are reading a play or a movie script, so that the names of people are listed next to their quotes. It contains a section that also lays out what you thought other people said behind your back at the time and compares it to the actual dialogue of what was said. There is also a section that includes every thought every other person ever had about you whether positive or negative. If you forgot who a person in your life was, there is an appendix of short biographies of everyone quoted that highlights the association they had with you to jog your memory. It's incredibly comprehensive," The Lion explained.

"How many pages is this?" Joy asked, looking wide-eyed at The Book of What Everyone Else Ever Said or Thought About Her.

"Too many to count," The Lion reflected. "I've checked. There are no page numbers in it. Instead of page numbers, it has the date and the time that the conversations and thoughts took place. If you look at it long enough, you might notice the size of the book keeps getting larger since people keep talking about you and thinking about you. I've noticed it's added pages every day. You wouldn't think that people would talk about you or think about you every day since you have those days when you stay in your room. I also know you think that nobody cares enough to think about you or talk about you, but you'd be surprised."

Joy was expressionless as she thought about what he said. The Lion couldn't get a read on her as he waited for her to respond.

"It's not worth it," The Lion added. He was becoming unusually unsettled by Joy's lack of response. "I don't think I'd ever want to see something like that written about me."

Joy was still quietly staring at The Book of What Everyone Else Ever Said or Thought About Her.

"You can read the book, Joy," The Lion offered. "But the only rule to it is, that if you do decide to look at it, then you must read each new entry line-by-line every day for the rest of your life when you wake up each morning to re-gain access to the real world."

"Well…" Joy began before descending into a long pause.

Although The Lion was waiting patiently for her to continue, she felt pressure to tell him the truth rather than dance around it.

"…what if I don't want to access the real world anymore?"

"That is an option…I am sure by now you've been in the real world long enough to know that there are people who simply exist there and do nothing more other than exist in it. Their minds, their hearts, and their souls are completely somewhere else to the point where it seems like they have only left the physical body behind."

At first, Joy looked like she may have had a response but instead appeared to delve deeper into thought.

"Joy?" The Lion nudged her leg with the side of one his paws.

Joy slowly turned to him. "If I read the book and stayed here then the new pages would gradually stop accumulating as I spend less time in the real world. As I read the book, I'd get to know everything terrible that was ever said about me in the real world, and I'd be more justified in my decision to stay here and read it. Eventually, there would be nothing more added each day for me to read in case I did want to keep my access open to real world. By then, I'd be so happy with my life here that I wonder if I'd want to keep my access."

"It's more complex than that," The Lion replied as though he had already prepared a response to that exact point. "There are also a lot of good things that are said about you in that book. There are. Believe it or not, your parents do love you and care about you.

And yes, I'm including your mom. Keep in mind, you'd be limiting or losing your access to them. You are also a very kind person who has done a lot of nice things for a lot of people, even strangers. You've made more of a positive impact than you think. Remember, this book covers your lifetime, not just high school."

The Lion had more to say, but before he could continue, he smirked.

Joy immediately took notice: "What?"

The Lion continued smirking. He looked so silly doing so that Joy couldn't help but laugh.

"What?!" She laughed. "What, Lion?!"

"Real love," The Lion mumbled.

"What?"

"Real love," The Lion repeated, this time with a little more clarity and volume, "you know you want real love. True love."

"Well, yeah...but we have love here. I get the sense that you love me, and I feel in my heart that all the others here do too, but—"

"It's not quite the same, is it?"

Joy nodded and took a deep breath.

She took an involuntary step back from the display table but as she did so, a loud thundering explosion that sounded like it was downstairs reverberated through the entire tower. The tower shook like it was experiencing an earthquake. Joy took another longer step backward to retain her balance.

As the tower continued to tremble, she crouched down to the floor, placed her hands over her head and closed her eyes.

"Joy!" She heard her mom's voice and felt both her mom's hands on her arm.

She back in Ms. Jewell's office, standing in front of the burning candle, with her mom now standing impatiently beside her.

"Come on, I'll take you home," her mom muttered.

1.12

"Joy, I don't know if you mean to disappoint people, but you do, and when you do, you seem to be relieved that you aren't the one being disappointed. It bothers me that my daughter might be one of 'those' people. You're at least better than that."

Joy listened quietly to her mom as they sat in the car on the way back to their house from the school. She was trying to block out the sarcastic responses that kept popping up in her thoughts as potential responses to her mom. She glared out the passenger-side window, not really observing anything within her view. On the way out to the car in the school parking lot, the dark clouds had seemed to indicate that the rain had stopped, started again, and then stopped again. It was a peculiar day weather-wise.

Her mom had been waiting for a response and the tense energy in the car indicated that she was losing patience. Joy could feel her mom observing her between glances at the road in front of them, the rearview mirror, and the side mirrors. Her mom seemed much more focused on her than on her driving. She was driving more slowly than usual, and the trip back home seemed much longer than it should have been.

"Sweetheart..." Her mom sounded concerned, but to Joy it also sounded kind of sarcastic and insincere. "I don't know what to do with you. I've bought you make-up and you don't wear it. I bought you nicer clothes and you don't wear them unless I beg you to when your grandparents come over. I feed you smaller portions at dinner time and I don't know what you are doing, because you have this extra weight on you that you shouldn't have. I've even searched your room to see if you are hiding any extra food, but I never find anything. I don't know what else to do. But if you want to get by in high school, you have to make friends. You must look like you care about yourself if you want anyone to like you. I mean look at you...you aren't going to make any friends wearing those clothes and not doing anything with your hair when you get up in the morning."

"I care about myself...This is who I am right now." As Joy finished speaking, she regretted responding at all.

Her Mom laughed. "You are going to have to change that, and you can do that easily. I had to. The bridge between junior high school and high school, especially those first couple years of high school, can be tough. You have to adjust to everyone around you. The whole world around you changes. You're running out of time. I was hoping you would have made all the adjustments you needed to make during your freshman year. Right now, you're in the critical stage."

"I don't think I need everyone to like me."

"Yeah honey, but do you have anyone? You haven't had anyone over for three years at least. What happened to Lizzie or Kaela? Kaela was your best friend. I haven't heard about her since you've started high school."

"Um, oh, yeah...well, they are all different now. They got all weird and mean. I don't understand how they can all be so mean to me."

"No sweetie, they aren't weird. They're normal. They've changed because they are supposed to and that's their way of trying to get you to grow up with them. You haven't grown up."

Joy's mom looked at Joy and she couldn't help but feel as though her daughter was already a failure. In her mind, you either understood life early on, and if you didn't by the end of the first year of high school, you were a lost cause: *For everyone and anyone, how you spent your time in high school was going to decide the rest of your life.* She couldn't believe that even though she had only one child to put all her energy into, she still had failed as a mother. She blamed her husband not doing more to help her and she also blamed his genes for Joy's bad luck with genetics. She obviously didn't feel her husband had the bad genes of his family (she wouldn't have married him otherwise), but she had observed these bad genes in his mother's appearance and in the appearance of one of his sisters. She fought the urge to give up on Joy.

"Joy, you know I love you and I still want to believe you have potential, so I'll let you in on another secret that most women never completely learn or have to learn the hard way: It's not about your education, your intelligence, your character, or your kindness. The key to success is your ability to manipulate other people, to push their buttons, and it's about having a dynamic personality to get them to do what you want them to do. I know you have it in you because your grandmother had that ability, as do I. Even as I drive you home right now, I know you'd rather be home. So, I know you know how to get your way without appearing as though you are trying. Imagine if you consciously applied that ability and used it to your advantage in ways that are truly helpful to you. You don't need to have the looks that usually help other women get their way as long as you have that innate skill."

Joy felt nauseous as though a flutter of butterflies had suddenly entered her stomach upon hearing this. If she had wanted to respond (which she didn't want to), she would have struggled to vocalize a thought because opening her mouth would have meant she might throw up in the car. Instead, she breathed a little harder through her nose.

"I know women have come a long way toward equality in our society," her mom continued with a tone that suggested she was somehow unaware she had made this statement several times before to Joy, "and you are fortunate enough to be growing up in a better world for women than the world I grew up in and your grandmother grew up in. But, as you know by now, the brutal reality is that despite some changes for the better, we still live in a cut-throat, unforgiving world that places women who look and act a certain way automatically above the others. The way some women are elevated so high above others in our society is like the difference between how we regard a rare exotic flower compared to a common ugly weed. I know you think I'm hard on you, but the world is much harder on us and I'm trying to help you grow into one of the women who will be in the upper tier because otherwise you'll live a very lonely and unfulfilling life. So many women I've known live in fear and are traumatized by the way they've been treated by men and other women. That's the way of the world we live in. I know women who were incredibly beautiful and were some of the most intelligent people you'll ever meet who gave up on themselves in the way you are starting to. They had everything, but in the end, life still took it away from them. Unless you find a way to take control of your environment and give yourself an advantage, you'll live every day of the rest of your life being beaten down by the world."

The stomach feeling hadn't passed for Joy. She quietly opened the passenger window slightly to catch some of the fresh but chilly December air for relief. She thought her mom might protest her opening the window and allowing cold air in since they had the car heater on, but her mom was still lost in thought as she drove. That's how she knew her mom wasn't finished; she was coming up with the next set of points she wanted to make. She didn't notice that Joy had opened the window or notice any of the cold air that had filtered in.

"It's strange the way time passes," her mom reflected, as if talking to herself. "We all are at least partially aware of how time passes so quickly as we get older, but we aren't always aware of how other people are evolving around us or how we've evolved. I look at myself in the mirror thinking I still look like the same person I did 10 years ago. But the reality is that I'm not anywhere close to that when I really think about it or look at old photos. I am no longer entitled to what the world had to offer me ten years ago with the way I have aged. I may like to think I still am, but I know the world has passed me by. That's the way of the real world, Joy."

Joy didn't respond as she gazed out the window at the same boring familiar places that she had grown so tired of looking at on any ride to and from school.

"Aren't you going to say anything?! You are just like your father with these non-responses when I am trying to have a conversation with you."

Joy still didn't respond. She had felt some relief after getting some air through her window. She opened the window further and closed her eyes as she allowed the piercing cold air to consume her face. The blowing air pushed strands of long hair off her forehead and cheeks.

"I really don't understand genetics," her mom continued, still unaffected by the cold air rolling into the car. "I wish I had known more about science; I really should've gone to college instead of marrying your father. I was so intelligent. I married an idiot, and now I have aged like this because of being married to him and starting a family with him. I also have a daughter who at least has my brain but looks like the women in his family and acts more like him."

Joy didn't know what to say at first. She did want to say something this time.

She had not heard her mom identify this regret so directly to her before, although her mom had hinted around it constantly. She had a lot of things she wanted to say to defend herself and her dad but knew she couldn't just say those things directly.

Her mouth even opened a little, she could feel the anger that she wanted to vocalize moving up her throat. She bit her lip and as she did so, closed the passenger window completely.

She chose not to say anything. She knew from experience that anything she said to disagree with her mom would simply make her mom angrier. Saying what she wanted to say didn't feel like it would be the right thing to do anyway. If she said what was on the tip of her tongue, she'd be insulting her mom and even though her mom had said something insulting to her, she had decided not to do the same in return.

But the unsettling silence that followed deepened the tension and something needed to be said. She went with the most diplomatic response she could think of while trying to keep her tone as neutral-sounding as possible.

"You really shouldn't say those kinds of things, mom."

"I shouldn't get mad at you about that," her mom concluded, as she pulled into the driveway of their home. "Once you get to my age, Joy, you'll know that there is no way to rationalize your own insanity. You either have to learn to accept it on your own, or if you are lucky, you find someone who loves you enough so that you don't have to accept it within yourself."

"I don't think—"

"Let's be real, since we have been having a real conversation here for once," Joy's mom interrupted her, "you are probably one of those people who will have to accept it on your own. A girl like you isn't going to have what I had. I know a girl like you would die to have what I had: both intelligence and beauty. But the truth is, you are better off having one or the other. You should consider yourself luckier than me in that sense. The beautiful woman in me wanted to get married, have children, be part of a world created by a successful husband who ideally would come from a successful family. At first, I thought I did that."

"Where is this—"

But her mom interrupted her again: "Joy, I know you were acting like you weren't paying attention and I know you opened that window. But I didn't yell at you this time because everything I have shared with you today has been the most important advice I can ever give you and I could tell you were listening. I want you to go to your room and spend the rest of the day reflecting on what I've told you. I know you'll think about it."

Joy nodded in agreement and tried not to look confused.

Before Joy had completely shut the passenger door behind her, her mom instantly backed the car off the driveway. The wheels initially released an obnoxious squealing sound before the car sped back down the road. She had never seen her mom in such a hurry to return to work.

She stood there for a while looking down at the cracks in the driveway beside her shoes. She listened to the echo of her mom's car engine become increasingly distant until it faded away entirely.

She then slowly made her way into the house, shut the door behind her in bedroom, locked the door even though no one was home, and closed her eyes as she laid down in her bed. She plunged face first into her pillow and then angled her face on the pillow just enough so that she could breathe.

She could sense The Lion beside her, "It's okay, Joy," he said, "we should head back downstairs."

1.13

She opened her eyes and stood back up in the blue tower. She was still in a heightened state of anxiety from the blast. Nevertheless, before they left the room, she took one last glance at The Book of What Everyone Else Ever Said or Thought About Her. It appeared slightly larger to her than when she had last looked at it.

She quietly followed The Lion down the spiral staircase and through both sets of double doors. Upon opening the second set of doors that The Lion had identified as leading to the great hall of the castle, they were consumed by a heavy fog of smoke and dust. The fog was gradually clearing to reveal the damaged details of the corridor. Below them they could vaguely see that there were hundreds of fragments of stone of various sizes scattered around the mosaic-embedded stone flooring. The outer wall immediately in front of the entrance had been split open. Joy walked gingerly up to and peered through the large hole in the outer wall and discovered a gorgeous view of a glistening sea. Looking through the cloudy haze of dust and around the debris, she saw that this outer wall was lined with windows and realized the castle was positioned on a low cliff that was directly up against the sea. On the sea, she noticed a distant large fleet of wooden ships that were positioned in a narrow line that was roughly parrel to the castle wall.

"We can resume our walk, that was a stray shot," The Lion said nonchalantly.

As she looked at him and then down the corridor in the direction they would be walking, she started to see how the interior wall was lined with torches as the passageway had been but were more spaced out. Incredibly, none of these torches had been affected by the blast. As the dust continued to settle, she was able to observe more of the details of the corridor at further distances. She could see how the torches shared the wall with various forms of artwork. Like the flooring, the interior wall of the corridor differed from the passageway to the cave in that it contained finely decorated mosaics portraying various social scenes (e.g. a scene at a marketplace, a scene of city street with various shops, a scene of a celebratory feast). On the interior wall, these mosaics were interspersed with maritime themed flags, paintings (e.g. a painting of a ship being constructed, a painting of a merchant ship being unloaded at a dock) and even objects (e.g. a ship's anchor, crossed boat oars).

Joy looked back again at The Lion, clearly still in awe of everything she was observing, and then pointed to the ships through the newly formed hole in the wall.

"I forgot to mention that your castle is currently under siege," The Lion explained flatly.

Looking out of the hole in the wall again, she was able to discern bursts of smoke emerging from each of the ships.

"I..." Joy paused. "I know I don't remember much. But I definitely don't remember there being cannons in existence when we used to visit here."

"Technological advancements," The Lion muttered. He motioned her to continue their walk.

She looked around as they walked through the rubble into the undamaged section of the corridor. She noted The Lion may have been overstating how the condition of the castle had declined, as it appeared to be relatively well-maintained. She could sense, however, that it had lost an energy it once had. She felt like she did whenever she entered a store that she sensed was probably going to go out of business soon but hadn't announced it yet. The more she saw of the details of the architecture and artwork, the more she was able to vaguely remember some events of her childhood here. From what little she could recall, she could remember a much livelier and more robust social scene in the castle. *Maybe that was what Lion meant earlier about this place not being the same. You can never underestimate the energy and positivity that having more of the right people around can bring to a place.*

"I remember this place more as we walk around. It's sad to see it so dead around here. We used to have so much fun," Joy reflected, touching part of the outer stone wall beside a window. "It was one my favorite places."

"It was fantastic," The Lion replied with the tiniest hint of wistful reflection in his voice, "we did have some good times here."

Joy thought of her mom, and how she talked about how she used to be beautiful and would wake up every day feeling like a princess. She was now realizing that there was a time when she kind of felt that way too in her own way.

"Where exactly are you taking me?" She heard another thundering roar of distant cannon fire beyond the outer wall. "And do we have enough time?!"

"We have enough time," The Lion answered calmly, "some of those cannons you are hearing belong to us."

"Are we going to win?" Joy heard herself ask before feeling surprised she had asked it.

The Lion stopped. He looked uncharacteristically surprised by her question.

"Win?" he asked.

She looked at him blankly.

"We are going to surrender to keep the castle and the village intact as much as possible."

Joy didn't say anything, but inside she started to get angry and feel saddened all at once. She had been able to visit her castle for the first time in years and now she was about to lose it. She finally had the opportunity to be somewhere that made her happy just when she had reached a point in her life when she had started to believe that a place like that no longer existed for her.

Now it was going to be gone.

The Lion still seemed surprised by her reaction and looked like he hoped he could contain it before it got any worse.

"They are only out there resisting the siege," The Lion started, looking at her as she failed to make eye contact, "because they knew you were coming."

Joy was looking down at the mosaic tiled flooring, it was a scene of a large group of knights and guardsmen bowing down and kneeling to a princess.

"Joy, look at me," The Lion whispered.

And after some tense hesitation, Joy looked up at him with her resting-frown.

"They all talked about how honored they were to serve you one more time. Everyone, even people who have had no battle-experience, joined the defense force when they heard you were coming. They've kept the enemy fleet at bay for several days. But we are running out of ammunition and as you know, to make matters worse, we are also dealing with a mysterious flood in the underground caves beneath the castle."

"Ohhh..." Joy murmured, trying to let that old feeling of being appreciated come back to her. "You keep mentioning a village. There's a village too?"

The Lion looked at her oddly as though he wasn't sure how to reply before turning his attention back to the direction they were originally heading in.

They resumed their walk, turning out of the corridor down a long stone staircase in a narrow, dimly lit passageway that led down to a boat house with docks directly on the sea.

The boat house was fully constructed within a small cave below the castle and was an artisan-crafted masterwork of maritime-themed interior design with various oceanic scenes and designs carved into its beams and painted onto sections of its walls. Various worn and tattered banners of different shapes and colors were hanging from the rafters. The boathouse was filled with the cool scent of the salty sea. Across the surface of the water, there was still the lingering mist of a slight sea fog that she imagined must have thickly coated the sea earlier that morning. The only boat in the boathouse was a small wooden rowboat.

The Lion gestured toward the rowboat.

"Prior to your arrival, we had been asked to meet with our enemies on one of their ships to discuss surrender terms," The Lion explained as he boarded the rowboat.

"Wait, they knew I was coming?"

"They knew you were coming."

"They know who I am?!"

"They know who you are."

"Shouldn't I be dressed like a queen for this?!"

"You're fine."

She looked at herself after she had joined him on the rowboat as though she had expected to have transformed back into royalty from being in her own castle. Much to her disappointment, she was still wearing her school clothes. But by now, she had at least mostly dried off from the flood in the cave.

"Joy," The Lion added. "I'm honored to serve you again. We all are."

Joy stopped focusing on her clothes. She looked down bashfully, closed her eyes and smiled.

She wondered if she could ever believe that she deserved to be treated this way.

1.14

There was someone not only knocking on the door to Joy's bedroom but also testing the doorknob by twisting it (and subsequently discovering it was locked but then twisting it a little more anyway as if to double-check).

"Who is it?" Joy asked in a half-muffled tone as she lifted her head from the pillow and looked at the door. The room was dark, and she wondered if she had fallen asleep or simply lost track of time. The sun had set as there was no evidence of daylight coming through her window. *Have I really been asleep for that long?* She felt the odd tired feeling she would get on some mornings when she wasn't clear on how much of the time she had been sleeping through the night and how much of the time she had been laying there on her bed awake but was so tired that it felt like sleep. Nevertheless, it was clear by the darkness that at least eight or nine hours had passed.

"Baby, are you okay?" Joy's dad asked behind the door. "It's Daddy. You missed dinner tonight and your mom told me you weren't feeling well today so I wanted to check in with you."

Joy hesitated. She didn't feel like answering the door for anyone. But this was her dad, and she couldn't remember the last time he had ever knocked on her bedroom door to check on her. In fact, this may have been the very first time since she started high school.

"Your mom went over to Aunt Katrina's house; it's just me here."

"Give me a minute, Daddy, I'll join you downstairs."

"Okay," she heard from behind the door.

But she sensed him still standing there, hesitating. He breathed on the door with the heavy kind of deep breathing that was his way of breathing when he was confronted with a problem that he couldn't mechanically fix.

"I'm okay, Daddy," she added.

"Okay sweetie," he said against the door, "see you downstairs."

When she went downstairs to the living room she saw her dad, sipping a beer and staring intently at a game on their television. She deduced it was a game by the commentary she could hear but couldn't totally understand since she never watched sports. The television was angled where she couldn't initially see what sport he was watching, but she suspected it was probably football with one of his favorite teams playing because he was so focused on it. He used to play football and was a star quarterback in high school. He also played briefly in college before he had to stop due to injuries.

"There is a football game on Wednesday night?" Joy asked.

"It's great, isn't it? This is the time of the year that the college football teams in the smaller conferences play some of their games on weeknights. I don't always watch them, but daddy's old team is playing tonight."

Her dad had turned off the living room lights because, much to her mom's displeasure, he liked to watch TV as though he was in a movie theater. Sometimes he would make the lights as dim as possible as a way of compromising with her mom, but this time they were completely off. She watched him as he focused intently on the television, and she could see the blue light of the screen engulfing him through the darkness. It was like the bluish light turned him blue. As she looked more closely at her bluish dad, she blinked and suddenly saw him in a helmet and shoulder pads, wearing a worn-out uniform covered in a blend of blades of grass and streaks of mud that included some specks of white yardage paint.

A few blades of grass fell off of the face mask of his helmet as he turned to her.

"Why are you looking at me like that?" He asked.

"Like what?" She responded, before taking a deep breath.

She looked down at her feet and realized she was standing on a football field wearing a helmet and full uniform herself. The grass was wet beneath her cleats, and a light rain was falling on her through the stadium-lit darkness. It was a chilly, rainy night game. She could see in the distance that there was a full, bundled up crowd with umbrellas and hot chocolates that had filled the bleachers.

She stood with the rest of the offensive line on her dad's high school team. She recognized her Uncle Tony, looking at least 40 pounds lighter and much younger, in a confident stance beside her, ready to protect her dad who stood behind them, waiting for her to hike him the ball. Her dad was starting to call out numbers and words she couldn't understand. Uncle Tony observed her looking at him through the corner of his eye and he turned to her. They briefly made eye contact before he returned his focus to the opposing player on the defensive line facing him. Uncle Tony then did a double take in her direction, but realizing the play was about to start, shook his head and turned his attention once again to the opposing defensemen.

The ball was wet and slippery in her hands, and she was afraid she wouldn't feed him the ball correctly. She was also afraid of the large opposing player immediately in front of her, who was twice her size and had an expression on his face that suggested he would run right over her as soon as her dad called for the ball. The rain felt nippy on her neck and the back of her bare arms. She felt uncomfortable from crouching so long and couldn't think of a plan of how she was going to react to the opposing player charging at her.

She took another deep breath.

"Joy, are you okay?!" Her dad was looking at her intently with his brows furrowed with concern.

She was back in the living room with her dad. She walked closer to him and sat down on the end of the couch that was closest to where her dad was sitting in his favorite recliner.

"Did Uncle Tony have freckles when he was a kid?"

Her dad's eyes lit up and he set his beer down on the end table that was situated between the recliner and the couch. "Yes, he did, and you know? I don't what happened to them. I guess sometimes when you get older those kinds of changes can happen to you."

"Were you off from work today?" Joy asked.

Joy noted that in addition to the current beer her father had been drinking, there was a crumpled empty beer can on the end table next to it. She also remembered he had been present during the bathroom episode that morning when he otherwise would have been at work.

"I gave everyone the day off today," he replied, "we worked through the weekend and barely finished that project in time yesterday before we start two new ones tomorrow. A real big one and a smaller one. I still got up at the usual time and went out to do a little work in the main office for an hour and then dropped off supplies over at the new sites. I was back here around 6:00am and beat most of the traffic and the rain. After that, I mostly tinkered around in the garage. I would've picked you up from school earlier in the truck, but your mom insisted on getting you. It kind of surprised me because she is often telling me about how much they micro-manage her breaks and lunches there."

Joy sighed and then defaulted to her usual resting-frown.

"Honey, could you go get daddy another beer?" Her dad asked as he turned his attention back to the television screen to check on the score of the game. At first, she felt a ping of annoyance that he was asking her for a beer when he had just been up to her bedroom door. She looked at him though and realized what a sad figure he was watching television in the dark alone drinking the cheap beer that she had heard him once say he didn't really like the taste of. She was unsure how long her mom had been away and was still surprised he had reached out to her. Moreover, he looked uncharacteristically nervous. She was also unsure if she had ever seen him nervous like this before.

"Of course, dad."

Her dad leaned his head back after Joy had walked out of the room and he tipped his beer can up so he could quickly gulp down the rest of his second beer. He hadn't really needed a new one yet, this one had been half full, but he had felt like he needed a quick moment alone before he faced Joy again.

Joy arrived back quicker than he expected; just as he finished the last drop of his previous can. He crumpled the can in his fist and placed it on the end table next to the other empty can. He then pushed the empty cans toward the other side of the end table closer to where Joy had been sitting to make more room for his new beer can.

He studied her as she handed the beer to him. He took a deep breath himself before speaking this time, hesitated, and then pointed to the TV first instead.

"You know, there is a rhythm to sports," he said as he opened the beer can, "and the older I get, the more I realize that same rhythm can be applied to life..."

He lifted the beer thoughtfully to his lips, considered drinking it, but then changed his mind and placed the beer on the end table.

"...because the world has only a few of what I would call 'true winners.' Anybody can be considered a 'winner' and some of them are lucky because they were in the right place at the right time by being on the right team. But the heart of a 'true winner' is so rare and something entirely different than a 'winner'. In sports, if you are lucky, you happen to have one of those individuals on your team. That's the only way most of the other players will have a chance to win a championship or a medal to become 'winners'. I've played and watched sports long enough now to know that it's not just about winning a championship to become a 'true winner.' It's about the ability for a 'true winner' to have the absolute confidence to take over a game, come from behind in the final minutes to win, never lose composure, stay focused, never get down on themselves, and never let their teammates down. That's a 'true winner.' All the rest of us can only sit back and watch something like that, even other 'winners.'

"But also, in life outside of sports, there are the 'true winners' in this world and then there is everybody else. We often assume that 'true winners' are always winning, and we easily forget all the adversity that 'true winners' have to go through like everyone else. What a lot of us don't realize is that 'true winners' will often fall behind and life will give them scenarios like everyone else goes through where they can be in a losing situation for an extended period of time. But a 'true winner' can maintain a high level of confidence throughout the course of losing to still eventually have a chance to win in the end. Even spectators watching who don't know sports or don't realize they are watching a 'true winner' will sense that the 'true winner' will somehow find a way to win the game they are watching when the odds are stacked against the team the 'true winner' is a part of. It's like a 'true winner' radiates this kind of rare unexplained energy to everyone no matter what kind of adversity they are going through. 'True winners' know they must take advantage of those rare crucial moments when the game...or life...can go either way but can still turn back completely in their favor. There is nothing else like it and I truly believe it applies to everyone in life." Her dad was looking into her eyes as he shared this, as though he intended to relay his message to her beyond his words.

"I thought I was 'true winner' because we won a championship in high school. But then I stopped putting the work in, got distracted, and didn't think I had anything more to learn. I started doing things that went against what my gut-feelings told me to do. It was only after I got injured in college that I realized I had become ordinary. There is nothing wrong with being ordinary, sweetheart, because the world also needs ordinary people. But I know I had a greater path, a higher road that I could have taken, and I stopped being patient. I stopped putting the work in and wanted to enjoy all the rewards that came along with the effort that I had put in up to that point. I stopped way too soon and started enjoying those rewards that immediately came along with it instead. Next thing you know, I had lost my motivation and my passion. It was like I had become a whole different person instead of the one I grew up dreaming I would be. I could've stayed a 'true winner' after high school, but after we won the championship, I let myself be content with being called a 'winner' before I realized I'd never stay content with that."

"Wow, daddy, I had no idea you felt like that."

He raised his brow. "Have you been losing weight?"

"I don't know," Joy answered, no longer making eye contact. She touched her stomach and when it trembled under her soft touch, she quickly pulled her hand away and proceeded to squeeze the couch pillow beside her instead. She closed her eyes. She hated lying so much to her dad who she probably loved more than anyone other than Gray. It seemed like every conversation she had was starting to feel like this.

"You gotta eat, baby. You're still growing. You really are. You're still our little snuggle bug."

"I can look like the other girls..." Joy tried to smile, but she fell short of one. She momentarily looked lost as though she had never sat down in her own living room before. "Wait, did you just say I was a 'little snuggle bug?!'"

"No."

"Daddy!"

"No, sweetheart. Don't know where you got that, maybe from one of your friends or your mom or somebody..." He was now looking at the football game again with a smirk developing. He picked up his beer.

"Daddy!"

"Not me."

Joy laughed. She leaned over to her dad and tickled the side of his arm right above his elbow.

Her dad started laughing so hard, that some of his new, opened, but unconsumed beer spilled on his white T-shirt near where his belly button was. He held Joy's ticking hand with his free hand to stop her, but with a soft gentle hold.

"Sometimes you stick with someone who doesn't deserve you because it was hard for you to open up and you invested so much, but it's okay to let go," he said quietly, as if he didn't want anyone else but Joy to hear (even though there was no one else in their house at that moment).

Joy looked down at her bare feet, at the chipped and peeling dark purple nail polish on her toenails.

"I don't have a boyfriend, dad."

"You don't have to be with someone to hold on to them in that way," her dad said as he released her hand. "You may not have a boyfriend, but you can still be somebody's girlfriend and he doesn't even have to know it. He doesn't know it, does he?"

"No, dad."

Her dad put his beer on the end table next to the two empty cans. He still hadn't taken a sip out of it. The beer can itself already looked like it was "sweating" in a thin layer of condensation. He was not known to engage in these kinds of conversations regularly and as she thought about that, she figured her mom would probably be jealous that she was having this type of a conversation with him.

"You should let it go because even if it feels like you got nothing back, you did. You learned how to open up and invest in someone for when the right person does come along and trust me, the right person will come along as long as you keep your heart open."

Tears were now developing in Joy's eyes: "I don't think everybody has a right person, Daddy."

Her dad looked at his beer and picked it up. He took a pensive swig and turned to Joy.

"Not everybody ends up with their right person, Joy," he said, "but I believe everybody has a right person."

Joy looked at him as he lowered his eyes. He had been losing weight himself for the past few years. He still maintained somewhat of an athletic build. He kept barbells, dumbbells, and a weight bench in his workshop in the garage that he now rarely used. He also didn't really go running or biking like he used to. His weight loss seemed like it had more to do with stress. He looked eternally tired and his years of 10-hour workdays over six-day workweeks of doing hard labor had etched wrinkles in his face and exposed veins in his arms and legs. He was wearing a dirty ballcap and a five o'clock shadow (relative to the limited amount of facial hair her dad could grow). She had never seen him looking as sad as he looked that night. Usually when she was around him, he was calm and joking around much more than he was with her now.

"You didn't end up with the right person, did you?" Joy asked in a high whisper that was barely audible over the commentators on TV calling the football game.

"No, sweetheart, but I have you and because of that alone, I have no regrets. And that doesn't mean I still can't help you on your journey to find the right one for you."

"Who was she?" Joy asked in the same high whisper.

But her dad ignored directly answering this question and instead he continued with what he wanted to share: "Patience is so important. I still think it's the most important quality any person can have, and I know you have it. 'True winners' have it. And that's what you need most of the time. But every now and then life will shake things up for you and you have to be ready to the take initiative and grab a hold of that rare life-changing moment when life offers it to you. You may be tempted to think you already have everything you need or have earned. You may also be tempted to think you aren't worthy or deserving of the moment that comes your way. No matter what, you'll have to keep working as hard as you can because you'll probably have to fight for whatever life is offering you when you're in that moment much more than you expected. You may have to do extraordinary things you thought were completely beyond your capabilities, things that you never thought you'd be able to do. As long as you don't give up, it will all be worth it and it will change your life beyond your wildest dreams. I feel like you are getting closer to one of those rare moments that could change your life as you know it."

Joy looked confused. "Did you ever have those moments?"

"Of course!" Her dad closed his eyes and smiled warmly at memories she had never seen pictures of or could try to imagine.

"Your Daddy..." He hesitated. His eyes remained closed. His smile had over-extended itself into an exaggerated smirk.

"Daddy?"

"You can't ever tell your mom I told you this story."

"Daddy!"

Her dad laughed with his eyes still closed: "Promise me."

"I promise..."

He opened his eyes and took another sip of his beer before he continued: "Daddy is not proud of this, but I was dating another woman at the same time as your mom. I know it's inexcusable since neither woman knew about the other at first. I was in high school, very popular, a great athlete, and felt like I was unstoppable. I thought I could do pretty much anything I wanted to and did. I dated whoever I wanted to. I got away with not doing homework because the teachers gave me passing grades on assignments that I probably should have failed, or I had other people do the assignments for me. I dated your mom on and off through most of high school. There were occasionally other women and I'm pretty sure she knew about all of them, because you know how sharp your mom is. I wasn't mature even though I knew deep down I was going against my values. Then there was one woman I met my junior year, and she changed everything."

His eyes had widened as he said "everything."

"Wow..." Joy gasped. She was listening with her highest possible level of attention while also in complete shock to hear about this other version of her dad that she would've never have imagined existing.

"This new woman made me question everything about myself. She started to change my attitude. I started to pay attention to things I never paid attention to before, and I wanted to make changes for the better even though before her I had told myself that everything had been perfect. This woman immediately made me better just by being in my life and I knew she was the love of my life. I eventually broke up with your mom and spent all of my time with her. Then one night during our senior year, I went to her house with a ring, and I asked her to marry me."

Now Joy was wide-eyed like she had seen a ghost.

Her dad took another deep breath before moving forward with the story: "She cried when I proposed...we had been dating for a year. She said she'd love to but then she said the word 'but' and when she said that one word, I knew it was over. She told me she had recently found out that I had still been seeing your mom for part of the time I had been with her. It was true...I had continued seeing your mom on and off for the first six months I was with her. When I explained I had completely split up with your mom to only be with her, she said she would still have to learn to trust me again and said that I needed to learn more about respecting her. She then told me that she wouldn't be fully respecting herself by continuing to be with me and that she couldn't trust me. I found myself crying along with her because I understood— she deserved better than that. We hugged and then went our separate ways. It was the last time I ever spoke to her. She gave me that opportunity to earn her trust in order to potentially get back together with her, but I ended up going back to your mom instead. When I went back to your mom, your mom told me she had never said anything to anyone about me dating multiple women at once because she knew I would eventually come back to her. Your mom also made me promise there would never be with another woman, and I've kept that promise ever since. I always catch myself looking back on my relationship with that other woman though. I still think about her a lot.

"The day when I proposed to her was my moment. It was that life changing moment that takes place once or twice in your lifetime that changes everything. How you respond to it will determine the course of the rest of your life. I had my chance to prove myself to this woman, but I took the easier route and went back to your mom. Even after I went back to your mom, a part of me still had this feeling that if I split up with your mom again and went back to this woman then maybe I'd have a chance again. It was a very strong magnetic pull for me to go back to her. It was like I knew she was thinking of me every day too. I could still feel her energy every day for a long time, and I almost went back to her several times. I stayed with your mom because even though I tell myself it's because I made that promise to her, I realize I was also really scared of taking that risk again and getting rejected. I stayed with your mom because it was easier to stay with her, and your mom has been loyal to me. I stayed with your mom because I also knew I had wronged both women and I felt guilty. I couldn't get myself to leave your mom too after already hurting the other woman. I stayed with your mom because my friends told me it would be much better for my reputation in school. Not long after we graduated, I stayed with your mom because we got married and then, of course, I stayed with your mom because we had you. I had my moment though, and I didn't live up to it when life got hard."

"But how do you know when it's your moment?"

"You'll know in your heart when life is offering you a rare gift and you'll sense that you have only a short window of time to accept the gift when it is offered it you. I know not everyone would agree with me. A lot of parents wouldn't be telling their children everything I'm telling you because they wouldn't want to hurt them. I can't regret my story, Joy, because you came out of this. As I tell you this story, I realize maybe things happened the way they did for me so I can make sure they don't happen to you. I do believe things happen for a reason and maybe I can help you live your moment to the fullest when life gives you that opportunity. I have this feeling in my heart that you'd rather me be real with you...and that feeling also tells me that you can handle it. Like I said, you have to take what life offers you. I believe life gives everyone moments at one time or another. It's up to you what you do with it. It's this feeling you get, maybe you knew it was deep inside of you all along but one day it hits you and it hits you so hard it feels like it came from out of nowhere. But somehow, you also have the potential to be ready for it to take you wherever you need to go. The only thing that can stop you is your own mind and your own fears. It's magical when it happens and not everyone accepts magical feelings like that. I think a lot of people miss their moments because they aren't fully conscious of the fact that they were offered a gift. I want to make sure you're ready when yours comes along, so you don't end up like me."

Joy looked down so her chin touched her chest and smiled at the thought of "magical feelings." If those feelings were what she thought he was talking about (intuitive feelings), she had been feeling them all her life. Even so, she couldn't imagine life offering her a "moment" too.

"The older I get, and as time goes on, I look more at my relationship with your mom and at the relationships our friends have had over the years, and I realize a lot of people really end up settling for someone they can act like a fool with. That's how your mom and I ended up together. We were just kids fooling around and we realized we can still act like complete fools around each other and still be together. That's how most of our friends ended up together and many of them are now unhappily married or divorced because that works out pretty well when you are young but not so much when you are older. When you are young you are a fool in so many ways, but you feel like it's okay if you have somebody to be a fool with you. That way you feel less ashamed about being a fool and when you are being hard on yourself for being a fool, you have someone right there either being foolish in their own way along with you or at least indirectly supporting you in your own foolishness. But the older you get, the more particular and stubborn you are about the things you choose to act like a fool about and well, your mom and I have completely different things we choose to be foolish about now. So, it becomes much harder to be fools together."

"Why are you saying the word 'fool' so much, daddy?" Joy laughed. "I don't think you're a fool."

"I know honey, but I am trying to make a point about settling for something less than what you need in life and how that makes you settle for someone that maybe you shouldn't be with in the first place." Her dad then paused to clear his throat anxiously before he continued: "I find some peace in knowing I accomplished everything I needed in a relationship at least once: I knew what it was like to fall in love, I knew what it was like at least start to make some sacrifices for a person you deeply love in a romantic relationship, and I briefly experienced what it feels like to commit yourself entirely to someone else you are truly in love with. I experienced the three most important things I think you can get in a relationship. I know I had the one brief experience with it for only six months, but I think so many people don't even get that or they had it but never realize what they are truly missing once they've left it. It took me several years after the relationship to realize it myself."

"So you've experienced none of those things with mom?" Joy asked.

He took another swig of his beer until it sounded like it was nearly empty by the echo the remaining liquid made as it slid back down to the bottom of the can when he placed it on the end table.

"None of those things with mom," he finally said.

She stood up and they hugged as he remained within his chair. She asked him if he wanted another beer and he declined. He thanked her for meeting with him and she assured him she would think about his advice. As she was about to leave the living room, she turned one last time to say goodnight but discovered her dad was back in his high school football uniform. She was in a uniform again too and the television light had turned into stadium lights penetrating through the rainy darkness.

Her dad called the signal for the ball. The ball instantly slipped through her fingers into his direction and a split second later, the opposing player in front of her crashed into her arms. She tried to hold him, but her grip quickly slipped over his bare wet arms. The opposing player then rolled his way past her, but it didn't matter because her dad had already thrown the ball. She turned and watched the ball fly in a spiral that sliced through the rain, the wind, and the dark before landing perfectly into a wide receiver's arms as he cut through the end zone for a touchdown. Her dad walked up beside her and placed his hand on her shoulder with a broad smile as they stood together in the rain. As they stood in silence, the rainy high school football field transformed back to her living room and she realized her dad had turned the television off, must have thrown the beer cans away in the small recycle bin they had in the kitchen, and was now standing beside her with his hand on her shoulder.

"Thank you again, sweetheart, for the talk," he said. "I hope you have a goodnight."

"Goodnight, Dad."

As they hugged a second time she inhaled a mixed scent of sawdust, paint and beer. It was a familiar musk her dad carried with him.

"I'll be rooting for you, Joy," he said with a smile.

She walked behind him on the stairs and noticed he was slightly off balance and moving in a wobble. She had seen him move like this enough to know that this was partly due to his body gradually breaking down from all the hard labor (on top of his old football injury) as well as from being buzzed from the beer he had consumed.

After one final extra "goodnight" with her dad before he went into her parents' bedroom, she returned to her room and noted on her phone that it was only 7:09pm. That made sense for her dad, because he usually went to bed at around 7:30pm on his worknights and would get up at 3:30am to get ready for work. She placed her phone on her nightstand and decided to go to bed herself, knowing that she probably wouldn't be able to sleep since she had apparently been in bed sleeping for most of the day. But at this point, she didn't feel like doing anything else. She laid back down in her bed in the dark. As she reflected on how her day went, she allowed herself to breathe a sigh of relief that as strange and crazy of a day it was, she hadn't been beaten up in gym class that day.

Part II: Wednesday (again)

2.1

The entire bedroom door was vibrating in place under the continuous pounding by the bottom of her mom's surprisingly strong fist.

It had initially pulled Joy out of a deep sleep, but she remained half-asleep. She was drowsy enough to only vaguely hear the pounding on her door, even as it was reverberating across her bedroom walls. She wasn't sure exactly when she had fallen asleep, but it had to have been somewhere between 1am and 2am. Every time she had tried to close her eyes to sleep, she kept imagining herself getting beaten up in the locker room and whenever she opened her eyes, she kept thinking about ways she could try to get out of getting beaten up in the locker room.

"Joy, you missed the bus again!" Her mom shouted from behind the door.

With her eyes still closed, Joy moaned and rolled around under her sheets onto her stomach. She sank her head face first into her pillow before reluctantly turning it to the side to breathe.

"You're killing me, Joy!" Her mom cried. "I have to be at work on time...you've got like 10 minutes to get ready!"

"Today is Thursday," Joy asserted in a kind of lingering moan with her eyes still closed. "I thought you have Thursdays off."

"Today is Wednesday, and you actually have more like eight minutes," her mom clarified sternly through the door but at a lower volume.

Joy opened her eyes, and the first thing she noticed was that it was darker than usual in her room again (even for what would be a normal cloudy day). She looked over to her window and noticed that the rays of light coming through it seemed different again.

"Yesterday was Wednesday," Joy said as if more to herself than to her mom.

"No! Yesterday was Tuesday and I had to drive you to school yesterday too. Please, Joy, I'm not going to have this ridiculous debate with you. Hurry up and get ready," her mom's voice had lowered even further this time to her usual volume. It sounded resigned and tired.

Joy looked at her phone, which was turned off on her nightstand. She then glanced in the direction of the window again and saw that the dim stream of light had vanished, just like it had on the previous day she thought was Wednesday.

If it was Wednesday again, that meant the light switch wouldn't work when the world went dark, but her phone would still work. She picked up her phone, turned it on, and glared at it impatiently as the phone's logo screen flashed on. As she waited, she imagined the screen flashing "Thursday, December 9th" and hoped that by imprinting in her imagination, it would somehow be reality.

"Joy? I don't hear anything in there," her mom was now twisting the doorknob, which Joy had locked again. "Why do you always have to keep this door locked? What are you doing in there?!"

She eagerly looked at the home-screen of her phone as it flashed on, but just like it had on the day before, it clearly stated "Wednesday, December 8th."

It can't be Wednesday again.

But unlike "the previous version of Wednesday," she had slept-in this time, and the clock read "6:37am." Since it was one of the first stops, the bus usually arrived at her bus stop (that was at least a five-minute walk away) around 6:40am (and got her to school around 7:10am).

She would miss the bus again like she did on Tuesday.

It can't be Wednesday again.

She sat up and sighed.

She looked at her phone to again: "Wednesday, December 8th – 6:38am."

She laid back down and sighed again.

She wasn't sure if she had truly fallen asleep until around 2am. Since she had slept through most of the previous Wednesday, she had done a lot more of what she now called "deep thought dozing" that night up until she had finally reached a period of deep sleep. She had come up with the term "deep thought dozing" that night after talking to her dad. She determined that "deep thought dozing" occurred when she would lay in bed, doze off for a half-hour to an hour and then wake up with her mind racing for an hour or more after that before dozing off for a short period of time again and so on. In addition to thinking about the note in her locker and the inevitable upcoming fight, she had spent much of the night thinking about the conversation with her dad and of course, thinking about Gray.

She lifted her head up and gazed in awe through the darkness that was now only vaguely lit by the glow of blue light from her phone screen. She held on to the faint hope that maybe her phone had the date wrong: *It can't be Wednesday again.*

"Mom, I'm not feeling well," she suddenly said aloud without thinking about it.

She was looked down a third time at the "Wednesday, December 8th" date on her phone.

She actually felt sick.

She laid her head back down on the pillow.

If it really was the exact same date, that meant that Casey's ghostly reflection may be waiting for her in the bathroom, that there would be a note waiting for her in locker telling her that she was going to get beat up that afternoon, and that her mom was going to give her a lecture again. She wasn't sure about all the other events repeating themselves, but she was oddly certain about the note in her locker and the lecture from her mom.

She felt sick at the idea of having to try to interact with people who were either waiting to criticize her and/or trying to convince her to be someone she wasn't. She didn't want to interact with the people who made her sick to her stomach because just thinking about interacting with them already gave her that feeling: *Haven't I already survived "today?"*

She knew facing reality was an inevitability but, at that moment, she didn't have the energy. She didn't have the energy at all.

There was still silence from the other side of the door.

"I am not feeling well today, mom," Joy reiterated at a higher volume and a slower pace to emphasize her words.

"Okay," her mom said softly from behind the door, "I'll call the school. Try to feel better for tomorrow."

Joy was stunned by her mom's reply as she had expected full resistance from her. Before Joy could utter "thank you, mom" like she wanted to, she could hear her mom already walking down the stairs and then going out the door to the garage. She could hear her starting the car and then hear the sound of the garage door closing after she had backed the car out.

All that was left were the sounds of the house itself as it's central heating system hummed in the cold December morning emptiness.

She remembered from what her dad had told her on "the other Wednesday, December 8th" that he must've been in his workshop in the garage at that point. The silence in her house made sense, since her mom probably told him in passing that Joy was staying home sick while she was getting into her car in the garage. Her dad consciously focused on quieter activities in the garage on previous days when he was home and Joy stayed home sick so that he wouldn't disturb her rest.

She looked around her darkened room again as it remained slightly lit by the glow of blue light from her phone. Her head remained on her pillow as she scanned the room. She thought about how the world had become dark again even though she would've slept through the onset of that event if it really was the exact same Wednesday. *Did the world becoming dark align with what time she got up in the morning? Was it really Wednesday again?* She wanted to go back to sleep and not think about it.

She wanted to sleep and hoped to have one of those dreams where she was living a better life that felt like it was in real life instead of being a dream. She had experienced that type of dream before and then had the mornings when she woke up and thought life had improved so much at home and at school only to eventually feel that miserable feeling in her chest and stomach that life was still the same as it was when she had gone to bed. It was only a very realistic dream, but those few minutes of hope after waking up when she still thought the dream was real made the whole experience worth it to her despite the disappointment that followed.

A smile suddenly tore open her resting-frown like a gift. It was the kind of sudden smile that only accompanies an epiphany.

She sat up in her bed, turned on the flashlight to her phone and placed it on the nightstand with the beam of light facing upward toward the ceiling.

Now she had her "beautiful glow'" again.

She rolled out of bed and searched among her clothes scattered around her floor among other various things. There were shirts folded inside out, chap sticks with missing caps, and the leaky bottles of lotion.

There.

She found the same white miniskirt she had located on "the first version of Wednesday" to put on again. This time, however, she changed out of her pajama pants into black leggings she also located to wear with the skirt. She was surprised she felt brave enough to wear the black leggings she had only tried on once before, but she went with it.

She climbed back up on her bed, turned to her mirror, and started with a gentle bounce. But soon she started jumping harder and higher until she jumped higher than she ever had before on her bed. Finally, she jumped up and rotated her body in midair so that her miniskirt twirled in the mirror. Once she completed the jump, she remained standing on her bed and looked at herself directly in the mirror.

She couldn't believe it at first.

She finally did it.

This time it was a perfect 360-degree twirl!

She laughed to herself like she couldn't believe it.

"That was perfect!" Gray's voice observed from beside her.

She nearly fell off the bed when she heard his voice but was able to side-step on the mattress to catch herself with a couple of light bounces.

She looked slightly to her right within the mirror and got a better look at the figure that had appeared beside her: his textured messy hairstyle, his muscle curves, his jawline, and his smiling eyes. He started jumping on the bed beside her and she joined him. She had never jumped with someone on her bed before but found the size of her queen-size bed accommodated both of them jumping on it.

He looked even more beautiful himself in the "beautiful glow."

"Really?!"

"Amazing," he verified, "incredible...you know, I have always secretly thought you were beautiful..."

She smiled but didn't answer him.

She took a deep breath and let the exhale remove the smile so that her face returned to the familiar resting-frown. She slowed down to a softer bounce.

He was still looking at her for a response while shifting to his own gentle bounce.

Instead of responding, she slid down off the bed and walked to the window.

"Hey! What's the matter?!" Gray shouted incredulously as though she had walked much further away from him.

But she ignored him and didn't turn back to see how his demeanor had completely changed to anger and disdain.

Joy blinked as she peered out into the empty darkness outside her window, listening to the faint morning traffic noises and a nearby bird singing.

She imagined a first date with Gray, feeling that kind of anxiety she would probably only feel on a first date but more so because it was with a person she really, really liked for so many years of her childhood.

Joy blinked again.

She saw him proposing to her on a rocky mountaintop overlooking a beautiful view of a green forest surrounding a deep blue lake.

She blinked a third time.

She saw him smiling at her and she smiled back at him as he approached her at the altar on their wedding day on a beautiful tropical beach with the clearest seawater she'd ever seen.

She blinked a fourth time.

She saw him holding their child not long after birth, leaning next to her as she managed a smile through her exhaustion while resting on a hospital bed.

She blinked a fifth time.

She saw herself crying as she stormed out of their bedroom while he was burying his head in a silk pillow on their king-size bed right after she had told him she was divorcing him once and for all.

She blinked a sixth time.

She saw herself reconciling with him as he embraced her in a gorgeous, futuristic-looking kitchen and told her he would never let her get that upset again.

She blinked a seventh time.

She saw herself admiring the clothes the other woman had left behind in their bedroom. The woman Gray had cheated on her with apparently wore a black lace-trimmed silk dress. She attempted to try it on, but it didn't fit.

She blinked an eighth time.

She then looked back to see that his shadow had sat down on the bed. She could faintly observe through the darkness that he was glaring back at her in disbelief.

She blinked a ninth time.

She looked back at the window as a stream of warm sunshine flooded brightness all over her. She could also sense it filling her room behind her.

The brightness caused her to take a half-step back, and she squinted with her hand partially shielding her eyes as she looked through the window.

The world was full of light again!

She blinked a tenth time (this time involuntarily) and she turned toward Gray again, but he wasn't there anymore.

She looked outside once more. There was a tree right outside her window that partially obscured the view it had of the busy city street beyond it.

She couldn't see the bird, as he was hidden within the foliage of the tree, but she could still hear him sing over the sounds of early rush hour traffic.

She closed her eyes and listened to the bird.

The song sounded so beautifully familiar to her and instantly filled her with hope.

2.2

When she opened her eyes, she was standing on the wooden walkway of a narrow suspension bridge that was anchored at various points to douglas fir trees in the middle of a massive forest. It was just before sunset. Both the steel railings and the trunks of the trees anchoring the bridge were decorated with swirls of glowing white string lights.

She was alone.

She also noticed she was still wearing her white miniskirt with black leggings along with her long-sleeved pajama top. She couldn't help but laugh a little to herself that she was still dressed that way in the new setting she was in. *Well, at least I'm here alone.*

She stood quietly in the moist humid air that felt like a first warm night in spring. The bridge appeared to be over two hundred feet above the ground and surrounded by hundreds of other douglas fir trees, western hemlock trees, and western red cedar trees. Although lacking in string lights, these trees surrounding the bridge were surrounded by thousands of fireflies that emitted a white light similar to the tone of the white string lights. She could hear the unified ensemble of hundreds of crickets performing below. More prominently heard was the singing of a single bird in the distance. It was a familiar song and sounded like the bird she had heard outside her bedroom window. She searched for but couldn't see the bird among the trees.

She grinned at the beautiful nature around her. It was one of those grins she only felt comfortable having when she was alone.

As she stood there, she felt lucky, but soon found herself being surrounded by different thoughts about luck: *Some people were lucky, they were lucky to have all the right people around when they needed around them— every step of their lives. They were lucky to have that loyal group of lifelong friends: the same group of friends that stuck with them no matter what, that stuck around for several years after much of their lives had changed and stuck around if a great distance separated them more from one another. Some people were also lucky to have the right sized nose, the right sized chest, a pretty face, the ability to maintain a great figure, an outgoing personality, and a likable first impression. Having all of these things increase a person's luck with finding love. Basically, they were lucky to have all the things that I either struggle with or don't have. Of course, carrying the weight of this knowledge only seems to make me more awkward to people when I enter the room. So much for my luck.*

As she got lost in her thoughts and pulled away from observing the nature around her, her trademark resting-frown had gradually made a sub-conscious return.

Without thinking specifically about Gray, she imagined the type of man she would want to be with: *He'd be handsome and masculine but also gentle and kind. He'd be versatile in the sense that he could be the strong, no-nonsense type but also be a teddy bear type (depending on the setting and the situation).*

She then pictured the guy she would probably end up with. She imagined a sadder, fatter version of her dad. The guy she'd end up with might probably be one of the weird, divorced, and depressed guys that often worked for her dad. They usually only lasted several months to a year before they quit. It would be a guy like that, who probably didn't have any friends himself either. His only friends would probably be his video games, his sports teams, his beer and/or his marijuana. *Casey was probably right.* She'd be lucky if the guy she ended up with overdid it with the booze or weed instead of venturing into the harder drugs. He'd probably still be in love with another woman from his past and he would use the alcohol and drugs to numb himself of the pain he still had related to loving that woman from his past.

She cringed at the thought that the only real friends her dad had left were his TV, his sports teams, and his beer. Of course, he was very personable and talked to everyone with genuine kindness. He had a lot of acquaintances, but his television, his sports and his beer were the only real friends he had left. Her mom claimed she had a lot of friends, but they didn't seem genuine. It was as if they knew that her mom didn't really respect them but kept them around because her mom no longer had the friends from high school she really wanted in her life. Her mom no longer had her friends from high school because they all had married rich husbands and her mom resented that. Like her dad's "friends," her mom's current "friends" were essentially acquaintances too.

Joy wasn't sure if it helped her to put her own struggle into the context of knowing that her parents were also not among the lucky ones to have the right people in their lives or if it made her feel worse.

"The people in your life may not remain the same anyway, not as long as you stay true to yourself and continue evolve," a voice suddenly replied aloud to her thoughts from among the trees.

The singing had stopped.

Joy was startled enough upon hearing another voice that she grappled both ends of the railings on the bridge to reset herself. As she did so, a bright red northern cardinal flew within her line of sight and perched relatively comfortably on the shaken railing a few feet in front of her to her left. She looked at him and gradually recognized him as she continued to hold on to both sides of the railings.

"Are you able to read my mind, Cardinal?" Joy eventually asked.

The Cardinal laughed.

Joy realized she had been in another one of those situations where she had so overindulged herself with deep thought that she had forgotten where she was. She was amazed at how a beautiful moment could easily venture into another downward spiral of recurring doubts and negative thoughts.

"Isn't this a fantastic place?" The Cardinal asked, changing the subject. "I love this place."

"It really is." Joy released the railings and walked closer to The Cardinal. "Was that you singing?"

"It was," The Cardinal sang, "you know it was."

They looked out at the fireflies surrounding the pine trees.

"Life is crazy in the way that you think you know everything and have everything you need but it turns out you knew hardly anything at all and don't feel like you have anything at all," The Cardinal mused. "Every time you think you've reset, and you think have everything together again is usually the right time to go through yet another period of feeling like you really had no idea about life to begin with. So, you start to question whether all the effort you have put in up to that point is worth the investment relative to what you've gained. As long as you keep growing as a person, life does that to you again and again."

"I don't feel like I'm growing..." Joy began.

"...but you are," The Cardinal finished.

"I don't feel like I'm going anywhere in life," Joy whispered.

"You are," The Cardinal reiterated in a whisper.

"I can't," Joy groaned.

Joy waited for The Cardinal to respond but he didn't. She didn't add anything herself either, because she could tell The Cardinal was lost in thought himself.

"You think too much, Cardinal."

The Cardinal laughed and Joy found herself laughing along with him.

"You think too much, Joy," The Cardinal laughed.

"Probably," Joy laughed and then smirked as she said: "And I would think that's a sign that I'm not really growing."

Joy looked down over the railing to her left and saw there was a smoky white fog developing below her with numerous fireflies moving in and around the fog. The glow of some of the fireflies faded gradually and then disappeared once they were enveloped by the rising fog. The air had a misty, refreshing woodland musk texture and scent to it. It was the kind of feeling Joy would normally get near an ocean, but instead she experienced it among an ocean of trees. She could sense how alive the trees were. She could also sense the trees breathing among the layers of fog and among the glowing of fireflies.

"Do people always have to grow?" Joy asked as she looked down at the trees, the fog, and fireflies.

The Cardinal looked like he didn't initially know what to say to that.

"I mean, I miss being a little kid. Now that I'm in high school, I can't seem to completely love and appreciate things like this sunset, this beautiful forest, these fireflies, or this bridge the way I did when I was little kid. No matter how hard I try, I am starting to think I'll never be able to again. Maybe that's a gift you only receive when you are a kid. I miss it so much. Right now, I can't seem to love you the same way I did as a kid, Cardinal."

The Cardinal looked like he was about to reply but Joy continued before he could: "The scent out here, Cardinal. You know? This smell. It's so incredible. It's so rejuvenating. Can you smell it too? Do you have a sense of smell?"

The Cardinal nodded, but Joy couldn't tell if one of those nods that people do when they don't want to respond or if he really did have a sense of smell. It was the type of nod that people also did when they aren't really listening, but Joy got the sense he was listening. Nevertheless, she continued as if he had confirmed he had a sense of smell: "Remember when you were young and you loved the sweet smell of something so much that it feels like the greatest gift you'll ever receive? It's just a scent and a scent is something fleeting that usually only lasts for a brief period of time. But to experience that same feeling as an adult, it's like you have to receive the new car you really wanted or get into a relationship with someone you genuinely love. When you are a little kid it's like you can come to a place like this and only have to enjoy the scents of the nature around you to feel completely fulfilled. When you are a little kid, the smell of your favorite foods, or the smell of a new candle, or the smell of freshly washed bedsheets means everything in that moment. It's like you don't know it at the time but you are able to love and appreciate things at a level that seems to be impossible to reach later in life. Just look at these incredible trees..."

"Well, I think—" The Cardinal started to say, but before he could go any further, he stopped as he realized Joy wasn't finished.

"...And these beautiful fireflies," Joy continued, looking around them with wonder. "There must be a million of them. I see them and I know they are amazing but now when I see something like this it's like my mind can only say 'oh, that's really nice' and most of the time it can't go any further than that. It's like my heart wants to enjoy it more but I can't, Cardinal. I can't enjoy it like I did when I was a little kid. Is this what growing is like?"

Joy and The Cardinal made eye contact, but Joy couldn't get a read out of The Cardinal. The Cardinal remained expressionless. She was led to wonder if The Cardinal thought she still had more to say.

"Well?" Joy added to prompt him.

The Cardinal continued to make eye contact with her for several seconds and then looked away at the trees and fireflies.

"Yes," The Cardinal answered as he watched the fireflies.

Joy looked at him with wide-eyed surprise at how simple his answer was.

"See, you are growing," The Cardinal added.

Joy erupted with laughter.

The Cardinal was so astonished by her reaction and that he jumped from his perch on the railing and started flapping his wings to regain composure in mid-air about a foot above his original position. Once he recovered from this initial shock, he started laughing again along with her as he returned to perch on the railing.

"Oh stop! Just stop, Cardinal," Joy giggled, "you may be right but that doesn't make it any better, right?"

"Well, aren't you enjoying yourself now?" The Cardinal asked.

"It's not the same," Joy reflected. "I thought I only experienced that difficulty loving and appreciating life around me in the real world. But I am feeling it here too. It's like an emptiness that can't be filled by anything anymore; not even the things I loved as a kid. I find myself loving people I don't know and things I don't have and I wonder if I would really love and appreciate those people and things if I knew them or had them."

She noticed the thinnest top layers of fog had started rising above the bridge. Rays of sunlight were fading over the treetops, leaving the string-lights and the fireflies to illuminate the onset of an increasingly foggy night.

"I feel like one of the rare times I get amazing moments like I used to get as a little kid is when I first meet new adults who haven't yet talked about me with my mom or when there are new girls at my school who meet me first before they talk to the other girls. I know they are strangers, but the way they would look at me and treat me at first is so...wonderful. They look at me and treat me like I'm normal person. They would complement me on my intelligence, on my personality, or my smile. Those interactions mean everything to me. Sometimes I wish I could simply hit a pause button to hold on to them."

The Cardinal smiled at first as if to hold back laughter, and then he laughed.

"Funny you bring that up," The Cardinal laughed, "we can help you with that."

"Funny?!" Joy asked with a tone of uncertainty as she wondered what was so funny.

The bridge started vibrating and shaking.

Joy held on to the railings again and The Cardinal leapt up from his perch again to a position of suspended flight just above the railing. They both glanced further across the bridge from where Joy had been facing and noted an adult asian elephant lumbering across the bridge through the fog and illuminated darkness toward them. Joy was stunned an elephant could fit on the bridge and that the bridge could handle an elephant's weight. The suspension bridge was apparently more than strong enough to handle the weight. The width of bridge however, barely and awkwardly fit an elephant. The asian elephant's tusks remained above the railings as it was moving swiftly and confidently given its size relative to that of the suspension bridge.

Upon making eye contact, Joy recognized The Elephant by the gleam in her eyes. The Elephant frequently had that gleam in her eye when she interacted with her as a little kid. If it was really possible for eyes to smile, The Elephant's eyes were almost always smiling. The Elephant's eyes also used to often suggest that she had something planned for Joy. She was able to remember how The Elephant would often arrange something fun and exciting for Joy to do or have an activity or a discussion planned that was meant to challenge her as a learning opportunity. Sure enough, as Joy was thinking about this, she noticed there was a small, taped package wrapped in The Elephant's trunk. She then recalled how The Elephant consistently had a calming way and energy about her that could put Joy at ease. When The Elephant reached Joy and The Cardinal, the bridge stopped shaking and The Elephant gently released the package onto the bridge in front of them.

"Joy!" The Elephant exclaimed after releasing the package. "How've you been?"

Joy looked at the package with her mouth slightly dropped open and then at The Elephant.

"She looks great, doesn't she?" The Elephant said to The Cardinal, who had returned to his perch on the railing. "She's one of those kids that you can tell will keep getting better as they get older and obtain more life experience. But we both knew in Joy's case that she has been great from the very beginning...just as she is."

"She really does," The Cardinal confirmed, "and let me tell you something, Elephant, I'm finding out she still literally has no idea of how great she is."

"No idea?!" The Elephant asked.

"Maybe a little bit." The Cardinal smirked.

"What is in the package?!" Joy wondered, glaring at it on walkway of the bridge. She felt uncomfortable with the compliments and was trying to change the subject.

"Go ahead, open it," The Elephant offered. She watched with The Cardinal as Joy kneeled down, opened the package, and then stood up with a tablet device that was almost entirely covered by a flat screen. The tablet had a few buttons along a narrow panel at the bottom of the screen.

Joy looked at it with curiosity. She looked both excited and confused like a kid who had just opened a new expensive-looking gift but had no idea what it was.

Joy then looked at both The Elephant and The Cardinal while maintaining this mixed expression in her eyes and throughout the rest of her body.

"This is a moment-capturing device that enables you to take a positive interaction with any individual in your life in the real world and freeze that interaction you had with that person so that you leave a lasting positive impression for the rest of that person's life," The Elephant explained. "The tablet enables you to take a photo at the end of the positive interaction you are having with that person and that person won't even realize you are taking a photo of the of them because the use of the tablet's camera includes a special scientific ambient noise element that neurologically re-maps their brain to cement that lasting impression of you they had right before you took the photo. The ambient noise occurs simultaneously with the camera click, is subtle, and has no impact on you or other people around you other than the person you are aiming the tablet's camera at to preserve the positive interaction with. When you use this device, it initially gives them the impression that you are simply taking a photo or video when in fact you are permanently triggering their neurons to develop positive pathways specific to that favorable experience they had with you. There is the added bonus that they will have no recollection of you taking their photo with the tablet. They only remember the positive impression they have of you from that interaction you had with them."

Joy lifted it up and tried to use it on The Elephant and The Cardinal, but she wasn't sure how to turn it on and when she pressed the buttons, no flash was produced.

The Elephant and The Cardinal looked at each other and laughed.

"It doesn't work in this world and it doesn't work if you try to use it on us even when we visit you in the real world," The Elephant laughed.

"Plus, you don't need to use it on us," The Cardinal added, "we will love you no matter what."

"True," The Elephant agreed.

Joy looked blankly at the device with her default resting frown: "Hey...it doesn't turn on?!"

The Elephant and The Cardinal looked at each other without responding.

Joy recalled her conversation with The Lion about The Book of What Everyone Else Ever Said or Thought About Her. She squinted as she exchanged glances with both of them.

"Okay, what's the catch?"

"You will lose the ability to interact with that person again for the rest of your life if you use the tablet's camera on them," The Cardinal acknowledged. "In other words, that person will always remember you positively but if you see or run into them again it will be like you are invisible to them. So, you give up the opportunity to have more potential positive interactions with them. But the trade-off is that you also prevent any potential negative interactions too."

Joy looked first at The Cardinal and then looked up to The Elephant with searching eyes. Behind them, Joy noted that the very last signs of daylight had become a mere fading glow beyond the trees along the horizon. Meanwhile, they had all become completely enveloped and surrounded by a very thin but discernible layer of fog.

"Yes, Joy," The Elephant replied to her gaze, "that includes using it on your parents, using it on Casey, and yes, using it on Gray."

"You also still have the ability to say things sometimes that makes me think you can read my mind, Elephant," Joy observed.

The Elephant laughed.

"I could use it on Casey and the other girls at school who want to beat me up if I can come up with a way to have a positive interaction with them that will make them change their minds about beating me up in gym class," Joy speculated. "Your timing is perfect in showing this to me. I can take it to school and use it on all of them. I don't care if I never speak to them again after that. I know with the way they have treated me since we were in middle school that they'll eventually come up with another reason to want to beat me up again in the future even after a positive interaction. They would finally, finally, finally leave me alone. They would leave me alone for the rest of my life."

Joy paused and looked down at the tablet.

"I could use it on Gray," she added. "He will never love me the way I hope he will. Deep down I know that. But if I get a good positive interaction with him. I could hold on to that instead. At this point, I think I might be willing to take that. It's better than him thinking I'm a loser."

Joy sighed to prevent any possible tears from budding in the corners of her eyes.

"I could use it on my mom," she continued, "maybe that would mean the end of our interactions, but she is so disappointed in me most of the time that I would rather leave her on one positive interaction than continue to disappoint her. Most of the time, she looks at me like I'm a failure. It might be worth capturing a small positive interaction that I could leave her with."

Now the tears were starting to form.

"Maybe I could use it on almost everyone except a few people I need to pass messages along to others. I'd keep my dad and maybe a few teachers that like me enough at school, but I could use it on everyone else. I'd be okay. There are only a few people who I don't have to worry about when I talk to them anyway and with everyone else, I wouldn't have to worry about saying the wrong thing or doing something embarrassing in front of them ever again," Joy's voice was now cracking at times as the tears were starting to leave the area around her eyes and travel slowly down her upper cheeks.

The last remaining daylight had disappeared into night and the white fog surrounding them gradually thickened. The bridge was only illuminated by the glow of string lights and fireflies.

The Elephant and The Cardinal looked at each other with concern as though they hadn't quite anticipated this level of detail and emotional intensity in her response.

"I could finally be me," Joy concluded, still gazing at the device.

"But how would you potentially experience real love with any of the new people you would meet? How would you make new friends? How would you confirm that you may have met your soulmate? How would you explain the tablet to your kids?" The Elephant asked. "You know you do deserve to experience all of that…"

"It's like I was telling Cardinal before you got here, I'm starting to realize that knowing real love mainly happens when you are a kid. And even if you are a kid, you're lucky if that real love involves other people and not just stuff like your favorite game or your favorite kind of pizza. I've watched my mom and dad grow apart from all their friends. I've heard other adults admit that they wish they never had kids. Everybody who thinks they experience real love as an adult is probably faking it unless they found true love with a soulmate; but that is so rare and only happens to a few lucky people. Even some of those lucky adults don't seem to know how to appreciate it when it's right in front of them. It's not fair. I know I would totally appreciate it. I'd embrace it. I'd love it. But it won't happen for me."

"It can still happen, and you deserve all the different kinds of real love," The Elephant asserted.

"Even if I find real love with my soulmate, I will still probably be sad because I will be surrounded by so many people who don't have it, so what good is it?" Joy wondered.

The fog had picked up the pace of growing denser so that string lights and fireflies had begun to vanish in its haze.

"You're the type of person who would share it with others and gently show them the way," The Elephant responded. "I know it wouldn't be easy, but all of us know you have the strength in you to not only acquire it but also share it. Bet you hadn't thought about it that way yet. But we know you'd reach a whole other level beyond just acquiring it."

"Now that must be really rare to find..." Joy started to say before trailing off.

"You have it," The Elephant pointed out, "...you can help make it less of a rare thing."

"I can't," Joy said.

"Why not?" The Cardinal asked.

Joy looked up and could barely see the Cardinal through the fog. If it weren't the fact he was such a bright red color, she wouldn't have been able to see him at all. The Elephant had also almost completely vanished in front of her. She could only see The Elephant's eyes and the very end of her trunk. She could now only see a few fireflies and the string lights immediately on either side of her. The Cardinal noticed her squinting at them and flew up to perch on a part of the railing that was closer to her so that she was able to see him better.

Instead of responding to the Cardinal's question right away, Joy sighed as she looked again at the moment-capturing tablet. This time she wasn't playing around with the buttons trying to turn it on and she was no longer looking at it like it was a new gift.

"It's like there is a dark energy inside of me and I must learn to use that dark energy to be a better person. It's ironic, because without that dark energy, it's like I can't truly remain a good person when life gets hard. That's what I think a lot of people are missing: they think they are a good person who is always right about everything without acknowledging the dark energy that is inside all of us. I don't think you can completely defeat the dark energy during your life; I think that dark energy is there no matter who you are or how long you live. But you can manage the dark energy to do more good for people on a level you couldn't imagine as opposed to only ignoring or resisting the dark energy while telling yourself that you were already a good person who can do no wrong. The dark energy can balance us to be a better version of a good person. This won't help me find that balance," Joy reasoned. She held the tablet up, hesitated for a few seconds, and then offered it to The Elephant.

The Elephant stepped forward and wrapped her truck around the tablet to accept the return.

Joy turned to the Cardinal, who was no longer perched on the railing, but perched on a tree branch. Upon noticing the tree branch, she realized it was much brighter again and there was now a window between them. She was back in her room, looking out the window at The Cardinal, who was now in the tree in her yard.

The Cardinal resumed singing again and Joy watched him for a moment. She smiled as it suddenly occurred to her that The Cardinal was singing the melody she used to ask him to sing when she was a little kid. She shuffled a half-step closer to the window as she remembered the first time she ever heard it.

For the first time in years, she pictured herself clearly as a little kid back when she first started playing soccer for an organized team. She remembered a specific day when she had been on a practice field by herself shooting the ball in the goal from long distances and then running to retrieve it after she either made or missed. She would then set the ball at a longer distance once she made a goal from a previous shorter distance she had marked with a fallen tree branch. She remembered she was intent on trying to see how far she could make a goal. She was fully dressed in her soccer uniform, and all of the other girls on her team were scattered around on neighboring practice fields. Most of the girls had remained near where their coach was on a practice field at the other end of the large park they were in. But eventually a small group of girls came over to her, took her ball away and said they wanted to shoot at the goal she was using. When she asked if she could join them, they said she couldn't. When she then asked if she could share the goal with them, they said "no" and then added, "you'll never be allowed to play with us, loser."

She recalled how she then walked to the sidelines, sat under a tree, and had started crying when she suddenly heard that melody for the first time. She looked at the tree and saw The Cardinal perched on the tree's lowest branch singing directly to her. He had winked at her as they made eye contact, and she remembered how she couldn't help but smile. She smiled even as the tears were still falling. Ever since then, she would often ask him for that particular song, especially when she was feeling down.

Back in her room, The Cardinal winked at her upon observing that she seemed to have finally recognized the song. He bounced his body up and down with his feet still planted on the branch out of excitement for her recognition. Then, just as any ordinary bird was inclined to do after making eye contact with a human, he abruptly flew away.

2.3

Before Joy walked downstairs to see if her dad had made coffee and if so, left any extra in the coffee pot, she debated whether she should change out of her white miniskirt and pajama top. After a minute or so of rigorous internal debate, she decided against doing so since she realized she was actually comfortable. She had never imagined she would be this comfortable in a miniskirt before (even though it was still over her black leggings). She wanted to ride that feeling for as long as she could. Her clothes didn't match at all, but she was comfortable, and she was safe at home.

Upon opening her bedroom door to go downstairs, she was surprised to hear commotion downstairs in the kitchen. It sounded like it was some kind of get-together or party. She could vaguely hear voices, the sounds of dishes and glasses clinking, laughter, somebody washing something in the sink, and some background music. On the way down, she stopped on a step in the middle of the staircase and leaned over the banister in the direction of the music. It sounded like some kind of low-key electronic music. It sounded futuristic and inviting. It sounded familiar, like the type of music she would like. It also didn't sound like something her dad would listen to.

As she entered the kitchen area, she first recognized The Bear. He was standing at the kitchen counter with a to-go cup of coffee beside him. She then noticed two figures were sitting at her family's round kitchen table near where The Bear was standing.

Among those sitting at the table, she recognized The Penguin first, an emperor penguin, who was standing on a chair with a plate of tiny stones and Joy's Stanford University coffee mug in front of her. Her mom had bought her that coffee mug because that was the college that Joy dreamed of one day attending even though her parents couldn't afford it. Joy then recognized The Wolf, a Eurasian wolf, who was sitting on a chair across the table from The Penguin. The Wolf had been using one of her dad's coffee mugs that had a picture of a wolf on it. The Wolf also had a plate in front of him, but he had already finished what he had been eating. By the plate's syrupy appearance and the smell of bacon in the room, Joy assumed he had pancakes, bacon and possibly eggs.

They had moved her mom's portable speaker into the kitchen and were playing the music from Joy's laptop computer which was sitting open and plugged in beside a speaker.

"What is this?!" Joy asked in a half-startled and half-excited tone.

"A little breakfast party celebrating you!" The Penguin declared.

"Celebrating me for what?"

The Penguin looked at her blankly.

"You brought us back," The Bear explained.

"No, all of you guys' just kind of started showing up again"

The three animals looked at each other in confusion.

"Seriously, how did you all manage to set all of this up?! None of you really have..." She hesitated because she didn't want to offend anyone. "...I mean you have paws, claws and flippers."

Before anyone could respond to Joy, she could hear the refrigerator door close (the refrigerator was out of her line of sight) and her gaze settled on a figure that had emerged into view at the other side of the counter from where The Bear was standing. Despite all the crazy surprises she had experienced over the past 24 hours or so (according to her timeline, not what the rest of the real world was apparently going by), it was a figure she hadn't expect to see at all. After a double take for recognition purposes, she took an involuntary step back with a clenched fist and a heavy feeling in her throat that felt like she had consumed the entire plate of stones that were sitting in front of The Penguin. Fear emerged right at the top of her neck and as it tingled down her spine through her back, she took another more-conscious step back. She felt much safer than she otherwise would have been since the animals were there, especially with The Bear pretty much in between them.

She looked squarely at The Bear.

"And you invited him?!" she asked indignantly.

The Toilet Monster didn't make any further movements in response to Joy's fear of him.

"Actually, he invited us," The Bear clarified. "He reached out because he overheard our conversation in the bathroom yesterday...I mean, heard our conversation this morning, or um, you know what I mean."

Joy couldn't believe what she was hearing.

"You lied to me, Bear. You said you had never seen The Toilet Monster and now I see you guys hang out."

"No, I had never seen him until this morning...this morning as in 'Wednesday Part II.' I didn't believe he existed. He told me he had always been too afraid of me before," The Bear added. He looked like he regretted not going into further detail in his initial response to her.

The Bear's answers didn't seem to have any impact on Joy, who looked increasingly livid.

"How could you all do this to me?! You all know how I feel about The Toilet Monster," Joy turned her attention to The Penguin and The Wolf.

The Penguin was about to say something when she stopped herself and glanced at The Toilet Monster. She gave him a nod that suggested to him "you've got this."

The Toilet Monster very slightly nodded back and cleared his throat: "Joy, even this world you have with us wasn't and isn't perfect. You still had doubts and fears that come up here too. Obviously since you are still standing here and maybe a little anxious, of course, but still standing here, you know that I am not as bad as you thought I was when you were a little kid. I overheard the conversation between you and Bear and I think I can help you now too. Whether you like it or not, I was a big part of your life too."

Joy hesitated and then admitted: "You were."

"I was," The Toilet Monster laughed awkwardly. He appeared quite uncomfortable himself. The Toilet's Monster's presence explained how the coffee was poured, how the dishes and coffee mugs were obtained from the cabinets, how breakfast was made, and how The Penguin was able to get up into her chair. Unlike the animals, The Toilet Monster had hands. The Toilet Monster had a cyborg body that resembled a cross between a human being and a seahorse. Both his bionic and non-bionic body parts were completely covered in a dark purple color, with exception of his neck and head which were a dark pink color. The only parts of his head that weren't pink were his eyes (they were the same dark purple color as the rest of his body below the neck). He was partially covered in mechanical scales (over the upper right quadrant of his torso). He had a robotic head designed like the head of seahorse. He also had a robotic arms and hands designed like that of a human being. The non-mechanized parts of his body were scaly like that of a sea-creature (even though real seahorses don't have scales).

The Toilet Monster cautiously walked around the counter to sit between The Penguin and The Wolf at center of the kitchen table opposite of where Joy was standing. Joy noted that his legs and feet were also robotic but resembled the legs and feet of a human being.

The Wolf dipped his muzzle into his coffee mug and took a sip of coffee. He looked at Joy after he had finished. "Well, we've been completely rude to Joy about one thing," The Wolf realized, "this girl loves her coffee and we haven't offered her any."

"Oh no, you're absolutely right, Wolf!" The Penguin looked like she wanted to get out of her chair and glanced at the floor as she said that. She was contemplating jumping. "Joy, we are so sorry about that. This is our first time drinking coffee so we are still kind of new to this."

"I got it," The Toilet Monster said as he rose from his chair.

"Wait!" Joy yelled.

They all froze and looked at her.

"Toilet Monster, I know we have had a bad history and I understand that you want to help me now, so I really don't want to offend you, but I have to bring this up."

"Go for it," The Toilet Monster replied.

"I mean, has it occurred to anybody here that you are being served coffee and food by The Toilet Monster? Is this sanitary?!"

The Bear, The Wolf and The Penguin looked unsure of what Joy meant by "sanitary" so they all turned to The Toilet Monster to defer to him.

"I have a built-in electric shock sanitizing system throughout my entire body that I use whenever I emerge from a sewer or a toilet. It works automatically when I transition to my full body form once I've emerged from the pipes. I use it an extra time before I'm about to work in the kitchen. It's perfect because I've discovered recently that I love cooking, it's become a hobby of mine. You all dug the pancakes, right?"

"They were excellent," The Wolf gushed. "I loved how you threw in the pecans and the bananas. It's like you knew I wasn't getting enough variety in my diet. I have really been slacking again on the fruits and vegetables. The banana-pecan pancakes have got me rethinking my whole approach to eating moving forward."

"Whatever, Wolf, you aren't changing anything," The Penguin laughed.

"I don't know, this Toilet Monster guy is a culinary genius," The Wolf asserted, "while you are sitting there eating stones."

"I had my pancakes and bacon already. They were fantastic. Eating eggs would be a little too weird for me, so I passed on them," The Penguin replied.

"Makes sense," The Bear determined. "But seriously, what is with penguins and stones? I never understood that."

"That's a secret penguin thing," The Penguin responded with a tone meant to sound intentionally mysterious.

"Ahhh," The Bear acknowledged. "Well, you've got to do you."

The Penguin and The Wolf laughed. Meanwhile, The Toilet Monster had left the table to get a mug of coffee for Joy. He approached her slowly with it and remained at a distance as he handed it to her. It was her favorite coffee mug that had a large picture of a purple orchid flower on it. The Toilet Monster also brought out a mug of coffee for himself (he used one of her mom's white mugs that said "MOM" on it in bold black lettering with several red hearts surrounding it).

Joy still hesitated to drink a coffee served to her by The Toilet Monster, but then she remembered she had accepted a coffee recently from Casey (who would probably spit in anything served to Joy if she had the chance). At the thought of that, she shrugged her shoulders and took a sip.

It was even better than the coffee she had with Casey: "Mmmm…"

She took the remaining chair closest to her at the table beside The Wolf and The Penguin and across from The Toilet Monster (who had returned to his seat). She had looked at The Bear before she sat down, and he simply motioned for her to have a seat. She realized that The Bear was probably afraid of breaking the chair if he tried to sit down on it.

"Isn't the coffee amazing?" The Penguin asked Joy before she bent over for a pecking sip of her own coffee.

"It's made with love," The Wolf raved. "That's the difference in what this guy does. He made this stuff with real love."

"You sure it isn't the brand of coffee beans that Joy's mom bought?" The Bear asked.

Everyone laughed, including The Toilet Monster.

"It never ceases to amaze me how sometimes you only sort of know someone a little bit or maybe you just hear about them, and then they end up being far more than you could ever expect once you actually sit down and spend time with them," The Wolf mused. "You can ask the others here, Toilet Monster. I don't usually throw out praise without it being completely earned and especially not right away, but you are totally an example of that."

The Wolf then turned to Joy: "And so are you."

The Bear raised his to-go cup coffee with both paws. "Cheers to that!"

The Toilet Monster and Joy lifted up their mugs while The Wolf and The Penguin nudged their mugs forward on the table with muzzle and beak respectively.

"Cheers!" Everyone called out so that their unique blend of distinct voices created a strange sounding one-word chorus.

"Look, I really appreciate it. But I've obviously made my share of mistakes and have more than my fair share of regrets, especially with the way I scared Joy all those of years," The Toilet Monster acknowledged after everyone had completed their sip of coffee.

"I think when people..." The Toilet Monster paused and looked around at his audience before continuing: "...I think when people, animals, or monsters change for the better, they like to act like someone waved a magic wand and boom— they've completely transformed for the rest of their life. I believe anything is possible, but for most of us it doesn't work out that way. I have my good days and my bad ones like everybody else. It's been a long, tough road and I'm still on it. Maybe this whole situation with Wednesday repeating itself will work to my advantage and I can keep making changes over a 'shorter' period of linear time."

"I really don't get this whole thing about reliving the same day all over again," The Wolf admitted. "We never experienced that before, right Joy?"

"Is it because we came back into Joy's life?" The Bear asked. "I noticed this time-loop thing coincided with our return. Should we really be celebrating?!"

After having her celebratory sip of coffee, Joy had been looking intently at the orchid flower on her coffee mug.

"Joy?" The Penguin asked. "Are you still with us?"

"Uh oh, I think we've lost her." The Wolf said.

"She does this sometimes," The Bear explained, looking at The Toilet Monster, "the kids these days are so different. I think it's a generational thing."

2.4

The orchid on her coffee mug had become a real orchid that was joined by several other real orchids and then joined by other different types of flowers: irises, peonies, daffodils, marigolds and lilies. These sets of flowers were then revealed to be among various other species, some of which Joy had never seen before. They all appeared in full bloom. The flowers were beaded with early morning droplets. She realized she was now surrounded by hundreds of different types of flowers in an elaborate, impeccably manicured garden that was covered in a sun-kissed mist.

Joy walked deeper into the garden along a pristine path of decorative stone tiles of various shades of muted colors that subtly accentuated the rugged texture of the stones.

She walked slowly, noticing how the plants morphed and shifted in form all around her as she walked by them. They each were growing and retracting in size, changing colors, changing species, and moving unevenly at varying speeds. Every time she scanned the full the garden landscape, it changed completely and felt like she was in a different part of the world with a broad view of different exotic plants each time. Yet, she wasn't perturbed or unsettled by the situation, embracing the beauty as she slowed down to take a longer look at how the enchanting landscape was transforming around her. Some of the plants were sparkling like glitter while others were shining like the sun through multi-colored stained glass.

She felt that feeling again that she'd felt often as a little kid when she was really excited about something. It was a feeling that she had rarely felt anymore as a teen. She had wondered aloud to The Cardinal on the bridge if she would truly ever feel that kind of feeling again, and right now she did. She felt the instantaneous excitement flow outward from her heart through her arms and legs to her hands and feet then back up through her body and spine into her head. She almost jumped, but instead just bent her knees and straightened them quickly with her feet still touching the ground. She was overwhelmed with happiness.

That smell.

That familiar smell in the garden was rejuvenating. It felt like she was smelling a dozen different types of flowers and trees all in one. It was a scent that was familiar to her, but she hadn't encountered it like this in years. It felt like this scent opened up every pathway circulating through her body as though both her respiratory and circulatory systems had been completely renewed. She had talked about how there was something about the way one's sense of smell operated as a little kid that was purer and more compelling than any of appreciation of different scents one could have after they reached adolescence. But in this strange scenario, her sense of smell was functioning at the level it did when she was a little kid.

As she took a deep breath of what felt like heaven manifested in the form of the air she could breathe, she felt a sudden droplet of very light rain on her arm and then on her forehead. When she looked up, she observed how the raindrops were glinted with bright light. She couldn't tell if it was from the sun's reflection because the light in the raindrops seemed brighter than that as if each drop of rain somehow conspicuously generated its own light. Despite the presence of this light, the rain felt cool against her skin.

As she continued walking among the changing plants, she noted that they were increasingly exotic in more colorful forms that were somehow futuristic appearing. Meanwhile the raining lights started to fall a little heavier and a little harder, but she was still relatively comfortable.

She turned the corner and noted a figure with a ball cap and a hoodie (with the hood on over the cap) standing in the middle of the path holding a large smartphone and glancing at it. She could identify that the figure was a male around her age but couldn't tell who it was. The figure and his phone seemed to be unaffected by the rain.

She felt safe enough to continue moving cautiously toward him.

As she did so, the raining lights completely stopped pouring down on and around her. This stoppage was so abrupt that she stopped moving herself and looked up at the sky. She observed that thousands of raindrops froze in the process of dropping in the air above and around her. They all remained lit like fireflies suspended in motion.

She was afraid to walk into any of the frozen twinkling droplets that surrounded her.

The suspended light drops were now changing colors to every conceivable color in the spectrum and continued to twinkle in these new colors. She felt surrounded by hundreds of strands of untethered Christmas lights. The different colored lights illuminated the area so magnificently that she no longer noticed the figure in front of her or the garden around her.

It was so illuminatingly beautiful she no longer cared where she was.

But just as she was about to wish she would never have to leave this place; she heard a familiar voice that made her blink.

"Hey," the voice of the male figure had said to her.

And with the sound of his voice, all the lights were gone.

The smells were gone.

The garden was there, having returned to its original form in the morning light when she arrived.

"Gray," she responded, recognizing the figure.

"What?" Gray was curiously studying her like she was a stranger.

Joy was surprised by his response and took a step back. She was already feeling rejected simply because he had only responded with "what?". It became apparent that he really didn't know who she was. She had always said he may not know who she was and suspected it, but she still had an underlying hope that he could still recognize her. *Was this not the guy who was jumping on my bed with me earlier, or was that just another reflection like when Casey's reflection appeared in my bathroom mirror?*

"It's Joy."

"Who?!"

Joy closed her eyes for a moment.

But even with her eyes closed, she still sensed she was in the garden, and she still sensed that Gray was there. The fact that Gray didn't recognize her had been painful in a way she hadn't expected, as the pain strangely felt like it would only temporary. Maybe it was because they weren't at school and in some weird garden where light rained down on them. Maybe it was because she still felt re-energized and re-vitalized from the experience she had immediately prior to their encounter. Whatever it was, she felt emboldened in this moment to tell Gray everything she had ever wanted to say to him. Everything that had been bottled up for years was ready to burst out of her.

"I would love you more than anybody else. I have so much love I haven't been able to give to anyone and I want to give it to you," Joy heard herself say. It wasn't planned and she was embarrassed upon pronouncing the first word she said. Normally she'd frown and/or look down at her feet, but she did neither of these things. Instead, she continued to gaze hopefully at Gray.

Gray stared at her blankly.

Joy wondered if they still were currently on the same planet or if she had become a ghost trying to communicate to someone who was alive that couldn't see or hear her in the form she saw and heard herself in.

Regardless, she felt the need to try to explain herself further: "Nobody could really love you the way I can because I saved myself just for you and I have loved you for a really long time."

Gray's right eyebrow perked up.

"A really long time?"

She looked at his lips as she spoke to him, and she found herself thinking about that moment when she was watching Natalie making out with her boyfriend in the hallway near her locker.

"Yes, since kindergarten."

"You knew me in kindergarten?"

Joy's eyes widened with disbelief.

"You were in the class next door to my class in kindergarten and then in the sixth grade we were in the same class. We sat catty corner from each other for part of the year."

Gray laughed. He initially tried to cover his mouth at first to hide it, but quickly relented on the effort.

Now came the familiar permanent-feeling sadness, loneliness, and doubt, hitting her like a powerful dark ocean wave engulfing her and then sweeping her deep underneath it.

She stood there silently.

And he continued to laugh.

As he laughed, she noted that his skin started changing color. The suddenness of this occurrence distracted her from the onset of horrible feelings she had started to feel. She looked at her skin and saw that it wasn't changing color. It was only happening to him.

The change of color started at his hands and mouth and expanded outward around across his arms and cheeks, converging underneath his clothes. The color was a vibrant red.

Gray looked at his hands, "What is this?"

At first, he laughed nervously. He was trying to play it cool and show even Joy (someone he could care less about), that nothing phased him. But once he saw the red was all over his arms, he lifted up his pant-leg and saw it was on his leg too.

It was then that he panicked.

"What did you do to me?!" He yelled at Joy without looking at her. He was fixated on how the vibrant red color now covered his entire body.

Joy was speechless, overwhelmed by the bizarre change of color to his skin.

She was so stunned that she couldn't keep her mouth closed.

The vibrant red gradually transitioned into a dark purple. Gray rolled up a sleeve on his hoodie and tried to rub the purple off of his right arm with his left hand. The friction created a gray color on the spots of his hand and arm that had been rubbed together. This new gray color, in turn, spread from these places of origin on his right arm and left hand and spread all over the rest of his body. He gasped but then took a deep breath. He took another deep breath and seemed to regain most of his composure.

As Gray stood there for a moment, reviewing himself, it appeared the dull gray color had settled as the permanent shade for his skin.

"What did you do to me?" Gray repeated in a softer, broken mumble. He turned his attention to Joy and saw the expression of awe and wonder in her face at his transformation.

As they looked at each other, he continued to calm down until finally, he smiled.

"Now I know what you're doing to me," he said.

She looked at him curiously. She was unsure of how she could respond and unsure of if she should respond.

"I'm not who you think I am, not at all," he added.

Her curious expression widened as a silent invitation for him to explain himself further.

"I'm changing now in front of you because I'm talking to you for the first time. The more I talk to you, the more you are realizing that the person you think I am is just a fantasy. It's not a real person, it never was. I know you've liked me since kindergarten or something like that. Of course, I noticed the way you've looked at me. It was so obvious, I'm sure everybody has. I pretended I never noticed because it was never worth it to me to acknowledge you. Whatever you thought of me when you didn't even know me was never my problem. There was never anything for us to talk about anyway."

His voice sounded deeper and much older as he said this. It barely sounded like the Gray she knew. She noticed wrinkles spreading on the surface of the skin of his face, arms and neck. His belly protruded outward. The hair on top of his head thinned and his forehead grew larger at the expense of some of the hair, which disappeared entirely. Gray had aged to appear as he would at seventy years old.

"This isn't you, Gray," Joy said.

"Tell me who I am," the older Gray responded sarcastically.

"You have so much going for you."

"Just because you like me?!"

"Well, you get good grades, you play soccer, you are in the highest math class there is at school..."

Gray's clothes had changed. They looked more like they matched his seventy-year-old appearance, but they were also dirty looking, stained in places and a size too big. He reached into his back pocket and pulled out a crushed-up pack of cigarettes. He took out a cigarette and a lighter that was stored among the few cigarettes left in the pack. He held out the pack to her and she shook her head to decline.

He lit his cigarette and sighed. His sigh released a puff of smoke in Joy's direction.

"That was all in elementary school," he muttered with the cigarette dangling out of his mouth. "Where have you been?"

Joy was bewildered. She couldn't believe Gray smoked. She had never seen him smoke before. She immediately started justifying his smoking in her mind to reconcile with herself on how it didn't fit her image of him up to this point. But before she could get too far into thinking about it, she realized that her stomach was still in knots and getting worse (not so much because of Gray's presence anymore but because the smell of cigarette smoke made her feel sick). She started coughing from the secondhand smoke. She closed her eyes.

"Joy?!" It was The Lion's voice. "Are you okay?"

2.5

"What's wrong with her?" Autumn asked. "She was fine when I saw her at school. Is she sick or something?"

"She'll be fine," The Lion replied, looking at Joy with a level of concern that didn't seem to match his words.

Autumn continued to glare at Joy, and it was unclear if she had heard The Lion speak.

Joy was distracted by a coughing fit upon entering the captain's quarters in the flagship of the enemy fleet that was attacking her castle. Autumn was so infuriated that she could barely tolerate the situation. Not only was she concerned that Joy was sick and potentially exposing her to some kind of illness, but she was even more upset that Joy had unwittingly hindered her planned introduction. Autumn had been looking forward to revealing herself to Joy as the commander of the fleet besieging the castle for some time. But here Joy was, coughing uncontrollably.

"You've got to be kidding me," Autumn scowled. "Joy, you are as weird and awkward in this world as you are at school. Why am I so surprised? You never cease to disappoint me."

Joy finally stopped coughing and looked at The Lion to give him silent reassurance she was okay before turning to Autumn.

"Hi...Autumn," Joy stuttered as she cleared her throat. "You hang out here too?"

Autumn rolled her eyes.

Through the corners of both eyes, Joy noted there were six guardsmen clad in armor and helmets carrying halberds lined up behind her and The Lion. Autumn also had three guardsmen also carrying halberds behind her. She observed how all the guardsmen were carrying swords in scabbards on their belts. Autumn herself was dressed in her school clothes that Joy had seen her wear on the morning of the first version of that Wednesday they had experienced together. Joy was now somehow in her white skirt, black leggings and pajama top despite being in her clothes from the previous Wednesday during the boat ride over to Autumn's ship. She looked at her own clothes after viewing everyone else in the room and looked embarrassed.

"Joy, you have to understand that girls like us will never make it in the real world," Autumn explained in a more amiable tone. "Your mistake is that you are still trying to make it there. You'll never be happy. But there is a world for us, a world where we are in charge and never have to worry about anything. It's a world that will forever be better than their world. You see, that's why the other girls don't mess with me nearly as much as they do with you. I am not trying to be anything in their world. I've found a world that is so much better that I don't have to try."

"You mean this world?" Joy asked sarcastically.

"This world," Autumn confirmed, ignoring Joy's sarcasm. She gestured toward the various accessories and decorations that made up her elaborate and fanciful captain's quarters.

"I thought you said I just have to make a few changes and I can be beautiful in the real world." Joy recalled. "You said I could be one of the most beautiful girls in school."

"That's just my opinion, but you and I know both know you're too different to be considered beautiful in their world regardless of what you and I think," Autumn clarified. "It's in this world where our opinions matter. In this world, you and I matter. In this world, you are beautiful to everyone here— well, except me, until you make a few changes."

"This world?!" Joy asked again.

"Yes, this one! The one you should've never left in the first place. And that was your second mistake: leaving this world behind. Look at your friends here. You have a castle and an army of knights, soldiers and villagers that are doing a brilliant job of defending it right now considering they are hopelessly outnumbered and have no chance at winning. But I see what you've done here. You built up quite the little empire here when you were younger. But that's the difference between you and I. You see, I never left it, Joy. Look around you, as you get older, it gets better."

"No," Joy muttered, without being entirely clear on what part of Autumn's statement she was saying "no" to. She thought about what to say next in a tense pause before continuing: "Something doesn't make sense; you take pills to lose weight to try to fit in the real world too."

"I take the caffeine pills to keep my weight down and to stay awake enough in their world to get by. They energize me. Do you notice how social I pretend to be at school? That's the caffeine. I take them so that the other girls and my family will leave me alone so I can spend more time in this world. See, my parents still think I'm trying to make it in their world, but the other girls know I am not really trying so they all leave me alone. The other girls know because I praise them and make self-deprecating jokes to give them the impression that they are better than me. There is a balance. And that's your third and final mistake, Joy. You clearly haven't learned to balance the two worlds. But I can't blame you, I struggled with it through junior high school myself. Trust me, there is a way to have full access to this world but still manage just enough in their world to get through it and embrace this one."

"More pills?!" Joy quipped.

"Now you're finally thinking," Autumn laughed. She signaled two of her guards to go to the bookshelf behind her that was filled with old hardcover books interspersed with piles of rolled up scrolls. They stood on each side of the bookshelf and as one guard pushed the edge of the bookshelf inward, the other guard pulled it outward on his end so the entire shelf moved in a circular motion. As the bookshelf side revolved inward, an identical set of shelves on the other side of it was revealed. But instead of books and scrolls, these shelves were filled with an array of hundreds of bottles and jars filled with various potions and solid medicinal-looking items.

"You see, as you get older in their world, it gets harder to access this world as often as you want to. But I found a way to access this world whenever I want to, and I can come here anytime like we did when we were younger."

"But don't you want to get married someday and have a family?" Joy wondered.

"Maybe someday when I feel like it." Autumn laughed in a way that sounded so fake that midway through her laughter she started to sound like she was laughing at how fake her laugh was. "Well, I don't know about kids, but I'd love to have a partner at some point. Like I said to you earlier, Joy, you still have to get by in their world to fully embrace this one. You'd be surprised at the number of guys our age who also choose this world over the real world. You don't know, because you are so focused on guys like Gray who are lost in the real world. I can be in a relationship anytime I want here, but I am having so much fun on my own right now that I don't think about it much. Maybe next year."

"But what about love?" Joy asked.

"This is better than love," Autumn contended. "As long as you embrace this world, you'll never get hurt here. Love can't promise you that."

Joy looked at The Lion, who made eye contact with her but remained stoic.

"Joy, we've specifically designed our initial attack to act as a warning. The bombardment of your castle has only been operating at about a quarter of what we are truly capable of in terms of our firepower. I'll admit that we weren't expecting your castle to be armed with cannons as well. We have had to pull in and out of their range to fire upon your walls but trust me, you don't have nearly enough to stop us once we put up a full siege on you. We are preparing a landing party that will outnumber and easily overwhelm your defense force no matter how much they surprise us with their will to fight. We put in a lot of preparation in anticipation of this day while you look like you still can't believe that I'm even here."

Joy had looked over to The Lion when Autumn had admitted she was surprised that Joy's castle had been armed with cannons. The Lion winked upon her gaze.

"Even the sea appears to be on our side," Autumn continued, "as we've observed rising sea levels flooding into the caverns embedded in the cliffs beneath your castle... Do you believe things happen for a reason?"

Joy hesitated in surprise at the unexpected question and then nodded that she did believe things happened for a reason.

"Almost everyone you meet in the real world is trapped and locked away in mediocrity. They live their boring lives trying to believe they deserve to be one level higher in life than where they are. If they are lucky and move up a level, then they immediately look at the next level they perceive as coming after it. They never see the big picture. It's a boring miserable lifestyle that makes them that much more subconsciously depressed. They consistently think they deserve or will attain a slightly higher status that they'll never reach because they can't get out of their own way with their own simplistic thinking. They are entitled and ignorant because they can't see past what they don't have and what they think they should have. They are also short-sighted because they never see beyond that next rung of the ladder that they think they deserve. They don't ever think about climbing beyond that. Haven't you noticed that? I listen to people in the hallways at school and its always people talking about wanting a new car or wanting a new partner or wanting new clothes. They never think outside of box. Even at our age they give up on the idea that their true passions and dreams will ever come true. They live their lives in a way only to please the other people who happen to be around them, and they never appreciate what they have, or remember to use their imagination. Is that the kind of life you want to have, Joy?"

Joy didn't respond.

"See, what I actually like about you is that you aren't like them. I know you are so much more than that. The potential is there. Your main problem is that you still let yourself get all caught up in the daily grind of unnecessary distractions that keep you from really enjoying your life here where you belong. You try to be like them, but you aren't like them, Joy. You can think outside the box, you are deeper than they are, and you deserve a comfortable place here where you can be happy. They'll never allow you to be happy in their world. They'll keep trying to change you and still tell you that you aren't good enough even after you've made the changes that they want you to make. Why live the rest of your life in a world where everybody thinks they are better than you when you can be here in a world where people know your qualities and appreciate you like me and your lion buddy."

The Lion put his head down. He looked increasingly uncomfortable and had held a stance that implied he wanted to draw as little attention to himself as possible in this situation.

"Remember when you were a little kid and almost every adult you met seemed cool and interesting?" Autumn asked. "It was so easy to look at everyone you met so positively. It was like you trusted everyone because you didn't know any better. You think everyone is great, especially your parents. But we all go through it in one way or another, Joy. Eventually we all realize how brutal life really is. It's like one day you suddenly learn all the dark secrets of what it means to be an adult and know all the things adults know. You learn how most adults are only out for themselves and just trying to selfishly get by. You learn how many adults don't really know who they are or what they're doing. You find out the world isn't nearly as positive and beautiful as you thought it was. You find out no one is really an expert at their expertise. You realize you can't ever get that perspective you had as a little kid back because you're lost trying to make money, trying to make other people happy, and trying to meet society's expectations while struggling so hard to figure out your own expectations of yourself underneath all of that. But here in this world, you don't have to worry about any of that. Look at your lion here, he loves you for who you are unconditionally, and all your friends and acquaintances here do too. Why throw all of that away?"

"If this world is better than love, why would I need love here, then?" Joy pondered with a tone that suggested she was half-serious and half-sarcastic.

Autumn quietly but tensely responded to Joy with a piercing stare.

Joy met her stare with a reluctant, though steady gaze.

"Think about how you are really somebody here and how you feel like you are a real person when you are here. I know you never feel that way otherwise. Take time to think about how much better your life would be if you joined me here full-time. Surrender your castle to me and I'll let you use it as often as you want as a first-class citizen of my empire. I'll handle all the administrative responsibility for you, and you can just relax, enjoy your friends here, and be on a lifelong vacation."

Joy maintained silent eye contact and resisted the habit to look down at the floor.

Autumn turned back to the guards near her and motioned them toward her and The Lion. "Please escort them off the ship and allow them to safely return to their castle. We'll give her more time to think about it. She is being stubborn like she always is, but I still think she will make the right choice."

The three guards approached Joy and The Lion. A guard took a position on each side of them and the third stood immediately in front of them. Joy and The Lion turned and started walking toward the door. The other six guards that had been behind them formed two separate lines of three guards each to form an honor cordon that flanked their path to the exit. Joy and The Lion couldn't tell if they were being treated as foreign dignitaries or prisoners who were being sent on a temporary release in a semi-ceremonious fashion.

"And Joy, I'm being generous and giving you twenty-four hours from now to think about it," Autumn announced from behind them,

Joy stopped and looked back at Autumn with a confused look.

"I mean twenty-four hours from now relative to your subjective experience of time elapsing."

Joy pondered this, but Autumn showed her no patience.

"Yes, I know…You're a mess when it comes to keeping track of time, but you've got your lion here and he'll help you."

The guard now walking behind them placed his hand on Joy's shoulder to keep her moving along as they were escorted out of the captain's quarters.

"Joy are you okay?!" Her dad's voice asked.

2.6

oy turned and realized that her dad had placed his hand on her shoulder while standing behind her. She then noticed she was still sitting at the kitchen table. She was holding the handle of her orchid coffee mug as it remained on the table with coffee still in it. She wondered if her dad would say anything about her having on coffee on a weekday.

The way the daylight was coming in through the window had completely changed and it looked like the clouds had come back in. She couldn't immediately tell, but it may have started raining again.

She squeezed the handle of her coffee mug without lifting it up to drink it.

"Oh...yeah," Joy mumbled, "what time is it?"

"It's 8:35," her dad replied, glancing at his smartphone to check the time (there was a microwave clock in the kitchen, but it was out of their line of sight from where they were positioned at the table).

Joy looked up at him.

"In the morning," her dad added. Her dad smelled like a combination of sawdust, paint, and the hair gel that still made his hair look wet even though he had applied it hours ago.

Joy sighed.

"Are you okay, baby?" Her dad asked, looking concerned as he sat down where The Wolf had been previously sitting. Joy noted that the animals and The Toilet Monster had vanished, and the kitchen looked exactly as it normally did. It looked as though the little breakfast party they had earlier hadn't occurred. As far as Joy could tell, the only remnants of that experience were her orchid coffee mug (still filled with some of the coffee that The Toilet Monster brewed) and the fact that she was still sitting in the same seat at the kitchen table.

"I should take a shower," Joy determined.

"That's a good idea," her dad agreed, "that will help you feel better."

Her dad got up from his chair and picked up her orchid coffee mug: "You know your mom and I want you to take easy on the coffee."

Joy smiled meekly at him as he took her mug back around the kitchen counter toward the sink.

After some hesitation, she finally got up and left the kitchen.

As she climbed the stairs, she heard her dad washing out her mug and she silently grieved the loss of the opportunity to drink the rest of coffee that The Toilet Monster had so masterfully made for her.

2.7

Joy entered the bathroom but after she turned on the light and shut the door behind her, she found herself standing in a luxurious glass elevator. The closed bathroom door had transformed into closed stainless steel elevator doors, and the light switch had disappeared. It was the kind of elevator one might find at a fancy mall, a corporate headquarters, or a downtown hotel.

She must have been on a ground floor because immediately beyond the elevator's glass walls was an enclosure of futuristic-looking metal walls. With the exception of the doors and control panel, the elevator was completely encased in glass (including the floor and the ceiling). Joy glanced at the control panel and found it had hundreds of floor buttons to choose from with no numbers assigned to them. The control panel was so long that it went all the way down to the floor. As she looked at it intently, the elevator doors suddenly opened.

Behind the doors she saw The Penguin. This time The Penguin was wearing silver aviator sunglasses with purple mirrored lenses. The scene behind The Penguin wasn't the upstairs hallway of her house but instead looked like some kind of futuristic office corridor.

"Joy!" The Penguin jubilantly greeted her as she entered the elevator and stood beside her to face the closing elevator doors.

"Hi, Penguin."

After the elevator doors had closed, Joy observed as The Penguin pressed about ten different buttons on the panel within her reach. The buttons she chose with the tip of her flipper had no discernible pattern to them and seemed random.

"Where are we going?" Joy inquired.

The Penguin was flabbergasted.

"Are you joking?!" The Penguin started laughing but stopped when she looked up and saw that Joy genuinely looked lost.

"We used to do this all the time," The Penguin added.

Joy anxiously curled a lock of her long dark hair around her finger and mumbled: "It's been a while."

"True," The Penguin agreed, and then responded to her question: "We are going to your space station."

"My space station," Joy whispered to herself in awe with a surprised grin she wanted to hide. She bent her head down so that her chin rested on her chest and her long hair rolled down her cheeks.

Joy looked up again as The Penguin hit several more buttons on the control panel. The elevator hummed for several seconds before it started moving upward. She was captivated by the 360-degree views of the sky after the glass elevator had moved rapidly beyond the metal walls surrounding it through at least fifty floors and then went up out of the futuristic-looking skyscraper it had been in. They had emerged from beyond the rooftop into a mostly cloudy sky at sunset with rays of twilight reflecting various colors on cumulonimbus clouds. A few of the fading rays of sunlight met Joy's forehead and cheeks as she looked out at the colors of the sky. There were shades of red, orange, purple, pink, blue and white intermingled into a perfect masterpiece. It was one of those once-in-a-lifetime twilights of a sunset that will pull a person so deeply into it that they don't want it to ever stop because they realize this may be the best sunset that they'll ever experience.

"Um... wow," Joy murmured.

The Penguin laughed: "It's fantastic, isn't it?"

Eventually they could see no ground or city below them— only glowing clouds and the sky above the clouds.

It wasn't clear to Joy how they were able to elevate as there was no clear elevator shaft, no rocket engine, no jet propulsion, or any kind of pulley. There was nothing connected to the elevator so it must have appeared to have simply been a glass box rising through the sky. As the elevator entered into the stratosphere, Joy noticed it was gradually building up speed as though powered by unseen rockets, but it remained steady.

"It was getting dark down there," Joy observed. "I thought it was still morning?"

"The elevator to the Space Station is in Malmö, Sweden."

Joy looked at her with perplexed, searching eyes. But she then noted that she could see her reflection too clearly in the darkened glass behind The Penguin and in The Penguin's sunglasses, so she made a point of directing her focus down to the floor, where the brightness of earth below made her reflection unnoticeable.

"Remember? You all left it up to me to decide the location." The Penguin smiled without Joy noticing her smile. "It's a nice city and the climate suits me. It's cheaper than Copenhagen."

As the elevator rose above the earth through the outer edge of the stratosphere and into the mesosphere, the details of the clouds and terrain became less and less apparent as the earth transitioned into a clouded blueish hue glowing against the surrounding darkness of space.

"It's getting kind of chilly in here," Joy indicated, folding her arms over her chest. The Penguin responded with a look of quiet embarrassment (unseen by Joy) and then hit another button on the elevator control panel.

"Mesosphere climate control option engaged," a robotic female voice stated through the speaker above the first row of buttons within the control panel.

"I'm so sorry, I forgot we put this in for you," The Penguin explained. "The space glass insulates the outside temperature enough for me."

But Joy had been startled into unfolding her arms (while still looking down). "Did the elevator just talk to us?!"

"It did. That is the Space Station Elevator computer. You named the computer 'Sura.' I think you chose that name because you said that was a name of a girl you were friends with in your kindergarten class."

Joy perked up at the mention of a familiar name she hadn't thought about for several years. The thought of Sura distracted her enough that she was indifferent to the reemergence of her reflections in walls of the elevator and in the Penguin's sunglasses by looking up again. Sura may have been her best friend in kindergarten and was definitely one of them. She was a girl from Turkey that Joy had instantly connected with on their first day because they seemed to be the only two kids who didn't know anyone else in the class. Sura's family moved away back to Turkey before Joy started the first grade. Joy felt like that had been the story of her life in school: everyone she ever connected with moved away to another school in a faraway place. The remainder of friends she once had that were still at the same school might as well have moved away too because not only did they not want to be her friend now, but they didn't want to acknowledge their past friendships with her either. She wondered if any other student in high school ever had this same experience.

"Sura," Joy acknowledged, as if to herself.

"Approaching destination: Alis Volat Propriis Space Station," Sura reported.

The glass elevator slowed down it's pace until it felt like it was steadily floating upward through space. The ride was so smooth that this sudden drastic change of speed had little to no impact on the occupants of the elevator as though the elevator could have been moving at a regular pace like that of most elevators climbing floors through skyscrapers. The speed of the ride could only be seen through the glass walls of the elevator as it was barely felt in the mild vibrations through the floor beneath their feet.

Joy looked up through the glass ceiling of the elevator but didn't see the modular space station she had prematurely envisioned. Instead, they appeared to be approaching a large gray circular object. The Penguin took note of Joy's wide-eyed curiosity (the kind that only a person seeing something for the first time would have) and by now had accepted that Joy apparently had no recollection of her Space Station. Joy was so interested in the appearance of the Space Station that she was oblivious to her reflection in the darkened ceiling.

"The Space Station is situated on that floating platform," The Penguin indicated.

As the platform drew closer and appeared larger, its shadow gradually filled the elevator completely and replaced the remaining light from the glowing earth with flickering navigation lights that were flashing simultaneously at various points at the bottom of the platform.

Joy closed her eyes as though her thoughts required that of her for clarity.

"Penguin, I used to have friends in elementary school and at the beginning of middle school, but I don't have any friends anymore," she shared with her eyes still closed.

As Joy opened her eyes again, The Penguin slowly removed her sunglasses with both flippers and then looked up at Joy: "I am still your friend."

Joy was astonished by The Penguin's use of her flippers: "Penguins can't use their flippers like that!"

"I am the only one who can," The Penguin boasted. "You taught me."

Joy closed her eyes again to let The Penguin's comment of "I am still your friend" sink in.

"You..." Joy started to say.

"Me?" The Penguin asked.

"I mean the generic-you..." Joy clarified with her eyes still closed, "...you want to believe you can grow up like everyone else: have a house, a family, and go on nice vacations. Once you have all of that, you want to believe you can do whatever extra things you'll want to do like renovate your backyard, add a room to your house, build a pool, and throw nice parties for your friends. I want to believe that someday I can be a part of all of that too even though everyone else in my life doesn't seem to think it will happen for me. But as I get older, it is like there are less people my age who are willing to talk to me. It makes me feel less like any of those dreams will eventually happen for me when I'm adult. It's like I already know it won't and my path will be weird and different from everyone else's path. Maybe it really is like my mom says when she reminds me that 'it doesn't happen for everyone.' Some people are going to be left out and maybe I really am one of those people. I'm finally accepting that today."

The elevator stopped once it had completely entered the bottom of the platform into a steel-walled docking station. Joy opened her eyes and saw that appeared almost identical to their point of departure at the building in Malmö, Sweden.

"Joy..." The Penguin whispered as she continued looking up at her with the hope that she would return her glance. When that didn't happen, The Penguin put her sunglasses back on, approached Joy, and touched her leg with one of her flippers as a show of empathy as a series of docking sounds vibrated around the elevator. The Penguin then offered the same flipper up toward Joy's hand to "hold hands."

The elevator then suddenly sped up again as it resumed moving upward. It became clear that they were moving rapidly up another steel-walled elevator shaft in a skyscraper that was also several stories high. Joy reached down and gently held The Penguin's outward flipper for the remainder of the elevator trip.

They quietly looked around once the glass elevator stopped. Looking up, Joy observed a steel ceiling that indicated they must have been on the top floor.

Joy released The Penguin's flipper and sighed.

The elevator doors opened and revealed that The Dolphin had been standing there waiting for them.

"Hey every— Joy! Are you okay?!" The Dolphin's tone of initial excitement quickly tumbled into serious concern when she noticed Joy's sadness.

Joy saw that The Dolphin was in the same customized dolphin-shaped spacesuit she had observed her in before when they were floating in outer space. But this time she could also see how The Dolphin's spacesuit contained two tiny jet engines on each side of her body beneath the sleeves for her pectoral fins. The tiny jets enabled The Dolphin to have the appearance that she was "standing" upright just as any dolphin would when emerging upward over the surface of the ocean. The jets gave The Dolphin enough lift so that she was floating over the ground and also gave her the ability to move in any direction she desired. Her tail flukes hovered several inches above the floor. The jets made only a slight sound that sounded like a gas cooktop flame burning. The sound reminded Joy of the massive, frequently used gas cooktop at the house of one of her old friends who didn't talk to her anymore. As if to further demonstrate how efficient they were, the jets showed no flame. Since they were in the space station, The Dolphin wasn't wearing her space helmet this time and Joy could see electrodes attached to The Dolphin's head. These electrodes gave The Dolphin the ability to control her movements on land surfaces by utilizing the movable jets.

At first, The Dolphin waited for Joy to respond, but once it became apparent that Joy was locked in an odd expression that mixed her own self-doubt with her curiosity and awe of The Dolphin's outer-space attire, she turned her attention to The Penguin instead: "We going to show her the robot?"

"Showing her the robot," The Penguin verified.

"The what-now?!" Joy asked, sounding exasperated. She was still thinking about how she used to have friends and be able to visit them in their homes too. She couldn't remember the name of the girl who lived in the house that had the elaborate gas cooktop.

"Oh, trust me," The Penguin assured her, "you'll love it."

They walked (or in The Dolphin's case, hovered) down a main corridor of multi-colored glittering lights that were embedded in walls, ceiling and flooring. The walls, ceiling and floors were all made of steel. The walls included various control panels and monitors that contained real-time typing on their screens in a strange computer-language that was foreign to Joy. The walls also contained occasional steel sliding doors on both sides.

As they reached the end of the corridor to a large set of steel double doors, the multi-colored lights began swirling in beautiful waves as if in acknowledgement of their approach. Joy could hear the sound of doors opening as she stopped in front of the double doors and looked at The Dolphin and then The Penguin in confusion as the doors in front of them weren't opening. The three of them stood (or hovered) there in silence, with Joy standing between The Dolphin and The Penguin. She then looked up and saw a small set of steel double doors within the ceiling opening above them. Behind the sliding ceiling doors, there were rows of track lights in a compartment that was just large enough to cover their heads.

Just as Joy turned her gaze back to The Penguin, a beam of purple light covered The Penguin's entire body and formed a glowing cylinder of light in the area immediately around her straight up to one of the light bulbs in the ceiling. Then when she looked over to her other side, Joy observed the same occurrence happening to The Dolphin before it started happening to her too. She couldn't feel anything at all upon viewing the purple glow all around her but nevertheless, she froze in fear and then closed her eyes.

"Scan completed. Access granted. Welcome back, Joy," a man's voice with what sounded like a French accent said over what sounded like an intercom. She opened her eyes, and the lights were gone. She looked up and the ceiling doors were closing.

Joy remained frozen and looked bewildered.

"That's Gabriel," The Dolphin acknowledged upon noticing Joy's lack of recognition of Gabriel's voice, "he's a computer system that operates and protects the entire space station. He does an excellent job around here."

"Thank you, Dolphin," Gabriel said from somewhere above them.

The double doors in front of them slid open and revealed a very large space that looked like an oversized hotel conference room (but if it was a hotel in a space station). The room had three steel walls that were similarly covered with control panels, sliding doors to other corridors and rooms, and computer screens like the walls in the main corridor. But the fourth wall in the room was a massive window that covered the entire left side of the room from the floor to the ceiling. There were also a few long rectangular tables with chairs scattered around the left half of the room.

Joy walked up to the window, put her hands up against the glass and looked outside in wonder. The scene outside of the window revealed what looked like a small city of skyscrapers and smaller buildings covering nearly the entire circular platform. The buildings were all underneath an overarching glass dome and were lit in various neon colors that were striking against the backdrop of space beyond the dome. It looked like it could easily have been an underwater city or a city on a distant planet. The vantage point from the window suggested that they were around 80-100 stories above the platform and must have been in the tallest building of the space station.

Due to the level of brightness in the way the room was lit relative to the darkness of space outside, it enabled Joy to become aware of her vague reflection in the glass of the window. To Joy, it wasn't her definition of the "good lighting" that her reflection required. Upon seeing her reflection, she released her hands from the glass, and she took a step back in disgust. Her curiosity permitted her to continue looking outside though, and upon doing so, she noticed a much better reflection of herself in the window. *Did that step back give me the right lighting?* She also wondered how many people worked and lived in the space station. She turned around and saw that The Penguin and The Dolphin were still standing at the entrance to the room, looking at her oddly.

"How many people work in the space station?" Joy asked them. "It almost looks like as if there are a million people living here."

The Penguin and The Dolphin didn't immediately respond so she turned back to the window again.

Her reflection was beautiful. She looked at it for a moment in awe. The lighting was perfect. It was kind of like it was on some early mornings before school in her bedroom mirror. It was strange though because this time there were two reflections, and she realized the better, clearer one was now directly to her right. She still smiled at this more preferable version of her reflection anyway.

The reflection didn't smile along with her (but the other one she turned away from did).

"The population varies. This is because a lot of the same people who live in and around the village near the castle also live and work here depending on where you are and where you've focused your attention. Think of it as people working different shifts depending on where they are needed. But right now, just about everyone is over at the castle because it has been under attack," Joy heard her own voice say.

Joy took another step back upon hearing her own voice despite the fact that her lips hadn't been moving. She also didn't have the knowledge to share that information.

She slowly looked further to her right and became aware of a better looking and better dressed version of herself gazing out the window beside her.

Joy looked at herself and screamed.

The Dolphin and The Penguin immediately went up to her to console her.

"No, no, Joy, no need to panic! This is the robot version of yourself. This is Robot Joy." The Penguin tapped the human Joy's knee with her flipper and pointed at Robot Joy with her other flipper.

Robot Joy calmly turned to Joy with an empathetic look of concern.

"Better turn off Robot Joy," The Dolphin managed to say to The Penguin over Joy's screaming, "it's really freaking her out."

The Penguin waddled as quickly as she could back to a control panel on the lower half of the wall next to the door that they had used to enter the room. She pressed a button on the tablet screen of the control panel.

"Robot Joy deactivated," Gabriel's voice echoed through the room.

Robot Joy's eyes suddenly closed and she remained still in her standing position facing Joy.

Joy stopped screaming but still took a couple more steps back away from Robot Joy and then as she continued to curiously study it silently, eventually took one step closer.

Robot Joy was fascinating in how closely it resembled her but with very slight variations that made her look more appealing physically.

"You know when someone takes a photo of you either individually or in a group picture and you see yourself in it and you're like 'oh wow, I never look this great'? That's how we created this robot. The robot looks like you, but you at your absolute best. This robot has your best hair, makeup, and clothes. This robot always looks like the way you do in photos taken at all your best angles. It is like that favorite photo you have of yourself but as a walking and talking reality of that photo. Its voice sounds like your voice but only when you are energized and in a good mood because the robot has the best sides of your personality in any given situation," The Penguin explained as she approached them again.

"I get that you wanted a robot version of yourself, but I've wondered what it was supposed to do for you, Joy," The Dolphin queried.

"I can't believe it's finally here. I wanted this for so long," Joy murmured, as if to herself. She was still in awe of Robot Joy's presence. "How long have you had it here?"

"This model was just recently completed," The Penguin answered. "As you can imagine, since you keep growing up, our team of engineers keep having to update it for you. They keep modifying it, even though we weren't sure if you were coming back."

"But why didn't I ever get to use my robot back when I used to be here?" Joy wondered.

"It was here," The Penguin replied, "but you never chose to use it the way you originally intended to use it. It was an idea you were excited about but then once you understood the ramifications of using it, you moved on to other things. It was kind of like opening a Christmas gift and saying you can't wait to use whatever it is but then putting it away in the closet somewhere for several years and eventually forgetting you had it."

"Wait," The Dolphin said to The Penguin, "does that mean I'm a robot too? Are we also robots that Joy created? We've been kind of stored away for the last several years too."

"You aren't a robot," Joy reassured her. She then hesitated before continuing: "At least I don't think so, I didn't ask to build you. But for real this time, I am going to use my robot. I want to send it to school in my place as I originally intended. That way, I never have to go out unless I want to. I can hang out here or go anywhere else I want while the robot takes care of everything. I could go to Spain!"

"Why wouldn't you want to go to school?" The Dolphin asked. She then paused in the moment as new thoughts seemed to arise within her: "So you would want to change your whole life then? Does this mean you also wouldn't have us around either anymore?"

"Of course I'd still keep you around!" Joy answered. "You're my friends. You would travel the world with me."

"I still don't get it," The Dolphin admitted, "you want to leave the rest of your life behind to Robot Joy?"

"The robot would go to school in my place, and she would be smarter than me so she would get better grades again like I used to get when I was younger and that would make my parents happy. She would take all the bullying and abuse I get without getting hurt like I do. She wouldn't have to worry about feeling pretty because she wouldn't feel anything and she looks like the best version of me anyway. She wouldn't worry about getting in trouble with my parents either because she would have common sense and always say and do the right things."

"So..." The Dolphin began, "do I get to have a robot too, or just you? Because I am not sure if it's fair to Robot Joy that you get to have us and she doesn't have any robot animals to chill with."

Joy stared blankly at The Dolphin.

The Dolphin laughed awkwardly, then added: "And if we are dividing our time, I also don't know if I can handle double duty being friends with you and Robot Joy. It sounds like a lot of work...I know

I'd want more time off. We have already been in your life longer than I thought we would be."

The Penguin laughed along with The Dolphin and Joy kind of awkwardly giggled along with them a little bit.

"Actually," The Penguin began, "if everything goes according to plan and Joy sends Robot Joy to the real world to replace her, we won't have to visit there. She wouldn't be there either, she'd be here full-time."

Joy looked a little confused and concerned: "But what about Spain?"

"Well, you wouldn't be able to go to the real Spain, per se," The Penguin responded, "but we do have our own kind of version of it here."

"The food isn't as good," The Dolphin added.

"No, the food isn't as good," The Penguin confirmed.

Joy sighed.

"But Robot Joy would still be able to go to the real Spain back in the other world," The Penguin continued, "and we would be able to watch it here. Here, we'll show you."

The Penguin returned to the same tablet panel she had used to turn off Robot Joy and hit a different button with her flipper. A large flat screen came down from the ceiling against the wall opposite from where The Penguin was standing. The massive screen was about 9 ft wide and 7 ft high. Once it was completely lowered, the screen was initially black but after The Penguin hit another button, a live video appeared of Joy standing in her bathroom looking at herself in the mirror with an expression on her face that even Joy herself found difficult to read.

Joy was stunned, the kind of "stunned" that caused her mouth to slightly open involuntarily.

"I know, it's incredibly creepy," The Dolphin laughed upon observing Joy's reaction. "You're in two different places at the same time."

"It's your very own reality show you get to watch here for the rest of your life," The Penguin offered.

Joy was speechless.

"You would be able to watch this anytime you want if you chose to activate Robot Joy to take your place," The Penguin added, "and if you activate Robot Joy, you'd also be able to read the book of what everyone else has ever said or thought about you that we used to keep in the castle and have now transferred here for you."

The Penguin pressed another button using the same control panel and a secret doorway to the left of the large video screen opened in the wall. This hidden doorway slid open like the other doors at the space station and revealed a small closet-sized opening that contained a display pedestal. It was a similar set up than Joy and The Lion had viewed in the castle. The Book of What Everyone Else Ever Said or Thought About Her was in the same display case as before.

"You'd have access to all the relevant information you could imagine in your life that you otherwise wouldn't know about," The Penguin said, "and you could do it all from the safety and comfort of being here. I am thinking if you transition to Robot Joy, it would be about the robot's life, not really your life, but it's still kind of your life, right?"

"Kind of, right?" The Dolphin semi-repeated.

"Kind of," Joy responded. She sounded like it was more of a response to herself than to the others.

The Penguin pressed yet another button on the control panel and a small compartment opened in the wall next to the control panel (on the other side of the doorway). It contained an opened sunglasses case. The sunglasses case was uniquely shaped for The Penguin's ease of use. The case was larger than any normal glasses case and enabled The Penguin to set the sunglasses with the temples still unfolded directly into it.

"You get a first-hand viewing from a more objective perspective of how they react to the robot version of you whenever you want to," The Penguin continued as she removed her sunglasses with both flippers and placed them in the case. "It's like an out-of-body experience. You'd have all the answers you ever really wanted to know about everyone in your life and everything they'd ever think about or talk about involving you. Can you imagine that?"

"But Robot Joy wouldn't know these things, right?" Joy asked. "It would just be me sitting here watching it, and I couldn't do anything about it."

"Right," The Penguin replied, "you would be giving up any control you have in the real world for the rest of your life and wouldn't be able to return there, but you'd still get to watch it here whenever you want to."

Joy was in deep discernment.

The Penguin pressed the same button on the tablet screen that she used to access the sunglasses case and the sunglasses case compartment closed within the wall.

"I can't have a free trial for a limited period of time with Robot Joy and then decide if it works out for me not?"

"No, we can only turn her back on one more time now that you know your options. Once she is turned back on and you say, 'yes or no' to having her in your life, there is no going back on either option you choose," The Penguin warned her. "Once she is turned back on, you will have to tell her 'yes or no.'"

The large wall-screen flashed and the image of Joy standing in the bathroom looking at mirror disappeared without The Penguin touching any of the buttons on the control panel.

The screen was blacked out for several seconds before it flashed again and revealed a new live video of Casey talking to a group of four other girls in the gym locker room at school. Joy shivered at the reminder that she would have been there right now getting beat up if she didn't have her mom call the school to tell them she was out sick.

Joy, The Penguin, and The Dolphin gathered closer to the screen to watch it together (with The Penguin first turning the volume up on the panel before joining them):

"Joy played sports when we were in elementary school and part of middle school. I think she was on my traveling soccer team up until like the fifth or sixth grade and she still looks pretty strong, you probably wouldn't win," Kaela warned, looking at Casey with concern.

Joy's heart sank whenever she saw Kaela; even now as she saw her on a screen. Kaela had been her closest friend in elementary school. But in middle school Kaela had gradually stopped inviting her to hang out and then after that, gradually stopped talking to her altogether. It was at that moment that Joy remembered that Kaela was the girl who had the gas cooktop at her house.

Joy started to sigh but caught herself.

Kaela had kept her hair relatively short, but she had started continuously bleaching it blonde around the time they were in the seventh grade. Since they had started high school, Kaela also frequently tanned at tanning salons (even during the winter months), wore heavy make-up, and had recently obtained eyelash extensions. All of these cosmetic changes had made her look unrecognizable to Joy at times when she saw her in the hallway without hearing her voice.

Kaela was sitting on a wooden locker room bench with three other girls beside her. They were looking at Casey, who was standing in front of them, with a row of gym lockers right behind her. Joy then noticed that one of the girls was Natalie, the girl who had been making out with her boyfriend in front of her by her locker.

"Not if I have help," Casey asserted. "Like I said before, when she finally does show up here, I plan to jump her with a bunch of you guys after everyone else has gone to gym class. Joy won't have anyone to help her. I'll make sure I still do it on a day when you all are here. The five of us can take her easily."

"Oooh.. you are so smart, Casey," Natalie said. "No one will hear us if all five of us can keep her trapped back here and no one ever stays behind with us once class starts."

"I know." Casey smirked. "Well...except Joy sometimes, because she's so ridiculously slow."

The four other girls laughed.

"People always talk about how pretty you are, but they never talk about how smart you are, Casey," another girl added. Joy recognized it was Lizzie, who teased her but only if one of the other girls she was currently with were around. Lizzie probably came from the wealthiest parents of the group and kept her long hair beautifully highlighted in varying shades of color depending on the season. She was one of those girls who had a mom who looked and dressed just like her in expensive flashy clothes to try to relive her youth. Joy had seen Lizzie's mom pick her up from school in her luxury convertible back before Lizzie learned how to drive. Joy remembered Lizzie's mom liked to keep the top down on her car even on days when it was probably a little too hot or too cold to keep it that way.

Joy's mom had characterized Lizzie's mom as being only marginally popular when they were together in high school, with the other girls often teasing Lizzie's mom because of the larger size of her nose. Joy's mom also had once told Joy that she thought that the reason why Lizzie's mom had Lizzie go to their old public high school instead of a private school the family could easily afford was because, unlike Lizzie's mom, Lizzie had the benefit of wealthy parents and Lizzie's mom wanted to show all the parents that she had made it big by marrying into a rich family (who had also financed a business Lizzie's mom started that made them even wealthier). Joy's mom had indicated that Lizzie's mom was reliving her high school years in this way through Lizzie and noted how no one gave Lizzie a hard time about her nose, even though Lizzie had inherited that exact same nose from her mom.

"Let me tell you a secret—" Casey began.

"Oh wow, really? You are going to tell us a secret? Does anybody else know this?" Natalie interjected.

"Just my mom," Casey sighed impatiently.

"Tell us, tell us," The fifth girl whined inauthentically. Joy recognized this fifth girl in the group was Madison. Madison was a newer girl to school who initially introduced herself to Joy during her first week and talked to her for a while before she realized how Joy was regarded by the rest of the school. After that, she started completely ignoring Joy, like she didn't exist. Madison was probably the most naturally beautiful girl in the group next to Natalie. Madison literally looked like she was probably approached by representatives from talent and modeling agencies whenever she went to a grocery store or a restaurant. Unlike Casey, Kaela or Lizzie, she seemed to have naturally tanned skin, minimal makeup, and seemed to downplay her beauty intentionally by wearing a hoodie and having her dark hair up in a bun. Joy wondered if she was trying to downplay her beauty as a way of showing the other girls that she was so beautiful that she didn't have to try like the others did.

"I act like being beautiful is everything, and it is here. But being as smart as I am will eventually end up being much more important to me. Of course, I love being both, it doesn't get better than this," Casey beamed.

"Wait... what? Why? How is being smart more important?! You're the most gorgeous woman in school," Lizzie countered. "You could easily be a like a model, make tons of money doing that and not have to worry about how smart you are."

"Because being smart is what is going to help me the most in life in the long run. Right now, being pretty is my biggest advantage because it connects me to people at this stage of my life and you need as many connections as you can get during every phase in life to maximize your chances of being successful. My mom taught me that. You need as many people on your side as you can get and that's my biggest advantage I have over Joy. But I'll let her think it's all about just being pretty. She has no chance against me as long as she doesn't have people around her that will help her."

"Why are you so obsessed with hurting Joy?" Kaela wondered. "She is already pathetic, she's a loser. She has no friends and nobody likes her. Even the teachers don't like her because she reads random books at her desk, stares off into space, and doesn't pay attention in class but still somehow gets good grades. She doesn't get straight A's like she used to, but with the way she is now, I am amazed she still occasionally gets the best test scores in some of the classes I've had with her."

"That's exactly it. She's thinks she is better than us," Casey remarked.

"You think so?" Natalie questioned. "She seems clueless to me. I caught her staring at me and Bradley when we were making out in the hallway yesterday. It was so creepy. She looked so sad when she was watching us, like she was at a funeral or the dentist or something."

"I still don't get it." Madison looked as lost as her voice sounded at that moment.

"Well, I am not finished, Madison," Casey scoffed. "I need you all to shut up and listen. I'm sharing my secret with you that could change your life forever if you actually listened to me."

"Oh wow, really?" Lizzie asked (repeating part of Natalie's earlier reaction to Casey's revelation that she was sharing a secret). Casey thought about how much she hated Lizzie's tendency to echo what others said as her reaction to everything she ever had to say. She already knew there was no way she'd continue to be friends with people like Lizzie after high school and they were barely halfway through their junior year.

Casey looked at the four other girls one at a time and ensured she made brief eye contact with each of them before proceeding: "You see, people like me are rare. You don't come across a person too often who is as beautiful and as intelligent as I am. Even among the people who are both beautiful and intelligent, not all of them are also smart enough to let their beauty get them everything they want without having to demonstrate how smart they are. This is an important skill to have if you are a brilliant person like me. This is because if you show how smart you are all the time, you can turn some people off no matter how attractive you are, especially guys and other beautiful women you may want to keep in your network. And this is all because I have an important underlying quality that you all wouldn't completely understand: I am always thinking two or three steps ahead. I play the game to win. Even though you are also popular and possibly as pretty as I am, I don't have to worry about you because none of you are nearly as smart as I am.

"That, and each of you date the deadbeat jock type of guy who will be lucky to play second-string in college and will end up selling t-shirts and bottled water in little tents outside of stadiums before big events. Not only that, but he'll also probably end up blowing all your combined income on starting a small business or two that will end up failing because he is too broken and too lazy to get them off the ground. You'll get tired of his smoking and drinking. You'll also get tired of depending on one undependable guy to tell you how beautiful you still are, so you'll end up divorced. You'll end up losing out on investing in a guy I could've told you wasn't worth investing in.

"Once you're divorced, you'll end up stuck with two or three kids that you could barely handle the responsibility of to begin with (even when you were still married to him) and end up being a slut who sleeps with either really older rich guys or much younger guys who think you are hot enough to have one night-stands with before they ditch you. But you'll need them because they'll make you still feel like you are beautiful– even as you are starting to lose your looks and get older and older. Meanwhile, you yourself will be smoking your lungs out and drinking yourself to death just like your ex-husband and your kids will eventually start doing the same thing once they're old enough. But if you are lucky, and when I say that– I mean relatively lucky, because you'll still be miserable– but if you're lucky, you'll have a daughter that will at least be as half as pretty as you were that you can take pride in. Maybe if you have a daughter like that, you can relive the best years of your life vicariously through her at least temporarily, before she ends up being a loser like you will be."

The four other girls glared at Casey as she finished and then looked at one another as if to try to read the true feelings that each was trying hide.

"Wow," Kaela finally reacted, "you've really thought this through..."

"I already knew the thing you mentioned about hiding your intelligence. I play dumb all the time, especially for my parents and boyfriend," Natalie tried to reply without sounding defensive (but still did).

"Casey," Lizzie whimpered in a concerned tone that didn't sound genuine to Casey, "I'm confused, I thought we would be friends forever."

Casey debated telling her the truth, but upon further consideration, reminded herself that Lizzie always seemed to be jealous and resentful toward her anyway, so she wouldn't be changing anything by revealing her actual plans.

"We will be," Casey reassured her before deciding to slip in the truth, "until I move out of state and go to college."

"Wait, what?" Natalie laughed uncomfortably as though she was hoping it was a joke and was still waiting for a punchline from

Casey. "You won't be friends with us after high school, and you are asking us to help you beat up a girl who comes to school every day looking like she already beats herself up?!"

"Wait, do you really think Joy thinks she is better than us?" Kaela questioned. "I'm getting the feeling here that you think you are better than us."

Casey knew she had to be more careful with her words this time. She had to tried to get away with too much and she had to acknowledge to herself that she underestimated the intelligence of her entourage again. So, she contemplated briefly how she would respond.

She decided to default to a fake apology.

She gave her friends that look she gave her parents whenever she wanted something from them, and they were initially hesitant to give her what she wanted.

"I'm so sorry, you guys, I didn't really mean that I won't be friends with you anymore after high school. I know Madison is new here but how long have I been really close friends with the rest of you now? Since like fifth grade?! And honestly, Madison, I feel like we have been super close like I've known you that long too. You all know how much I can't stand Joy and sometimes even when we are just talking about her, I can't think straight. I also get frustrated with you guys when you don't understand how much of a threat a girl like that is to us. Trust me, she is a serious threat to us. You know why she was staring at you, Natalie? She wants your man. That's right I said it. She wants Brad and maybe you think she'd never be able to get with him, but I know better. I know most guys are animals and will get with literally anyone that remotely shows any interest in them—"

"That's not true," Natalie interrupted, "she's loved Gray since when? Like she's loved that guy since they were like five years old and everybody knows it. He knows it. She loves him even though he's never looked at her for more than five seconds."

Casey smirked. She was prepared for this kind of a retort.

"And how do you know that, Natalie? How Gray acts around school and around us is no reflection of how he really is behind closed doors. You of all people should know that about guys. You went through it with Trevor last year. And you remember that girl he went behind your back with? What was her name?! Vanessa? Something like that. But let me tell you something, Natalie, I said it once and I'll say it again: that girl Vanessa has nothing on Joy. Like you all were saying earlier about Joy, she is super-intelligent and at least played sports when we were younger. Vanessa didn't have any of those qualities. The one thing she had going for her was her ability to distract Trevor from you."

"You promised you wouldn't bring Trevor up again!" Natalie cried.

"Oh, it's okay, babe," Casey said, "you have Brad now, so you have nothing to worry about. I personally don't think he's any-thing to write home about either but he's still a nice upgrade over Trevor. You're on the right track. You are moving forward. But you have to be careful, especially with people like Joy. I'm trying to protect all of you and your boyfriends."

Casey looked at each of them briefly again with a smug expression that oozed the kind of confidence that the other girls thought they needed more of.

"I'm trying to help each of you and be the best friend to you I can be. I am telling you that we have to do something about Joy. She has the ability to disrupt each of our lives like ten Vanessas' rolled into one. Trust me, Joy will know she did wrong by staring at Natalie and Brad because she will see my note in her locker. It will still be there if she hasn't seen it already. I have a feeling she saw it and then ditched class to avoid us. Either way, she will have to show up here eventually."

"But wait, shouldn't we be beating up Vanessa then? Joy was just staring at them. Vanessa is the one Trevor hooked up with when he was cheating on Natalie, right?" Madison asked.

Casey violently pounded the front of a locker beside her with the bottom of a rolled-up fist, causing the locker and a few lockers in the same row to rattle and vibrate.

"You guys aren't getting it!" Casey yelled in an echo through the desolate locker room. Up until this point, her voice had been oddly lowered to an often furious but hushed tone. She looked at Madison as if she wanted to scream at her but then appeared to have a counter-acting thought that instead led her to a prolonged sigh.

"Okay Madison, I remember now that you weren't present when we took Vanessa down last year. You didn't move here until over the summer, right? But I still think you've been around us long enough that you would've known the story."

"I had no idea," Madison pleaded, "you guys have beaten another girl up before?!"

"Oh yeah we did," Lizzie giggled. "We not only made Vanessa regret what she did with Trevor behind Natalie's back, we made her regret even being born. We beat her up in an empty classroom after we jumped her in the hallway sometime around Valentine's Day. She went down easy, and she had some bumps and bruises– nothing serious physically. But, Madison, it destroyed her emotionally. She disappeared from school after that. I heard they ended up sending her to some type of alternative-school about a month later. But we don't know for sure, we haven't seen her since."

"You all really had my back last year," Natalie recalled.

"That's exactly what we need to do Joy," Casey proclaimed. "She doesn't belong here either and if she stays, I promise you she will do the kinds of things Vanessa did, or worse."

"Now don't get angry at me when I say this, Casey, because you know you're my best friend, I love you, and I am not saying you're necessarily wrong..." Kaela started out her disclaimer as diplomatically as she could. She had been contemplating this response for a while. "...but it's really hard for me to think Joy would do the same thing to any of us that Vanessa did to Natalie. I mean, Joy was my friend back when we were in elementary school, and she always had a good heart. Even though I know she was watching Natalie with Bradley, I think she was probably doing it more out of curiosity since she has never experienced it herself. Knowing Joy, she was probably in her own little world wondering what that experience was like and didn't realize she was staring at Natalie."

"I wasn't friends with her as long as Kaela was, but Joy was my friend too when we were little kids," Lizzie reluctantly acknowledged, "and if anything, I remember thinking she was way too nice."

Joy noticeably grimaced when Lizzie said that, as she didn't like to admit to herself that she was once friends with Lizzie (especially after seeing the person she had become in high school), but it was true.

Casey gave Kaela the dirtiest look that Kaela had ever seen out of her. It was filled with an unprecedented level of anger and disdain that shook Kaela's core. It made her feel like she was shrinking down into her seat on the locker room bench. She wanted to be anywhere but within Casey's line of sight. The seconds of enduring the extreme tension felt like years. She got a little relief when Casey eventually redirected some of that piercing glare in Lizzie's direction as well.

Both Madison and Natalie felt pressure to say something to try to help them. They looked at each other.

"Look, Casey...we know you don't like Joy, and we are totally on your side here," Natalie whispered. "We are just making sure that you really want to do this, I mean—"

"Oh, I want to do this," Casey snapped, "remember how badly you wanted to do it with Vanessa? It's like that!"

"Oh...it's like...that?" Natalie stuttered.

"It's like that," Casey groaned.

Casey continued to stare at Natalie. Natalie couldn't tell if it was a conscious stare or if Casey was lost in thought.

"So, she called out sick to avoid this happening today?" Lizzie asked to draw Casey's attention away from Natalie. "How do we know that she did that, I mean, maybe she's somewhere around here?"

"She's in my history class and in my study hall before this," Madison said. "Today, she wasn't in either one."

"Other than taking sick days, Joy has never skipped class in her life," Kaela added. "She takes sick days a lot lately, but she still would never skip class if she was here."

"What would boring people like Joy do if they skipped class anyway? They wouldn't know what to do themselves," Natalie joked and then laughed at her own joke. The others, including Casey, laughed along with her and that alleviated some of the tension.

"Trust me, we will get a re-do," Casey asserted, "and if you help me take down Joy, I promise you that I will be your best friend through high school, college, and beyond. But you need to be 'all in' with me on this, like we were for Natalie last year. I want you to help me make Joy regret that she even gets out of bed in the morning."

The rest of the girls looked at one another and there was a collective understanding that they would each have to move forward with this plan to remain a part of Casey's inner circle.

"We're in," Kaela finally confirmed.

The screen went back to black.

"I guess maybe we could still watch Robot Joy travel the world, if it chose to," Joy suggested after a long pause. "Maybe we could program in a greater desire to travel."

The Penguin looked anguished over how to respond to this. Earlier she had been going through the motions of feigning enthusiasm while describing the options that Joy had with her robot and The Book of What Everyone Else Ever Said or Thought About Her while feeling like a bored and slightly overworked tour guide in need of a new location to work in. She did not expect Joy to think about it so much.

"You are really considering this?" The Penguin asked timidly.

"She's really considering it," The Dolphin verified.

"I could just be here," Joy said aloud to herself. "I wouldn't have to deal with school, I wouldn't be beat up, laughed at, and teased anymore. I wouldn't have to deal with my mom being disappointed me, and I'd know for sure that people really didn't like me anyway. I'd be totally justified being here with you guys. If I ever miss anyone, I can tune in to what Robot Joy is up to and if I don't want to see a difficult situation the robot has to deal with, well, then I can shut it off."

The Penguin and The Dolphin looked at each other as though they preferred the other to respond first. But before either could react any further, an alarm sounded throughout the space station. The alarm was relatively pleasant and had a synthesized futuristic sound to it. The volume of the alarm also wasn't that loud, but Joy covered her ears anyway out of habit to be safe. There were blue emergency lights spaced out along the top edges of the walls below the ceiling that correspondingly flashed along with the sounds of the alarm.

"What's going on?" Joy asked as she uncovered her ears to make sure she heard the response to her question.

"Joy, your mom just arrived home from work to check on you," Gabriel reported over the alarm from somewhere overhead.

Joy sighed and covered her ears again as though she wanted to avoid anything she might start hearing from her mom.

"Joy!" Her mom yelled from behind the bathroom door while simultaneously knocking on it. "Joy?!"

2.8

J oy reluctantly uncovered her ears again.

She was back in her bathroom alone and could no longer hear the alarm. She looked away from the mirror and down at the sink.

"Joy are you in there?! Your father told me you've been there for an awfully long time!" Her mom hollered. Her mom then knocked a few more times.

"I am in here, Mom!" Joy called back to her. "I'm about to get into the shower."

"You haven't showered yet? What's the matter with you?" Her mom was starting to sound angry, and Joy felt an extra knot being added to the others that were already in her stomach. "What are you doing there?!"

Joy didn't know how to answer in a way that would satisfy her mom. She still hadn't learned and wasn't sure if she would ever learn what to say to her mom to make her any less angry or disappointed in her whenever she sensed anger and/or disappointment in her mom's voice.

"Joy? I need you to either come out right now or answer me!"

Feeling the pressure to say something right away to avoid having to face her mom, Joy decided to go with the first intuitive response that had come to mind: "I really wasn't feeling well this morning, but I feel a little better now so I can go in and take my shower."

There was a long pause.

Joy knew her mom would think it was a physical illness that she was referencing. Joy also knew her mom would consider it a lie if she knew that Joy was primarily referencing her mental health (which she was) but Joy didn't consider it a lie. This was another one of those days where she felt so bad mentally that it did make her feel ill physically. In addition to the knots she felt in her stomach, she had a dull headache.

"Okay, I came here on an early lunch break to check on you and have a chat with you, if possible. We'll probably miss each other; I can't stay here too long."

"It's okay, Mom," Joy replied, "I'm okay, I'm feeling better now. I think I'll feel even better once I take a shower. I'll be able to go to school tomorrow."

Joy really wanted to avoid talking to her mom beyond the minimum requirement, so she had tried to say everything she imagined her mom wanted to hear. She rationalized taking this approach as she felt she had already endured everything her mom had planned to say to her on the first version of this Wednesday, December 8th.

"Alright," her mom said. There was a tone in her voice that suggested she may have been rolling her eyes behind the door.

After listening to her mom's footsteps travel back through the hallway and then down the staircase, Joy locked the door. She was both surprised and relieved that her mom hadn't barged in on her. She then finally proceeded to take her shower, and it was a long one. Despite meeting The Toilet Monster earlier that day for the first time, she still felt uneasy being in there alone. She wasn't sure why she felt this way and wondered if part of it was from encountering Casey's reflection in the mirror. About midway through the shower, she cautiously poked her head out around the curtain to see The Bear loyally sitting on the closed toilet seat watching the door. He turned to her and quietly waved. She looked relieved to see him there before disappearing back behind the curtain to re-sume her shower.

2.9

J oy could hear her mom downstairs in the living room talking on the phone from where she stood in the upstairs hallway after she had finished her shower. The sound of her mom talking on the phone was loud enough that she could tell the conversation was animated, but distant enough that she couldn't decipher the words. She went into her room and changed into the clothes that she had worn on the first version of this Wednesday. She initially had wanted to keep her pajamas on but opted to change in case she encountered her mom. Her mom would absolutely say something to her if she was still in her pajamas, even on a day when she called out sick. She was disappointed but wasn't surprised her mom was still home despite her mom's earlier assertion that she couldn't stay long before returning to work. She always wanted the guarantee that it would be a good interaction with her mom even though she also knew there was never any guarantee what kind of mood her mom would be in. It wasn't like her dad, who always seemed to light up when he saw her as though he was perpetually in a dim mood without her in the room.

When she emerged back into the hallway from her room, Joy could still hear her mom talking on the phone and the conversation still sounded intense. She climbed halfway down the staircase to try to understand what her mom was saying. Her mom was using her more positive, energized tone that she only seemed to reserve for interactions with her friends. She sounded like she was in her favorite spot at the end of the couch in the living room (farthest away from where her dad's chair was).

"Ha! Amber, we've been talking about this subject since we were in high school, nothing has changed since then. No matter how old you are once you are an adult, there are women and then there are— well, what did we used to say?! Oh, yeah, 'eternal girls.' There are women and then there are 'eternal girls.' High school is still the place where a potential woman finds out which path she is going to take, and I did my best with Joy. You know that as well as I. Now that she is on her third year of high school, I must accept that all my fears have come true...she'll never be a woman...And I have to find peace with the fact she will be nowhere near the kind of woman, you know, that we are," she overheard her mom telling Amber on the phone. Amber was one of her mom's best friends from high school that her mom kept in touch with but rarely spoke to. Joy had never overheard her mom talking to Amber on the phone before. She had only heard about Amber whenever her mom would talk about her high school days.

There was a pause for several seconds as her mom was apparently listening to Amber's reply. Joy suddenly felt like she couldn't breathe and also felt her knees start to buckle. She crouched and placed both hands beside her on one of the steps. She then allowed herself to lean into a sitting position on another step below the one she had placed her hands on. Amber was obviously trying to give her mom some reassurance as the silence was eventually broken by the occasional "uh huh," "oh" and "ahhh'" by her mom. This went on for several minutes, which felt like an eternity to Joy.

"Well, you have a different situation with Natalie. I mean I wish Joy had spent more time with her when they were younger. But for one thing, Natalie is the perfect prototype for a thin body. That right there puts her head and shoulders above Joy. I don't think Joy will ever get her weight right again. I also can't figure out what she is doing or not doing with her hair, but whatever is going on, she is obviously doing it wrong. I wish she would let me help with her it. She spends all day on the weekends in her room and hardly speaks to either her father or me. She almost never wears makeup and won't let me teach her how to apply it properly. She doesn't seem to care that she doesn't have any friends anymore. She obviously is becoming more and more like the way her father became after he gave up on himself too. But going back to Natalie...another thing about her is that she sounds like she has a lot more self-awareness than Joy so—"

There was another pause, as her mom had been interrupted mid-sentence by Amber. Joy had not known that Amber was Natalie's mom. She had known that Natalie was the daughter of one of her mom's old friends but didn't realize it was Amber. She felt an empty feeling in her chest as if her heart had relied on electricity to keep it running but someone had unplugged it from an electrical outlet in the wall.

"I understand you can only have a certain level of expectations for girls their age," her mom said, sounding agitated that Natalie's mom was giving her more opinions and advice when she only wanted someone to listen to her and empathize with her, "but I am talking about her wild, ridiculous hair, the stuffed animals, the weird clothes, the stickers, and the anime pictures on her wall. All the stuff I have been telling you about that I can't convince her to get rid of. But as long as her father goes along with it, I am limited in what I can do. It kills me because her father of all people knows what it means to build and maintain an image in school. I don't know how a winner like he was can tolerate the idea of having such a loser as a daughter..."

Joy abruptly became more aware of the central heating turned on in the house as she sensed a thin layer of sweat over her skin. Her breathing slowed down and felt much heavier. She kept blinking to prevent any excess liquid from forming around her eyes. Her throat was too dry for her to swallow, and it felt as though her tongue has disappeared somewhere down her throat. Her stomach started to purr, and she didn't move. But then the purring gave way to an unforgiving growl that caused both hands to clench and then squeeze her belly in an effort to muffle these sounds with limited success. She shifted uncomfortably around the stair and nearly slipped down a step.

An intolerable pressure erupted within her head as the word "loser" echoed though her mind: *Loser... Loser... Loser...*

She covered both of her ears as though she was still hearing that word being used about her externally. She wobbled as she stood up on the stairs (nearly slipping again as she did so) and then gingerly slogged her way back up the staircase. She kept one ear covered as the other hand alternated between covering her ear and grasping the staircase railing. *Loser... Loser... Loser...*

She briefly stopped at the top of the staircase and realized she was covering her ears not just to try to silence the internal echo of "loser", but also because she couldn't bear to hear any more of the conversation her mom was having with Natalie's mom.

She covered her mouth with one of her hands as she started to sigh. *Loser... Loser... Loser...*

She lifted the hand covering her mouth back up to covering her ear and trudged toward her bedroom.

As she entered the doorway to her room, she felt the urge to slam the door behind her but having managed to somehow make it this far without her mom hearing her, reminded herself that she didn't want to be heard.

She wanted to be alone.

She closed the door gently behind her and locked it. She collapsed on top of her bed, landing on her stomach with her face hitting the pillow.

She lifted the sides of her pillow with each hand to wrap them over her ears.

When she turned over to breathe, she realized the echoes of "loser" had subsided and she could no longer hear her mom on the phone.

She sighed as though she was finally releasing the sigh that she had muffled earlier. She then closed her eyes, and pulled her knees close to her as she rolled into a fetal position.

2.10

When Joy opened her eyes again, she found herself curled up on the dark oak hardwood floor of an immense majestic room that looked like it was in a library or a museum. As she stood up, the first thing she noticed were the large floor-to-ceiling windows in place of a wall at the far end of the room. Through these distant windows, she could see dozens of beautifully night-lit skyscrapers of a city that didn't look familiar to her. She observed how the lights of the skyscrapers illuminated what appeared to be a steady snowfall.

The other walls of this massive room were almost completely made up of bookshelves with thousands of books piled hundreds of feet high up to the ceiling. The room wasn't so large in floor space as it was in height. The bookcases required a series of built-in platforms and dozens of long wooden ladders with wheels to be able to access all the books. Strategically zigzagged and scattered throughout the center of the room were large glass display cases with shelves that featured trophies, degrees, plaques, medals and ribbons. On one side of the room, Joy saw a large electric fireplace with two large leather chairs facing it. Each chair featured a neatly folded fuzzy white blanket that looked very warm and comfortable to her. The electric fireplace included crackling and popping sounds like a real fireplace. It also had a warm glow that filled the immediate area as an added source of illumination since the room otherwise primarily depended on dimly lit chandeliers. The chandeliers were hanging on chains from a ceiling that appeared to be miles above them. White string lights that swirled around the upper reaches of the glass display cases, that stretched along the edges of the bookshelves (as well as the edges of their ladders and platforms), and that were down along the floorboards had a glow that was accentuated by the dimmer surroundings. The ambiance of the room gave Joy the mixed feeling that was she was either cozy while alone in the safe comfort of her room or alone in the unfamiliar but inviting front room area of an otherwise crowded social event taking place in the next room that she would want to avoid.

"What is this?" Joy asked aloud to herself.

There was apparently no one around to answer.

She started walking among the glass display cases after noticing there was a single small glass display case right in the center of the room. Unlike the other larger display cases, this small display case had a circumference of space cleared out around it as if to stress its importance given its modest size. She gradually noticed the shadow of a small figure on top of the glass case. As she drew closer, a muted warm light turned on within the case and remained glowing as though it was activated by a motion sensor.

She stopped when she recognized The Cardinal was the figure standing atop the display case. The display case was stained-glass in a dark purple color so she couldn't see what was inside even when she was close to it.

"This is the library warehouse of all of your accomplishments, your positive life-changing events, and your favorite heartfelt moments so that you can re-experience them," The Cardinal revealed. "If you touch or read any of the items in here it will reactivate the full experience for you as if you are back in time reliving it."

"I mentioned something to Dolphin about this..." Joy started to say before drifting into a state of hypnotic bliss. She felt as though she had just won every award and accomplishment that was in the room in that single moment.

"Yes, it really exists," The Cardinal said as a way of gaining back her attention.

"Where are we?" Joy asked after she blinked a few times and re-focused on The Cardinal.

"Seoul, South Korea," The Cardinal answered, turning briefly to look outside the wall windows at the skyline.

"Wow..." Joy replied, looking around all over again as if she hadn't already looked around. "I know I don't remember much, but I would think I would remember having something like this."

"This is your first time here," The Cardinal indicated, "It's pretty cool, isn't it?"

"But I haven't really accomplished anything so far."

"Sure you have," The Cardinal retorted, "you have done many good deeds for people when you didn't have to, you have been an honor roll student pretty much all of your life, and you have made a positive impact on people just by surviving all of the pain you've been through without even knowing it."

"So, everything in here documents all of those little, tiny details?!"

"You can see they add up," The Cardinal observed, "but that's not all. These various books and awards also document your potential future as well as your past. This includes your dreams, the best ideas you've ever come up with but haven't applied to your life yet, and all the options and possibilities for your future. This includes the different colleges you might attend, the different careers you might pursue, the different homes you might purchase, the different relationships you may or may not have, and all the different people you've met and will meet throughout your lifetime with details on how you would and would not benefit from associating with them. If you touch or read any of those items than they take you into the future to experience them as like a free trial."

Joy laughed the kind of prolonged laugh that subsides into a giggle.

"Alright, Cardinal, what's the catch to being able to stay here and look at some of these things?" She giggled.

"There is no catch like that this time, you're free to look at everything in here," The Cardinal responded before joining her in laughter. "The book of what everyone else ever said or thought about you isn't here. That's stored at the Space Station now. Everything that is here is readily available to you at any time. If there ever was one, I suppose the only catch to being here is you might not want to leave because you can easily get lost in here. There is really a lot to look into and think about here."

"So, what is in the display case that you're on then?" Joy asked. She had initially assumed that it contained a copy of The Book of What Everyone Else Ever Said or Thought About Her.

"It's the mystery case and so I'm honestly not sure myself. I was hoping you'd ask," The Cardinal admitted. "You're welcome to take a look and see."

The Cardinal flew off of the display case and onto Joy's shoulder. He watched intently as Joy carefully removed the purple glass display case to reveal a small hand mirror that was face-down and covered in a diverse blend of different types of rare seashells.

Joy flipped it over and looked at her reflection in the mirror.

She saw what felt like the most beautiful version of herself possible. Her reflection was in flawless makeup, with voluminous, highlighted hair, glitter on both her hair and skin, and long, sparkling earrings on her ears. She was wearing a beautiful exotic dress that looked like it was tailor-made specifically for her body. She was mesmerized, she couldn't believe how good she looked in this reflection. This version of herself was more beautiful than the morning twilight glimpses of herself in the bedroom mirror, more beautiful than the reflection she saw of herself in the cave, and more beautiful than Robot Joy.

She felt like a celebrity. She felt like a celebrity with billions of dollars at her disposal to invest in improving her lifestyle, her health, and her appearance. She felt like a celebrity with such a high reputation that she only met with the most successful people she could learn from and knew all the right people she needed to know to maintain her prestigious position in society. She felt like a celebrity capable of attracting royalty from all over the world while living in a fairy tale dream that had come true in real life. She felt like a celebrity who lived in one of those modern-day mansions with architecture that incorporated elements of a medieval castle.

But then she noticed how the reflection also appeared subtly cartoon-like. It was upon that last observation of her reflection that she remembered that she looked exactly like she did in her bathroom mirror just before her reflection transformed into Casey. Up until that point, she had lost the one positive memory associated with the event due to the bizarre and frightening outcome of it.

Her entire body was suddenly shaken as though she had seen a ghost. She dropped the mirror at the thought that her reflection might transform into Casey again.

When she instinctually reached down to catch it before it hit the floor, she observed that the floor had transformed into a blank white surface.

She watched in awe as the seashell hand mirror disappeared into this void without a sound. When she looked up, she realized the entire warehouse of accomplishments had likewise transformed into this white void. She no longer felt The Cardinal on her shoulder, and she checked both shoulders to find that he also had vanished.

She was back in her regular clothes and back to feeling ugly.

"Where am I?!" Her voice echoed.

2.11

There was no response.

She had even waited a little longer hoping for another delayed response from The Cardinal.

She started walking, but it was so white that she didn't know where she was going and after a few minutes, she wasn't sure if she was moving forward toward a potential destination.

She stopped.

She decided she might as well keep going.

She continued.

Upon resuming her walk, she started to hear crunching under her shoes that sounded like snow. She suddenly felt cold upon hearing the crunching sounds. She could see and feel particles of icy moisture start to appear in scattered areas all over the bare places on her skin, including her hands and face. They felt like snow flurries, but she could only observe them once they reached her skin and clothes due to the bright white environment around her. She folded her arms as her teeth started chattering and she found herself picking up her pace.

She soon noticed a distant black dot and oddly felt a sense of relief at the sight of it despite not knowing what it was. She made a point of walking toward it and as she did so, she seemed to rapidly approach it in a way that didn't measure up to the initial distance that she seemed to be away from it. Each step she took was like the equivalent of several miles traveled on a high-speed bullet train.

However, the pace slowed to a regular walking rate once the black dot turned into the figure of a person, then that of a teenage girl dressed in a heavy winter jacket, winter cap, and gloves, and then that of Autumn once Joy was close enough to recognize her face. Joy stopped once she found herself within her usual safe conversational distance from Autumn.

Autumn quietly looked Joy up and down (then up and down again) with a smirk on her face.

"What took you so long?" Autumn asked.

"Uh, mmm, ummm," Joy initially struggled to talk as shivered and looked around the white void that surrounded them as though she was trying to see something more beyond it.

Autumn laughed.

"Where are...we?" Joy stuttered, ignoring the initial question.

"We are here in nothing," Autumn casually replied, "it's a really cold place."

"Really, really cold," Joy agreed.

"This is exactly the place that your whole life is turning into, and unsurprisingly, I see that you are completely unprepared for it," Autumn sneered.

"Look, Autumn, you can have the castle." Joy was hoping that would end the encounter before Autumn launched into another full one-sided conversation about how everything she thought that Joy was doing with her life was wrong. More than anything, she wanted any discussion to end as soon as possible so she could return to a warmer place. "I obviously wasn't really using it anymore anyway."

Autumn was astounded by her reply. "You mean, I can have everything?!" she gushed.

Joy looked down at her white void below her for several seconds as she pondered Autumn's question and then looked back up at Autumn with an expression of confusion: "Are you also talking about the space station?"

Autumn's mouth involuntarily dropped open: "You also have a space station?!"

Now Joy was even more confused: "You seem to know about everything else about me, but you didn't know about the space station? How do you know about the castle?"

"I have a castle of my own," Autumn responded with air of defensiveness as though insulted that Joy was still unaware of that at this point, "I have several castles. But I don't have a space station yet, I never thought of having one. But I'll gladly take yours."

"I'm good with that—" Joy started to hear herself say but then paused when she thought about how she'd still want to keep Robot Joy and The Book of What Everyone Else Ever Said or Thought About Her (just in case). "...as long as I get to visit it one last time before you take over so I can take a few things with me I'd like to keep."

Autumn smirked.

"If we are in agreement," Joy continued, "then this was much easier than I thought it would be." She was somehow hoping Autumn's smirk may have been a good sign despite the familiar bad feeling it probably wasn't.

"You don't understand Joy, I want everything," Autumn demanded, "and that includes all of your animals"

"What...animals?!"

Autumn scowled at her impatiently. "Don't be ridiculous, Joy," she scoffed, "I know about the animals, your lion was with you when you visited me earlier on my ship and your enormous Elephant is sitting right there beside you right now. I can see them too."

Joy looked to her right to find The Elephant was in a seated position right beside her, seemingly unaffected by the cold. The Elephant turned to her with a meek expression.

"What are you doing here?" Joy whispered to her even though it was clear that Autumn could still hear her anyway.

"We try to make sure one of us is with you when you go to these weird places," The Elephant whispered back.

"This isn't a good time."

"Exactly, that's why I am here," The Elephant whispered back, "I'm here to help protect you when it isn't a good time. I've got your back."

"Noooo, you don't get it!" Joy exclaimed with an unintended exponential increase in volume. "She literally is talking about—"

"You don't want to let them go, do you?" Autumn interrupted her.

Joy and The Elephant looked away from one another and back to Autumn as though they each wanted to hide the fact the other was still there in Autumn's view.

"I suppose there is an Elephant in the room," Joy finally acknowledged, laughing awkwardly with no immediate reaction from Autumn and a sheepish grin from The Elephant.

"Then you still have fourteen hours remaining to think about it a little more," Autumn indicated flatly.

"Fourteen?!" Joy protested. "That doesn't seem right."

"Are you sure you didn't fall asleep again?" The Elephant asked.

But as Joy was about to answer "yes" to The Elephant, the white void suddenly turned black, and she could see neither The Elephant nor Autumn.

She blinked.

She found herself laying in the darkness of her room. As she looked around, she was barely able to make out the details of her bookshelf, her desk, her nightstand and bedroom mirror. She felt the grogginess of a long "deep thought dozing" kind of nap.

She sighed and rubbed her eyes as she shifted her head against the heat of her pillow.

She was poisoned by the specific type of lazy guilt that one experiences when they had either slept too long and/or had fallen asleep when they didn't intend to.

2.12

It was so dark in her room that at first this scared her into thinking it was another blacked-out Wednesday morning, but she was relieved when she was able to turn on the lights.

She checked the time on her phone: It was 6:37pm.

She wanted to go back to sleep, but she also knew that wouldn't be possible: *Here comes another sleepless night and it's all my fault again.* She couldn't hear anything upstairs but could hear the vague muffled sound of the television on downstairs. She thought of her dad being down there by himself from the first version of this Wednesday night.

When she opened her bedroom door, the upstairs was dark and once she arrived downstairs, the living room was dim.

The glow of the football game on the TV was the primary light that filled the living room. Her dad was staring blankly at it as though he wasn't following the game at all. He didn't seem to notice her entering the room and looked like he was so lost in thought that he may have lost awareness that he was even in the room. Unlike the first version of this Wednesday night, he had the lamp on the end table beside his favorite chair set on the dimmest possible setting. The lamp was so dim, that it only seemed to illuminate the end table. Her dad mostly kept the lamp off when he was alone watching TV, but he turned on the lamp at the dimmest possible setting to appease her mom whenever he anticipated she may be coming home soon. Joy would often hear her mom yelling at him from up in her room whenever her mom caught him watching TV in the dark. This time there were three crumpled beer cans scattered around the end table, and he was holding a fourth one on his lap.

"Dad?" Joy stood at the edge of the living room.

Joy's dad didn't move.

"Daddy?!" Joy raised her volume this time.

Her dad blinked and quickly turned to her, nearly spilling his beer in his lap in the process. He looked at her, then glanced at the beer cans, and then looked down at his lap and appeared embarrassed.

"Are you okay?" Joy asked as she approached him. She stopped a few feet away from him and remained standing.

"Your mom went over to Aunt Katrina's house," he said, without answering her question.

"I know." Joy studied him intently. "What were you thinking about?"

Her dad looked up at her like he wanted to say something but hesitated. Then, just as she was about to accept that he wasn't going to tell her, he shared: "A girl I knew when I was in high school."

The tone of his voice had slightly changed when he admitted that. He still sounded somber but now there was a trace of relief, as though a thorn had been removed from the left side of his chest, but the pain was still lingering.

"A girl other than mom?" Joy already knew the answer but still felt obligated to ask.

"I was also thinking about change..." Her dad replied without answering her question again. He had sounded like he intended to say a lot more than that but instead trailed off into a silence that lasted several seconds. He then gestured to Joy to have a seat on the couch. As she sat down at the spot on the couch nearest to her dad, he turned the television volume all the way down and increased the brightness setting on the lamp beside him.

"Are you okay, sweetheart?" he asked, "Are you feeling better?"

"What do you mean thinking about change?" Joy asked, without answering his question.

Her dad laughed: "Okay, okay, you win."

"I always win, Daddy." Joy joined him in laughter.

"You always win," he acknowledged, before taking a swig of his beer.

"I never knew it before like I do now…" He placed his beer on the end table beside the crumpled cans. "…but change is really everything. I realize it's the secret to life. Change is the fulcrum of determining whether or not you are happy. If you are able to change and adjust, you are happy. But if you can't and life has something better in store for you, you'll stay miserable. I am convinced everyone knows this at least to some extent but so many of us still choose not to change. They are the saddest people of them all. They can only find occasional comfort in their immediate surroundings that they either don't want to or can't leave behind because it has become all they know. There is a powerlessness they feel when thinking of any effort to leave it all behind. The longer they stay, those moments of occasional comfort and happiness grow fewer and farther between. People like that feel trapped for the rest of their lives and wait for something that can only be found in their past."

"Daddy, you never talk like this…" Joy whispered through the tense silence.

"I am one of those people Joy," her dad confessed.

"Dad, no…"

"Sometimes you meet people in your life, and you know they'll make your life better, but the tragedy lies in the fact that you don't appreciate it because you are not ready for them, so you end up living separate lives…" her dad trailed off again, lost in thought. Eventually, a half-smile appeared on his face that he seemed to be unaware of. Joy waited at first for him to continue, but after about thirty seconds of waiting, she had enough.

"Okay, now what are you thinking about dad?" Joy tapped his forearm. Her dad blinked and turned to her.

"I just thought of something I hadn't thought about in a long time," he answered.

"What is that?"

Joy's dad didn't respond. He turned his attention back to the muted football game. He stared intently at the TV screen, but it was clear from his detached, wistful expression that he wouldn't have known what the score of the game was.

"Daddy!"

Her dad winced, blinked his eyes, and rubbed his face before he picked up his current beer can and had another sip.

"What is the memory?"

Her dad cleared his throat as a very brief delaying action before responding: "Something my dad told me before he died. I try not to think about it, but it still comes to mind every now and then. When I think of him when I'm with you, I think of how you two would get along great. I wish you had the chance to meet him. He was such a deep thinker like you are. I never said a word to him about how sometimes I would regret certain things like not taking better care of myself when I was playing football in college, the way I gave up on college because I couldn't play football anymore, and..."

"Dad..." Joy laughed. "Give me details. You still haven't really told me the memory."

But her dad was stone-faced. His eyes were on the football game, but they were not watching it. He looked like he was lost in whatever destination his thoughts had transported him to, like he might as well have been staring out at the ocean during a sunset while standing on a beach or looking out at a sunrise over the hori-zon from a cabin high on a mountain.

"My dad wanted me to play baseball or basketball instead of football and of course, that's why I chose football," her dad recalled after the prolonged pause. "He was never really into sports himself. I'm not sure if he ever played them. So, it took me off guard when he said to me: 'Son, the ball was always in your court, you just lost sight of the ball.'"

Joy pondered this and when she thought she was done, she pondered it some more. She unsuccessfully hoped he would continue without her having to prompt him further.

"You mean because you got injured playing football in college and didn't finish your degree?" Joy eventually asked.

"I didn't know he knew. It was like he knew even though I never said anything to him about it. I never said anything to my mom, or to my wife, or to my friends that it still bothered me that I didn't make it in football, that I didn't finish my degree, and that..."

"What is it, Dad?! That's the second time you've stopped on the third thing you were going to say."

Her dad gulped air.

"The girl?" She asked.

"The girl," he confirmed as he turned to her again.

"Well?"

"I don't... don't want you to think that I regret having you," he stuttered. "You...you know how much, how much I love you and..." As he spoke, he maintained eye contact with her this time as if to tell her he didn't mean to have so much difficulty with his words. She couldn't stand to let him continue this way and wanted to help him.

"I know all of that, daddy."

He took a deep breath.

"It was like your grandpa was also saying the ball was in my court to be with the girl that I loved, to focus more on taking care of my body to prepare for college football, and to take being the first person in my family to ever go to college more seriously. He was saying I had my fate in my hands to achieve all of my dreams and I completely lost sight of that. I lost my focus and got caught up in all the attention I was getting as the 'star high school quarterback.' I really was a star. I was the most popular kid in school. It was like I had everything, but that still wasn't enough. I wanted more, and I also needed that assurance that I would always have what I was already receiving. I was dating your mom, but since I thought I could get away with anything, I started dating this other woman too. I loved this other woman, Joy. I did this for six months and when I could no longer take it anymore, I decided to be only with her instead of your mom. The next six months of exclusively dating this other woman ended up being the best time of my life. I loved her so, so much, and I already knew I wanted to marry her even though we were still so young. Joy, I bought a ring and everything! But—"

He paused and took a final swig of his beer, closing his eyes as he did so as if he wanted the need to continue the conversation to have disappeared once he opened them again. But when he opened them again, he found Joy was still there and so were his memories. The beer can sounded empty as he placed it back on the end table beside the other cans.

"...when I proposed to her, she responded by telling me that earlier that day, she had found out about me still dating your mom when I first started dating her. But then she said she was willing to stay with me even though she was declining the proposal. She said I had to earn back her trust before we could get married. When I realized my girlfriend was different than other girls I had dated and was going to challenge me to be better, I ended up going back to your mom instead. I couldn't let anyone tell me 'no' at that time, Joy. My ego couldn't take it. I also was worried that your mom would eventually shame me in front of everyone else if I didn't get back with her. I knew that she expected me to come back around. Your mom was the most popular girl in school and had been wanting to get back together. I started to think about my reputation and all the mutual friends your mom and I had. I know everything happens for a reason and it all worked out because I have you, I have your mom, and we have the construction business. But still, every day I know in my heart that I hurt her, I hurt your mom, and I didn't rise to the occasion when life gave me one of those rare once-in-a-lifetime moments to be something more than I ever thought I would be."

Joy turned her attention to the football game as she let everything he had shared continue to sink in. She watched as a play unfolded that resulted in the quarterback on her dad's former team throwing an interception that was returned in the opposite direction for a touchdown by the other team. She looked at the score and saw that the touchdown along with the extra point by the kicker had now erased the lead of her dad's former team and tied the game.

She cringed and looked over to her dad. But he hadn't joined her in watching the game. He was looking at her with glassy eyes. As they made eye contact, Joy realized she had mixed emotions after hearing the story the second time. The first time, she was more confounded than anything by the story and had still naturally sided with her dad. She had justified his actions with the way he treated her mom in high school based on the way he had always been kinder to her and more empathetic than her mom ever was. But this time she could see things from her mom's perspective. She had always seen her dad as "the good one" between her parents. But now that distinction was less clear to her. She realized she wasn't as close to her dad as she liked to think and say she was. She realized she couldn't really relate to or understand either of her parents. It was like they both inhabited an entirely different world from her and continued reliving their lives in past events that happened before she was born.

"I know, Daddy's not perfect," he said as if he had just read her mind directly or had consulted his own book of what everyone else had ever said or thought about him.

"I don't know you to be the type of person who would've done that," Joy determined. "The dad I've known wouldn't cheat on his girlfriend or wife."

"You're right," her dad replied without hesitation. "I was wrong, and I regret that. A lot of people say they don't regret anything, but we all regret something that we wish we had done differently. It wouldn't be 'life' if we didn't regret something because we all make mistakes and should all take ownership of that. I believe you can regret things you did in the past but learn from them every day as you try to live your best life in the present. As for my life now, it depends on what you think it means to cheat, does thinking of another woman from the past more than my own wife qualify as cheating in a sense? I ask myself that. I also ask myself if I have learned everything I was supposed to learn from my mistake."

Joy couldn't help but wonder how many people in the world have unknowingly or even knowingly maintained relationships and marriages in which one or both partners involved had set aside their hearts and minds for someone else. She concluded that her mom has sensed her dad still felt this way about the other girl in high school, like her grandpa did.

Her dad looked up at a family photo that her mom had placed on the wall near where the TV was. The photo was a professional portrait they had taken when Joy was six years old.

"Growing up, I noticed how other kids seemed to either put their parents on a pedestal or thought they were evil. Sometimes, I would catch myself doing the same thing. While that will be true for some kids for the rest of their lives, I think a lot of kids eventually discover their parents really fall somewhere in-between those two extremes. Most kids learn that their parents are flawed people who have done the best they could do relative to how they were raised by their own parents. No one is perfect. I tell you all of this, Joy, because I see how you look at me and how you look at your mother. She's still your mom and believe it or not, she loves you in her own way just as much as I do and wants what she believes is best for you."

Joy wanted to reply but didn't know what to say. Normally, she'd speak up and say something like "don't defend her" as she had whenever dad tried to explain her mom to her in the past (which wasn't very often because they rarely had conversations that lasted this long). But on this occasion, she was seeing her mom a little differently. She still didn't like the way her mom treated her, but now she understood it more without agreeing with it.

"Why would you and mom have a kid if you always felt this way inside?" Joy heard herself ask and then wondered if she should have asked it.

"I didn't want children with your mom," her dad answered bluntly. "We were at the point of discussing a divorce when she became pregnant with you. We never talked about it directly, but I think that was her way of keeping me around. She wanted more kids at first, and after having you and meeting you, my perspective changed, and I wanted more kids too. But I think the responsibility of caring for a baby was overwhelming to her, almost to the point that she regretted having one because I should have done so much more to help her with you. So, we just had you, and you've been the greatest gift either of us could ever have. I believe that for both me and your mom, whether your mom will ever tell you that or not. You know she isn't the best at expressing herself in that way."

Her dad looked at her and smiled as he picked up the TV remote. He turned off the TV without checking the score of the game (which was very unusual for him). He yawned as he collected the empty beer cans from the end table.

"Some periods in your life will appear to be a waste of time but one day you'll realize, for better or worse, that they were necessary for you to become who you are now. You will then decide if it was for better or worse, depending on how you choose to look at your life and choose how you are going to proceed from there. You'll potentially realize that each of these life events, good and bad, are like essential building blocks that are necessary for you to take on any challenge that is front of you or ahead of you. You may eventually realize how much you needed all those experiences to reach your greatest goals in your life, and yes, those experiences include your deepest regrets. I believe that's the mentality we all must have to reach the highest levels of potential in our lives. It's all a matter of whether we are willing to learn from every event we experience and grow from them. I haven't completely learned yet from my experiences, but I know I will keep trying until I do. I know all this that might sound like it's hard for you to believe right now, but I know someday you'll look back on what I just said, and it will make complete sense to you," her dad shared before spontaneously breaking out into another yawn.

"Anyway, Daddy's going to get ready for bed, I have a long day ahead of me tomorrow. I hope you feel better and get some rest. Goodnight, Joy."

He stood up from his chair and walked toward the entryway that led to the kitchen.

Joy still hadn't responded as he reached the entryway. He flicked off the wall light switch to the living room lamp and only a nearby nightlight that was activated prevented Joy from being consumed by total darkness.

"Wait, Dad!" Joy blurted out before involuntarily covering her mouth out of embarrassment from how unintentionally loud she was. Her dad stopped as he stepped into the hallway that led to the kitchen and flipped on the light to that hallway. The hallway light created a dim glow through the living room.

Once he had flipped the hallway light on, Joy was startled by her dad's appearance. He was wearing his full high school football uniform with pads and cleats. There were grass stains streaked all over the white and blue jersey and pants. The bottoms of his cleats were caked with grass and mud. As her dad looked in her direction, she noted how he still had the beer cans cradled to his chest with his right arm, but his hand that had flipped the light switch now held a grass-stained and mud-streaked helmet. Her dad still appeared the same age despite this metamorphosis, and it wasn't surprising that the uniform fit him as her dad had maintained a tanned slim build from all the labor he did outside for work.

He stepped back into the living room just beyond the entryway.

Joy looked around to confirm that they were still in the living room and not back in the football stadium again.

"What makes me a gift to you and mom?" She asked as her gaze settled back on her partially transformed father.

"You are one of those people who offers a rare gift to everyone you meet whether we want it or not," her dad laughed. "Like my old girlfriend tried to do with me, you challenge all of us to be better people. You do that by being your real, authentic self. You do that by having the kind of heart you have. It's the strongest heart of anybody I know. That's a beautiful gift, Joy…"

He winked at her and then disappeared down the hallway to take his beer cans to the recycling bin in the kitchen.

Part III: Wednesday
(one more time)

3.1

J oy opened her eyes and rolled over in bed to face her bedroom window for an indication of what time of the morning it was.

The window was still dark and gave her no clue.

She felt oddly more rested but still unrested in a way as she had slept for several hours but could have slept for several more. This was enough to give her the sense that it was morning.

She sat up but remained in bed.

Given her recent experiences with morning darkness, she sighed.

After she sighed, she unexpectedly yawned.

Once she yawned, she sighed again.

With her fingertips, she timidly searched the general area of her nightstand where she knew her phone was until she found it. She tapped the phone's touchscreen to illuminate her locked home-screen display, and it slightly lit up her face and the hand that held it.

She dropped her phone on the bed once it revealed the date and time: "Wednesday, December 8th – 5:29am."

She fell backward into her bed with her head reaching the pillow and pulled her covers over her head (and over the phone).

She allowed herself to stay in this position for what felt like several minutes. She felt overwhelmed by the fear of getting beaten up in the locker room and the fear of Autumn taking away the animals and the places she had loved when she was a little kid just as she was getting reacquainted with them. She recognized that feeling overwhelmed by these two primary concerns along with both the revelation that the day was repeating itself in a time loop and the fact that she had not slept well the previous two nights prior to last night (based on her real-time experience, not the calendar date) had all led her to completely passing out once she had arrived in her room after visiting with her dad again. Yes, she had crashed the previous night even with all the recent napping she had indulged in.

She took a deep breath (which was now somewhat difficult under the covers, so she pushed them down from over her head).

She took a second deep breath without the covers over her.

She knew then in her heart that the day would simply keep repeating itself unless she faced these fears. When this intuitive clarification came to her, she felt a complicated array of emotions that combined a jolt of rare confidence with a familiar sense of dread. This strange and sudden epiphany made her think of all positive experiences she had with the animals and even The Toilet Monster on the second version of Wednesday and how they stuck by her even though the day repeated itself. *They are going through this with me. They deserve better than to relive the same day over and over. They believe in me. They think I'm better than this. I used to think I was better than this. I may be ugly, but they are beautiful. I have to fight for them. I don't want to fight, but I have no choice. I don't want to get out of bed. I want to sleep more. I wish I could sleep one more Wednesday, but I only have like three hours left or something like that before Autumn tries to take over the castle. Did I really sleep like ten hours straight last night after that long nap earlier in the day? I wish I didn't get that tired feeling after sleeping too much. Shouldn't that make me feel more rested? Why is it so dark every morning like this? What can I do to make this all go away? I have to end this.*

She thought about her dad would have already left to go to his office at this time of the morning. Meanwhile, the door to her parents' bedroom was still closed and her mom was probably back in the master bathroom getting ready for work (assuming the world was dark for her mom too, her mom was known to follow all her beauty routines with candles lit if the power was out).

Joy picked up her phone, turned on its flashlight and slowly made her way out of her room while making as little noise as possible. As she came out into the upstairs hallway, she tiptoed by her parent's bedroom door and could faintly hear the shower running from the master bathroom. She moved as quietly but as quickly as she could downstairs, through the living room, the kitchen and then out to the garage. They had a massive garage that could easily fit three or four cars into it, but it only housed her mom's car. Her dad had built on an addition to the original garage to create a workshop for himself that took up half of the original garage space as well. He had also added heating and air conditioning to the garage when he was working on the addition. The entire garage had such a clean, fanciful and organized presentation that it could have been used as a studio set for a TV show featuring a handyman showing off his favorite gadgets and side projects. Her dad loved metal work, woodwork, and mechanical work and used the workshop primarily for his personal projects and side-projects.

Anyone who visited the family on a regular basis over the years or otherwise knew them well enough would have observed that the garage workshop arguably saved the marriage of Joy's parents. Her mom had hated when her dad was always out working when Joy was little. Her dad was working extra to expand his construction business, but then when he was at home there was tension, and they frequently argued. Typically, her dad complained about her mom spending more money than what they had on herself while her mom complained about her dad spoiling Joy too much when he was around. She also complained that he was not helping enough with raising Joy.

The creation of the garage workshop gave her dad his own space so that he and her mom mostly stayed out of each other's way while they were both at home. Her dad was usually in the workshop when he was at home. As his business rapidly expanded and he was able to hire a construction manager to oversee his work sites, her dad was able to spend more time at home but still feel productive working on his side projects. Joy's mom liked this arrangement because he wasn't immediately in her space, but much more available to her at home when she needed him. He also made a point of creating furniture for the house, toys for Joy, and making various upgrades around the house using his workshop.

Among other things, the workshop included various steel storage cabinets, a massive pegboard for tool storage, three work benches, an air compressor, welding equipment, various saws, a drill press, a router table, a refrigerator for beverages and even a bathroom with a shower and sink in it.

Joy went straight for the bathroom.

The workshop bathroom was her dad's primary bathroom for his morning routine since her mom didn't want him making too much noise at 3:30am when he was getting ready for work. He kept most of his hygiene products and medicine in the workshop bathroom.

Once she walked into the bathroom, she took note of her beautiful version of herself in the mirror of the medicine cabinet. Her smartphone flashlight generated just the right light for her to allow herself a heart-hearted smile to her reflection in the mirror. This was the first time she had tried looking in the medicine cabinet mirror in the workshop bathroom with this kind of lighting. But she couldn't truly feel good about her reflection this time, because she had never seen the beautiful version of herself in the mirror look so sad. Her half-smile slipped back into the resting-frown that was so familiar to her when she wasn't the beautiful version of herself.

She yawned and opened the medicine cabinet.

Once she shined her phone light into the medicine cabinet, she spotted the medicine pill bottle of her dad's most recent prescription of pain pills (from when he hurt his back again at a work site in mid-November) sitting prominently among other various medicine bottles.

She bit her lower lip.

She started to reach for it but hesitated.

She swallowed air.

She took the medicine pill bottle of pain pills and closed the medicine cabinet. She stood there for a moment as she thought about rearranging the bottles in a way to make it less noticeable that there was one missing but felt too guilty to do that.

She already felt guilty enough doing what she was doing. This wasn't like her at all, and she felt like a completely different person doing what she was doing.

She thought about how she might want her dad to notice. She knew, however, that he didn't often go into his medicine cabinet as he tried to take medication as little as possible. Unsurprisingly, the medicine pill bottle she held felt like it had never been used. *This would be more than enough.*

She took a deep breath that triggered tears that formed at the corners of both her eyes. *This is it. It may come down to this.*

Then, as quietly as she could, she nearly ran back up to her room and immediately put the pain pills into her backpack once she arrived there.

Before she went to her bathroom to start getting ready for school, she sat on the floor next to her backpack for a few minutes. She had that rare unique empty feeling in her stomach and her throat that only happened on the mornings of days of big events when she had a feeling that she would remember that day for the rest of her life. It was like her body cleansed itself into an empty slate with the knowledge that for better or worse, something major and life-changing was going to happen within the next twenty-four hours. Just like the mind and the soul, it was like the body needs to prepare itself for those once-in-a-lifetime type of "moments" her dad had told her about.

3.2

Joy used her phone flashlight to navigate her way to her own bathroom. She closed her bathroom door behind her and locked it. She flipped the wall light switch in the bathroom, and as expected, the light didn't turn on. She set the phone face-down where she could find space on her bathroom counter so that its beam of light faced upward.

With her phone flashlight shining enough light to generate a reflection, she looked at the bathroom mirror. She expected to either see Casey or the princess version of herself.

Sure enough, there was Casey.

Casey was in a beautiful black V-neck shirt dress and was holding a to-go coffee cup with a label printed on its sleeve from a coffee shop that Joy didn't recognize.

"Happy Wednesday, Joy," Casey greeted her in the fake, cutesy voice that Joy had seen her use with teachers and other adults she wanted approval from.

Joy wanted to verbalize a response, but as she opened her mouth, a long yawn involuntarily emerged from it. Casey was immediately appalled by Joy's yawning response and demonstrated her outrage with an exaggerated facial expression.

Joy looked at Casey's coffee, wondering where she got it from so that she could potentially visit there. The label on the coffee cup was in a strange font and far enough away that it was difficult to read.

"Tired of it being Wednesday, yet?" Casey smirked.

Joy didn't respond. She was feeling fatigued from thinking about the day she had ahead of her and was genuinely concerned that if she tried to open her mouth, she would yawn again.

"You know you could make this your last day of a repeating Wednesday. I have two ways I could make that happen for you. You can either sign the contract and join me, or you can meet me in the locker room during gym class like I have so kindly requested," Casey offered.

There was a knock on the bathroom door.

Joy opened the bathroom door expecting her mom or dad with the hope that their arrival would end Casey's mirror visit. Instead, it was the server from the morning of Casey's future wedding reception standing in his full tuxedo and apron at her doorway, holding the contract with the clipboard and pen again. The setting behind him remained the familiar darkened upstairs hallway in her house.

Joy had the sense that she should have been more surprised upon seeing the server in her house, but by this point she recognized that anything was possible.

"No coffee?" Joy asked the server as he handed her the contract and pen.

The server remained expressionless and gave Joy a slight bow before he headed downstairs.

Joy sighed. She closed the door again and locked it. She placed the contract and pen on the counter to her left beside the sink (near where her toothbrush and toothpaste were after brushing a few other bathroom items aside to make room for it).

"People like you who have their hearts broken are always miserable no matter what they try to do about it," Casey sneered from the mirror. "Some of them stay trapped alone and are only ever accompanied by their own bitterness and resentment. Others spend their time desperately surrounding themselves with other damaged people who use them while they fool themselves into believing they're really helping those other people from being more broken like themselves. Then there is the third category of people like you who just stay numb and clueless. Heartbroken people can also become different combinations of each of these three categories or fall into all three categories at different points of their lives. I put you in the numb and clueless category. When I think of 'numb and clueless,' I think of you and that girl in our chemistry class who has multiple pairs of the same t-shirts and jeans because she likes to think she is a cartoon character who can dress the same way every day and get away with it."

Joy knew exactly who Casey was talking about but couldn't remember her name. She squinted as she strained her mind trying to remember the girl's name. As she did so, she became aware that The Bear was now standing next to her to her right, facing Casey in the mirror as well.

"Do you even know the name of the other girl I'm talking about?" Casey asked. "I don't think you do. You see, Joy, everyone doesn't quite remember her the same way they don't quite remember you."

Joy looked to The Bear, who returned her gaze.

"She can't see me at all," The Bear laughed.

"Really?" Joy wondered.

Both Casey (inaccurately) and The Bear (accurately) thought Joy was talking to them.

"Don't be ridiculous and pretend you don't know that," Casey scoffed, somewhat confused by the fact Joy was no longer looking in her direction. "I know you're smarter than that. You're on the road to being a lifelong loser like her, but I know you have the potential to at least be a little bit more than that. But the only way it can happen for someone like you is if you join the circle of someone like me. That's why you have that contract in front of you. I am giving you one last chance to sign it. If you have it signed by the time of our meeting in the locker room, you won't run into any more problems today— or for the rest of your life. It's up to you."

"Yeah, she can't see us like the rest of the people in this world can't see us even though she can do this bizarre mirror thing and can do the wedding reception waiter stuff," The Bear concluded.

"But what about Autumn?" Joy asked The Bear.

"Autumn," Casey repeated. She looked increasingly uncharacteristically nervous and uncomfortable, "I don't know who that is. Why are you being all weird and looking away from me like that?"

Joy turned to face Casey to make it less awkward. They briefly made eye contact before Joy looked down at the sink.

"Autumn can see us in the other world, because she knows about the other world, but even she can't see us in this one because we are with you and not with her. This girl Casey doesn't know the other world, she just knows this one, but it seems like she can somehow manipulate time and space within this one. I don't know, it's crazy to me too. But most people in this world don't know the other world or at least aren't nearly as conscious of it as you and Autumn are. I'm hoping this all makes sense," The Bear explained, still looking at her.

Joy nodded in the direction of the sink, even though she was still kind of confused. For someone who apparently only knew of this world, Casey sure gave her the impression that she knew everything in every world with her intelligence and intuition. Joy wondered if Casey's awareness of everything went beyond that of The Bear. Either way, she was still relieved that Casey couldn't see The Bear. She knew if she could see The Bear, she would probably want The Bear in her entourage like Autumn did. She also felt a little empowered that there was at least one aspect of her life that Casey didn't seem to know about.

The brief eye contact and sad response of Joy looking down at the sink seemed to satisfy Casey despite Joy's otherwise odd behavior to her. Meanwhile, Joy's acknowledging nod seemed to satisfy The Bear. Joy got the sense that she was sufficiently acknowledging them at the same time again.

Joy looked up and saw Casey drinking her coffee. Through the corner of her eye, Joy could see The Bear turning his attention back in Casey's direction as well.

"I'll tell you a few secrets that I haven't even told my own close friends," Casey offered once she had completed her dose of coffee. "Most women our age, including you with Gray, don't really love the guys they are interested in. You love your love for the person more than you love the actual person. You love the way you feel when you love Gray but don't know what you love about him. You don't know him well enough to like him, much less love him. That's the only way losers like you know how to love because you don't have the real-life experience to learn about love through the trials and errors of real relationships. It's not totally your fault, because I know your parents are losers who didn't set any example for you since they don't love themselves anymore or each other."

Joy remained quiet, with tears forming again at the corners of her eyes. She thought about the pills in her backpack.

"Let me tell you another secret," Casey added. "Making out and sex mean nothing nowadays, it's something we do to get something else we want or need. I know you've never even kissed anyone so you're excited to learn what that will be like. But I'm here to tell you it's entirely meaningless beyond being something that might temporarily make you feel good if you are lucky and doing it with someone who happens to be good at intimacy. Most people aren't, and they don't have the potential I see in you to understand love. True love is rarer than the world will ever want to admit. A lot of people you know probably think they have or know true love, but deep in their hearts they know they don't. I'll tell you this though, understanding love in a deep way is a mixed blessing because it's so rare that you may never find it. Even I will be lucky to be with someone at my level, if they're out there. So, if I were you, I'd start accepting what I am telling you right now and stop attaching any meaning to the love you think you've been experiencing with Gray. You know nothing about love."

A tear made it halfway down Joy's left cheek. She remained still and made no effort to wipe it away. She was hurt by Casey's insults, awed by Casey's intelligence and insight gathered from her years of dating experience, and disturbed by her apathy as a result of those experiences all at the same time.

"Have you ever had a period of time in your life when you never wanted it to end?" Casey asked without giving Joy time to respond. "That's brings me to the last secret I will share with you before I give you time to decide on the contract. This is another one that my close friends don't know. When we were in freshman year, you may remember I hung out with a lot of the seniors. My favorite person from that senior class was this beautiful woman named Whitney. I wanted to be closer friends with her, but she was so different from the other popular people in that class. She was gorgeous, but she was also intelligent and seemed to know a lot more about life than the others her age. I remember I looked up to her but wasn't sure why.

"Anyway, her parents were out of town for her last day in the United States that summer after school ended and she needed a ride to the airport because she was going to college in Switzerland. My mom ended up giving her a ride and I was there with her in the backseat. I remember her telling me on the car ride how she had approached high school differently from all her friends by staying focused and taking school seriously. She said that almost all her friends had changed by the time they reached high school by partying and ditching class, while she remained the same by staying consistent with her studies. Even so, most of them were pretty much going to the same college and wanted her to join them. But she picked Switzerland and sort of alienated herself from them that summer. She tried to explain to me how Switzerland had one of the best educational systems in the world and there was so much more to life than what we experience in high school and experience in the place we grew up in. To be real with you, I was really turned off by that conversation with her myself.

"I thought she was weird for wanting to go to Switzerland and I actually didn't want to go on the car ride to the airport. But my mom loved her and made me go along with them, so I played nice. She encouraged me to stay in touch with her before she left, and I didn't reach out until two years later to no response. You see, I never understood what she meant until two years later and it was too late because I'm sure she sensed I didn't respect what she was doing and now she has long moved on to a much better life. I find myself feeling the same way she did back then. I wish I had stayed in touch with her because I literally can't relate to any of these idiots you see me hanging around with. I feel like everyone I'm friends with and nearly all the people we know in our class are morons who have no idea what life has in store for them after we graduate. You still aren't nearly as smart as I am, Joy, but I know you are smarter than most of them. I think you might get it.

"We could be friends for the rest of our time in high school and maybe go to college in Switzerland together. Either way, Gray will go with me. He will follow me anywhere and will do anything I want him to do. I am not sure he knows where Switzerland is, but when you get a guy who will do anything for you and shape his whole life around yours, you know he's a keeper. I'll be honest with you and tell you I can't guarantee that even if we become friends, that you will get to experience that with a guy. I'll do the best I can to help you, but some of us were born to be extraordinary and it's impossible for most other people to learn how to get my level. You have always been a loser and I can understand why you would hesitate to be friends with me. You don't know a good thing when it comes along because you only know misery. I can guarantee you that if you don't take my offer, you'll remain a loser the rest of your life. I don't even know how you can go on living day-to-day at this point. I'm giving you until gym class to decide, but why don't you do yourself a favor and sign that contract for me now?"

Joy turned for a moment to The Bear and he returned her glance. She had a second tear running down her right cheek.

She returned her attention to Casey, and they quietly made eye contact. This time, Joy maintained eye contact with her resting-frown.

Casey smirked.

"The last time you tried to convince me to sign the contract, I got a coffee too," Joy said.

Casey laughed inauthentically and then without warning, ripped off the plastic lid to her coffee, pulled the nearly full cup of coffee back so it was behind her and then thrust the cup forward while maintaining a tight grip on it. This caused the coffee to splash through the mirror and partially soak both Joy and The Bear, as Casey had partially aimed the 20oz round of coffee to her left. With only seconds to react, Joy had managed to turn her face away to her left while The Bear had remained still and continued to face the mirror. Immediately following the impact of the coffee, the mirror flashed brightly for several seconds so that both Joy and The Bear were forced to shield their eyes.

When the flash ended, Joy looked up again and saw that Casey had vanished, and the mirror just had a reflection of her and The Bear. The usual bathroom lighting came on since Joy had flipped the switch earlier. They were both dripping wet with coffee. Casey had mixed a great deal of cream into her coffee, so fortunately for Joy and The Bear, the coffee wasn't too hot by the time it had struck them (and therefore, wasn't the scalding, super-hot coffee anyone having coffee thrown at them would be concerned about).

"Well, that was a little intense," The Bear quipped, turning to Joy.

"People keep saying that want to help me, but then they end up getting angry with me and insulting me," Joy contemplated aloud as she turned off her phone flashlight now that the bathroom light was working again. The phone had only been hit with a few drops of coffee. "It's not helping."

"So, two fights today?" The Bear asked.

"I wish you could fight both of them for me."

"I wish I could too," The Bear sighed. "But I don't think that is going to get us out of this time-loop thing if I fight them for you. Having said that, you know we will be doing everything we can to support you."

Joy's eyes widened.

"Us," she softly repeated.

The Bear assessed the coffee in his fur that was scattered around various parts of his upper body. "I think I'm going to use the shower after you are done," The Bear laughed. "We really need to get your parents to get you a new mirror in here."

"I think she only took a couple sips of that large coffee," Joy reflected, with coffee dripping down the right side of her face, down her neck and from her hair. Her pajamas were drenched on her right side from her neckline and shoulder down to her elbow and belly button. She had clearly received the bulk of the coffee-splash compared to The Bear.

"It's not so bad," The Bear decided, "she gave you a pre-shower."

Joy laughed. Her body felt strange as she laughed, as though she hadn't laughed in years, and it wasn't sure how to respond even though she had already laughed a number of times over the previous 24 hours.

"True," Joy agreed, "the timing was good."

"She aimed it just right," The Bear observed, pointing at the contract with his paw, "there isn't a spot of coffee on that thing."

The Bear took a couple of towels from the towel rack and presented one to Joy while keeping one for himself.

As she started dry her the side of her face and neck, Joy leaned over to the contract for a closer look.

"If I did sign this, I could avoid one fight and concentrate on the other one, Bear. At least this potential fight doesn't involve me possibly losing you and the others like the other fight," Joy considered, as she started thumbing through the pages. "It might be worth looking further into and thinking about. I mean, what would I really have to lose if I signed it?"

"Maybe your self-respect?" The Bear quipped as he awkwardly fumbled around with his towel in an arduous effort to try to dry himself with his large, clawed paws.

As Joy flipped through the pages, a section she hadn't seen when she was previously looking at the contract titled "Beauty" caught her attention.

3.3

J oy revisited the contract during her 8:30am study hall and again, had the page turned to the section titled "Beauty" on page 19. She was wearing a snowman-themed "ugly sweater" that her mom had specifically requested she not wear to school. It was her favorite sweater because the cartoon snowman on it made her smile. She still wore the same pants she had been putting on the previous Wednesdays (they were clean again with the renewal of each Wednesday).

She had completed her morning routine on time (therefore avoiding any interaction with her mom or dad), made it to the bus (and sat in a front seat to be the first one out of the bus), found Casey's note in her locker again before the morning rush of students settled into the hallway (successfully avoiding any interaction with Autumn in the process), and made a point of giving Mr. Kingsapple the impression she was paying attention in history class without incident. She moved swiftly to and from her locker after history class and interacted with no one as though she had been invisible. She was the first one to arrive in study hall and she immediately placed the contract in front of her to give Mr. Green- roads, her study hall teacher, the sense that she was thoroughly invested in it so he wouldn't approach her. She had wanted to look at it on the bus or in history class but didn't want to draw any un- wanted attention from either the other students or Mr. Kingsapple. She had put the "new" note from Casey in her pocket and upon doing so, realized that the "old" note had disappeared.

The study hall was strangely located in the cafeteria, which was completely decked out with holiday decorations. Joy wasn't entirely sure why her study hall was in the cafeteria, but overheard other students once discuss how it was because their school was overcrowded, and the school needed to utilize any extra space it had throughout the school day. The cafeteria chairs were rearranged so that there were chairs on only one side of each table with all the tables and chairs facing a single table at one end of the cafeteria where Mr. Greenroads was stationed. Joy was sitting at a table on the far-right end of the cafeteria, three rows back from where Mr. Greenroads was. There were two extra chairs at the other side of his table for students to approach him with any homework questions. More often than not, these chairs were filled with female students who had a crush on Mr. Greenroads. Mr. Greenroads would indulge himself with their attention if there wasn't a student who approached him for actual help (and there rarely was). Some of the other students referred to these girls who had a crush on him as his "groupies."

Mr. Greenroads was a well-dressed, attractive, 26-year-old man with an athletic-build and a boyish face who looked like he could easily be a model, athlete, or actor instead of a teacher. He was one of those rare people that made all heads turn to him when he entered a room and had a strong, dynamic presence wherever he went. He made anyone who encountered him at the grocery store or the post office wonder "what is he still doing here in our city?" and also wonder "why isn't he in Los Angeles or New York?" while glaring at him with an awe that would make most people uncomfortable. But like real celebrities, Mr. Greenroads seemed to be used to the attention as he was unaffected by it as though he expected it.

Joy and Mr. Greenroads had little interaction as Joy never approached him and he only approached Joy if he thought she was sleeping or daydreaming more than usual. She grew to resent this a little because he didn't seem to do that with the other students (even if they were obviously sleeping or daydreaming). However, she knew that once he got locked in conversation with one of his "groupies" that she was pretty much free to do whatever she wanted. For this particular study hall, she planned to do something she had never done before and leave it early. To help facilitate the process of leaving early, she only brought the contract with her and left her backpack in her locker. She figured if she had her backpack, she would look more suspicious trying to leave study hall early.

As she waited for Mr. Greenroads to get approached by a "groupie" she looked up at the digital clock that hung on the wall behind him.

It read: "8:32."

She sighed.

They were only two minutes into the study hall session but usually there was already a "groupie" distracting Mr. Greenroads by now. Autumn was going to start her attack on the castle in a matter of minutes.

She defaulted to her resting-frown, and returned her attention to page 19 of the contact:

Section XXXIX -- Beauty

You will be permitted with my approval, to select your favorite photo of yourself that you have deemed to be the best version of yourself. Once approved, you will undergo a makeover to as closely resemble this version of you as possible and will be provided instruction on how to maintain this appearance on your own. During this initial makeover process you will also be assessed by a nutri-

tionist and personal trainer for dietary changes and fitness train-
ing recommendations you will be required to follow. New photos
may be taken of you to select as your baseline photo if you demon-
strate improvement in your appearance. Any corresponding ad-
justments to your required clothing and accessories will be made
accordingly. Failure to adhere to these guidelines after two warn-
ings will result in immediate termination of the contract and per-
manent banishment from my inner circle.

Joy looked up from the contract and closed her eyes.

After taking a deep breath, she opened her eyes and saw Madison sitting in one of the chairs opposite Mr. Greenroads at the front of the room. She couldn't hear what the conversation was about, but Madison appeared to be in a very animated discussion with him. Joy observed that Madison was using enthusiastic hand gestures to help convey whatever she was sharing and occasionally interrupted herself with laughter. For his part, Mr. Greenroads looked completely engrossed in whatever the conversation was about and even seemed to be providing courtesy-laughter along with her.

Joy knew this was her chance.

She got up from her table and started walking down the right side of the room toward the double doors at the "back" of the cafeteria (opposite of where Mr. Greenroads was) with the contract in its clipboard. The clipboard gave her the appearance that she was working on some kind of interview project or completing a form for the front office at school.

Her study hall was usually what one might call "quietly loud", as the many whispers of her classmates in side-conversations were intertwined to form a continuous, pronounced, indistinguishable babble throughout the cafeteria. But as she got halfway through the room, the cafeteria suddenly fell eerily silent. Her heart skipped a beat with that specific type of rhythmic interruption that was reserved for moments when she was caught doing something she wasn't supposed to be doing.

Joy stopped and nervously turned back to look at the rest of her study hall.

To her surprise, she saw that everyone and everything in the room except herself were completely frozen in the form of whatever action they were engaged in when the room unexpectedly fell silent.

Mr. Greenroads, Madison, and all the other students were frozen in place as though they had instantly turned into wax figures of themselves or realistic humanoid statues. Joy looked around cautiously and suspiciously with increasing awe at the bizarre spectacle before her. Mouths hung open, arms were raised, eyes were closed, and stares looked permanent. There was a book page being turned at mid-turn, a student laughing with another student next to him with their mouths wide open, and even a pencil in mid-air that had been thrown by a frustrated-looking student looking in its direction from several feet away. They were all lifeless and yet were collectively demonstrating the full spectrum of life with their facial expressions, hand gestures, body postures, and chosen proximity from one another.

She decided that since the room was frozen, she would exit out of one of the double doors at the designated "front end" of the cafeteria instead, as her locker was closer to that side.

She started to walk back toward the front of the cafeteria, timidly studying the details of the various poses of her frozen classmates in passing as her shoes squeaked and scuffed across the floor. She wanted to walk up and down the aisles among them to get a closer look but also felt afraid that they could immediately become unfrozen at any given moment.

As she approached the set of double doors near where Mr. Greenroads was, she observed that he had remained immersed in whatever it was that Madison was discussing with him with a slight grin. Madison had placed her two hands together to form a shape of a heart in front of him as a hand gesture to illustrate whatever she was telling him about while her mouth was open in mid-sentence.

No, he hadn't noticed Joy getting up to leave at all.

As she walked through one of the doorways with her head down, she found herself stepping onto grass instead of stepping onto the tile flooring of the hallway.

3.4

Joy looked up and saw The Elephant, The Lion, The Wolf, The Cardinal and The Penguin standing in front of her. Behind them she had a distant view of the ocean. Except for The Cardinal, they were each wearing various forms of armor that was designed specifically for their bodies. Due to their respective sizes and body types, The Elephant was the most heavily armored knight while The Penguin was the least armored among them. The Elephant was draped in chainmail in addition to the massive armored plates that covered much of her body. There were smaller plates of armor linked to chainmail that aligned down her trunk. The Penguin was wearing no body armor but had a heavy specially made helmet over her head. The Lion and The Wolf were moderately dressed in armor around their bodies with no protection on their heads, legs or tails. The Cardinal had tried on his suit of light chain mail that protected his front torso and the mantle area of his back between his wings but opted not to wear it because he didn't like how it slowed him down, especially in flight. He acknowledged he hadn't kept his body in shape the way he used to and subsequently endured a good-natured ribbing from the others.

The warmth of the morning sun was slightly offset by a light spring breeze. White cumulus clouds were gently moving at a slow pace overhead. The air smelled like it had drizzled overnight but the ground had mostly dried.

Joy could hear the distant sounds of cannons firing, explosions, the sounding of horns, and faint battle cries. They were in a meadow situated high above the ocean and seemingly at the same elevation as the castle, which Joy could see several hundred yards away jutting out into the ocean on a bluff to her left. The castle looked magnificent from this distance, as though it hadn't suffered from the recent bombardment or years of neglect. She looked in its direction with wonder before she returned her attention to the animals.

"You guys look...different," Joy said.

"Don't we look amazing?" The Penguin asked from inside her helmet. "All of our armor was still intact at the castle armory."

Joy quietly nodded in agreement with The Penguin. She then looked further out to the ocean to her right and spotted a large armada of ships that had formed a long firing-line parallel to the coast.

She bit her lip as she observed that there were dozens of ships firing away at the coast below.

"So, this it, huh?" she asked nervously (and rhetorically).

The Lion stepped forward and proceeded to give Joy an update on their defense plan:

> The castle was on a bluff at the end of the peninsula they were on and was naturally protected by sea cliffs on three sides. On the fourth side, the land bridge to the castle was also flanked on both sides by sea cliffs. These natural defenses would force an attacking army to try scale them in addition to the castle walls. The rest of the peninsula was primarily covered by a forest that limited access from the mainland to a narrow dirt trail through the forest. Judging by the movements of her fleet, Autumn wanted to move her invasion force overland quickly and take the castle relatively intact, so she had planned to land her army on the

beach nearest to the castle. The nearest beach that was adequate for a landing party was midway down the peninsula between the castle and the village. The village was located on the coast of the peninsula close to where it converged with the mainland. The village was surrounded on land by the forest and only connected to the castle by the narrow forest trail. The decision was made to evacuate the village as the defense force wasn't large enough to protect both the castle and village. However, every knight, soldier, and villager available volunteered to fight. Anticipating that the main fleet was going to attempt a landing on the beach, the defense force dragged a few of the castle's cannons to the beach. The cannons were positioned within makeshift earthworks crudely constructed out of sand, rocks, shells, and dirt. Once it was confirmed that the main fleet had shifted its focus to the beach, the castle itself was left only lightly defended and was also reserved for those who were either unable to fight or too young to fight.

The Lion motioned for them to follow him, and they walked to the edge of the meadow near where it descended into sea cliffs. From where they were standing, they had the perfect view to see the invading armada as it was firing away at the beach. The ships appeared as though they had bursts of tiny flames erupting from their sides. But even though the beach was nearby, he indicated that the sea cliffs were so high and angled in such a way that it couldn't be seen from where they were standing. Therefore, he pointed with his paw in the direction of the entryway to the meadow from the beach before he continued:

The cannons had limited ammunition, and the defense force had planned to use them to try to keep the ships away from the beach until they completely ran out. They planned to then proceed with an orderly retreat to the meadow to set up the next line of defense there. They were able to sink one of the first ships that approached the beach with the element of surprise but were unable to delay the overall attack because the firepower of the enemy vessels was overwhelming. Once the ships got close enough to start firing their cannons at the beach, Joy's defense force took cover in caves and various hiding places among the rocks at the bottom of the sea cliffs just beyond the beach. As a result, the defense force was forced to abandon its own cannons before they had used up their ammunition. Given their dire circumstances, they now plan to re-emerge from these hiding places once the troop transport vessels reach shore and the cannon fire from the ships has subsided. They have been instructed to hold out as long as they can on the beach and then make a gradual fighting retreat up to the meadow where they will make a final stand.

The Lion's briefing was interrupted by several gasps among the group as they witnessed dozens of smaller troop transport boats were now heading from Autumn's main fleet toward the beach. The ships that weren't in the process of lowering transport boats were still blasting away at the defenses on the beach.

The Lion turned to The Elephant and gave The Elephant an upward nod. The Elephant then picked up where he had left off in explaining the battle plan and how it related to the landscape:

The meadow was considered the best position for a defending force to make a stand against an enemy attacking from the beach because it left the enemy with only a narrow outlet for retreat if the defense force was able to keep them contained along the edges of the sea cliffs. To reach the meadow from the beach, the enemy soldiers would have to go up a spiraling inclined pathway of sand, rock, and dirt to reach a small entranceway situated well above them. This passageway was ideal for delaying actions during a retreat since it was narrow at every segment, walled in by cliff rock, and flanked by steep sea cliffs. The passageway from the beach continued as a thin dirt trail through the meadow before linking up to the main trail that stretched across the peninsula. The plan was to allow Autumn's army to position themselves on the meadow once they reached it, regroup the remaining defense force, and launch a counterattack that would trap them with their backs to the edges of the sea cliffs. Part of the counterattack would strike the right flank of the invading force, to attempt to cut off their escape through the passageway back to the beach.

After The Elephant had finished her portion of the briefing, Joy turned to the meadow and saw how purple wildflowers were scattered in dense patches throughout the grassy landscape from the sea cliffs back to the dense forest that surrounded the other three sides of it. Autumn's army would still have to cross part of the forest from the meadow to reach the castle, but over a much shorter timeframe than if it had come in from the mainland and had to go down the whole length of the peninsula. There was one small distinct grove within the meadow, several yards to the right of where The Lion had pointed out the entryway from the beach with his paw.

"That sounds like the perfect plan to me," Joy responded, before pausing with a curious expression on her face. "Um, have you all planned battles before or something?"

The animals looked awkwardly at one another.

"This is our first time," The Cardinal admitted. His nervous demeanor suggested that he felt like someone else should have replied for them.

"First time!?" Joy asked.

"You really can't underestimate Elephant," The Wolf rhapsodized. "The woman is a genius. She came up with most of the plan and then the rest of us hashed out the details with Lion over breakfast at your place."

"You guys had breakfast at my place again?!" Joy asked.

"Of course," The Penguin echoed from under her helmet, "you have a great kitchen. We also had to get The Lion out of the castle, he's constantly hanging around there, even though it's empty and depressing."

The Penguin poked at The Lion's side with her flipper. The Lion acknowledged her with a half-grin.

"Well, I wasn't there," The Elephant pointed out. "I was here keeping an eye on things. It was the only way we could get Lion to go and obviously, as you know Joy, I can't exactly fit in your kitchen."

They all laughed.

"But my dad was home, right?" Joy noted. She then paused as another thought occurred to her: "Wait, were you guys hanging out with The Toilet Monster again?"

"He does make excellent coffee," The Lion affirmed.

"See, I told you," The Wolf jested. "Why couldn't you admit that during breakfast?"

"Your dad always eats way early," The Penguin said.

"He can't hear or see us anyway," The Cardinal added, "he was in the garage the whole time."

"Well, I'm happy you all had a good time," Joy chuckled.

"The food was even better than yesterday's version of Wednesday," The Penguin remarked. "It helped having Dolphin there too. The Toilet Monster incorporated a couple of seafood dishes into his breakfast buffet for us."

"Where are Dolphin and Bear now?" Joy asked.

"Bear is commanding the defense force on the beach," The Elephant replied sheepishly. "I guess we should've mentioned that earlier."

Joy gasped, "The Bear?!"

"He volunteered," The Lion added, "and Dolphin is in the sea scouting out Autumn's ships for us."

"We've got this, Joy," The Penguin beamed.

Joy smiled meekly back at The Penguin before she closed her eyes and took a deep breath. As she did so, the sounds of cannon-fire faded into emerging sounds of wheels turning across tile-flooring. The smell of wildflowers moistened with the last hint of morning dew gave way to the smell of bleach. The air felt colder.

3.5

"**J**oy, are you okay?" An unfamiliar female voice asked her.

Joy opened her eyes and found herself standing right outside the closed double doors of the cafeteria in the hallway at school. She saw The Custodian standing in front of her with a concerned look on her face. The Custodian was wearing nitrile gloves and a dark blue uniform. Joy had seen her around many times before over the past two and a half years, but they had never interacted. Joy felt like she had never seen The Custodian this closely before.

She was astonished by how beautiful The Custodian was.

The Custodian had the appearance of a woman in her early 40s who looked like she could be ten years younger in nearly every way except for the maturity Joy observed in her eyes, which revealed her true age. Joy found in them that she had the life experience and wisdom of someone in that age range. She could see that The Custodian took immaculate care of herself and despite the responsibilities involved with her vocation, she looked like she had just walked out of a spa in a custodian's clothing. She had long, flowing dark hair with blonde highlights that appeared to be glowing beneath the otherwise bleak glimmer of fluorescent lighting above them. She had an athletic figure and a vibrant energy that only people who took care of themselves with diet and exercise seemed to have when they were also comfortable with who they were. She had a large, empty gray trash can on wheels along a mop in a yellow bucket on wheels beside her. She was holding the mop handle in one gloved hand, and the rim of the trash can in the other.

"I'm okay," Joy murmured after taking another deep breath.

The Custodian looked skeptical.

"Are you sure?"

"Yeah."

The Custodian remained where she stood. She was waiting for more than just "yeah" and Joy sensed it. Joy struggled to come up with something else to say to reassure her. Her mind kept returning to the question she really wanted to ask The Custodian, so she decided to ask that instead: "How do you know my name?"

The Custodian looked away from her briefly before resuming eye contact.

"Well, since I work here, I get to know some of the names of the students around here over time and some tend to stand out more than others," The Custodian laughed. "In this job you overhear a lot of conversations and see a lot of things between the students, the teachers, and the administrative staff."

Joy looked at her curiously as though she needed to hear more to understand why The Custodian would know her name but perceived no further information was forthcoming.

"I am still surprised you know my name," Joy anxiously blurted out to her own surprise. "People don't really talk to me. I don't have a lot of friends like you do."

The Custodian laughed: "How do you know I have a lot of friends?"

"You do the job you do in this miserable place, and you look happy. You're always smiling and laughing."

The Custodian smiled one of the most beautiful and engaging smiles Joy had ever seen.

"I don't mean any disrespect when I say this," Joy began carefully, "but most people that I see at their jobs either aren't happy or are too serious all the time. You seem to be doing your job like you are supposed to, but you also look so happy even though you are stuck doing it. You are doing this even though other people think it's disgusting and would look down on you, but you do it as if you were meant to...like you love it."

The Custodian paused thoughtfully as though not expecting Joy to engage in her this way. She released her grip on the trash can and leaned slightly in the direction of where she was holding the mop in the bucket with her other hand.

"I don't know if I can say I am always happy cleaning up around here, but I am happy to be alive," The Custodian explained. "Each day will bring something new to you if you stay open to it."

Joy responded to her with a mixed facial expression, suggesting it was hard for her to believe her, but wanted to.

"That's true for me," The Custodian added, "even though I do this job."

Joy stayed quiet.

"You didn't really answer my question though, how do you know I have friends?" The Custodian asked.

Joy hesitated and then cleared her throat before speaking: "Like I said, because you are happy."

Joy looked down at her shoes with her resting-frown.

"I have seen you around here for the last year or two. You usually have that same frown you have right now. You're easy to spot because you are always by yourself here," The Custodian reflected. "I get it. But may I share something with you about having friends?"

Joy looked up at her oddly and hesitated a second time: "Um, okay."

"Joy, there aren't many people like you. There aren't that many people committed to do the right thing who have a heart like yours. So many people don't really live the right way and deep down they only do right for themselves, even at the expense of other people. But you are unique. You are a treasure. People like you are so vulnerable to those other people who mistreat others. You have to value yourself and you have to love yourself because a lot of people won't know how to value you. They'll see you as a threat, because you are like a mirror to them. You are mirror that makes them look at themselves and see in themselves who they should be but haven't been. You make them realize they can be better people when they don't want to be or think they aren't able to be. You are so special, and unfortunately a lot of people like you don't always make it in our world because of how cruel it really is. A lot of people like you disappear and hide away to get away from the world, when really you have so much to offer to it, and when really, it needs more like you."

Joy looked at The Custodian like she was a saleswoman still trying to sell her something even though everything about Joy's body language indicated she was no mood for any kind of verbal interaction: "What does that have to with making friends?"

The Custodian laughed.

"Don't resist kindness from others when it's genuine," The Custodian recommended, still smiling, "otherwise you will keep resisting being kind to yourself too. Did you really listen to anything I just said?"

"I did." Joy didn't know how to take The Custodian's positive responses to her. It wasn't believable to her that anyone could be this positive.

"But?"

"I don't believe you."

"You don't believe me because...?"

"You don't know me at all," Joy scoffed, "you might have seen me around, but this is my first time ever talking to you."

Joy looked down the hallway like she wanted to leave. She felt like she wasting her time talking to The Custodian. She had trouble with people complimenting her in general, but especially people who didn't really know her.

She sighed and looked up toward the ceiling. But instead of the ceiling, she saw a bright blue morning sky with thick white clouds. Among these clouds, she observed a strange flying object moving toward her.

3.6

Despite witnessing his approach, Joy didn't recognize The Toilet Monster until he landed in front of her with smoke lingering out of his jetpack. She was back in the meadow with The Cardinal, The Lion, The Elephant, and The Penguin. The Wolf was noticeably absent this time. The sounds of cannons had stopped. She observed that the number of boats in the invading fleet had doubled with several more troop transport boats heading toward the beach. She could now hear distinct battle cries over the continued echoing of horns and could hear faint sounds of metal clashing against metal.

"Autumn has landed a much larger army than we anticipated," The Toilet Monster reported, looking at both The Elephant and The Lion, "but they've left their ships mostly unguarded. Dolphin and I have stored the bombs in the rowboat at the boathouse. Dolphin is there now. We will be able to attach them underwater to her ships undetected upon your order."

"Did you check in with Bear?" The Lion asked.

"Yes, and I'm not going to lie, Bear and the others are barely holding on down there. Our defenses drove back the first wave of enemy soldiers, but they were also able to land their archers. Their archers rained arrows all over the beach before they deployed a more powerful second wave of their knights and elite infantry. They are driving us back. I've got to say, I'm amazed we've made it this long. We have about two hundred people left down there, and they have at least a thousand attacking them. They should be here any minute. Are we kind of meeting them here?"

"First and foremost, we want to spare the castle for Joy," The Elephant began, "but I'm a little surprised we haven't seen any of our group head over to the castle to be with their family members there. Did any of the villagers on the beach choose to retreat in the other direction toward the village to protect their homes?"

The Toilet Monster glanced wistfully in the direction of the beach.

"They stuck around," The Lion read from The Toilet Monster's non-verbal reaction.

The Toilet Monster turned to Joy: "They all have chosen to stay together and keep fighting to protect Joy too. They know she's up here now and, they know what she is going through."

The Toilet Monster then added to The Lion: "They will need all the help we can give them."

The Lion looked up to The Elephant, who acknowledged him with an approving nod. The Lion then faced The Cardinal, who was now hovering beside The Elephant.

"Cardinal, we are going to deploy your secret weapon once Autumn's full army arrives here," The Lion told him.

Joy became aware of The Wolf walking up beside her. He had a pair of hearing protection earmuffs that he was carrying by the headband in his mouth.

"Joy, you'll need to put on these earmuffs for your protection during Cardinal's siren," The Elephant explained to Joy before turning to the rest of the group. "Wolf and Penguin, I want you two to take cover in the grove and hit their right flank after they've all entered the meadow. Let the Cardinal's siren call be your signal to attack. The rest of us will move back down the main path toward the castle and take up our position at the edge of the forest. Lion and I will lead the counterattack head on with our remaining forces. Cardinal will stay back with Joy and once Bear arrives, he will stay back as well to protect Joy. I have a feeling Bear will need a break anyway, so we will keep him back as Joy's bodyguard. Toilet Monster, I want you to return to the beach to update Bear on our plans. Once you've accomplished that, you will rejoin Dolphin and attach the bombs to all of Autumn's ships except her own flagship and detonate them as soon as you can. We want Autumn to have a way back to her own castle after this is over. We will handle everything here in the meantime, but we still need you and Dolphin to join us as soon as you can."

"Sweet," The Toilet Monster winked at the group and then immediately shot upward with his jetpack. Once he had reached about a thousand feet above them, he darted downward diagonally in the direction of the beach.

"Race you there!" The Penguin exclaimed as she tapped The Wolf on the shoulder with her flipper. Joy was still in the process of taking the earmuffs from The Wolf's mouth when The Penguin suddenly flopped down on her belly in her tobogganing position and shot like a rocket across the meadow toward the grove.

"Isn't that cheating?" The Wolf wondered once Joy had removed the earmuffs from his mouth.

"How does she do that on anything other than ice or snow? Has anyone figured that out?" The Cardinal inquired.

"Extraordinary moments like this call for extraordinary gifts," The Lion replied to The Cardinal, "and we will be relying on yours to make all of this work."

"You know you still have it in you, buddy," The Wolf added to The Cardinal, "I'll see you all in a bit."

The Wolf sprinted after The Penguin toward the grove.

"Alright everyone, let's head back to toward the forest quickly, they'll be here any minute," The Lion ordered.

As The Lion, The Elephant, and The Cardinal all set out toward the forest, Joy took one last look in the direction of the beach before she joined them. She thought about how immense and powerful the invading army was and how they were all coming for her castle and her animals. Autumn had made that clear. But now that battle had begun, she couldn't help but feel like they were also coming for her.

"Joy? Are you still with me?!" The Custodian's voice asked.

3.7

Joy was back in the school hallway again. Through the corner of her eye, she saw that The Custodian was looking down the hallway in the same direction that she was now looking in.

"Are you waiting for someone?" The Custodian wondered.

Joy had turned away from gazing up at the ceiling and was glaring down the hallway in the direction of where her locker was. She had an awful empty feeling in her stomach, and it simultaneously felt like her lungs lost at least half of their capacity to take in air. Meanwhile, a throbbing pressure in her head started to expand across her face to her eyes and nose. She could subsequently feel tears streaming down both sides of her cheeks and experienced sudden nasal congestion as though this pressure had caused the discharge from her eyes and within her nose.

She turned back to The Custodian.

"You are crying," The Custodian observed with increased concern, looking around the hallway in vain for a tissue box as though one might magically appear.

"You wouldn't understand," Joy cried. She pulled her sweater up over her mouth, and then her nose, and then her eyes until the collar strained to expand over her forehead.

"I might not," The Custodian responded to Joy's sweater-covered head, "but I do understand crying and how it can be healthy to let it out in a place where you feel supported and safe. I know I don't know you well, but I'm here for you now. I can take you down to see Ms. Jewel if you think that will help."

"I thought maybe I was going to be somebody great," Joy reflected in a lowered muffled tone from beneath her sweater.

"You are great. You know how you meet someone for the first time, and you sense how they are different, like you already know they have greatness? That's the experience I am having with you right now even as you are hurting. You are great," The Custodian asserted with enough heartfelt sincerity that Joy was comfortable enough to pull her sweater down to reveal her red-face and continued tears despite her embarrassment from revealing herself in that condition.

"I am not pretty enough," Joy sobbed, surprised at how straightforward she was with The Custodian.

The Custodian looked down at the mop bucket in which the mop head had drowned in bleach-based floor cleaner. She was deliberating on how she wanted to respond.

But before she could respond, Joy continued: "I always wanted to feel like I was beautiful. I know you don't have to be beautiful physically to feel that way because I've been around other kids who aren't seen as beautiful by other people but feel that way about themselves and lead beautiful lives. Maybe I missed my chance to know what it was like to be beautiful because I didn't feel that way even back when I had friends. All of my friends I made in school when I was little stopped talking to me in middle school. Some of them are in my classes or I see them in the hallway...It's like I don't exist anymore at all, but here I am. I'm still here. I don't know what it's like to fit in anywhere. I don't know what it's like to be a cheerleader, or to go out somewhere with a group of friends without parents around, or to go to a high school dance, or to go on a date, and I'll probably never know about any of those things. All I can do is watch or hear about how other people enjoy them. I get to watch other people lead beautiful lives.

"For as long as I can remember, both my mom and dad told other people about how they gave up their beautiful lives to get married and start a family. I know about this, because I often overheard those same other people talk about how my parents once lived beautiful lives and how my parents wish they could get those lives back again. Now that I'm older, I know it's true because lately they have basically admitted that to me...separately. It's like I failed them by being born. Not only did their daughter turn out not to be beautiful, but I took away how they felt beautiful within themselves. Sometimes I wish I was born all over again, so I can try again to be beautiful, so beautiful that my parents are reminded how they are beautiful too. But I realize it would still be very hard to change my nose, my mouth, my ethnicity, my hair, my stomach, my shyness or my personality if I got that second chance. I may never learn how it is to feel like 'I'm beautiful,' and I wish I had just one moment to truly know what it feels like."

Joy didn't allow herself to see The Custodian's reaction. She didn't want to see it. Instead, she looked down at her shoes and her whole body shook a little a bit as she made an unsuccessful effort to hold back her tears.

"You can't be so hard on yourself, Joy," The Custodian whispered, as she set the mop handle carefully against the wall and looked at Joy with a maternal aura of profound empathy.

"You wouldn't understand," Joy cried. Her voice cracked as she said this. She was still struggling to mitigate her crying.

"It isn't fair to you to put what your parents have been through on yourself like this," The Custodian cautioned. "I knew both of your parents well enough to assure you that neither of them felt as self-assured as you are saying they were before you were born."

Joy suddenly stopped crying and turned to The Custodian in shock: "Huh?! You what?"

Joy then hiccupped at the abrupt stoppage of her crying. She breathed more deeply as if to prevent another hiccup and started wiping her tears.

"I grew up in the same neighborhood as your mom and knew both your mom and dad in high school," The Custodian revealed. "We were all in the same grade. I haven't spoken to either of them since we graduated from here, but I thought you might be their daughter right away by how much you resemble your dad. It's ironic I am talking to you now, because I happened to see your mom drop you off in the front parking lot yesterday morning when I was on my way in to work. It was my first time seeing her in almost twenty years. I didn't see her up close, but I couldn't believe how she looks almost the same as she did back then."

Joy initially maintained a blank expression as she processed the unexpected information The Custodian had shared. A strange feeling in the form of a burst of invisible electricity emerged at the back of her head, before flowing down a tingling current through the back of her neck. She naturally reached up with her left hand and held the back of her neck as if to interrupt the flow of this rare but familiar sensation that seemed to happen whenever she was on the cusp of an epiphany. She had remained locked in eye contact with The Custodian long enough to see the glassy change in The Custodian's eyes at the mention of her resemblance to her father.

"You are the woman my dad dated before he went back to my mom," Joy whispered.

The Custodian's look of concern for quickly disintegrated into a flat, wide-eyed stare downward toward Joy's shoes and then at her own. The Custodian was momentarily unnerved as though Joy's father had just split up with her all over again by virtue of his daughter being aware of it. Her reaction was so abrupt and intense that it was like she was reacting as if Joy wasn't standing there with her at all. She remained speechless as she gradually became aware again that she was in Joy's presence. Joy sensed a tension within her, a struggle to remain composed before she could fully return her attention to Joy.

"I'm sorry," Joy said softly. The expression of concern that The Custodian had previously shown to her had now shifted over to her face with a similar level of empathy.

The Custodian slowly raised her head back up and made eye contact with Joy. Joy could see how tears had welled up in her eyes and how she was now partially biting her lower lip.

"I guess maybe I should've known he would tell you, but it was never really his way to share anything like that, I mean that wasn't..." The Custodian trailed off.

"... his personality," Joy finished. "No, it's usually not at all. I'm surprised he told me too."

The Custodian didn't say anything but looked like she wanted to say something.

"We don't have to say anything more about it," Joy offered. "I won't ever mention we ever had this conversation to anyone, including him."

The Custodian continued to remain silent. Her eyes seemed to be telling Joy an entire story as though her lips were no longer capable of parting to sound out words.

"I should really get going," Joy indicated, looking down the hallway in the direction she needed to go in to get to her locker. "You don't have to worry about me, I'm okay. But let me know you'll be okay too before I go."

"Your father was my first and only love," The Custodian recalled. "I haven't seen him in twenty years. I never bothered to look him up or anything, because he hurt me so much. If anything, I've avoided him."

Joy bit her lower lip, perhaps as a subconscious reaction to recently watching The Custodian do the same when distressed. There was a part of her that was completely fascinated and curious about what The Custodian had to potentially share with her while the other side of her was also wishing she hadn't mentioned anything at all to The Custodian about her dad.

"Well, that's not entirely true," The Custodian acknowledged, correcting herself. "I do know a few things. I do know he's still married to your mom and that he has his own construction company..."

"...and that I'm his daughter." Joy added once she noted how The Custodian had trailed off again.

"And that you're his daughter."

"You still love him," Joy deduced.

The Custodian was blindsided by Joy's forwardness and reacted with a shocked, wide-eyed seriousness that made Joy regret saying that. Joy was about to apologize again, but then to her surprise, The Custodian unexpectedly started laughing.

"I suspected you might have been his daughter when I first saw you but told myself I was crazy for seeing him in you," The Custodian laughed. "I didn't know if he had a kid for sure. I then told myself you might have been a relative of his, maybe one of his nieces or something. Like I said, I haven't been exactly seeking him out or asking questions. I knew about the construction company from looking for a contractor to do some repairs in my home a few years back. I only confirmed that you were his kid when I saw you and your mom yesterday. I still can't believe how she looks the same to me..."

"You still love him," Joy repeated and smiled.

The Custodian laughed but with the kind of conscious laughter that suggested that she was laughing it off both to avoid responding directly to Joy's statement and to help her cope with the situation.

"I probably shouldn't be talking to you about all of this," The Custodian conceded.

"But how do you..." Joy hesitated in a thoughtful effort to ensure that she was going to ask the question with the right words that would minimize potentially offending The Custodian.

The Custodian caught the gist of what Joy was going to ask her.

"Not all of us need to be in a romantic relationship, Joy," The Custodian explained. "There are many people out there who are perfectly happy being single. There also those of us who are even more content because we know about what I call 'the deep love'. Very few people ever really get to know the deep love. Your Dad didn't know it, but he helped me discover this deeper form of love. It's an ongoing, conscious effort to know, to learn, and discover more of the deeper love within you. There are people out there who never learn about it. There are those who look to other people to copy their lives without knowing their own dreams. There are others who are simply living for or through other people without acknowledging their own internal wants and needs as individuals.

"The secret of living with others, being present for others, and helping others is learning to live with yourself, being present for yourself, and listening to yourself as you grow as a person. You are going to have those vulnerable moments when you realize you got wrapped up in everything going around you or wrapped up with what's going on in another person's life. Knowing the deep love within you will enable you to acknowledge when you've strayed too far away from who you are. Knowing the deep love will help you avoid becoming one of those many people who have fooled themselves into thinking they have reached their full potential or have only made it as far in life as they can possibly go. Knowing the deep love awakens you into knowing that love never ends and neither does the process of finding it in new and different forms as you recognize that learning more about love itself never ends in this life."

Joy wasn't sure how to respond. She tried to conceptualize "deep love" and it felt both overwhelming and unattainable to even think about it. But at the same time, it also felt like it was already something dormant inside of her. She felt uneasy, as though her mind and body had lost their sense of gravity. She looked down to find her feet were still planted on the ground. But the ground had become grass again.

3.8

When Joy looked up, she immediately collapsed to the ground in fear. She was still in the meadow, but at the edge of it in front of the forest and there was a group of villagers, soldiers, and knights running desperately towards her as arrows rained upon them from behind. They were young, old, and every age in between. They made up the remainder of her retreating defense force. The Elephant and The Lion lunged past them to enter the fighting to help cover them. Meanwhile, The Cardinal called to them and flew back and forth signaling to them to pick up protective earmuffs (just like the ones Joy had been provided) from a pile of earmuffs the animals had amassed in a line at the woodland edge.

Once some of the soldiers and villagers had put on or had begun the process of putting on the earmuffs, The Cardinal then started ordering and signaling them to regroup and to form a line of defense near the end of the meadow in front of Joy. The knights removed their helmets and started putting on earmuffs as well before joining the line of defense.

Joy remained low in the grass through all of this, with a view of the battle beyond the thin line of defense forming in front of her. She saw an arrow strike one of the retreating soldiers in her defense force from behind and watched as the soldier suddenly vanished in thin air. She blinked twice out of disbelief and noticed that the space the soldier previously occupied remained clear. She then saw a villager in her defense force disappear in the same way after getting slashed in the back with a sword by an invading knight while stumbling toward the new defense line. The same enemy knight was then hit so hard by one of The Lion's front paws that the knight's helmet flew off his head as he tumbled to the ground. The Lion roared and leapt on top of the enemy knight before striking him in the head. As the invading knight was hit this second time, he disappeared from underneath The Lion, causing The Lion to drop back to the ground.

The Cardinal looked at Joy once the new line of defense had formed enough to indicate to any stragglers within the defense force retreating to it on what they needed to do to regroup. The Cardinal couldn't tell if Joy saw him, so he flew over to her.

"Let's get back into the forest behind the trees," The Cardinal requested, sounding out of breath.

With the Cardinal flying beside her, Joy ducked back into the forest behind a tree with a large protective trunk that was surrounded by several other trees of slightly smaller but similar sizes. The tree that Joy hid behind had such a massive girth that it could have also safety protected two or three others of her size.

"I saw Bear heading this way, I'm going to direct him back here to join you." The Cardinal said once she was behind the tree. He then flew back toward the battle.

Joy wanted to look back through the trees at the battle but was now much more afraid she would get hit with either an arrow, spear, halberd, or sword, so she settled into a seated position on the ground with her back leaned up against the tree. She took a deep breath as she heard the sounds of the battle beyond the tree drawing closer to her.

As she about to take another deep breath, The Bear nearly made her jump up as he collapsed beside her to her left.

The Bear had an arrow in both his left shoulder and in his right leg.

Joy gasped at the sight of him and his wounds.

"It's okay," The Bear moaned as he tried to catch his breath, "we're kind of immortal, we always end up self-healing in situations like this. I know this even though I can't really say I've been in a situation quite like this."

The Bear sat next to her with his back mostly up against the tree and grimaced. He first held his leg as he tried to place it into a more comfortable position on the ground and then held his shoulder as though he couldn't decide which hurt more.

"It hurts though. Do you mind pulling them out for me?"

Joy raised an eyebrow as part of the quizzical response on her face before reluctantly sliding forward to his leg and grabbing the arrow. She closed her eyes before pulling. She turned her face away as if her eyes weren't already closed as she pulled at the arrow.

"Kind of immortal?" Joy grunted as she pulled the first arrow successfully out of The Bear's leg.

"Yeah, only you can make us disappear," The Bear grumbled after cringing in pain as the arrow was removed.

"But our soldiers and her soldiers are disappearing," Joy pointed out as she stood up beside him to take hold of the second arrow in his shoulder.

"Yeah, but they're all different than us animals." The Bear responded as he braced himself for another arrow removal. "Everything else can come into existence or disappear relatively easily here, including the castle. I thought you already knew that."

Joy was perplexed: "There is apparently a lot of things you guys think I should know about that I don't know." She then pulled the second arrow out of his shoulder with a similar approach she had used with pulling out the first. The Bear whimpered in a way that suggested he was in much more pain than he was letting on.

"Is this one of those times when you are going to make me guess?" Joy asked once The Bear had regained some of his composure.

The Bear somehow manage to laugh despite his pain: "You've always been smarter than you think. You've also always been smarter than you over-think"

"Okay, okay, just tell me, what is the difference between you animals and everyone else here?"

"Love," The Bear replied.

In an instant, as The Bear uttered the word "love" he gleamed as though all his pain had temporarily vanished.

Joy looked down at the ground with a half-grin and found herself looking down at tile-flooring.

3.9

"Love," The Custodian said softly and thoughtfully as if to herself, "the love inside of you."

Joy looked back up to her with a half-grin. It was that kind of half-grin that just appears involuntarily when she least expects it.

"That's what I mean by the deep love," The Custodian continued. "You aren't in control of anything that's going to happen to you in this life. It's all about how you handle what's immediately in front of you. You may not like what is in front of you, you may not like what is going on inside of you or how you were made. But if there is one thing you can still grab on to, something I still see in you, that's love. You can start there and find it can gradually make things better all around you if you embrace it to its full potential. You do that, then one day, you can finally look in the mirror and love what you see."

Joy maintained eye contact with The Custodian as her half-grin dimmed back into her resting-frown.

"I can't...." Joy began, but hesitated.

"Trust me, Joy," The Custodian continued after giving Joy a moment to try to finish her thought, "hear me out. Everywhere you go, you hear people talk about trying to change something about themselves. But often the most profound change that can happen in someone's life isn't the type of change that you notice right away or that happens overnight. It happens as a result of accessing the love already within you. It happens on a sub-conscious level. You slowly start noticing a change in your habits, in your thoughts, and in the way you deal with specific people and situations. You may change the way you do something on a regular basis and not realize it at first. It's happening, but you don't notice it right away because you have other things on your mind. Even once you realize it's happening, you may not know why it's happening at first. You might just be happy that it's happening, so you go with it. That's how generating real positivity within yourself works."

"I don't..." Joy began and then hesitated again. But this time, the words came to her more quickly: "If anything, I don't think I'm changing, I feel like I'm still stuck in the same place I've always been in...um, I might be drifting backwards."

"That's also a part of process," The Custodian insisted, "that's why you hear that saying about how sometimes you must first go backward to eventually move forward. When it comes to the love inside of you, you usually have to go backward first. But I can see it in you right here and now. You're close. There'll be a moment when you'll feel love bursting out of you and it won't be directed to anyone in particular. It will come from within you and only you will experience the gift of it. It will feel like it has inhabited every cell, like the universe is embracing you. Few people know love at that depth. They think just loving themselves is enough or they think this type of love is only love they can experience for their partners or children or specific material things. But it's a deeper love only some people will ever know about, and they are even better off if they learn it at an early age. I didn't know until I was 39 years old. But since I've known about it, I've had no difficulty with identifying other people who have it or are close to it. You, my friend, are close to it. The other girls that you may think are beautiful are nowhere close to it, but they can sense you are on to something because even though few embrace it, I believe we all have the ability to be aware of and access deep love."

"I don't..." Joy began again.

"You're close," The Custodian reiterated before she could continue, "you're right there."

"How do you know?!"

"You've always had it," The Custodian contended, "I bet the other girls here at school see it in you too. They don't want to realize it. They don't know what it is that they are seeing that you can't see. They just know they are threatened by it because they can't find it within themselves. They are nowhere near as close as you are."

"Okay," Joy muttered, looking pensive, "I think you've lost me"

"The deeper love," The Custodian emphasized, "the deep love."

"Yes, you keep talking about this deep love," Joy groaned, sounding fatigued by the topic, "and you talk about a moment just like my dad talked about."

"I was there for his moment," The Custodian reflected, "and then he walked away from it."

Joy's eyes widened with a gleam of renewed interest.

"He came close himself and he probably knows it. It's unfortunate, but few people ever embrace deep love," The Custodian reasoned. "You'll meet people who think they already know what love is or what it means to love someone else, but they have no idea and don't ever learn why they have no idea. They simply go on living believing they know love while thinking the emptiness they feel inside is a part of it because they are in relationships that would appear in every other way to be a relationship that should cultivate a deeper love for them. In other words, few people know deep love but so many others think they've either found it in someone else or at least experienced it at one time in the form of lust. But they were never open to knowing deep love within themselves. They never learn the true vulnerability, gratitude, sacrifice, openness, humility, compromise, and inner growth required to know and honor deeper love. They choose to live in a fantasy while settling for something far less than the love they are capable of. But Joy, trust me when I say, 'you are close'. You may be suffering, and you may be in pain, but the struggle is necessary to know deep love. You will only find it in the struggle."

A long silence followed. There was enough time for one tear to slowly navigate its way down the side of Joy's right cheek and another to gather in full form at the corner of her left eye.

"You're ready for your moment, Joy," The Custodian declared, breaking the silence.

"I don't..." Joy started to mumble, sobbing softly, "...know."

"Your moment will often happen when life gets hard to handle," The Custodian continued in a softened, calming tone. "It will often happen when you feel tired and aren't quite ready for it. But when it happens, you have gained enough knowledge and enough strength to take control of your moment, if you choose to. What you decide in that moment will affect the course of the rest of your life. It is one the most important decisions you'll ever make. It can determine whether people can reach their full potential, whether they will find peace, joy, and true love in their lives, and whether they will be able to reach their goals and achieve their dreams."

"If I choose to?" Joy asked in a near-whisper. "Why wouldn't I choose to?!"

The Custodian smiled before responding: "People frequently choose not to take on their moment. Your dad chose not to. They choose to continue to allow their lives to drift in whatever direction they may or may not have chosen for themselves. They drift along not knowing their lives can change at any moment and may not even recognize a moment if it hit them over the head. They let it pass them by, or they run away from it into their own little fantasy world. The world that the popular girls at this school live in is a fantasy. But their type of fantasy world is more deceptive than most fantasy worlds because theirs is so cleverly disguised to them as reality taking place in the present moment. They think they are living their moment, but it's not reality because they haven't really opened their hearts to other people, nor have they opened their hearts within themselves. They are allowing their minds and their hearts to be guided by only what they think other people want them to think and do. That becomes a fantasy. When you only focus on what other people think, you lose sight of what their hearts are saying. What their hearts say may be totally different than what their minds are thinking.

"But if you are willing to change, if you are willing to grow, and if you are willing to do more, you create a window of opportunity to be open to your true moment when it comes along. You must accept reality, allow yourself to be grounded, and let go of your desires and attachments to acknowledge the world around you objectively as it is. When you do that, you are more mindfully aware of how what people are saying and thinking doesn't always align with what their hearts are feeling. You aren't inserting your own desires into theirs or theirs into yours. You can't love yourself or the world around you without accepting yourself for who you really are, accepting that the people around you are who they really are, and acknowledging the world for what it really is. When you are able to do those things, you put yourself in a vulnerable place. But I don't think it's a coincidence that those rare moments tend to come along when you are feeling most vulnerable. It can be scary, but it can also be magical."

"You're saying people just drift along...?" Joy started to ask before second guessing the question she was starting to ask.

"They do."

"What will make me any different?" Joy looked down at the floor as she asked this.

"You may not end up being any different," The Custodian admitted, "but I know you have it in you to be."

"I can't...." Joy began again before stopping to think about her response once more, "...but um, thank you for talking to me about all of this. I really have to go."

"Joy!" The Custodian called out to her from behind as she walked away. "The deep love is worth it. I know it sounds overwhelming, but your love will guide you. Trust me, it will be hard. Anything worthwhile is usually hard. But it's always worth it."

3.10

The journey through the empty hallways to her locker from the cafeteria involved taking a route through the school's second-floor skybridge that was surrounded by windows on either side. Joy avoided the skybridge as often as possible (like she did when going to Ms. Jewel's office on the first version of this Wednesday) but she noticed from a quick peek out a window that it was raining outside again and she was already running behind on her plans.

She tried to ignore her reflection in the skybridge hallway windows as she quickly scurried past them.

The skybridge felt endless as she was flanked by her walking reflection in the windows on both sides. Depending on the way both the exterior and interior lighting highlighted each window, she could see herself in these windows with varying degrees of clarity. On previous walks through the skybridge, the clarity had been so sharp in the windows that she felt like she could've been looking directly in a mirror if the lighting was just right for that during certain times of the day. It took every bit of her focus to ignore these "window mirrors" as much as possible each time she walked through it, no matter how much she wanted to stop to think or to look outside. She found it was best to look straight ahead, or as she preferred when she was walking around the school in general, with her eyes lowered.

This time she managed to get halfway down this hallway of mirrors when through the corner of her eye using peripheral vision she found increasingly impossible to ignore, she caught a perfect mirror-like glimpse of how she looked in one of the dark gray windows. Though she was able to continue walking, she found herself revisiting a previous conversation with her mom in her mind that dated back to her freshman year:

"Are some people meant to be alone and single for the rest of their lives?" She had asked her mom.

"I don't know," her mom had answered, "I've always had someone with me."

"What about Uncle Tony?"

"He's pretty weird," her mom replied. "He chooses to be that way. Your father did all he could to help him through high school and even got him a spot on the football team. If he didn't turn into the loser he's become since then, I'm sure there would be somebody out there for him. Some people never get it."

Back in the present moment, Joy swallowed air and sucked her stomach in as she caught a less favorable glimpse of her reflection in another one of the skybridge windows. She then heard her mom's voice again from later in that same conversation from her freshman year:

"You probably think you can change your life for the better overnight, Joy," her mom had told her. "But even at your age, life is too cruel to ever let you get away with that. There are your old habits, your old ways, your old feelings that are always there lingering, and they come out just when you start thinking you might be changing for the better. They push you back down into the hole you were in to begin with. There is nothing wrong with being in that hole, because that's where a lot of people end up. As you get older, your pain gets deeper. When you are older, you'll be wishing you had it as good as you do now when you are still young and don't have as much as knowledge as you will have later about everything that is wrong with society. After you get older, it will feel like it's impossible to change because the world all around you is moving too fast for you to keep up."

Don't look, don't look, look away...
She couldn't get herself to look away and took another passing glance at her reflection. She tried in vain to manage her frizzy long strands of hair as she did so. Meanwhile in her mind, her mom's voice trailed off and was gradually replaced by Ms. Jewel's voice talking to Mr. Kingsapple in a conversation she overheard them having two weeks ago as she arrived at her locker to retrieve a book. She vividly remembered them holding their coffees while standing a few lockers away from her as she overheard Ms. Jewel say:

"No wonder these kids are either so anxious or so tired all the time: they're overstimulated! I think it would take months or even years for their brains to unwind for them to attain the focus our brains had when we were in high school. Nowadays, we are given so much more of an opportunity to be involved in each other's lives by taking pictures of ourselves, pictures of where we live, pictures of what we eat, pictures of where we go out, and pictures of who we are with at any given second of every day with phone cameras, videos, texting, and selfies. We insist on letting everyone know on social media how wonderful or miserable our lives are and then compare how wonderful or miserable we are to how extended family, friends, celebrities, complete strangers, and AI profiles appear to be. It's like we know more about one another than we ever have but still want to know more. We may know more about the false versions of ourselves we want people to see, but that still says so much about a person and what they are hiding about themselves, if you really think about it. Our parents and our grandparents kept secrets about everything going on in their lives and it was understood that privacy was to be respected, and taboo subjects wouldn't be talked about, but that's all gone. There are no secrets, and everyone is up close and personal with you whether you want them to be or not. That would tire me out or make me anxious too."

Joy stopped at the end of the skybridge and opened her email inbox on her phone. She scrolled through to Tuesday evening's emails and saw several confirmation emails indicating she had deactivated or requested permanent deletion of every social media account she had ever created (even the ones she barely used anymore).

She sighed and then continued walking.

She turned the corner into the hallway where her locker was located and looked around until her eyes settled hypnotically on a couple facing each other in a partial embrace. She stopped and stared at them, despite being aware of how obvious it would look to them. They were standing about a dozen lockers away from where her locker was located and were situated about halfway between where she was and where her locker was. She had never spoken to either of them but knew so much about them that she felt like she spoke to them every day. She knew their first, last and middle names, knew which classes they had together (she was in a lot of them), knew which subjects they liked, and knew who each of them dated before they ended up together. She knew all these things because for some reason during that fall semester, fate had placed her in all these situations where she was constantly in the same room, the same line, the same hallway, and the same general area they were in.

Of course, that wasn't totally true, but it seemed like they were always hovering around her. Since she had no one to talk to herself, she would overhear what was going on with them. She also overheard the other girls talk about them and analyze their relationship in the locker room during gym class and while they were standing in the lunch line at the cafeteria (in those few moments she had in the lunch line whenever the couple wasn't around). The other girls would compare themselves to the girl, talking about how lucky and undeserving she was to be in that relationship.

Joy looked down at the contract she was still holding while maintaining a peripheral glance at the couple. He was feeding her a brownie, one partially gooey crumb at a time. Joy peripherally watched for several seconds until she realized the seconds had been minutes and at that moment, looked around to see if anyone else had entered the otherwise empty hallway and caught her looking at them for that long.

No, as usual, no one had noticed her, not even the couple.

The only part of her body she could feel at that moment was her heart, because it didn't seem to be beating correctly.

She looked at the couple again, focusing in on the girl, who had a wide-eyed, dimple laden smile that appeared to involve every muscle in her face. *Was that kind of happiness reserved only for some girls? Was it predetermined to be that way? Why was she so teased by their constant presence in her life?* She had been hungry, but the empty air of loneliness filled her mouth down to her stomach and pounded her chest.

She took a deep breath that seemed to only exhale halfway under the greater weight of a new heaviness that she now felt all over her body.

She started walking down the hallway while looking awkwardly at the row of lockers on the other side of the hall from where the couple was standing. It was a concerted effort to hide her curiosity and look away from them as much as she could. Even so, as far as she could tell from quick peripheral glances at them, they still didn't notice her at all, as though they had the hallway entirely to themselves. *Could there really be someone out there for everybody and some people just miss their opportunity? What if there could be somebody for me, but I am missing out because I am the way I am? It's never an issue if you don't ever think about it, right? But if you aren't thinking about it, does that mean you might miss out on your opportunity?*

After she stopped in front of her locker, she attempted another deep breath that seemed to prematurely exhale without her consent. As she worked her away nervously through her lock combination, she was so shaky that she needed three attempts to open her locker after entering the wrong combination the first two times.

When she opened her locker door there was a sudden flash of light that caused her to involuntarily close her eyes and turn her head to the side.

"Are you okay?" The Wolf's voice asked her. "You seem to be distracted. I mean, you know, more than usual."

3.11

As Joy slowly opened her eyes, she gradually became aware that she was now sitting at the same table as before on the beautiful mahogany deck that was decorated for Casey's future wedding reception. The setting was similar to what it had been when she had met Casey there before, but there were differences in how the sky appeared and how the birds sounded. The temperature was also different. It wasn't as cold (but it was still cool). The sun had just emerged over the horizon with its rays parting through some of the pine trees that surrounded the deck. The sky was filled with dozens of clouds that were highlighted in yellow, orange, pink, and purple hues. The scent of piney renewal was still in the air, and a light dew was fading on the deck boards. She also heard hundreds of birds chirping, tweeting, whistling or singing in the background. These divergent sounds from the birds were so multi-layered that they uniquely blended to create a calming ambient background. All the string lights along the wooden railings and in the trees situated along the edge of the deck were plugged in and twinkling.

The deck was still covered with red carpeted walking paths around long, rectangular, fine oak tables set with red tablecloths. Imaginative plates of appetizers, diverse sets of drinking glasses and perfectly positioned silver settings surrounded orchid themed floating candles that were glowing faintly against the emerging daylight.

She was sitting in the same exact spot she had been sitting when she had been talking to Casey. But there were two key differences at the table: 1.) the absence of Casey (whose table setting had been fully cleaned up and reset as though no one had been sitting there) and 2.) the presence of The Wolf (he was sitting beside Joy in the chair to her left). At his table setting, The Wolf had a large gleaming sliver bowl in front of him filled with water that also wasn't there in Joy's previous visit. Joy had a filled coffee cup in front of her. The coffee was in the same type of cup that had been served to her when she had met with Casey there.

"I'm feeling a little anxious," Joy acknowledged to The Wolf. She was trying to sound casual about it, but she could hear in her voice that she didn't sound casual at all.

"This is a calming place for that," The Wolf observed, looking out over the thin fog still interspersed among the pine trees.

The Wolf starting drinking from the bowl of water, but then stopped for a moment after a few sips and looked at Joy.

"And the water here is so pure, it's like I'm in heaven," The Wolf whispered.

Joy was perplexed.

"Aren't you supposed to be hiding with Penguin in the grove at the meadow to help defend the castle?" Joy asked.

"Penguin and the others know I'm here now," The Wolf answered. "You see, we try to make sure one of us is with—"

"Me," Joy interjected, "I know, I get it now."

The Wolf pointed his muzzle in the direction of Joy's coffee, and then gazed at her, encouraging her to take a sip with his eyes. He reasoned to himself that even though the caffeine wasn't good for her anxiety, coffee seemed to be good for her soul. He recognized this logic was the result of being a die-hard foodie and an aficionado of good taste.

The coffee itself was still steaming as though it was making a warm inviting gesture through the cool morning air. She allowed the steam to warm her upper lip and nose before taking a sip.

Meanwhile, The Wolf stopped himself before taking another drink of water as though interrupted by instinctively sensing something was nearby. He turned to look behind them.

"What's his name?" The Wolf asked as he looked behind them.

"His name?!" Joy's right eyebrow perked up, and she looked behind them as well.

She turned and saw Gray walking down the red carpet path on the deck toward them in a full tuxedo suit.

"He can see me," The Wolf realized, looking surprised. "Believe it or not, he's familiar with both worlds. Maybe we can recruit him to help us fight Autumn."

"Oh no...his name is Gray, and he's definitely not a friend; stay with me, Wolf," she implored, just before Gray was within earshot.

The Wolf laughed: "Um, absolutely. I'm going to enjoy this."

"Stop," Joy giggled.

Gray walked past them around the table and past the seat that Casey had been sitting in during Joy's previous visit. He instead sat down in the seat beside Casey's seat, which was directly across from The Wolf.

"What are you doing here?!" he demanded as he glared at The Wolf, making no initial acknowledgement of Joy.

The Wolf made an unusual growling sound to suggest he was trying to speak but didn't have that capability.

Gray then turned to Joy: "I thought I saw you talking to him as I walked up here."

Joy forcibly laughed as though she was trying to laugh off what he said: "I was talking to him, I'll admit, but well, he is a wolf."

The Wolf smirked.

"It is already weird enough that you both are here," Gray sneered. "I would've never have imagined in a million years that

Casey would invite you here but here you are with a wolf. It blows my mind. Is the wolf safe to have around?! It looks like a wild wolf that randomly crawled up the stairs from the forest to get up here."

"This wolf is a friend," Joy tried to reassure him. "Wait, so there are stairs to get up and down here?! I was looking earlier."

Gray grimaced as though interacting with Joy was the last thing on earth he'd ever want to do.

"How else could you possibly get up here?" He asked incredulously. "Of course, there are stairs, and they are very memorable ones since it seems like it takes forever to get up here. They are way on the other side of the deck. Do you want me to show you back down?!"

Gray's tone from the start, including the sarcastic way he asked her about being shown the way downstairs didn't seem to faze Joy. The new anxiety she had been experiencing since she realized Gray was there had augmented the anxiety that she already had in anticipation of the day's upcoming events. Half of this new anxiety was that type of anxiety she would get whenever she wanted to express her feelings to anyone, including her parents. Despite Gray's tone, Joy still saw this as an opportunity to continue what had she started with him when she had seen him in the garden. She had just started to express her feelings for him when they were interrupted by his sudden, rapid-aging transformation. But it was clear now that his metamorphosis was only temporary. The other half of this new anxiety was that usual anxiety she would get from simply being around Gray. She would get this type of anxiety around him even when she was passing him in a crowded hallway at school without him seeing her. When telling Joy about her own teenage love stories, her mom had told her that there was an intense form of anxiety unique only to teen love. Her mom explained that teen love had a blend of excitement and anxiety that adults couldn't replicate in later years because people become more desensitized to everything as they age.

These various forms of anxiety, along with being in the future circumstances of an upcoming wedding between Gray and Casey placed her in an unsettling fight or flight mode: *Should I really try to tell Gray how I feel about him again? It's now or never.*

As the pressure increased to tell Gray how she felt about him, she wanted to disappear. That feeling of wanting to disappear was always present within her, often lingering in the background. She knew this because it had the capacity to emerge without warning to poke and prod around the front of her mind in any given situation or circumstance. It was a feeling that was at once comfortably familiar and achingly jarring.

By her estimation, romantic relationships were a natural occurrence for 99% of the population. Meanwhile, here she was in the other 1% experiencing a cascade of never-ending anxiety from her mind,from her chest, from her stomach, and even from her toes. The anxiety was flowing from all these sources at an accelerated pace, as though her body was energetically aware of all the red flags from Gray that indicated she was doomed to fail, even though her mind was oblivious to those same signals.

"Um, are you okay?" Gray reluctantly asked.

It took every ounce of courage she had left in her heart to speak and when she did, words came pouring out without her thinking about them.

"Gray, I love you, I've always loved you and I want to be with you," Joy blurted out in a shaky voice that finally gained confidence by the time she had uttered "be with you."

"We will never be together," Gray snarled without flinching as though he already saw this coming, "I don't see that ever happening."

He looked at her strangely— up and down.

"I can't picture it," he snickered, "no way could I ever see my-self with you, even in my imagination."

She was trying not to cry while also reminding herself she wanted to sound strong when she spoke again.

"Huh? In your imagination?!" she asked with added curiosity and volume in her voice. Her voice had still cracked a little bit de-spite her best effort. She hated how that always happened when she was trying her best to keep herself together.

"You know what I mean," Gray muttered.

Joy's entire body was now shaking visibly within her chair. The Wolf placed one of his paws on Joy's left shoulder to try to help re-assure and settle her.

"Whoa, why are you shaking?" Gray asked, sounding uncon-cerned and exasperated.

"I'm okay," Joy murmured. She lifted up her right hand and placed it on The Wolf's paw so that her right arm fell across her chest.

Gray was increasingly incensed that Joy was reacting so emo-tionally toward him. He made silent piercing eye contact with Joy to let her know this. She looked like she wanted to let her eyes trail off anywhere else, but her feelings for him wouldn't permit her to do that.

"Joy, you live in a complete fantasy world," Gray scoffed. "I have no interest in being a real relationship with you but somehow you are already acting as if we are in one. It's really messed up and the most pathetic thing I've ever seen in my life from anyone. You don't realize how one of the biggest ways you can insult someone you love is to pretend that you are already in a relationship with them when you know they don't love you back. We have never spo-ken to each other at school, yet you have this whole idea built up in your head that we are going to fall in love and be together for-ever. It's never going to happen and it's a complete waste of my time and yours to discuss it. I used to kind of feel sorry for you sometimes because I lived in a fantasy world a lot too when I was a little kid dealing with my parents' divorce. But I moved on and grew up. Obviously, you haven't because you can't handle me being real with you and you even brought a wolf here. I realize now you are a bigger loser than I thought you were."

As tears formed along the corners and lower rims of her eye lids, Joy tried to blink them away and dropped her hand from The Wolf's paw on her shoulder. Joy then turned to The Wolf, who appeared stoic in the same way The Lion often did. Joy was appalled that The Wolf didn't seem to be surprised at all by what Gray was saying. The Wolf even seemed like he had been expecting it. Joy was starting to feel alone as she thought about The Wolf's lack of emotion. It didn't matter anymore to her that his paw was still empathetically placed on her shoulder.

She felt pangs in the area around her chest and her stomach that felt like they were pangs from her soul. These were pangs filled with wistful longing for a life she didn't think she could ever access yet seemed accessible to everyone else. These were pangs to be able to live her dreams and to feel connected to others. These were pangs of longing for a world so distant and foreign to her that viewing that world felt like looking at a distant moon in the night sky.

She turned to Gray as if he was the only one who could save her from the condition she was in.

"But I am open to hooking up if you are interested," Gray smugly offered after a long pause.

Joy froze.

The Wolf was startled by her sudden change in posture and involuntarily pulled his paw away from her shoulder.

"I mean, just because we will never be together doesn't mean we can't still hook up," Gray added, appearing surprised that he didn't get an immediate affirmative response from Joy.

Joy remained frozen as though she had encountered a dangerous wild animal on a mountain trail while hiking that could potentially hurt her.

"Haven't you wanted to get with me for like several years?" Gray continued. "I mean, I have seen the way you look at me. Everybody has, they tell me all the time. I can't believe you have no response to that. Joy, I'm basically saying, we can do it if you want to. We can hook up today. Obviously, there would be some ground rules: 1.) you won't ever tell anyone, 2.) I always have complete control of everything we do together, and 3.) you decline any offer to be friends with Casey because she has told me she has thought about adding you to her inner circle. If I am going to be with Casey it would be too awkward to have you that close to her."

Joy finally moved again by checking to make sure The Wolf was still beside her. The Wolf turned to her and as they made eye contact, he maintained the stoic expression that seemed characteristic for a wolf but uncharacteristic for The Wolf. Joy's eyes communicated how disturbed she was by Gray's offer.

Gray noted the eye contact between her and The Wolf: "Even your wolf friend here would understand where I am coming from. If you are attracted to someone, you might as well hook up if you both are down for it. It's instinct and it's natural. Animals do it all the time too."

"Actually, studies have shown that us wolves are actually mostly monogamous creatures," The Wolf whispered to Joy. He broke through his stoic demeanor with the faintest chuckle.

An attractive, inexpressive man wearing a fine black suit and apron suddenly walked up beside Gray and caught the attention of both Joy and The Wolf. Joy recognized him as the same young server from her earlier interactions with Casey. The server was holding a clipboard and a pen. He placed the clipboard and the pen in front of Joy again beside her coffee. Like the paperwork the server had presented to her when she was with Casey, the front page revealed it was a contract, and like Casey's contract, it was around 40 pages long. She started flipping through the pages, initially wondering if it was a trick and if it was just the same contract as the one Casey gave her. But as she skimmed through the pages, she noted the language frequently mentioned references to sex. She came across one section that discussed protocol if she were to become pregnant, another section on procedures if Casey discovered that they had hooked up, and still another section on how future hookups were a possibility if Gray had determined he wanted more of them.

At that point, Joy decided to read no further.

As she looked up from the contract, she saw that Gray had been watching her with a diabolical countenance. She was amazed at how much thought and effort had gone into the contract. She didn't know if Gray could create something like that on his own. She suspected that Casey may have somehow helped him without knowing the details that may have been later added to it.

"But you just called me a loser," Joy reminded him (and herself).

"You wouldn't be a loser anymore if you got with me," Gray quipped.

Joy turned to the Wolf again, who appeared perturbed.

"Now you are finally upset that he's been calling me a loser?" Joy whispered to The Wolf, trying to minimize the movement of her lips as much as possible in front of Gray.

"I've been upset this whole time," The Wolf muttered.

"You sure haven't looked like it," Joy quickly whispered back.

"Come on, Joy, I'm a wolf, we are supposed to be strong and always look the part, um, duh..." The Wolf tittered.

Joy cackled. She tried to suppress it at first, but that effort only seemed to make it louder.

Both the finely dressed server (who had stayed behind after delivering the contract) and Gray were looking at them curiously.

"Uh, are you talking to this wolf?" Gray asked. His curiosity reverted to revulsion.

Joy was initially unable to respond as she concentrated on curtailing her laughter. Meanwhile, The Wolf returned to his stoic posture.

As if to curtail the awkward energy around them, the server checked Joy's coffee and The Wolf's water dish. Once she regained her composure, Joy was tempted to order a second coffee again but reminded herself that she had barely acknowledged the coffee she had. It seemed to be impossible for her to enjoy the things she loved when she was feeling so anxious. After finding that Joy's coffee and The Wolf's water dish were still at least half-full, the server left the area.

Upon realizing he wasn't going to get a response to his question and deciding it didn't matter, Gray reached over and tapped the contract in front of Joy.

"This is the opportunity you've been waiting for," Gray insisted in his best sales-pitch voice. He had decided he would overlook almost any form of strange behavior in exchange for getting laid.

Joy picked up her cup of coffee with the intention to drink from it but noticed by the shakiness of her hand that it would be difficult to do with Gray now studying her so intently.

She was able to take a sip, but some of the coffee dripped onto Gray's contract as she returned the coffee cup back to the table.

Gray looked briefly agitated over the coffee dripping on the contract before resettling himself: "Don't you ever go through life wishing you were someone else? Or like a better version of yourself at least? Believe it or not, I wish I was more athletic and a little taller sometimes. I know if I have these feelings, you must have them too. If you get with me, that can help you feel like you are someone else. You could feel like someone else I would want to be with. That feeling may not last, but it's probably better than any feeling you've had so far. Someone like you will be lucky to get moments like that...oh no, are you crying again?"

"You are really breaking my heart," Joy mumbled, trying again to blink her tears away.

"You are breaking your own heart," Gray shrugged. "I didn't ask you to fall in love with me. I hardly know who you are and have no interest in getting to know you beyond what I am presenting you with here in this contract. You should be happy that I'm doing this for you. Sign it so we can get this over with and move on."

Joy was unable to look at him or The Wolf. She started wiping the tears that she was trying in vain to hide from him.

"You aren't being very nice about this," she heaved while trying to catch her breath to mute any potential crying sounds.

"That's the thing with girls: they expect us guys to read their minds and know what they want. See I know this, and that's why girls love me. I know they expect that from me, but I know better than to be nice about it. Girls want a guy who is a challenge. They want a guy who is exciting. I could be genuinely nice to you, and most girls in your situation would get bored and lose interest, but I bet you in your case that you'd still be interested because you are so lonely and inexperienced. Girls as hopeless as you never get opportunities like this. The smartest thing you can do is sign the contract and just be happy that I'm even considering this."

At that moment, a new epiphany occurred to Joy upon hearing Gray use the word "lonely" to describe her: She had apparently maintained a "good feeling" about Gray for all these years because it turned out he was open to hooking with anybody— it didn't matter who you were. He was even open to her. She had also liked the person he was when he was a little kid. He was a kid who also indulged in his own fantasy world and dealt with his own childhood pain (in his case, it was related to his parents' divorce). Back then there was a common ground and she saw from a distance how his experience mirrored her own in some ways. But Gray's personality no longer resembled that of the kid she initially liked in kinder-garten at all. In fact, he was the opposite. She had remained in-terested in him due to memories of who she thought he was and due to the openness that she had sensed from him. But as she was learning now, it turned out to be "the wrong kind of openness." To him, she was just another piece of territory he needed to try to check off on a travel map that he'd probably never complete be-cause it would always be expanding with new girls he would meet.

Joy turned to The Wolf with the intention of reassuring him that she had a better handle on how Gray was treating her but instead found that his ears were back and his lips were slightly curled as he was looking over Gray's shoulder at an incoming wave of darkness that filled the sky.

The approaching darkness was behind Gray and therefore, completely out of his line of sight.

She observed how the wave of darkness was pure black and moving rapidly but eerily toward them like an incoming sand-storm as it enveloped sky and trees in its path. This darkness resembled the unique early morning darkness she kept re-experi-encing as part of the time loop.

"No this can't be!" Joy cried frantically to The Wolf. "I'm start-ing to feel like maybe I can find peace in all of this…"

"How…what? Nobody likes you. I don't like you. There are cer-tain…" Gray hesitated in thought before coming up with the word: "…characteristics that I need in a girlfriend. You don't have any of them. I don't know how you get up in the morning. You don't have any friends. I don't know how someone like you could ever feel at peace, Joy. I don't know how you aren't, like, suicidal."

Upon his use of the word "suicidal" the darkness completely enveloped Gray. With only milliseconds to brace herself for the in-coming wave of darkness, Joy hugged The Wolf tightly (with The Wolf leaning in to comfort her) and closed her eyes as the wave of darkness also consumed them (along with the unsigned contract as well).

3.12

"Joy!" The Cardinal cried in her direction from a distance somewhere overhead.

"Help me out here," he added in a lower voice that was now much closer to her, "we need her to put on the earmuffs! It's time."

"Joy!" The Bear yelled in her direction from immediately beside her, "You still with us?" The Bear was close enough to her that her entire body seemed to vibrate from the amplification of his deep baritone voice. It sounded so unusual to her when it was heightened like that.

Joy looked up from the ground with a blank expression to find The Bear awkwardly holding up the earmuffs to her with both of his paws. The Cardinal was hovering beside him. Both The Cardinal and The Bear looked like they were ready for anything to happen and expected whatever it was to happen at any second. As Joy looked at them, she became increasingly aware of how much closer the sounds of the battle were to their position. The battle was going on immediately behind the set of the large trees that was shielding them.

"I'm going all out with my effort this time," The Cardinal informed The Bear. "This will almost kill me. You know I lose my voice whenever I do this, but this time, it might not come back."

"You've got this," The Bear assured The Cardinal as he still held the earmuffs up to Joy.

The Bear then turned back to Joy and added: "Whatever you do, leave these on no matter what for the duration of the siren. Worst-case scenario, if you need to communicate something to others, let me or one of the other animals try to translate for you. We all like to think we can understand all the different languages of 'Joy' even if we aren't always fluent."

They all laughed and then Joy started to smile before it slipped back to her resting frown.

She took the earmuffs from The Bear and put them over her ears as she remained seated against the same enormous tree they had been hiding behind.

Once he saw that Joy had safely put on her earmuffs, The Cardinal flew a few feet away from them and closed his eyes for a meditative pause before his big moment.

With his eyes still closed, The Cardinal then opened his beak and a blazing, unorthodox, shrill siren sound blared out of him like an expanding tornado of sound. It was so powerful, its impact continuously rustled all the leaves in every tree around them like they were experiencing an earthquake.

Once he established his highest pitch, the Cardinal bolted forward as though he had been shot out of a cannon through the trees toward the battlefield. He maintained his full siren sound as he entered the fray. The Bear, who was without earmuffs and seemingly unaffected by the siren, looked at Joy and pointed in the direction of the battlefield. As he started to walk in that direction, he signaled to Joy to follow him.

As Joy followed The Bear through the trees back into the expanse of the meadow, she witnessed hundreds of Autumn's invading soldiers, knights and archers collapsing to the ground as they dropped their weapons and clutched their ears. Some of them were rolling around on the ground while others were vanishing entirely just from the sound of The Cardinal's siren. The remaining soldiers, knights and villagers of the defense force had held a thin defense line a few feet in front of the edge forest and were all safely wearing earmuffs. A substantial number of them rushed out into the battlefield and collected the weapons that were being dropped by the invaders. A group of these raiders primarily collected bows and quivers still filled with arrows to form their own makeshift archery unit.

Like The Bear, The Elephant and The Lion were not wearing earmuffs as it became clear that all the animals were uniquely immune to The Cardinal's siren. The Elephant and The Lion stood in front of the defense line while Joy and The Bear remained behind it.

The Elephant stepped forward and raised her trunk as high into the air as she could as a signal for the defense force to counter-attack. Immediately after the signal, all the villagers and soldiers with a bow and arrow fired a volley of arrows into the compromised invading force before charging forward alongside The Lion, the knights, and the other soldiers and villagers. The Elephant quickly joined them.

The Bear and The Cardinal remained behind with Joy.

The Cardinal had continued his siren at his highest pitch and was now flying back and forth over them in a pacing motion as if the movement was necessary for him to keep the siren going.

The Bear gently tapped Joy's shoulder and pointed out to her how there were about a dozen black and gray smoke plumes rising and expanding through the sky from where they had previously observed Autumn's ships on the ocean. The Dolphin and The Toilet Monster had successfully completed their mission.

The Bear then signaled her to follow him, and they started walking briskly across the meadow behind the rapid advance of the counteroffensive. The Cardinal kept up with them from above as he maintained his piercing siren at uncompromising decibels. The three of them maintained a relatively safe distance behind the fighting.

Any organized resistance by Autumn's army was impossible due to the Cardinal's siren, and around 80% of them eerily vanished from the sound of the siren alone. Those who remained were swiftly overwhelmed as The Elephant trampled over everything in her winding path, while The Lion ferociously pounced on others nearby with his claws. In an advancing row that had fallen behind in trying to keep up with The Elephant and The Lion, the soldiers and knights of the defense force attacked with swords, arrows, spears, and halberds. The villagers had gradually formed a second row behind them that vanquished the few that remained with either arrows or spears. The Bear, The Cardinal, and Joy were only encountering abandoned weapons, rations, and equipment. The Cardinal's siren had been far more successful than anticipated.

About halfway across the meadow, they were joined by The Penguin and The Wolf, who had cut off and destroyed the rear-guard of the enemy force with such ease that they were now attacking the main contingent from behind. As one might expect, The Wolf was pouncing on enemy soldiers with spring-loaded precision but to Joy's surprise, The Penguin was fighting even more fiercely than The Wolf was. She watched in awe as The Penguin conspicuously slid on her belly to knock over the enemy soldiers before pecking them with her sharp armored beak.

The invasion force had been reduced to its last few remaining soldiers when Joy suddenly felt a wave of pain originate at the top of her head and then flow down her body toward her feet. Only the area of her chest around her heart was spared of this pain. Nevertheless, she started having trouble breathing. She looked up and saw The Cardinal stop his siren. He flew haphazardly in a circle over their heads before suddenly thrusting forward like he had been propelled by a slingshot in the direction of the forest area where the counteroffensive had begun. The Bear watched The Cardinal with concern and was considering going after him with Joy but when he turned to Joy, he found she had fallen to her knees and was holding both of her hands on her head (that was still covered with earmuffs).

"Joy! Joy, are you okay!?" The Bear hollered despite the fact that Joy was unable to hear him with her earmuffs still on. He knelt beside her. Seemingly unaware of his presence, she was now looking blankly at the sky over the sea.

At the same time, the last invader vanished beneath the spear of an elderly villager, but Autumn was nowhere to be seen.

Before they could celebrate, they all noticed Joy was down and rushed in her direction.

But Joy had completely lost track of their progress and had no awareness that they were trying to help her as she was still looking up at the sky beyond the meadow, beyond the sea cliffs, and beyond the plumes of smoke from Autumn's burning ships. She watched as an encroaching darkness was filling the sky over the sea and was moving in their direction mysteriously at a slow, calculated pace. She noted that unlike the sudden complete darkness she had been experiencing each Wednesday morning (or the rapid onset of darkness she had witnessed while she was on the mahogany deck with The Wolf and Gray) that this incoming form of darkness was still glinted by daylight. Even so, it still maintained an ominous and frightening aura about it.

She allowed her arms to fall to her sides and closed her eyes as she made another effort to breathe.

3.13

Joy was able to take a slow, prolonged breath that didn't bring her any sense of calm even though it brought along the knowledge that she was capable of breathing again. Her stomach was in knots, and she felt goosebumps covering her body from head to toe.

She opened her eyes and found herself standing in front of her opened locker. The usual disorganized contents were inside of it in addition to her backpack.

She looked around the hallway and discovered the couple was no longer there and she was alone. She placed Casey's contract inside of her locker. She was breathing but it was harder to breathe than usual.

The feeling of being in an empty hallway felt like a friend in that moment, but the kind of friend she wouldn't normally want to have.

She thought about checking the time but felt that intuitive feeling that she was running out of time and decided that the few seconds it would take would only set her back further. She took out her backpack and clumsily pulled out all the books, notebooks, folders, pens and pencils that were in it in haste and haphazardly placed them anywhere she could find space in her locker. She double-checked to make sure the only thing remaining in her bag were her dad's pain pills. Once this was confirmed, she didn't bother zipping up her backpack but instead held it tightly to her chest like she was trying to hide something with nowhere to hide it.

After closing her locker, she sped across the hallway into the girls' restroom nearby.

The odorous restroom smelled like it hadn't been cleaned since the previous week. Joy wondered if The Custodian was so happy and relaxed because she took it easy doing her job. But as soon as that thought entered her mind, she did everything in her power to ignore it because The Custodian had been so kind to her. Once she had reminded herself of The Custodian's kindness, she added further reminders of how terribly the other girls treated the restroom and how the school was one of those really old buildings with an overall stale smell that was more pronounced in the restrooms. The restroom was dimly lit by ancient, faint fluorescent lighting and muted streaks of sunlight coming from a very small window located just beneath the ceiling directly across from the entrance to the restroom.

She checked all the stalls to make sure they were empty and saw that at least three of the eight toilets had been used but not flushed. She thought about flushing them, but again, told herself that there was no time.

On the other side of the room from the stalls, there was a large full-length mirror over a counter that contained a row of sinks. Joy placed her backpack on the counter beside one of the sinks after taking out the pill bottle. Throughout this process, she avoided any sight of her own reflection in the mirror by keeping her eyes trained downward at the counter, then at her backpack and then on her hands holding the pill bottle over the sink.

She noticed how her hands were shaking as she held the pill bottle and wondered if she needed to hold the bottle awkwardly with both hands to make sure she didn't drop it.

She sighed.

She looked up at the ceiling with intention as though she could observe the sky on the other side of it.

3.14

"Joy! Joy, wake up!"

The Bear was facing her and had placed his paws gently on each side of her shoulders to potentially assist with easing her back up to her feet if needed. But Joy was still on her knees facing the distant darkened sky. The defense force had removed their earmuffs and huddled around her. A wise woman from the village had set aside the spear she had been carrying to carefully remove Joy's earmuffs. Everyone in the group was looking at Joy with profound empathy and concern as though they had forgotten that they had just won a decisive victory to save their homeland.

"Is she dead?!" The Wolf wondered.

"Well, her eyes are still open," The Toilet Monster observed.

"She's not dead," The Lion insisted, sounding annoyed that anyone would assume that.

"It looks like it's going to rain any minute here..." The Penguin pointed out, "...maybe we should take her back to the castle."

"No, she's just being Joy," The Elephant concluded, "she'll come out of it any minute now."

They all continued to quietly surround Joy, hoping she would acknowledge them at any second while trying to think of possible solutions of how to handle the situation.

"Joy! We did it!" The Penguin then cried out in jubilation to encourage a potential re-awakening from Joy. "They're all gone now."

"Joy, we won!" The Wolf nudged Joy's right arm with his muzzle before adding: "I know it might be hard for you to take in at the moment, I can't believe it myself."

Joy remained unaffected as she watched the blue sky and white clouds continue to be absorbed by a large floating carpet of gray-black clouds that appeared to be interconnected as one dark fog-like cloud that could singularly cover a planet. The progress of this methodical darkness had now reached the sky over their heads.

"I'm okay," Joy said aloud as though to herself. She looked around at the others surrounding her and finally noticed the worry on their faces and their tense body language. They seemed to be completely focused on her and still oblivious to the changes in the sky.

After witnessing Joy stand up on her own and hearing her verify to The Wolf that she was "absolutely sure" that she was okay, the group dispersed. The Elephant, The Lion, and The Wolf were all immediately tended to by The Dolphin, The Penguin, The Bear, The Toilet Monster, and the medical staff of the defense force to treat their wounds. The Elephant had been hit by at least three arrows and a spear that had penetrated her armor. The Lion had been hit with an arrow, and The Wolf had been hit with two arrows (one of which The Penguin was able to pull out with her beak after her helmet was removed by the blacksmith who created it for her). The Penguin wasn't hit by any arrows, but the removal of her helmet had revealed that one of her eyes was swollen shut from being hit hard in that area despite having her helmet on throughout the battle. Nevertheless, she declined any assistance and enthusiastically helped tend to the others. Everyone who had participated in the battle seemed to have superficial wounds from getting grazed by swords, spears, halberds, and arrows or hit by shields, fists, kicks and various other blunt objects. The ability of Autumn's depleted army to still inflict that much damage after being nearly wiped out by the siren was a testament to how well-trained and tough they were.

The Dolphin and The Toilet Monster were dripping wet from their underwater mission. The Dolphin was wearing a diver's suit version of her space suit with one major upgrade: the diver's suit included mechanical arms that resembled The Toilet Monster's mechanical arms. The Dolphin had additional electrodes attached to her head that enabled her to control the arms and hands to help tend to the wounds of the others. Otherwise, her diver's suit contained the same tiny jets beneath her pectoral fins to lift her several inches off the ground and propel her movement on land in any direction.

The Cardinal was still noticeably absent.

After spending some time quietly observing the activity around her, Joy walked through the fallen debris of the battle in the meadow toward the edge of the cliff overlooking the sea. The animals and the remainder of her defense force eventually took notice, stopped what they were doing and followed (with some of them limping) behind her.

As they were walking behind Joy, The Lion was looking curiously at The Dolphin's outfit and gear. The Dolphin had noticed The Lion doing this earlier when she had arrived from the sea with The Toilet Monster and felt the need to say something, so she turned to The Lion.

"Technological advancements," The Dolphin quipped.

For a split second, just long enough for The Dolphin to see it, The Lion smiled before defaulting to his usual stoic countenance.

Upon arriving at the edge of cliff, Joy looked out to the sea and saw that nearly all of Autumn's ships had sunk, with only three of them still afloat. Two ships were covered in flames. Only Autumn's flagship was unscathed.

The scene confirmed they had been victorious, but Joy didn't feel like they had won anything. She somehow felt worse at the sight of the burning ships.

She turned to the group, which included the animals (sans The Cardinal), The Toilet Monster and about fifty others between the remaining knights, soldiers and villagers.

"I don't feel like I have anyone left for me in the real world…" Joy began, before pausing to look up at the sky.

The others all looked at one another as though each wanted someone else to respond because whatever they had to say initially didn't feel like it would be enough at this point. Meanwhile, Joy observed how the carpet of gray-black darkness had now fully covered the sky for as far as she could see.

"…that's probably why you all came back," she added, turning to the group again. "I don't have friends anymore and I can't make any new ones. All my old friends found new friends, and they act like we were never friends."

There was another pause.

"Life is so much more than that, Joy," The Toilet Monster finally replied.

"I can't make it without any friends, Toilet Monster," Joy confessed, with tears budding in the corners of her eyes. "It's too hard."

"It will be hard," The Elephant acknowledged, "but you are stronger than you think."

"No, Elephant, I'm not," Joy cried, wiping her right eye. She looked down at the ground to avoid eye contact with anyone and minimize the sight of her tears. She was looking at an area of the ground where the grass of the meadow gave way to rock that formed part of a sea cliff.

"You created a whole world here," The Elephant continued, "and you can do the same thing there, and make new friends with the right people who will naturally come along like they did here."

"No, Elephant, people don't understand me there like they do here. Autumn is right: this place is better for people like me and her. And my mom is right about how some people never make it in the real world, like as if they were never meant to. And Casey and Gray are right: there is no way I'll ever meet someone who will love me and want to be with me. I'm too ugly and I'm too weird."

There was a third pause. This pause was twice as long as the previous two earlier in the conversation.

"You're more than this, Joy," The Dolphin proclaimed in a way that reverberated through Joy's core.

"What?!" Joy was both dazed and flustered. "More than this?!"

"There is so much more to you than just this place," The Dolphin clarified. "We had a lot of fun when you were a little kid, but even back then all the signs were there that you had the intelligence, had the depth, had the ambition, and had the love in you to create something far greater in what you call 'the real world' then anything you've ever done here."

Joy wanted to say something, and her mouth started to move a little bit, but nothing came out.

"The real world is cruel, but the real world is beautiful. It gives you life, brings you joy, and fills you with love. But it will remind you that the act of living does not exempt you from disappointment, trauma, and pain," The Elephant added. "Everything Dolphin said is true. You have a love within you that will manifest itself if you stay strong and if you stay persistent. It's true because underneath that surface of cruelty in the real world and in your own heart, you'll find real love. It's the greatest gift you will find in the real world, and you will never have full access to it here. It doesn't come from a romantic relationship, it doesn't come from a friend, and it doesn't even come from the combination of all the love you can experience from everyone you know who loves you. It can only come from the love inside of you."

"I can't—" Joy began.

"But you can..." The Penguin interjected.

"...but I can't." Joy continued.

"You know we are behind you no matter what, because we are always a part of you," The Penguin reassured her. "We've given you options to create a life again here as an alternative to the real world and it's clear now that deep in your heart, you know there's a better life for you there."

"I can't, Penguin," Joy tearfully replied. "If I stay in the real world, I'm afraid that I will always end up being alone."

"And you could easily end up alone," The Toilet Monster conceded, "but you don't have to be. When you open your heart, the right people will find you and you will find them. But if you choose to hide and deprive yourself of love, you'll live in self-doubt and most of all, you'll live in fear..."

"There is so much to be afraid of," Joy muttered. But then, as she finally looked up and made eye contact with The Toilet Monster, she started to laugh unexpectedly: "I'm honestly still kind of afraid of you right now."

The Toilet Monster genuinely laughed along with her before returning to his softened, serious tone: "Trust me, I know. But love can't fill your heart if you are already overflowing with fear. You may think love is the primary force in your life, but you are not allowing real love into your heart when you are always finding reasons to be afraid. That kind of constant fear holds the dominant place in your heart. Yes, fear can and will fill your heart if you let it. Once you know real love and let it into your heart completely, then fear has nowhere to go and will have nowhere to hide. People think real love can only come from other people you have relationships with. But real love isn't possible to have in relationships unless real love is first attained within both people individually. Real love comes from within you before you can experience it mutually with anyone else."

Joy turned to The Bear, who nodded in agreement.

"The real love is always inside of you," The Bear added, "but it's easy to forget that it's there unless you let it into your heart to remind you of who you are and what you can be."

"I hear what everyone is saying about love inside of me. But no one is telling me how I can find it," Joy grumbled.

"You have to face your fear," The Toilet Monster said.

Joy looked down at her both of her hands and found the pill bottle there cradled between them.

3.15

J oy was back in the girl's restroom observing the pill bottle, which remained cradled within her shaky hands.

She took the longest deep breath she had ever taken in her life, but it seemed to be ineffective at alleviating her shakiness.

She thought about how the bell for the next class was going to ring at any minute and time was running out. After fumbling around with the bottle for what felt like several minutes, she was able to open the cap, but when she attempted to dump as many pills as she could into her right hand, the cap and a few of the pills fell into the sink. She then accidentally caught a quick glimpse of herself in the mirror as she tried to retrieve the pills. She was immediately disgusted with how ugly she thought she looked.

She groaned.

None of the pills had fallen into the drain.

She carefully but nervously scooped up the pills that were in the sink into her right hand. Her right hand was already holding at least a half-dozen of them. She continued to hold the pill bottle in her left hand as she used a few of her left fingers in a scooping motion to fit the pills into her right hand with the others. She left the cap in the sink.

She looked at the fistful of pills and sighed.

"I wish I was someone else," she declared to the empty, dim, leaky restroom.

She had more she wanted to say, but before she could continue, she heard The Dolphin's voice: "Where's Cardinal?"

3.16

"He flew off into the forest after he finished the siren. Probably to rest somewhere safe where he could have some privacy," The Bear responded to The Dolphin back in the meadow.

Joy was still looking down at her hands, but this time they were empty.

"You know how self-conscious he gets about being so exhausted from doing the siren. This time must have really taken a lot out of him," The Bear continued, "I'm sure he's—"

The Bear stopped himself the moment he noticed a large group of people emerging from the forest behind them into the meadow and organizing into an attack formation. The Bear was shocked to see how they were entering the meadow from the area of the forest where he had been at earlier with Joy before the counteroffensive.

"Who are they?" The Wolf raised his tail.

"I think..." The Bear hesitated and continued staring out at what now appeared to be thousands of people flooding into the meadow from behind all the trees surrounding it. "...it's a whole other army."

"The biggest one I've ever seen," The Penguin estimated.

"Everyone, fall into the last stand formation around Joy." The Lion ordered.

The remaining soldiers, knights, and villagers formed a semicircle around Joy with their weapons drawn. The animals surrounded Joy within the semi-circle. Their backs were to the sea cliffs. An army that was ten times larger than the previous one they had faced was assembling rapidly in the meadow. As it grew in number, this army was expanding across the meadow in a similar way that the darkness had expanded earlier across the sky.

Joy suddenly felt something in her right hand. But when she looked down, she saw that the pills weren't there.

The Penguin had placed one of her flippers into Joy's right hand.

Joy turned to The Penguin and made eye contact with her.

"Never give up hope, Joy," The Penguin whispered.

"I wish I could have hope," Joy mumbled in response to The Penguin. But before Joy had completed the "I wish" part of the sentence, The Penguin's flipper had vanished and had been replaced with pills.

3.17

"**I** wish I could have hope," Joy requested aloud to herself in a way that echoed through the restroom. She clenched her right fist over the pills.

Her wish felt like an old familiar friend who had entered the room to comfort her but could only stay for a minute before it left her feeling even more lonely than she felt prior to its entry.

"I wish I could have love," she whimpered as she sank down slowly to her knees with her right hand still clenched over the pills and her left hand still gripping the half-filled topless pill bottle. The cap to the pill bottle remained in the sink. She held both of her wrists up against the edge of the counter but leaned her head down underneath it as if to hide as she started crying.

"I wish I could be beautiful," she cried.

As she finished her last wish, there was suddenly a rapid tapping sound from somewhere in the bathroom. Joy was shaken by it and nearly dropped the pills again (as well as the bottle in her other hand). Remaining on her knees, she hastily looked around but realized she hadn't caught the direction the sound was coming from.

She sighed and awkwardly stood up again with some difficultly as she continued to hold on to the pills with one fist and the pill bottle in the other.

Once she found her balance, the tapping returned.

It was overhead.

When she looked up toward the window, she saw The Cardinal perched on the other side of the window staring back at her.

Upon making eye contact with him, she involuntarily shielded her face with her arms out of embarrassment, with one arm over her mouth to try to muffle her sobbing.

The Cardinal started tapping the window a third time with his beak. Each round of tapping contained around a dozen window taps in rapid succession.

Joy realized she was holding up the pill bottle in plain sight of The Cardinal as she shielded her face from him. She lowered her arms and looked at The Cardinal again.

"I can't..." Joy cried to The Cardinal.

The Cardinal tried to speak but was unsuccessful. Undeterred, he simply tapped on the window with his beak again as a response.

"I..." Joy hesitated. She could feel the love in the concerned look The Cardinal was giving her. It felt like he wasn't just representing himself with the love she felt from him but was also radiating the love of all the animals who were not present.

The Cardinal opened his beak again, but he was again unable to generate a sound. Once it became apparent that he wasn't going to succeed, he tapped on the window again instead. This time, he only tapped a few times. They were slower, gentler taps.

Joy and The Cardinal then maintained eye contact in a tense silence.

Joy could feel her heart beating rapidly in her chest, it was so prominent that she felt like she could almost hear it going at the same pace that The Cardinal had used when he was initially aggressively tapping on the window.

The Cardinal started tapping rhythmically on the window.

At first it confused Joy, but she recognized over time how it sounded beautiful. It took her another moment to realize The Cardinal was tapping the melody he had created for her in the soccer field that day when she was shunned by the other girls as a little kid. He was intricately tapping the melody she loved and used to ask for whenever she was feeling down. She had never heard him do a "tapping version" before, but it sounded brilliant. It sounded as good as it did when he had sung it to her outside her bedroom window.

Joy spontaneously cried out as she listened to the song.

But for once in all the crying she had recently experienced, this was a good cry.

She was able to softly control her subsequent weeping in a more muted form and although the song didn't seem to immediately slow her heartbeat or clear her mind, it gave her a sudden sense of her own strength.

She finally looked away from The Cardinal as he continued his performance and carefully poured the pills back into the bottle. She then extracted the bottle cap from the sink and slowly twisted it back tightly back on the bottle.

"You did it, Joy," The Toilet Monster's voice echoed through the restroom.

3.18

"You did it, Joy," The Toilet Monster repeated, looking at her. She was back at the edge of the meadow, where The Toilet Monster was now standing beside her, holding a crossbow he had obtained when The Lion had given the order for the "last stand" formation. It was the first crossbow Joy had seen on the battlefield, so she wasn't sure if The Toilet Monster had picked it up from among the debris of the earlier battle or brought it on his own.

Joy was still holding The Penguin's flipper.

"Did what?" Joy smiled to The Penguin as she gently released her flipper.

There was no response.

Joy finally turned to The Toilet Monster and was baffled to see that he had tears in his eyes.

"Wait, are you crying?" Joy inquired, looking at him curiously with noticeable surprise that he was capable of crying. The Toilet Monster still didn't answer her and made no effort to wipe the tears that were now falling down the area she would have identified as his "cheeks."

The Toilet Monster then suddenly dropped his crossbow to the ground.

With his right hand, The Toilet Monster opened a compartment in the area of his left wrist that revealed a control panel with a touch screen. With his right index finger, he entered a complicated code on the touch screen that looked like he had to press at least fifteen different buttons.

"Self-destruct mode activated," an unfamiliar female robotic voice said from what must have been a speaker around the same wrist area where the control panel was. "You have five minutes remaining."

As they all turned to him, The Toilet Monster made eye contact with each of the animals individually, one by one. Meanwhile, the enemy army had fully assembled and advanced forward to face what was left of the defense force.

The defense force had reconfigured their position to add more defense in depth while keeping their weapons pointed in the direction of the enemy: There was a front row of soldiers and villagers kneeling in front of the group with bows drawn and arrows aimed. Behind them, the remaining villagers, soldiers and knights stood in a row in front of Joy with their spears and halberds pointed out above the front row. The animals and The Toilet Monster had held their position surrounding Joy as her last line of defense. Some of the remaining soldiers were still quickly finishing up tending to the wounds of some of the animals.

Once The Toilet Monster had connected silently with each of the animals, he took a few steps back from the group to address them. He stood at the very edge of the sea cliff.

"Make sure everyone on our side stays positioned behind our front line. No one move beyond it until I'm gone," The Toilet Monster instructed the group before looking directly to Joy. "It's time for me to go, Joy. Good luck in gym class today and remember, you're stronger than you think you are. Life will never stop giving you reasons to be afraid, but you also have the ability to always find reasons not to be."

The Toilet Monster closed the control panel on his wrist and blasted off with his jetpack. Joy and the animals watched as he stopped his ascent once he was around a thousand feet above them. As he hovered directly overhead, Joy wanted to try to shout something to him to ask about what he was doing. But before she could say anything she had the unique odd feeling of someone directly staring at her as if they were trying to burn a hole through her. When she looked ahead of the front line, she saw it was Autumn. They were able look directly at each other through a narrow gap that remained in place through the crowd that was positioned between them. Joy stepped out in front of the animals from in between The Elephant and The Bear for a better view of Autumn.

Autumn had approached the defense force with a contingent of knights, soldiers and archers that were standing or squatting all around her with their weapons aimed at the defense force. One of the soldiers standing beside Autumn was carrying a white flag to indicate they were interested in negotiating a truce. The size of the contingent that had accompanied Autumn was approximately the same size of what was left of Joy's defense force. Autumn's main force remained fifty yards behind them.

"Congratulations, Joy! You've actually impressed me. You fought off my diversionary attack!" Autumn exclaimed sarcastically.

"Diversionary?!" The Lion repeated as if to himself in disbelief and looked up at The Elephant with uncharacteristic angst.

"But no one opposed or even took notice of my main army that landed near the village that you inexplicably abandoned. We went up the other side of peninsula through the forest completely undetected. We chose to spare your pathetic castle that we would already have in our possession, but I realized I don't really want it after all...it's not worth all the repair it needs from being neglected for so long. Plus, I honestly felt sorry for all the people you had there who weren't in any condition to fight, though I admire that they would have. You really have a great group of people here, but I'm disappointed that you left none of them to defend either their village or the castle. I guess I'm not surprised. By the way, we didn't want your empty village either. Did you really think that my entire army was coming up from that beach?"

"Wait, how are you with them?!" Joy asked. "Your ship is down by the beach."

Autumn sighed.

"Again, Joy, that was a diversionary attack. It was meant to fool you, and it succeeded beyond what I could ever have imagined. That ship is just a look-alike I sent with the diversionary fleet. That is a decoy. Come on, Joy, you are better than this. You still look so lost here to me. It's like even when you are in this world, you might as well be at school."

Joy legitimately felt as lost as she must have appeared to Autumn. She thought about how to respond for a moment before determining that it would be best to be honest since Autumn seemed to read her so well anyway.

"I still don't understand why I am here," Joy confessed. "I don't know how I returned here."

"You never completely left," Autumn replied flatly. "You may not remember this place very well in your mind, but your heart never left here. In that sense, it's kind of like you never left at all."

"But I really don't remember—"

"That's just it, you didn't have to," Autumn continued, "that's why people like you who think they have no future inevitably look for and find comfort in the past. It's true whether you are conscious of it or not. Sad people like you are so unhappy in your present lives that you eventually find comfort in a revisionist nostalgia of those previous times in your life when you were ironically probably as unhappy as you are now. But your mind has even more control of how you view the past than it does of how you live in the present. Your mind can filter or block out so many of the memories, both good and bad, and you can choose to reflect only on those few moments when you felt great. You are already starting to do that, Joy. I knew you when we were little kids and you weren't happy at school back then either, even when you had friends. You were only happy here, that's why you are remembering this place again. At one time you thought you moved on from it, but no, here you are. So why not stay here with me where you can live a life truly worth living? You and I both know your life is a total waste in the real world and you are realizing it always has been."

"I don't—"

"Then you leave me no choice." Autumn interjected.

Joy took a step back and felt her back up against a wall. Realizing there was no actual wall behind her, she looked up in a panic and saw that she was leaning up against The Elephant's right front leg. She made eye contact with The Elephant's right eye before hugging The Elephant's leg with both of her arms in a backwards hug.

"All archers come forward and take your aim," Autumn ordered.

More archers within Autumn's negotiating contingent came forward in front of the knights and soldiers to join the archers that were already up front with their arrows aimed. Several of them took aim at the animals and Joy. A few of them also had their arrows aimed up at The Toilet Monster as he still hovered above the defense force.

The Elephant positioned her trunk across the front of Joy's body in a protective posture while The Bear also squeezed into a space immediately in front of her.

Joy braced herself as though she was caught in the middle of a desert in the face of incoming sandstorm and closed her eyes as she held on tight to The Elephant's leg.

3.19

When Joy opened her eyes, she was back in the school bathroom looking at the closed bottle of pills in her hand. She turned to the window and saw that The Cardinal was still there, gazing back at her. He had stopped tapping the song to her, but when she looked at him, he gently tapped at the window a few times with his beak again. He then started to try to sing to her.

No sound came out.

He stopped, looked down, and reset himself.

Joy opened her backpack and put the bottle of pills back into it. As she zipped up her backpack, she felt an immediate anxiety about the process of returning the bottle of pain pills to her dad's medicine cabinet without him noticing. But this was somewhat alleviated when she remembered that during that night, she will have a window of opportunity after her dad goes to bed early while her mom would still be away from home at Aunt Katrina's house.

It was at that moment she heard faint, melodious chirping coming from the window.

Upon recognizing her favorite melody, she looked up and saw The Cardinal moving his body up and down excitedly as he sang their song. His voice sounded thin and weakened from his prolonged siren "song" during the battle. Although he was moving up and down out of enthusiasm, it also seemed like a necessary action to propel the song out of himself as he struggled to hit the higher notes.

Joy started to smile as she picked up her backpack and clenched it securely but awkwardly against the front of her upper body. But she stopped short of a complete smile when the fluorescent lights in the bathroom started abruptly flashing in succession. As she looked up curiously to inspect them further, she found herself looking upward at lightning expanding across a dark, swirling sky.

3.20

Flashes of lightning unaccompanied by thunder had emerged at various points throughout the grayish-black cloud-carpet that covered the sky. This lightning added illumination and greater tension to the standoff in the meadow below. The darkness remained tinted in the context of daylight just enough that Joy was still able to clearly see The Toilet Monster hovering above them during the intervals when lightning wasn't present.

The Toilet Monster was looking off into the distance in pensive contemplation. He seemed to be unconcerned by the emergence of lightning in the sky.

Joy tapped on The Bear's upper back (as close to his shoulder as she could) and then nudged his right arm to move over to his left where there was still some space for him to stand.

"It's okay," Joy whispered to The Bear, "I have to face Autumn."

The Bear grunted and then groaned before reluctantly moving out from in front of Joy. The Elephant's trunk remained around her as a long, protective shield.

As soon as The Bear had moved away, it revealed how Autumn had continued to glare intently in her direction. Autumn smirked upon resuming eye contact with Joy.

The tension was all but suffocating as both sides stood ready to engage, with their weapons aimed at one another.

"You may fire when—" Autumn began while maintaining her burning glare in Joy's direction. But before Autumn could utter the word "ready," The Toilet Monster shot like a hypersonic missile toward the center of Autumn's main force well behind where Autumn was standing. Because it happened in a flash, Joy was only able to vaguely observe The Toilet Monster's body transform into a dozen bolts of purple lightning that eventually clustered together and moved at the speed of actual lightning. This phenomenon distracted both sides from firing at one another as everyone winced and covered their ears from the thunderous roar that was created from it.

Although it had sounded like an explosion had occurred, there was initially no actual explosion created. Instead, once the lightning struck the exact center of the Autumn's main army, a massive gust of wind blew throughout their columns, causing many of her troops to either tumble to the ground or drop their weapons. At first, the soldiers and knights in the immediate area hit by the purple lightning appeared to be unaffected but were nevertheless in a daze. The wind also reached Autumn's forward-detachment and Joy's defense force, but they only felt the peripheral impact of it and were able to mostly keep their balance.

There was an eerie silence for several seconds as both sides looked up at the sky and around at one other in confusion.

There was an ominous sense that this was only the beginning.

The silence was initially interrupted by what sounded like a jet flying in the distance and then followed by another clap of thunder that was equally as piercing as the initial sound. This time it was accompanied by a large explosion of faintly visible air that created a large wave from the site where The Toilet Monster had struck. The wave's visible air was minimally outlined by particles that gave the naked eye a view of its shape even with the darkened sky as a backdrop. The 360-degree wave spread as an expanding circle from this site of origin, and it appeared to be about three feet off the ground. It instantly caused all the knights, soldiers, and archers within Autumn's main army to vanish upon impact as it rapidly consumed their entire formation within seconds.

Once it had destroyed Autumn's main army, the visibility of the wave disappeared, and its force diminished significantly into the equivalent of another powerful gust of wind that shook the trees in the forest surrounding the meadow. The nearby grove within the meadow was rattled the hardest among the trees in the area but remained intact. This second gust of wind, however, knocked Autumn and several of those around her to the ground. The residual wind softened to a slight breeze just as it reached Joy's defense force, and they were able to regroup and re-aim their weapons at Autumn's disorganized contingent. As the breeze subsided, it became clear that only Autumn's negotiating contingent remained of her army.

"The Toilet Monster just totally saved us," The Penguin blurted out through the aftermath as she watched Autumn and the rest of her army either stand up or try to find their weapons, "I'm really going to miss him."

"Like Wolf alluded to during breakfast on our second Wednesday, he's an example of how you can't always judge someone by a first impression," The Bear reflected.

"Eeee," The Dolphin added as a sign of agreement.

"True," The Lion concurred.

"I tried to tell you guys he was special," The Wolf reiterated. "I think I'm the best judge of character in our group."

"The best?! No way," The Penguin laughed, "you only talked about his culinary skills and his coffee."

"Um, guys..." Joy mumbled as she pointed to Autumn and her forward contingent, "...look."

Autumn's contingent had resumed their positions and were now aiming or pointing their weapons in their direction again.

Both sides resumed a silent standoff, and the tension was even more palpable than it was before. Joy observed that Autumn looked like she wanted to say something but wasn't sure what she was going to say. Autumn's mixed facial expression seemed to indicate that she was trying to hide deeper emotions, such as sadness that most of her army had disappeared or anger that her plans were abruptly derailed by a mysterious supernatural experience that she couldn't explain.

Joy felt obligated to say something too, but as she was about to try to request a peace offering, a bell echoed in both of her ears as she opened her mouth to speak.

3.21

Joy was startled by both the school bell ringing and the sound of another girl rushing out through the restroom door to get to her next class. As she turned to witness the girl (who she didn't know) running out of the restroom, it occurred to her that it was the second bell signaling the start of the next period.

She was late to gym class.

She had been totally oblivious to the first bell to mark the end of the previous period.

She must have been standing there awkwardly in front of the sink clenching her backpack in a tight hug in front of the bathroom mirror the entire time there were other girls using the sinks and stalls around her. The scent of various perfumes intermixed with the usual unpleasant restroom smells along with freshly dripping faucets and the lingering intuitive feeling that people had seen her and judged her seemed to confirm this.

She felt a slight stiffness in her neck that reminded her she had also been looking at the ceiling for at least part of the time after she had seen the fluorescent lights flashing. She cringed at the thought of various girls observing her standing in front of the sink while glaring mysteriously at the ceiling and hugging her backpack. She decided to stop thinking about it and try to pretend it didn't happen as much as possible with the hope that this memory would go into the part of her brain that disposes of the tiny repetitive and inconsequential details of life that she forgets about before the day is over.

She looked over to the window and saw that The Cardinal had disappeared.

She looked at her backpack and sighed.

She exited the restroom and stopped by her locker. There were only a few remaining students in the hallway. A couple of them walked in opposite directions but moved similarly in a slow, reluctant pace to class. They were resigned to their fate of being late and unconcerned about the consequences. A third student with an overstuffed backpack that seemed larger than his small frame was running as quickly as he could through the center of the hallway as though his life depended on his arriving to his class as soon as possible (despite his tardiness). His overstuffed backpack made Joy think about how most of the time, her backpack probably looked that ridiculous to other people too.

Joy opened her locker and placed her backpack inside of it. She then stared into her locker for what felt like several minutes until she realized that she was now standing in an empty hallway looking at nothing specific among the cluttered mess inside.

She closed her locker.

She started to turn away from it when she turned back and opened her locker again. She searched through it until she found Casey's contract where she had stuffed it underneath several notebooks and folders. She took out the contract, removed the clipboard and placed the clipboard back on the upper shelf of her locker. She couldn't find the pen that went along with it and gave up trying. She then divided the contract into tear-able portions before tearing each divided portion in half. She allowed the halved pieces to tumble down to the tiled floor as she progressed. Once she ripped the last divided portion of the contract in half it suddenly vanished while still in her hands. She looked down at the remaining pieces of the contract on the floor and watched as they disappeared as well. She then turned back to her locker and saw the clipboard disappear as it entered her line of sight.

She blinked in amazement, but when she looked again, she saw that they were still gone.

She shrugged.

She wondered if the pen that went along with the contract had also vanished while lost somewhere within her locker.

She sighed.

As she closed her locker again, she heard Autumn's voice in her ears, but it sounded muffled and distant in a way that indicated that Autumn wasn't talking to her in the hallway. She initially couldn't distinguish what Autumn was saying until she heard her say: "There is more to you than I thought, Joy."

3.22

"I don't know what to make of you. You genuinely have no clue of how strong you really are. It's sad that other people also don't know how strong you are or if they do, they don't appreciate it in the way you deserve," Autumn pondered. As Autumn's voice became clearer and closer to her, Joy felt The Elephant's trunk shielding her body again. Autumn was looking at her curiously and everyone around them were still facing each other with weapons aimed or raised.

"I didn't think this would be easy, but I'll admit I thought you'd make it easier for me. I only have known the Joy from school, so it makes sense that I would think that way, right?!" Autumn casually laughed as she said this and then looked around to see if the others would laugh along with her, but observed that everyone else was silent, tense, and still ready for a fight to break out at any moment.

"I'd love for you to join forces with me here, but you don't have to do that," Autumn continued after that uncomfortable pause. "You can go ahead a live more of a miserable life again in the real world. I feel kind of sorry for you, but in the end, I really don't care. If you refuse to surrender though, I can assure you that I could come back here with even more soldiers and more ships. My empire is far larger than what you've seen today. That's the difference between you and I, Joy. You see, you think you left here years ago. But I never left and I know it. I have had time to build up something far greater than anything you could imagine."

"Did she just say there's more?!" The Dolphin blurted out unintentionally. Joy turned to The Dolphin, who was hovering nearby with a crossbow aimed at Autumn. The Dolphin had picked up The Toilet Monster's crossbow in her mechanical hand as her new preferred weapon over the spear she had previously obtained.

Autumn seemed to be oblivious to The Dolphin's rhetorical question.

"But I'll make you a deal, face me one-on-one in a sword fight right here and now. If I win, I take your castle and the village. You also give me this space station I've been hearing about and you..." Autumn paused and looked at each of the beat up and exhausted animals surrounding Joy. "...surrender all of the animals here to me."

Joy quietly glanced at each of the animals herself. In doing so, she realized that The Cardinal had returned without her noticing and was perched on top of The Bear's head. The Bear was still facing Autumn's army, but The Cardinal had turned around long enough as Joy looked in his direction that they made brief eye contact.

"If you win, I promise I'll leave you alone here and leave everything as it was. It will be like I never existed in your life here, unless of course you do something like try to hurt me at school or try to turn other people against me. But I know you won't do anything like that. Best of all, if you win, it will also be Thursday when you wake up tomorrow." Autumn initiated an intense squinting glare as though she was aiming for something beyond eye contact with Joy, as if she was trying to look directly through Joy's eyes. When Joy made eye contact with Autumn again, Joy did feel as though Autumn's stare was penetrating through her eyes as though they were windows to look through.

"I'll say one last thing before you decide. Don't forget that unlike the real world, that whenever you are here in this world, you are always beautiful, Joy..."

Joy turned her attention down to her shoes, which looked like she had owned them for a year too long by their wrinkles, cuts and creases. It was at that moment that Joy understood there was a more profound, underlying motivation within Autumn.

It all now made sense to Joy: Autumn bypassed both the castle and the village even though she was saying she now wanted them because, in the end, she doesn't really want them at all. She didn't take over the castle or the village when she already had the opportunity to. Though Autumn would've preferred Joy to stay in the other world, Joy understood why it didn't matter to Autumn if she did or not. Autumn's underlying motive became clear.

"I know why you are doing this," Joy determined, looking up at Autumn.

Autumn was taken by surprise.

"Because this world is better than the real world?!"

"You just want to be liked and to have friends too."

Autumn's mouth dropped open. "Are you kidding me?! I have a ton of friends. Way more than you. I am the one trying to help you."

"They aren't friends in real life. They aren't enough. If you can't have a friend in real life, you are going to keep collecting more and more friends here. But it will never be the same as having a real friend, so if that's what you want..."

Joy hesitated as though she wanted to be one hundred percent sure she believed in what she about to say.

"...then I will be you friend, Autumn," Joy offered. "We don't have to go through all of this."

Autumn was insulted before Joy had completed her last sentence and was incensed by the perceived counteroffer.

"Shut up, Joy, I never wanted to be your friend," she responded bitterly, "I never wanted to be friends with a loser like you."

"Then why do you want me to stay here with you? Why would you lock me up in a time loop in the real world so that I have to keep reliving the same day over and over again while time proceeds linearly here?"

Autumn abruptly smiled in that cruel, toxic way that some people are able to do in an instant even when they're still clearly angry and otherwise unhappy.

"You did that all to yourself..." Autumn snickered. There was a short pause before she added: "...and I'm giving you a way out of it."

Joy looked out toward the ocean, but the sky captured her attention. She couldn't help but notice how the lightning was now constantly flashing in alternating areas throughout the darkened sky in a way that gave the impression that the entire sky was continuously blinking. Autumn noticed how Joy appeared to be seriously considering her options and motioned to her army to lower their weapons. In response, the defense force also lowered their weapons. Autumn then boldly walked out beyond her front line of archers and stopped right in between her the remnants of her army and the depleted defense force with an aura of confidence.

Joy turned to Autumn while everyone else present turned to Joy in anticipatory silence.

"Okay," Joy agreed, "I'll face you one-on-one." Joy had spoken in such a soft tone that she found herself nodding along in agreement with her words to make sure she was clear.

There were audible gasps of concern around Joy from the animals, but Joy didn't seem to notice. Instead, Autumn's voice saying "you did that all to yourself" echoed through Joy's mind as she returned her attention to the flashing sky. *You did that all to yourself.*

$$3.23$$

"You did that all to yourself," Joy mumbled to herself as she looked up at the dull twitching, fluorescent lights overhead in the ceiling near where her locker was located. These words repeated themselves to her within her mind as she walked through the maze of hallways that led to the entryway to the girl's locker room.

By the time she arrived, it seemed like everybody else had already changed into their gym uniforms and exited the locker room to go to gym class. This wasn't surprising, as she had moved very slowly and reluctantly when walking to the locker room.

After she had changed her clothes, she sat alone in her gym uniform on the ancient, nicked up wooden bench in front of her closed gym locker. She could sense her resting-frown was pasted on her face. She had opted to change into her gym clothes even though she wasn't sure if she would make into gym class. She sat and listened to the silence for a moment before realizing there wasn't true silence, as she could the vague, distant sounds of kids playing some kind sport in the gymnasium next door. She couldn't tell what it was, but it sounded like basketball or maybe volleyball.

She felt tense whenever she was in the locker room. The humid aroma of stale body odor seemed to seep from the lockers, the walls, and the floors. This tenacious odor also seemed to be emitted from the endlessly twitching fluorescent lights (that twitched more than the other twitchy lights in the school). On this occasion, the tense feeling had hit her harder than usual when she had stepped through the entrance to the locker room. It didn't help that the locker room was somehow smellier than usual while also hotter, stuffier, and more humid. Even though there were winter-like conditions outside, anyone who entered the girls' locker room would have thought they were in a tropical location, as unnecessary heat from the dusty vents further perspired a room that already felt like it was sweating in its own way.

It also didn't help that Joy had been jumped by other girls before at various times in diverse circumstances since middle school and that made her feel like she could be jumped at any time, especially since she was always alone.

She took a deep breath.

She waited for a moment to determine if she was feeling any calmer.

She wasn't.

She took a second deep breath.

She hesitated again before taking a third deep breath.

Nothing yet.

She took a fourth deep breath.

Make this next one count.

She took a fifth deep breath, this time slowing down so this breath lasted twice as long as others. She then let out a loud, echoing exhale that she immediately regretted.

She had acquired this breathing exercise in 7th grade health class. She couldn't remember how much of it she had learned directly from her health teacher and how much of it she had later modified for herself. Either way, her full breathing exercise involved her taking five deep breaths in a row while making the fifth deep breath last twice as long as the others. It always helped, at least a little bit, in every instance she used it.

This was one of those occasions when it helped just a little bit.

She stood up from her seat and walked across the occasionally sticky concrete floor. The locker room was one of those rooms that turned out to be much larger in size than what one would expect when initially entering it. Her sticky footsteps echoed along the main walkway. To her left, there were the endless rows of gym lockers. To her right, there was a row of doors and windows to dingy but large-sized offices for the physical education staff. Further down the walkway to her right, there were also doors to a large storage room for gym equipment, to a shower room, and to a restroom. In addition to having a row of sinks inside the restroom, the locker room also featured a row of sinks integrated into a long countertop with an extra-large frameless rectangular mirror on the wall above them along the right side of the walkway. This mirror and row of sinks was positioned between the door to the restroom and the door to the shower room. The main walkway led directly from the entryway of the locker room to the double doors that led to the gymnasium.

Joy's gym locker was in the first row of lockers beside the front entryway to the locker room and she had started walking toward the double doors to the gymnasium. The windows of the offices for the physical education staff that looked out into the locker room were dark. As she walked past each of the aisles between the rows of lockers, she looked down them curiously as though she needed to make sure there was really no one else in the room.

It was at the end of the room where she spotted a familiar figure sitting alone on the bench in the aisle between the last two rows of lockers.

She took a step back in awe once she realized it was who she was really thought it was.

It was Robot Joy.

Robot Joy was somehow dressed in the school's gym uniform as well and was looking down at the floor as though it might be deactivated.

"You're...you're not in my gym class," Joy stuttered to Robot Joy with a tone that sounded like she was trying to be polite (but not totally succeeding at it).

Robot Joy didn't respond.

Joy nervously stepped toward Robot Joy to observe it more closely. Closer observation confirmed Robot Joy's eyes were open. Joy also noticed that Robot Joy had a large book on the bench beside it. The book was on the other side of Robot Joy from where Joy was standing. Joy leaned in and gazed at the book's familiar appearance for a few seconds before realizing it was The Book of What Everyone Else Ever Said or Thought About Her. After previously viewing the book displayed with a protective case around it, it was bizarre for her to see it on a grungy, old wooden locker room bench.

"What are you doing here?" Joy inquired, having disposed of any effort to convey a polite tone.

Robot Joy abruptly stood up and turned to her. As it did so, Joy blurted out a shaky "whoa" and backed a few steps away. She saw that Robot Joy had a tablet tucked in its arm. After briefly wondering why Robot Joy would have a tablet with it, Joy recognized that the tablet was the moment-capturing tablet.

"You know why," Robot Joy replied casually upon Joy's recognition of the tablet.

Joy looked at it oddly: "I thought you were supposed to be deactivated?!"

But Robot Joy didn't reply verbally, instead it offered her the moment-capturing tablet.

"Oh... no. No, thank you," Joy whispered.

Robot Joy looked a little surprised, and it waited for several seconds as though it thought Joy might say something more.

Instead, there were only the sounds of the creaky, heat-humming locker room interspersed with the distant clamor of the basketball or volleyball game in the gym.

Joy was still shocked at the fact that Robot Joy was somehow in the locker room during gym class wearing a gym uniform. It was a more extreme version of, but a similar feeling to finding out there was a new kid in one of her middle school classes after a week of being on vacation and discovering how the new kid had developed better relationships with all the other kids than what she ever had with them.

Robot Joy looked at her as though it was trying to understand how Joy was feeling without asking her how she was feeling.

Robot Joy then pointed to The Book of What Everyone Else Ever Said or Thought About Her.

"No," Joy whispered, but then hesitated with her body language as if to open the door to the idea that she might change her mind.

They made eye contact briefly before Joy looked away.

"No," Joy repeated softly, "no thank you,"

Robot Joy placed the moment-capturing tablet beside The Book of What Everyone Else Ever Said or Thought About Her on the bench. Just as it did so, both the book and tablet vanished.

Robot Joy turned to Joy, bowed to her and then smiled. It was a smile that looked so genuine that Joy wondered if it was capable of a smile like that.

But before Joy could think of how to respond, Robot Joy vanished as well.

Joy looked around the area for a moment as if to confirm they had completely disappeared. She then waited for a minute as if she was expecting that they would return, before finally, accepting there was no trace of them.

She sighed and involuntarily returned to her resting-frown.

She continued walking toward the double doors to the gymnasium but found no sign of Casey and her friends.

The last door on the right side of the hallway was to the restroom. Joy stood near this door but didn't hear any activity behind it. Even so, she was still too afraid to enter the restroom, anticipating it could be a trap. She wondered if Casey and her friends were in gym class or if they decided to skip gym class (which she had seen them do multiple times before). Either way, she had the faint hope that maybe they had forgotten about it.

The rows of lockers along the left side of the locker room ended at a point across the walkway from the door to the shower room. It was there that the main walkway of the locker room narrowed into a hallway that ended at the double doors to the gym. This architectural arrangement made the extra-large mirror above the row of sinks outside of the restroom impossible to avoid whenever Joy was walking between her locker and the gymnasium or the restroom.

As Joy stood near the restroom door, she saw a side view of herself in the edge of the mirror. She gazed at herself briefly before turning away. As she did so, she noticed a light switch on the wall of the left side of the hallway that she had never noticed before.

She walked over to the light switch and turned off the hallway light. She then approached one of the sinks in the middle of the row. She cautiously looked at the dimmer view she had of herself in the mirror.

She smiled.

The darkness of the hallway combined with the dull, grainy fluorescent lighting vaguely glowing from the rest of the locker room made her almost, but not quite, appear in the same way that she looked whenever she saw herself in her bedroom mirror on perfectly partially sunlit mornings before school.

She was about to turn her body completely around to have a full look at herself in the mirror when she suddenly had an idea.

She took another deep breath before she began to run around the entire locker room as fast she could.

She ran up and down along the main walkway, turning off every light switch she could find as the locker room gradually transformed from a dimly flickering fluorescent glow to a dark neon-lit labyrinth. Soon, the locker room was only lit by neon emergency lighting. There were the small spotlights created by the emergency exit signs above the double doors that exited to the gymnasium and above the front entryway that exited to the rest of the school. There were also several small emergency lights beaming down from the ceiling along the main walkway between these two exits at either end of the locker room.

Perfect lighting.

She approached the sink she had been standing at earlier and looked fully and directly into the extra-large mirror above it. The partial light of the emergency exit sign above the doors to the gymnasium gleaned off her left forearm.

She now looked exactly as she did in her bedroom mirror when the lighting was just right in the early morning.

She looked beautiful.

But I don't feel beautiful.

It took a minute of gazing before she realized for the first time in this light, she didn't feel anything.

Wait. This is supposed to help me.

She then lost focus as several thoughts hit her all at once.

She thought about how the few people outside of her family who do acknowledge her are often so open with her. It was almost always people she hardly knew or complete strangers. They would tell her about their feelings and themselves, like it was her job to simply listen to them and support them because she was an outcast with no one else to talk to. She was an outcast but was apparently a more approachable outcast to them. It felt good in a way to be approachable to them, and she wanted to help others, but it also felt like a sign that she was not supposed to have a life of her own. It felt like a sign that she only existed to make others feel better about themselves.

She also thought about how most of the other people who weren't open to her always seemed to be trying to put her down, as if they want to make sure she never had the opportunity to have her own life. It was as if they didn't want her to feel good about her own life so she could never potentially take away from anything they have.

And I thought because of the way I am, I was never going to have my own life and feel good about it. Instead, I thought I would only be allowed to see how other people have their happy lives. I thought I was just here to watch them feel good about themselves. It was like my only responsibility was to help them feel good about themselves again whenever they didn't. I wasn't supposed to feel good. I wasn't supposed to feel love.

But I know I have love inside me.

I have love.

I am filled with love.

Love.

I am love.

Joy now had tears streaming down both cheeks, but they were tears of joy. She stepped back several feet and flipped back on that first hallway switch that she had turned off.

Once that hallway light was back on, she no longer saw her own reflection in the extra-large mirror, but the reflection of the nine-year-old version of herself wearing a bright clean red and white soccer uniform.

The nine-year-old Joy was also crying, but they were tears of sadness. The nine-year-old reflection of Joy was crying so hard that it instantly put its hands over its face the moment they made eye contact.

"I can't play soccer anymore. I don't want to go the game today, they'll hurt me again," the nine-year-old reflection cried with its hands still over its face.

"Don't cry," Joy whispered, "it will be okay."

The nine-year-old reflection of Joy removed its hands from over its face revealing the tears streaming down its red face.

"They pick on me," the nine-year-old Joy whimpered, "they always pick on me. I don't know why. But they want to hurt me." The nine-year-old Joy's voice had cracked as it said "...want to hurt me" and it descended into harder sobbing again.

"It's because they know you are great," Joy heard herself say to her own surprise. "They feel intimidated or threatened because they see everything in you that you don't see."

"I'm not great," the nine-year-old Joy sobbed. "I'm ugly...and I'm uglier right now because I'm ugly crying."

"No," Joy said, "your beautiful, Joy."

"They want me to give up!" The nine-year-old Joy screamed.

"That stops today," Joy insisted, "they'll never try to hurt me anymore."

"They will try to kill you," the nine-year-old Joy cried in a much softer tone. "They will kill you..."

"Not anymore," Joy reassured her reflection, raising her voice to ensure she was heard.

Suddenly the door from the restroom opened further down the hallway and Joy looked down at the sink. She could hear the echoes of four pairs of sneakers walking and scuffing on the floor in her direction.

When she looked back up at the mirror, she saw her own present reflection.

Nine-year-old Joy had vanished.

She closed her eyes in anticipation.

3.24

"There is no way you can keep this lifestyle up for long, Joy…" Autumn warned her.

Joy opened her eyes and took an immediate step back upon realizing how the environment around her in the meadow had changed: both her army and Autumn's army had formed a large circle around her and Autumn as they stood several feet across from each other. Autumn was now wearing late-medieval armor that covered every part of her body except her head. Joy was also covered in similar armor without a helmet. They were both armed with swords.

"…you can't bridge the two worlds at our age, we aren't little kids anymore. You have to decide between them." Autumn added. She pointed her sword in Joy's direction.

"I have been doing okay with it so far," Joy tried to reason with herself, as well as with Autumn. She lifted her sword and hesitantly pointed it toward Autumn.

Autumn laughed. "Oh really?!" She sneered. "So reliving Wednesday over and over again has been working out pretty well for you, then?"

Joy took another step back.

She then looked behind her with her sword still pointed in Autumn's direction and recognized that she could only take so many steps back before she would back right into the solders, villagers, knights, and animals that made up her half of the circle standing behind her.

"I know you are wondering how I know," Autumn continued. "I've been there, Joy. I keep trying to tell you that. I've been through it. I'm trying to help you, so you don't have to go through months of repeating and reliving the same day like I did."

"Months?!" Joy shrieked as she turned back to Autumn.

Autumn shrugged her shoulders and laughed. Joy looked at her with a level of bewilderment that suggested that she was contemplating whether Autumn had lost her mind or she was losing hers.

"It's a life changing decision, right?" Autumn acknowledged. "But it was stupid of me to wait as long as I did. All that pain and suffering, what was it for? Why put myself through all that anguish over a world where I will always be different, never fit in anywhere, and be looked at like I'm in the way or blocking the view of someone else they'd rather pay attention to? I know...I wish it hadn't taken me so long to know my real home is here. But you know what? It could've been worse for me; some people go through what you are going through now for years. Some people never get it and relive the same day for the rest of their lives."

Joy looked down at her sabatons as she continued to hold her sword up in Autumn's direction.

"Why spend my life constantly trying to wear the right clothes everyone else wears, watch the right movies or shows, eat the right food that everybody else eats, get married when everyone else gets married, have children when everyone else has children, and say all the right things to anyone who, if I'm lucky enough, will half-listen to me," Autumn reflected with sadness.

When Joy looked up again, she saw that Autumn now had tears in her eyes.

Joy lowered her sword: "Maybe there is something deeper in the real world that is far greater—"

"No," Autumn interjected, "there is nothing!"

There was a sudden clap of thunder that echoed through the dark sky as bolts of lightning continued to illuminate it all around them.

FINALE: WEDNESDAY, 9:58 AM

Joy could hear the lingering echo of thunder in her ears as she stood tensely in the locker room with her eyes closed. She could also sense the toxic hatred of the other girls huddling around her, surrounding her like a slowly suffocating fog of bad energy.

"Talking to yourself again, Joy?" Casey snickered from close behind her. She was so close that Joy could feel her breath and speech up against the lower left area of the back of her neck.

"You could say that," Joy murmured, keeping her eyes closed.

As she sensed the girls quietly organizing into a half circle around her to enclose her against the row of sinks, Joy tensed up even more and grabbed the front edge of the countertop with both of her hands.

She suddenly heard footsteps echo at the other end of the locker room and Joy felt a tinge of hope that it was a teacher or even another student. She heard the person start running down the main walkway toward them. The light scuffling and squeaking sounds of sneakers indicated it was a student.

"Oooooh, what you have got there?!" Lizzie shouted excitedly to the incoming person.

"Shut up," Casey whispered aloud, "Ms. Glacier may not notice when we aren't in class, but Ms. Peppertree eventually will."

"You got her backpack?!" Kaela reacted in astonishment. "Did you like find out the lock combination to her locker or something?"

"Oh yeah, Bradley saw her use her combination when we were by her locker yesterday," Natalie explained as she approached the group, "but you won't believe what else I found inside of it..."

Joy's heart sank further.

Her heart sank not just at the fact that the person who came in the front entrance to the locker room was Natalie, but at the subsequent sound of the rattling pills inside of her father's pill bottle as Natalie showcased it to the others girls. She could then hear what sounded like the light plunk of Natalie dropping Joy's empty backpack on the floor.

"Did you think that Bradley and I were there just to give you a show, Joy?" Natalie muttered while leaning close by her right ear.

Joy didn't reply and tried to remain as still as she could, though she felt herself increasingly shaking. She couldn't tell how visible her shaking was to the other girls because she kept her eyelids tightly closed as though that would somehow make them go away.

"Well, well, look what we have here," Casey scoffed. Joy could sense her smirking behind her. "Why am I not surprised, Joy?"

"It doesn't look like she took any of them," Natalie observed. "Why have them if you aren't going to use them?"

"Maybe she forgot to take one before she knew she going to have to fight us today," Madison laughed. "Should we offer her one now?"

"Oh no, Madison, oh no," Casey replied. It sounded like Natalie had handed the pills over to Casey as Joy could now hear them being handled in the area behind her where Casey's voice was coming from. "See, you don't know Joy as well as I do. She wasn't going to take these to prep for getting hurt in the fight or for any kind of physical pain. You see, our friend Joy here was planning to kill herself. Weren't you, Joy?"

Because she wanted them to leave and hoped they would take pity on her, Joy opted to be open with them about the truth. She maintained tightly closed eyelids as she slowly nodded to confirm Casey's suspicion.

"Right? Well, you should've followed through with it because you are about regret it, loser," Casey scolded her with the lowered volume of a hushed tone.

Then, in a move that even the other girls in her entourage didn't seem to be quite ready for, Casey brutally sucker-punched Joy in the area of her closed left eye.

Joy fell sideways to her right, as she lost the grip of the countertop with her left hand. She fell on her right knee with her right hand still gripping the countertop. As she tried to blindly find the countertop with her left hand again, there was a vicious kick that struck the right side of her abdomen. Joy swayed back to her left like a pendulum. She was barely able to catch the floor with her left knee as she maintained her hold on the countertop with her right hand. She tightened her grip on the countertop like she was hanging by a thread.

"That's for being such a creep and staring at me and my boyfriend when you should mind your own business," Natalie snarled as she watched Joy struggle to recover from the impact of her kick.

As she regained a sense of balance on both of her knees, Joy could now hear Casey passing her dad's bottle of pills to someone else overhead.

"I'll make sure these don't go to waste," Lizzie giggled behind her.

"Be careful, guys," Kaela cautioned, "I know Joy better than all of you. She's stronger than you think."

"Oh, with all due respect, Kaela, will you shut up about that already," Lizzie managed to say between continued giggles before finally settling down. "She's going down easier than we all thought she would. She's so weak she brought these babies with her to school to probably try to avoid all of this from happening to her.

She's not the same kid you used to be friends with. She's even more pathetic now."

Lizzie leaned forward with the bottle pills in her left hand and struck Joy in her back kidney area with her right fist, causing Joy's forehead to hit the front end of the countertop. Joy was able to lessen the impact of the blow to her forehead by raising her left hand back to a grip on the countertop alongside her right hand just as Lizzie hit her. With both hands holding the countertop, she was able to somewhat catch herself from hitting it harder and possibly getting knocked out.

Joy moaned from the pain in her forehead as she continued to hold on to the countertop with both hands again as though her life depended on it. She shifted her left grip away from her right to give herself a steadier hold of the countertop.

"See, she's not fighting back," Lizzie laughed as she put the bottle of pills into her backpack. "Thank you Joy. That's my thank you for your death pills. You should be thanking me for saving your life by taking them away from you."

Joy finally opened her eyes but all she could see was the edge of the countertop right in front of her nose as she maintained her hold on it with each hand at either side of her face. She was able to regain full balance while still on her knees.

"Let's not get ahead of ourselves," Casey sneered, "let's see if Joy can survive through this. It's your turn, Kaela."

Joy closed her eyes again and cringed.

"Kaela?" Casey irritably inquired. "Are you flaking out on us?!"

"Don't flake," Natalie chimed in.

Kaela hesitated and glanced at each of her friends as they imparted looks of judgment and disdain in her direction. It was one of those strange moments where she felt she could lose years of friendship simply for refusing to participate. Because she hesitated and allowed this odd tension to permeate through the group, she realized she would have to hit Joy harder than she would have ever intended. She had to hit Joy that hard, otherwise they would primarily remember how she hesitated to hit Joy at all.

Kaela drew back her leg in an exaggerated pose and then kicked Joy as hard as she could in the right side of Joy's abdomen. Joy released the countertop and barely caught herself on the floor with both hands as she tumbled sideways. She opened her eyes just in time to see where her hands landed on the floor. She was able to remain on her knees with her knees still facing the counter while her face and upper body were now pointed to the left (where Casey and Madison had backed up a step from behind her in anticipation of her fall).

Joy started coughing up blood on the floor. She tried to muffle the moans that were emerging between coughing fits.

But despite all her suffering, there was a glow in Joy's eyes. Kaela's kick had momentarily put her mind in a strange, mysterious daze.

It was as if she was suddenly able to feel all of the pain she had ever felt from elementary school, from middle school, from high school, from her mom, from herself, from not being pretty enough, from being teased, from being beat up, from her friends that turned out not to be her friends, from having no friends, from being lonely, from being heartbroken, from all the previous attempts from other people to hurt her, and from these girls now standing behind her— all at the same time.

As she experienced this extraordinary pain, several random happy images from her life that she hadn't thought about in years flashed through her mind along with the more familiar happy images she frequently revisited. She remembered being a little kid and overseeing the construction of the castle with the animals, she remembered being slightly older and blasting off in a spaceship from a dock on her space station with The Dolphin, she remembered going to a baseball game with her Dad and then playing catch with him later that night in the backyard after they got home, she remembered laughing with her mom the first time her mom was showing her how to put on makeup back when her mom was more patient with her and still seemed to have some hope for her, she remembered a moment on the bus when she was in middle school and Gray arrived late for a field trip so he had to sit with her by default (but she still loved it so much), and she remembered laughing and kicking a soccer ball around with Kaela before a game when they used to play on the same team together. Then finally, she remembered the very first morning when the light of the rising sun shined in her room so perfectly that when she looked in the mirror, she felt like it was the most beautiful version of herself she had ever seen up to that point. She was late to school that day because she knew that moment would end, and she didn't want it to. She remembered how badly she wanted to feel like the other girls that day, who always seemed to feel like they were beautiful no matter where they were.

As Joy completed this final flashback, she started coughing harder, but this time there was less blood coming out.

Despite the uncontrollable coughing, she was suddenly able to somehow hear Autumn's voice in her ears clearly: "You'll spend the rest of your life having those little moments each day when you feel like you've hit rock bottom all over again because your life has remained unfulfilled, and you know there is nothing you can do about it..."

*** *** ***

"...is that any way to live?" Autumn asked.

Autumn then lowered her sword. She looked like she wanted to rub her eyes, but her armored gloves made it too challenging.

Joy looked out over Autumn's shoulder at the spectacular flashes of lighting in the sky surrounding the meadow. She was in awe of how the meadow she was standing in felt familiar to her again as she could now recall it from when she was a little kid.

"Answer me!" Autumn shouted as she lifted her sword again.

Before giving Joy another chance to respond, Autumn made a sweeping thrust toward her with her sword that was ironically synchronized with another loud burst of thunder. Joy was able to block Autumn's sword as it was bearing down toward her head with her own sword. Joy had perfect timing that she even surprised herself with. She then took several side-steps away from Autumn to another area of the circle and lowered her sword as if to try to show Autumn that there was no need to fight her.

"Keep your sword up, Joy," The Dolphin warned from a few feet behind her, "she has that look in her eye."

Joy lifted her sword back up and noticed it was shaking along with the rest of her body.

"The longing you have felt for Gray in the other world doesn't go away," Autumn asserted as she took a few steps toward Joy. "Even long after Gray is gone, it will stay with you and it will manifest in other unfulfilled areas of your life: like your other relationships, your career, your possessions, your finances, and even in your vacations. Just look at your parents. You may tell yourself right now that you will never turn out like your parents, but trust me, those seeds have been planted. I've seen it in Summer, the daughter of my mom's best friend. Yeah, my mom's best friend named her daughter 'Summer,' but my mom claims it's unrelated to me being named 'Autumn.' Anyway, she's twelve years older than me and ever since she graduated college, she's been a lost soul like her mom is. She's working a job that's unrelated to what she majored in, she's in a long-term relationship with a guy who won't marry her or commit to her in the other ways she wants him to commit to her, and she spends most of her time complaining to her friends about these things while they also complain to her about their lives. And you know what? Summer was popular in high school. Can you imagine what our lives would be like at her age then?"

Joy didn't respond as she struggled to steady her sword.

Autumn drew back her sword to her side before briefly taking flight in a running leap to slash toward the upper left side of Joy's body.

Joy was able to block Autumn's sword again with her sword, but the sheer impact knocked her over into the grass.

Joy was able to turn audible gasps of concern from her side of the circle into more open sighs of relief as she rolled into a kneeling position and blocked yet another attack by Autumn, this time aimed for her head again.

It was at that point when Joy realized her shaking had abruptly ended. She confidently held steady as Autumn's sword continued to hammer away savagely and impatiently at her own.

After Joy had successfully blocked Autumn's sword at least a dozen times, Autumn wearily took a few steps back while breathing heavily with occasional interrupted puffing.

They continued to point their swords at one another while maintaining eye contact as the others watched in an edgy silence.

With Autumn now at a relatively safe distance and clearly recovering, Joy stood back up again. As she did so, she tried not to make it look as difficult as it felt to stand up underneath the weight of her armor. She wasn't sure how successful she was in doing so.

"You ever notice how most people in the real world end up dying while living alone?" Autumn inquired rhetorically, still sounding like she was catching her breath. "We all die alone, but it seems like most people end up living their final years alone too. They either die in a nursing home, or they die on their own years after their partner has passed away. If they are lucky, maybe they live with their kids or grandkids, but even then, you can tell they look and feel helplessly out of place. It's like they don't want to be alive because they don't want to bother anyone or feel like they are burdening the people they live with. Even those people who live with others at that stage of their lives look and feel like they are alone. People live their lives living this fantasy that they will have someone by their side and that someone will love them for who they really are and not just for their looks, their money, or their position in life.

"That's what separates you and I from a lot of people, Joy. We get it. As outcasts, we were forced by society to step back and observe all the details that many people don't see or think about. That's why deep down, I know that you know what I am saying is true. Deep down you also know that if you stay here, you'll never be alone. Once you make a complete return to this world, you'll find your friends here will love you far more than any friends you make in the real world ever will." Autumn nodded upward to The Elephant, who towered above the others standing in the circle, and then turned back to Joy with a smirk: "And let's be honest, that's assuming you're able to make any friends out there. You don't have any friends anymore. You haven't had any friends since we were in elementary school."

"Middle school," Joy corrected her.

"Whatever," Autumn scoffed. "it's been a long time."

"It doesn't seem that long..."

Autumn snickered.

"You do have personality, I'll give you that," Autumn acknowledged, "and that's your best chance, Joy, if you want anyone in the real world to pay attention to you. You'll be one of those eternally lonely people who make other people laugh but also overwhelm them with your personality by talking too much in social interactions usually meant for nothing more than small talk or a quick greeting. You'll make a cashier at a coffee shop awkwardly try to politely end a conversation with you. You'll make a car mechanic smile for a minute but wish he hadn't worked on your car. You'll make anyone who manages to make it into your phone as a contact cringe when you call them or send them a text message. What you don't understand is that would be your 'best-case scenario' for the rest of your life. I don't know why you are fighting this or fighting me. You belong here...with all of us."

Joy didn't respond verbally, instead she lowered her sword a little bit while keeping it pointed at Autumn.

"It's like kids these days gain too much knowledge and are exposed to too much information that by the time they become adults, life in the real world is too much for them to handle," Autumn continued (by this point, she was no longer sounding fatigued and had talked her way into a second wind). "It's like their developing brains were scarred by the information overload they experienced as kids. So many people are happier when they are kids and are much happier when they remain like kids for as long as possible. That's why a lot of people take drugs, drink alcohol, eat junk food, get excited and nostalgic about pop culture from their childhood, and have child-like hobbies even when they're adults. They are all trying to recapture something they lost when they grew up. But here in this world, you can see that we never lose what we had as kids. This world stays with us as we grow up. It's perfect for us. Do you ever notice how adults these days act more like kids now more than they ever have? It's because the real world has become incredibly complex with all the media and immediate information that is available to them that overstimulates their brains, interrupts their sleep and convinces them to create unrealistic life goals. It's impossible to focus on anything in the real world or have the time to learn and understand who you are.

"People these days are barely disciplined enough to be in love with one person. They lie to themselves and others that they value their relationships, and that they value themselves. You ever notice how no one really takes advice from each other anymore? They just ask multiple people for advice on the same situation until they hear what they already know they want to hear from someone. People have commoditized each other without ever really getting to know each other and now similarly dispose of relationships the same way they would dump an empty to-go coffee cup or a used napkin. As soon as they have no use for someone anymore, that's it. But Joy, here you know that never happens. Here life is simple, here we are respected, and here we are everything to them."

Autumn spread out her arms as far as she could to her sides and gestured positively to the entire circle around them with both her sword and her free hand. Joy had never seen Autumn smile so broadly. Autumn gracefully made a 360-degree turn with her arms spread open as a grandiose gesture to display how wonderful their environment was despite the dark skies, the fierce battle that was waged there earlier, and the high-stakes sword fight they were apparently still engaged in.

Joy made a point of looking around individually at each of the animals who were standing in different parts of "her side" of the half-circle. She looked first at The Dolphin, then The Bear, The Lion, The Cardinal, The Elephant, The Penguin and then The Wolf. Each of them had a look of intense concern and anticipation in their eyes.

"I know there is a love inside of me I can only find in the real world," Joy concluded, looking back at Autumn. "I know I can only go so far living my life here and that I must go back to find a greater love there than anything I will ever have here."

Joy lifted her sword back up in anticipation of Autumn lashing out again in immediate anger. But to her surprise, Autumn remained still and was expressionless.

"You ever notice how Casey acts like I don't exist? People like her don't bother with people like me who choose to be here. Aren't you tired of getting beaten down trying to find this so-called 'love inside of me' that you so vaguely describe? Is it really worth it? Is that even scientific? How do you know it's there?"

Before Joy could answer, Autumn made another running leap in her direction, and this time struck Joy's sword as hard she could with her own. The intent was to try knock Joy's sword out of her hand, and though Joy nearly lost her grip, she was able to maintain it. As Autumn took two steps back to recover, Joy held her sword up again in anticipation of her next potential attack.

"Why aren't you fighting back?!" Autumn cried, as a uniquely bright flash of lightning illuminated the darkened sky behind her.

*** *** ***

"Why aren't you fighting back?" Casey cried before she kicked Joy in the left side of her hip. Joy redirected her hands to the floor on her right side to catch herself from collapsing completely on it. She was still on her knees. She was still coughing, but now there was no blood coming out anymore.

"Don't you think she's had enough?" Lizzie asked with a slight note of concern in her voice. "I don't remember us beating up Vanessa this badly. I mean, Joy has coughed up blood over the place. What if she dies or something?"

"Oh, we are just getting started. Do you have somewhere else you need to be?" Casey scoffed.

"I was hoping I could have time to go hide out somewhere and take one of my new pills to help me zone out before I have to sit through math," Lizzie confessed.

"Just getting started?!" Kaela spoke up after briefly hesitating. "I think you've made your point, Casey."

"Um, yeah, Casey," Madison agreed, "she was already broken when we found her."

"Are you kidding me right now?" Casey asked incredulously.

"Don't be ridiculous," Natalie responded to Madison, "if Joy didn't have any hope left, she would have killed herself before she came here knowing what was going to happen to her."

"Okay, I need to know right now if you all are still with me or not?!" Casey demanded with a discernible undercurrent of resentment. "Are you with me?"

*** *** ***

"Hey! Are you with me?" Autumn asked, taking one step forward as she continued to point her sword cautiously in Joy's direction. "Is that why you aren't fighting back? It seems like you're still thinking about it despite what you're saying. I'll give you one last chance right here and now to say you are with me since you obviously don't want to fight me."

After Autumn finished her inquiry, she tried to read Joy's mixed facial expression as Joy remained still. Joy was quietly looking out at the darkened sky as another uniquely bright flash filled it behind Autumn. Meanwhile, The Cardinal started softly singing Joy's favorite melody from where he was positioned in the circle to the left of Joy.

Joy turned to him and saw him lifting his feet up and down, one at a time, while perched atop The Lion's head. This time, The Cardinal's singing was amplified and full. He sounded like he had completely recovered from the use of his siren. Beneath him, The Lion was displaying his rare, full smile that instantly made Joy smile in the way that seeing anyone who rarely smiles would make someone else who knew them instantly smile at the sight of it.

The Lion started humming along with The Cardinal.

The other animals then joined along, one by one, from where they stood in different parts of the half circle around Joy: The Penguin first joined him, bleating along to the song. The Bear then added his own deep baritone humming. The Dolphin started in after The Bear with her distinct way of whistling. The Wolf then joined them with a lower version of his howl to blend with the other animals.

They all turned to The Elephant who initially looked hesitant and unsure how she could join them. She brushed her front right foot up and down across the grass thoughtfully for a moment.

"The love is inside of you, Joy!" The Elephant cried out along with the melody.

The Elephant then began making a series of unusual chirps and squeaks that somehow fit in seamlessly with the chorus. Each of the other animals, Joy, and even Autumn looked at The Elephant in amazement, as none of them had seen an elephant make sounds like that. As The Elephant joined in with the other animals to create this extraordinary symphony, Joy smiled the kind of smile when she doesn't realize she is smiling at first until almost a minute after it appears.

She continued smiling as she looked up and noticed for the first time that the darkness in the sky was slowly starting to fade back into a grayish-bluish hue.

*** *** ***

"What are you smiling about?" Natalie fleered after observing Joy's change in countenance. "Unbelievable, you guys see that? She's actually smiling."

Joy was still on her knees, but she had stopped coughing. As she grabbed a hold of the countertop again with both hands, her entire body clenched under the weight of the pain she felt everywhere as it seemed to now cover every part of her body.

And yet, through all this pain, Joy was smiling.

She whispered back the words that The Elephant had cried out, remembering they were also The Custodian's words, with the feeling of blood sliding off her lower lip as she did so: "The love is inside of me..."

From the moment she had uttered those words, the pain started diminishing and she began to feel a sudden ticklish swirling sensation around the area of her heart. This sensation immediately started flooding her upper body from its source and pushed its way up through her head while simultaneously moving down her torso and across all of her limbs. She started rising from her kneeling position slowly, as she had kneeled for so long that she felt like the sprout of a plant pushing its way through the dirt.

"The love is inside of me," she repeated in a murmur.

*** *** ***

"The love is inside of you!" The Dolphin yelled out emphatically to Joy before whistling along again with the melody. Joy noticed Autumn slowly backing away from her as the song of the animals grew in volume and echoed throughout the meadow.

The lightning in the sky abruptly ended.

The gray-black cloud-carpet splintered and separated into smaller individual gray clouds as the sky above them entered into a more rapid phase of transformation. These individual gray clouds then brightened into sun-glinted white clouds as blueness continued to fill out all the spaces of sky around them.

*** *** ***

"The love is inside of me..." Joy repeated to herself, but this time she was slightly louder with more clarity so that the other girls in the locker room were able to confirm that she was really starting to say something.

Joy was still making sense of what was happening to her body. It was like the conglomeration of pain that was once spread throughout her body had recentered itself at her heart and then transformed there into a different energy that swirled in a sphere before exploding like a star over and over again, racing in separating beams across her arms and legs, and through her head, before supercharging in her feet and her hands. This sensation, which she now recognized as love, was flooding her body from her heart a billion times over as if to account for each cell in her body. It no longer felt like she was defending herself and it no longer felt like she was under attack. It no longer felt like she was fighting as much as it felt like she was being loved, healed, and strengthened all at once. She felt goosebumps, but for once in her life it wasn't from fear, it was from feeling like she finally had the ability to stop them from hurting her. It felt like the type of goosebumps she imagined she would feel if she made it up to the top of a mountain after several hours of feeling like she would never make it to the top (along with the emotion of never wanting to go back down).

She had the confidence of knowing now, they weren't ever going to bring her down.

"What? What's she saying?" Kaela wondered. "She sounds so out of it; I can't understand her."

The amazing sensation Joy felt throughout her body continued to deepen in intensity with each word she uttered about the love inside of her. She felt it flowing like a replenished river inside of her body and filling every corner of it. She also experienced a magnetic pull, gathering strength around her head down to her shoulders that was pulling her upward.

Slowly, Joy lifted her legs from her kneeling position. She continued rising.

*** *** ***

"The love is inside of you!" The Wolf called out to Joy between howls as the song continued at what now sounded like the highest possible volume that the animals were capable of.

The sky was now completely clear of gray and bright with the sun filling the deep blue sky among white cumulus clouds that had fully regained their form.

The remaining members of Autumn's army quietly looked disconcertingly at one another within their half of the circle. One of them eventually pointed toward the lone remaining decoy flagship still positioned offshore from the beach among the graveyard of charred and sunken ships from the original diversionary attack. They appeared to determine that it was the quickest, most convenient way out before they all gradually broke rank and started walking toward the passageway that led back down to the beach.

While still maintaining their half of the circle, the knights, soldiers, and villagers of the defense force laid down their weapons once Autumn's side started their retreat. They then began to dance along jubilantly to the animals' song once the last soldier in Autumn's army left the circle.

"Wait, where are you all going?!" Autumn shouted in overwhelmed disbelief after her retreating army. By then, they had started down the passageway to the beach with their heads down. "I haven't given you orders to retreat. Get back here...I...I still need you here! What... What's happening?!"

*** *** ***

What's happening?!" Madison inadvertently shouted into the hair over the back of Joy's head as Joy continued slowly rising toward a standing position from being down on her knees. Joy had planted her right foot on the floor as she lifted herself up using both of her hands on the countertop.

"The love is inside of me," Joy repeated softly to herself without acknowledging Madison's question.

"Come on people! Take her down now!" Natalie pleaded. "Hit her!"

Natalie tried to punch Joy in the back of the head out of desperation, but her fist instead struck Joy directly in her upper right shoulder blade. Natalie cried out in pain as the blow appeared to hurt her fist far more than any pain it could have caused Joy. Joy, meanwhile, seemed unaffected by it.

"The love is inside of me," Joy said to herself in a near whisper.

"Shut up!" Natalie screamed at her as she held her throbbing fist tightly against her stomach before leaning back in agony against the wall on the other side of the hallway.

*** *** ***

"Shut up!" Autumn screamed at animals. "Make them shut up, Joy!"

"The love is inside of you!" The Bear belted out to Joy exuberantly before he resumed his humming.

Autumn turned and screamed in the direction of her retreating army as loud as she could. After none of them acknowledged her, she turned to Joy with newly formed streams of tears trickling down her red, enraged face. She pointed her sword directly at Joy and charged toward her as through the sword was a makeshift lance for jousting.

Joy gripped the handle of her own sword with both hands and drew it back to her right side.

As Autumn came within range, Joy struck the left side of Autumn's sword with a long wild swing like she was swinging a bat for a home run in a baseball game. Autumn instantly lost her grip on her sword, which flew out of her hands and rotated like a frisbee as it spun high through the air. The sword flew well over the heads of the remaining group still huddled around them, beyond the edge of the meadow, and then over the edge of the cliff into the sea below.

Autumn stopped in her tracks and then backed away a few steps in horrified shock. Joy resumed pointing her sword in Autumn's direction as the animals continued to sing and the rest of the defense force continued to dance.

As they made eye contact, Joy saw that Autumn had an uncharacteristic mix of fear and bewilderment in her eyes.

*** *** ***

Through the somewhat blurred corner of her left eye, Joy could discern an uncharacteristic aura of hesitation and anxiety in Casey's body language. Joy looked into the mirror and made full eye contact with Casey through her reflection in the mirror.

Casey blinked and shook her head before throwing a punch that harmlessly seemed to bounce off the left side of Joy's ribs.

Lizzie shrieked after Casey's punch appeared to be completely ineffective against Joy.

"The love is inside of me," Joy mumbled as she reached a full standing position. She remained unsteady however, as the girls surrounding her now simultaneously began to pummel her back, her hips, her obliques, her shoulders, the back of her head and her face in a desperate, coordinated effort.

At this point, the pain was completely gone.

"You aren't hitting her hard enough!" Casey cried out angrily as she projected her own lack of effectiveness on to the others. "Hit harder!"

"The love is inside of me," Joy whispered underneath her breath.

"Seriously, what is she saying?!" Madison whined as she threw a punch specifically aimed at the most battered side of Joy's face, around her left eye.

After absorbing Madison's blow to her face, Joy dropped back down to her right knee but she able to keep her left foot solidly on the floor to maintain her balance.

Joy started to try to rise back up but was nearly knocked over again when Kaela kicked her in the right leg in the area where her knee was touching the floor. She quietly took the hit while maintaining her balance.

"How is she getting back up?!" Natalie cried in shock as she stepped forward from leaning against the wall. Her hand was still throbbing, and she was motivated to strike with vengeance. She cocked back her remaining uninjured fist with the intent to hit the left side of Joy's face after observing how Madison's blow to the same area had been the only recent effective hit that Joy had sustained.

Joy continued rising.

*** *** ***

Joy raised her sword up toward the sky over her head.

Autumn and all the others watched in awe as Joy's sword flashed several times before settling temporarily into a warm glow as though it had absorbed energy from the sun. Autumn cautiously took a few more steps further away from Joy. The warm glow gradually brightened and swirled throughout the sword until it became so intense that it turned into a prolonged flash that was far brighter than before. Except for the animals, everyone (including Joy), winced and closed their eyes in response to this extended flash of dazzling light as Joy continued to hold the sword above her head.

The animals continued their song without pausing while everyone else present ducked down and continued to cover their eyes until the flash vanished.

Before Joy had opened her eyes, the weight of the sword felt much lighter, and the volume and texture of the handle had transformed into a very thin object. Once she did open her eyes, she saw that she was holding the stem of a large, fully bloomed purple orchid.

She smiled and lowered the purple orchid to her chest.

She looked to Autumn, who was standing back up from the crouching position she was in during the flash. Autumn briefly met Joy's gaze and then glanced over in the other direction to find that her retreating army had all disappeared down the passageway toward the beach.

Joy confidently approached Autumn, who then turned back to her but remained as still as a statue and expressionless.

Joy offered Autumn the purple orchid.

After a moment of tense hesitation, Autumn slowly lifted her right hand and took the orchid.

Joy gave Autumn a slight downward nod after the hand-off was complete. Autumn's gaze fluctuated between Joy and at all the spectators still standing behind Joy.

"The love is still inside of you, Autumn," Joy said.

Autumn finally observed the large orchid more closely in awe and wonder.

Autumn then looked to Joy and gave her a slight downward nod in return before turning toward the passageway to the beach. She called out to anyone in her retreating army who might still hear her to wait for her as she started running in that direction with her new purple orchid.

The remaining soldiers, knights and villagers of Joy's defense force turned to The Elephant, who nodded to them with approval while still contributing to the song. Some of them began to walk back toward the dirt trail that led to the village while others walked in the opposite direction on the trail toward the castle.

Only the animals remained, and they continued to sing, hum, whistle, squeak, chirp, howl and bleat their song to Joy as they formed a smaller circle around her.

"The love is inside of you," The Lion sang soulfully along with the melody as he joined the newly formed circle. After this display of unexpected vocal talent, he returned to his gleeful hum.

*** *** ***

"The love is inside of me," Joy yelled out as she turned and grabbed Natalie's arm in mid-air before Natalie was able to land her punch.

Natalie's arm twisted violently within Joy's grip as she desperately tried in vain to pull away. The strong pull of Natalie's arm enabled Joy to resume a full standing position. Joy was then able to resist an even stronger attempt by Natalie to twist her arm out of her grip by pulling Natalie back with her full weight.

There was a sudden snapping sound and Natalie bellowed out in pain.

"She broke my arm!" Natalie howled. She immediately started running for down the main walkway of the locker room toward the front entrance. Madison and Lizzie briefly made eye contact and Lizzie handed Madison the pill bottle. Madison then chased after Natalie.

Joy took a deep breath and as she exhaled, she could vaguely hear the song the animals were singing to her as a distant sound that apparently only she could hear. She started to smile a little bit but then involuntarily coughed in pain before she could complete her smile.

*** *** ***

The animals continued to sing in their small circle around Joy as the scene around them suddenly transformed from the meadow-by-the-sea setting into the white void that Joy and The Elephant had met Autumn in earlier. The song of the animals took on a more eerie echo given the mysterious acoustics of the white void. Joy also noticed how the entire bodies of each of the animals now appeared as dim holograms.

She defaulted inadvertently to her resting frown and started looking down after noticing this fading hologram effect.

Joy's lack of engagement didn't deter the animals, however, and the song seemed to echo even louder around her.

"The love is inside of you," The Cardinal echoed to Joy over the melody.

*** *** ***

"The love is inside of me," Joy yelled out again. She blocked a punch from Kaela and then pushed her forcefully backward as hard as she could so that both Kaela's head and back slammed against the wall on the other side of the hallway behind them.

Kaela slid down the wall as she dropped to the floor into a seated position with her head titled forward. She was initially motionless. Lizzie ran to her aid and started shaking her shoulders simultaneously with both hands.

"Kaela, talk to me! Tell me you're okay!" Lizzie screamed.

Kaela moaned incoherently.

"Oh, you are definitely dead now!" Casey declared.

Casey then threw a punch toward her reddened left eye, but Joy ducked down so that Casey missed her completely. Casey subsequently lost her balance, nearly stumbling to the floor. Joy stood back up and pushed Casey as she stumbled, causing her to tumble directly into Lizzie who was just helping Kaela up off the floor by putting Kaela's left arm around her shoulders. Casey and Lizzie directly bumped heads and Lizzie subsequently lost her grip of Kaela. Kaela grabbed the back of Lizzie's shirt with one hand and Casey's left arm with the other to try to stay upright, inadvertently pulling them both down to the floor with her. Casey tried to break her fall with both hands but was unsuccessful at trying to pull her left arm out of Kaela's grip. This caused Casey's left elbow to slam against the tile floor while bearing much of her weight as well as Kaela's.

Casey wailed in pain.

At that point, Madison returned to the scene without Natalie or the pill bottle and started helping them up.

"Come on, I am going to take Natalie to urgent care in my car. I can fit you all in there. Let's get out of here!" Madison bawled.

Joy could hear the girls' scuffle and stumble through the main locker room corridor and eventually out of the front entrance to the locker room. There was another door just a few feet down the hallway outside of the locker room's front entrance that led to a student parking lot where Madison would be able to get the girls off school property and then to urgent care undetected.

Joy could feel how bloodied and bruised she was, but still no longer felt any pain.

She quietly picked up her empty backpack up off the floor and put it on the countertop beside the sink.

She could still hear the faint sound of the animals singing to her.

"The love is inside of me," Joy said quietly to herself through her swollen lip.

*** *** ***

"The love is inside of you, Joy," The Penguin sang in an echo that Joy heard with equal clarity both within the white void as well as in the locker room.

The Penguin opened up her flippers with the intention of hugging Joy, but waited as the other animals slowly faded out their song. One by one, they also made gestures toward embracing Joy.

"The love is inside of me," Joy whispered in the center of the circle and again to herself in the locker room simultaneously.

She hugged the Penguin and was soon joined by the other animals in a group hug as they either hugged her or leaned into her. The Elephant joined the group hug with her trunk by wrapping it around both Joy and The Penguin. The Wolf leaned lovingly against her right side and The Lion leaned with the same sentiment against her left side. The Cardinal had flown up onto her right shoulder and was hugging her neck and the side of her face with one of his wings while also leaning into her lower cheek. The Dolphin and The Bear then joined the hug with their mechanical arms and hairy arms respectively at opposites sides of Joy where they could fit in.

Joy closed her eyes and smiled in what felt like the warmest, most loving hug she had ever experienced in her life.

When she opened her eyes, the animals and the white void had vanished and she was standing alone and bleeding in the empty locker room, but she still felt the warmth inside and all around her from the group hug.

She looked in the mirror.

Her gym uniform was covered in splotches of blood, especially around the collar of her t-shirt. She had a partially closed reddish-black left eye, a bleeding lip, and bruises along with streaks and smudges of blood on various parts of her bare arms, hands, neck and face (some of which she couldn't tell if they were the source of bleeding or had been in some contact with an area that had been bleeding). The hair around her face and over her shoulders had blood in it too.

But she saw something different in her eyes, they had a gleam like her eyes were somehow smiling. She could even see this smile in her partially closed left eye.

She smiled again too.

The features of her face that she hated, the way her body was shaped that annoyed her, the way too much light made her skin look worse, the way shirts she wore like her gym uniform shirt didn't seem to adequately fit her shoulders, the way her eyes were shaped, the size of her breasts, the size of her ears, the size of her hips, the way her hair looked too dry, and even the awkward, crooked way her smile looked when she smiled with her teeth exposed suddenly looked attractive to her for the first time, despite the blood and bruises.

She spun around slowly in front of the mirror while trying to maintain her balance with her bruised legs and completed a full turn after nearly falling to the ground halfway through it.

She resumed her hold with both hands on the edge of the countertop and looked at in the mirror again.

"The love is inside me," she whispered to her reflection in the mirror.

The double doors from the gymnasium suddenly opened and she heard footsteps stop momentarily just beyond the doorway before rushing toward her.

"Oh my... are you okay, Joy?!"

She turned toward the sound of a familiar voice.

"What on earth did they do to you this time?"

"It's okay, Ms. Peppertree," Joy said softly.

Ms. Peppertree was the assistant physical education teacher who was in her mid-20's and usually seen sitting in her office scrolling on her phone when the students were changing before and after class. She had voluminous, soft-looking long hair that looked like she applied only the most effective high-end products to it and wore heavy make-up to hide her freckles and pimples (Joy knew this because she had seen Ms. Peppertree once at the grocery store when she wasn't wearing makeup). Joy wondered if Ms. Peppertree ever really played sports or engaged in any recreational activities herself. She was one of those teachers you would expect would quit at a moment's notice and Joy wouldn't have been surprised one day to come to class and find she wasn't there.

Yet despite all of this, Ms. Peppertree really seemed to like Joy. Joy was convinced she was the reason why she had passing grades in gym class because she sensed that Ms. Glacier hated her. Ms. Peppertree also frequently looked out for Joy if she had any suspicion that the other girls were in the process of teasing her. If anybody from school was going to walk in on her in this moment, Joy was relieved it was Ms. Peppertree.

Even so, despite all the yelling and screaming that had ensued in the locker room, Joy wasn't surprised it took any teacher this long to find her. She knew gym class was loud when team sports were played in the gymnasium and fate seemed to frequently delay a teacher's arrival whenever she needed them around the most. It always took too long. But this time, it didn't bother her. For once, she had a moment where nothing seemed to bother her.

Ms. Peppertree studied her anxiously and gasped a couple of times in the process.

"We gotta get you to the nurse immediately," she squinted as she continued to inspect Joy's wounds, "or to the hospital."

"It's really okay, Ms. Peppertree," Joy laughed at the suggestion of going to the hospital, "I just have a few bruises here and there. They got my eye and my back pretty good, but I actually feel great right now."

Ms. Peppertree looked at her in amazement. She was used to Joy complaining. She was used to Joy crying. She was used to Joy being sad.

Joy and Ms. Peppertree gazed at one another in silence for several moments as each appeared to be initially unsure of how to proceed. Joy noted that Ms. Peppertree didn't appear close to breaking her stunned silence, so she knew she had to say something.

"Ms. Peppertree..." Joy began.

She paused for a moment because she couldn't help but smile.

"For the first time in my life..." Joy's voice cracked as she said the words "first time." She turned away from Ms. Peppertree to look again at her bruised, sweaty, bleeding, tearful, and smiling self in the mirror.

"For the first time in my life, I know I'm beautiful."